## "I'm going back to my r

"No, Jessie, you're not," Springer said quietly.

"Are you going to try to stop me?"

"No." The word was low and beguiling, and his other hand slid up her arm, lightly touching, tantalizing, but in no way restraining. "You can go if you want to. But you don't want to. Do you?" Springer's head moved closer, blotting out the light, his other hand holding her still for his kiss. The lips were warm, flesh on her flesh, a gentle exploration, a question, a soothing balm for Jessica's lacerated soul.

"Do you?" he whispered again against her lips.

She would have shaken her head in denial, but it would have broken the tantalizing bond. "No," she said silently against his mouth. And liking the way her lips moved against his as she formed the word, she tried it again. "No...."

## ABOUT THE AUTHOR

Anne Stuart had her very first work published by *Jack and Jill* magazine at the age of seven, and she has been writing professionally ever since. She is the author of five Gothic romances and two Regencies, as well as four American Romances and two Intrigues. A native of New Jersey, Anne moved to an old farmhouse in Vermont in 1971 and has been living on a mountain there ever since. She shares her home with her husband and their newest addition—a daughter.

## Books by Anne Stuart

# BANISH MISFORTUNE

## ANNE STUART

CHAMBREL

*Harlequin Books*

TORONTO • NEW YORK • LONDON
AMSTERDAM • PARIS • SYDNEY • HAMBURG
STOCKHOLM • ATHENS • TOKYO • MILAN

Published April 1985

ISBN 0-373-65005-1

*Part One*

# Chapter One

**The Slaughterer, vol. 43: Tombs of Blood**

*Matt Decker surveyed the carnage around him. He was a man's man, out to battle injustice and destroy it wherever he found it, with no weak-kneed government giving him limp excuses. Decker was judge and justice, an avenging fury, better known as the Slaughterer.*

*Slowly, carefully Decker picked his way over the bodies that littered the El Salvador sidewalk, his trusty companion, best friend and lover, the Smith & Wesson .45 by his side. His job was done here; it was time to move on.*

*Back to the real world, back to the compound hidden deep in the bowels of the ugliest, best city in the world: New York. He rubbed a bloody hand across his sweat-streaked face and looked north. It was good to be a man, in a man's world, he thought.*

*Who knows where his next assignment might come from? Wherever evil stalked the world, wherever injustice flourished, Matt Decker was there to combat it, to wipe it out in a blaze of gunfire. Someone once said there were eight million stories in every city. As of the last census they*

*might be down to seven million, but Matt Decker, the
Slaughterer, could seek out and find that one story that
needed his own particular brand of expertise. He gave his
smoking Smith & Wesson a fond look and moved into the
shadows. It was time to start.*

JESSICA HANSEN dropped the cheap paperback thriller
onto her desk and looked down at the thin fingers that
tapped the teak-and-mahogany surface in front of her.
The hands were curiously small for someone of her
height, the fingers narrow and nervous-looking, the
discreetly elegant rings hanging loosely. A perfect
pearly shade of pink adorned the long nails, nails that
were expensively maintained at a Madison Avenue
salon for a price that didn't bear thinking about. For a
moment Jessica stared at her fingertips, a sign of
pampered affluence that proclaimed her free of mun-
dane activities such as dishwashing, typing or gardening. *Like a Chinese empress,* she thought distantly,
turning the thin hands over to survey the soft, useless
palms. Not a sign of the calluses of her childhood, not a
mark anywhere. Except for the faint, spidery tracing of
scars across her delicate wrists. So faint that no one else
had noticed them or come up with difficult questions
she'd rather not answer.

She turned her palms back down toward the desk,
banishing the thought of those scars from her mind
with her customary efficiency. She leaned forward and
pressed the intercom buzzer. "Jilly, hold all my calls."
Her voice had its usual smooth, self-controlled calm,
never hinting at the turmoil that kept her stomach
knotted and her hands clenched in fists.

"Mr. Kinsey is expecting you in half an hour, Jessica," Jilly's efficient British voice returned, but beneath it Jessica could hear the soft note of concern. So much for the efficacy of her mask, she thought wearily.

"Which Mr. Kinsey? Peter or his father?"

"The old man himself. I don't know if it's important or not...."

"A word to the wise, Jilly," Jessica managed in a perfect drawl. "When the president of the company wants to see you it's always important."

"Even if he's going to be your father-in-law?"

"Especially if he's going to be your father-in-law," Jessica said. "Though you know as well as I do that nothing's official."

"Not yet." Jilly's voice left little doubt that it was just a matter of time. Whether that voice approved or not was another matter. "Shall I tell the old man you'll be up?"

Jessica hesitated. Never had she made a decision based on emotion rather than professionalism in her enormously successful career at Kinsey Enterprises. Indeed, there'd been no room in her life for emotion at all. Until recently, when she'd been unable to fight the wearying depression that kept trying to swamp her.

"Call Peter for me, Jilly," she said suddenly, giving in to temptation and despising herself for it. "Tell him...tell him something's come up. Have him head his father off."

"Something concerning the Lincoln merger?" Jilly suggested, understanding far too well.

"Yes...no. Then they'd want to know what it is. Tell him I'll explain later. He'll cover for me."

"Of course he will. Is there anything I can do, Jessica?" The concern wasn't even masked at this point, and at the other end of the disembodied voice, alone in her spacious office, Jessica grimaced in sudden pain.

"No, thanks, Jilly. I just...have a wretched headache and too much work to get done to deal with interruptions. I owe you one."

"Anytime."

The intercom went dead. It was already late Friday afternoon—almost everyone had left the headquarters of Kinsey Enterprises. Everyone but the workaholics. Her desk was clear, spotlessly neat, not a trace of work in sight, with Hamilton MacDowell's latest installment of *The Slaughterer* beckoning with all its gory glory. She turned to look out the wide windows, past the Turner landscape, to the New York skyline, never noticing that her hands had once more clenched into fists.

At the age of thirty-one Jessica had her life ruthlessly under control. She had climbed to just within reach of the top of her profession, that summit shimmering in sight, about to drop into her lap like a ripe plum. Vice-president of Kinsey Enterprises, Inc., she was about to become engaged to the president's charming, intelligent, cultured son, she was the pampered protégée of old Jasper Kinsey himself and she was in the midst of overseeing a merger with the Lincoln Corporation that would pull them back from a dangerous precipice and quite possibly double their already substantial profits. So why was she sitting at her desk, her hands clenched in front of her, wondering how in the world she was going to escape?

Could it be burnout? Jessica had taken seminars on

the subject, determined to avoid that seemingly omni-present threat to corporate success. Impossible. Financial and personal triumph loomed directly ahead, her past put firmly, completely behind her. The taste of success was sweet, she told herself, ignoring the flavor of ashes in her mouth.

One hand unclenched to push through her hair. What there was left of it. The wheat-colored tendrils were beginning to reach just below her small ears, and thoughtlessly, nervously, her hand clutched at the razored strands. She'd have to have it trimmed again, she thought absently, pushing it back as she ignored the sudden rebellious thought. She didn't want to go in for her biweekly trim, she didn't want Felipe nagging at her, forcing food on her, clucking in that maddening way as he sculpted the shining honey-blond cap.

"Only you could wear your hair this short and still look feminine, darling," he'd fussed last week. "But don't you think it's time for a change? Here, eat some cannoli." He'd shoved the rich pastry in front of her, and it had taken all her resolve not to throw up in his face. It would have served him right. "You're beginning to have a faintly concentration-camp kind of look to you, and the hair doesn't help. Eat, for heaven's sake!"

Even now, the thought of food made her gag. She hadn't eaten enough in the last few weeks to keep a bird alive, and she knew it. But knowing it wasn't enough to work up an appetite. Jessica had spent so much of her life fighting to keep off the extra pounds that could so easily creep up and turn her five-foot-eight-inch frame into a graceless lump that the thought of being too thin was incomprehensible.

Restlessly she pushed back from the desk to stride over to the windows. New York was dark and dirty that summer afternoon, the oppressive heat and humidity trapping the smog and smothering the city with it. Up on the thirty-seventh floor Jessica could feel the darkness invade her light, airy office, and not even the lemon-yellow carpet, her one concession to frivolity in the past ten years, could dispel it. Her feet were silent as they crossed the room, the tap of the leather shoes muffled in the deep buttery pile. The heavy weighted door to her private bathroom opened silently beneath her thin nervous hands and shut just as silently behind her. Leaning against the marble sink, she stared at her reflection.

The Snow Queen stared back. The Ice Princess, encased in her impervious calm. Large, assessing, chilly blue eyes filled her thin face, shadowed by pale mauve shadows that Elizabeth Arden couldn't quite disguise. The ruthlessly short blond hair stood in spikes around her small, well-shaped head, setting off her small ears, delicately pointed chin and nose. Her mouth was large and pale and unused to smiling, and the face she turned to the world was one of unruffled calm and control.

Her Ralph Lauren suit was hanging loosely around her tall, slender frame. Felipe, damn him, was right; she was getting too thin. At this rate anorexia was right around the corner. But somehow nothing could make her eat. And Peter seemed to find her slimness—no, her skinniness—attractive. Maybe she should gain weight, she thought, with a flash of mocking, uncustomary humor.

It must simply be nerves about the merger. A great

deal rested on its outcome. Her career, perhaps, her relationship with Peter, the future of Kinsey Enterprises. Once it was safely wrapped up, she'd feel more like herself again. Although who that self was, she couldn't quite say.

She looked up from her slender, elegant body. Concentration camp indeed! The ice-blue eyes looked into their mirrored partner; the cool, controlled, distantly amused false smile that she had perfected over the years played about her pale lips. And then, to her absolute horror, the face in the mirror crumpled suddenly in uncontrollable grief and despair. And Jessica quickly turned away, unable to witness her own naked pain, and remembered.

No one could have called it a happy childhood, not by the wildest stretch of the imagination. And yet Jessica had always comforted herself and her sisters with the doubtful assurance that others had it far, far worse. After all, their parents stuck together, through thick and thin, on the wagon or off, clinging to each other with what surely must be a deep, abiding love. Many of their friends' parents were divorced, the children forced to shuttle back and forth between two stilted, guilt-ridden households. At least they still all had one another.

And they weren't beaten, or abused. Certainly, Daddy had knocked Maren against the wall one night when he'd been drinking and she'd come in late from a date. He'd called her a tramp, ordered her from the house, and it had taken all Jessica's tact and diplomacy to soothe the raging belligerence of her father, the tearful defiance of her seventeen-year-old sister, while their mother kept silent behind the locked guest-room door. The little peacemaker, her father had called her during his sober days. The little mother, trying desperately to make things all right, he'd said, laughing and promising to change. And he would change, for weeks, months—even, on one glorious occasion, for two miraculous years of sobriety. But then something would happen and he'd be back again, the tearful, bellicose, sodden heap of a man taking over her father's charming persona.

And Jessica would tell her older sister, Maren, and her younger sister, Sunny, that they were better off. Some people's parents never stopped drinking, never even tried. Look at Uncle Bob Lemming's family. Not that he was really their uncle, just a drinking crony of their father's from way, way back. And at least it wasn't all bad. Mother and Daddy were never down at the same time. Once Daddy started drinking, Mother would become strong and maternal, the wage earner, the dominant force, relying on Jessica to keep the home going, the meals on time, her sisters in school. Until Daddy would begin to pull himself up again, go back to AA meetings. And then Mother's nerves would shatter, and it would be time for Daddy to be sober and strong. All the while the three children would cling to one another for comfort and safety.

At least there was enough money. And Daddy's drinking was never so bad that he lost a job. He was a very bright man, was Lars Hansen, a talented, charming engineer with an astounding ability to get the job done. Employers gladly overlooked his periods of diminished effectiveness, knowing from long experience that they didn't last forever.

Except that sometimes they seemed to. There were no dates for Jessica, who was too tall and too fat and too caught up in trying to hold her family together, in soothing her father's insecurities, in healing her mother's fears, in bringing up the family that would fall to pieces without her. There were no friends for Jessica, who spent her spare time reading and daydreaming when she wasn't struggling with the bland, packaged carbohydrate-laden food her mother bought for Jessica to prepare. And there was no peace for Jessica, who balanced her maternal concern between her parents and her rebellious sisters, Jessica who tried so desperately to make everything all right and who couldn't help but fail in the face of overwhelming odds, time and time again.

There was only this life and this family she had been born into, was trapped in. She used to daydream about going off to boarding school, being with other girls, away from the constant demands of an overwhelming family. She knew she could never go, even if her parents would part with the money. She wouldn't even go to college, not until Sunny and Maren had escaped and her parents had come to some sort of peace. They couldn't make it without her, could they? None of them could. No, her life could wait, just a few more years. She was only fifteen—Maren was going to the University of Minnesota that fall, Sunny was their high school's most promising track star. Jessica knew exactly what she was running from.

But when Jessica was sixteen everything changed.

Maren was away at college, and there were only the two of them. For a while things were more peaceful. Daddy wasn't drinking, and Mother, though lost in a chronic depression, seemed to have controlled her rages. Maren still bore the scar from one of those rages—the time their mother had smashed all the china, a large shard flying across the room and embedding itself in Maren's right leg.

And Jessica allowed herself to breathe a tiny sigh of relief. Until the afternoon when she came home from school and found her father passed out on the sofa, and Uncle Bob Lemming waiting for her, his reddened face wreathed in a smile, the look that she had come to expect and dread in his bloodshot eyes, the smell of Scotch on his breath.

SPRINGER MACDOWELL slid his long, long legs back down into the cramped confines of his 1963 Lotus Europa and started the engine, listening to the instant purr with a distant satisfaction. Satisfaction with his car, but not his life. Why was he doing this again? Why did he let himself in for the complete, unutterable weariness of driving cross-country every year, and for what? For the dubious pleasure of seeing the old man who by some accident had fathered him and then betrayed him, that twenty-year-old betrayal still raw in Springer's soul. Returning to New York every summer only brought back all the pain and doubt and anger that he usually managed to squash down, and even the presence of his mother couldn't prevent it all from spilling over. So why did he come?

The western Pennsylvania highway stretched out in

front of him, heat shimmering from the pavement, the lush greenery passing in a blur. His eyes were trained on the road with single-minded concentration, a concentration necessary after three days on the road with only the bare minimum of stops. He knew that if he took his time he might never make it to New York, might turn around and head back to the West Coast, and to hell with his father. But he'd promised his mother, promised Elyssa that he'd try one more time to heal the broken ties with his bastard of a father. And too many people had broken their promises to her—he wasn't going to be another one, even if it killed him.

And it wouldn't. He'd seen his father too many times in the past twenty years; he knew full well he could deal with it, even managing to be pleasant if the situation called for it. But Hamilton MacDowell wasn't fooled. He knew his son hated him, he knew why, and there was absolutely nothing he could or would do about it. Except stumble through Elyssa's periodic attempts at reconciliation with the same miserable grace that Springer mustered. And doubtless breathe the same sigh of relief that Springer did when they finally were released from each other's onerous presence.

Releasing some of the pressure from the accelerator, Springer stretched the long legs that had given him the nickname that still clung to him. John Springer Mac-Dowell, king of the Princeton basketball court, second only to Bill Bradley in the college's history, Springer MacDowell of the mile-long arms and legs and the devastating hook shot that had made more than one professional recruiter drool and then weep, as Springer calmly and resolutely turned his back on their lucrative

offers. Hamilton had been too proud of his son, too
eager for Springer to succeed. Once aware of his
father's belated paternal pride, Springer had done the
only thing he could think of to punish the old man.
He'd enlisted in the marines with the express purpose
of going to Vietnam and rubbing the liberal old man's
nose in it.

But that, too, had backfired. It wasn't Hamilton Mac-
Dowell who suffered from the deprivation, the soulless, violent agony that was war. It was Springer, who
since his father's betrayal had done everything he could
to squash down any signs of sensitivity, Springer who
had to deal with the soul-destroying despair warfare
brings. And still had to deal with it.

Reaching up one large, well-shaped hand, he pushed
the mirrored sunglasses up to rub the bridge of his
nose. It was a definitive nose, not quite Hamilton's imposing beak, but a determined, hawklike blade none-
theless, giving his face a brutal look not tempered by
the high cheekbones, deep-brown—almost black—
eyes and thick straight, silky black hair. His mother had
likened him to an Indian, knowing full well he got his
spectacular looks from her, not the father who had be-
queathed him the bladelike nose and a legacy of pain
and hatred.

Women had always responded to those looks, to
Springer's immensely tall, wiry body, the distant, beautiful face and those dark, unfathomable, lost eyes. And
Springer had always taken advantage of that response,
taking what was offered with pleasure and irresponsibil-
ity and a complete disregard for commitment. Even his
brief marriage hadn't curtailed his amatory activities.

Only a reluctant maturity had done that, so that now, at age thirty-five, he'd gone for the longest period of celibacy since the discovery of his father's betrayal. It had been five months since he'd slept with a woman, and he was in no mood to remedy that situation. He was mortally tired of faceless bodies, of casual sex, of the ritual mating dance that ended before it even began, ended in a tangle of sheets and limbs and performances. Maybe he was more like his father than he wanted to believe.

He'd promised Elyssa he'd stay for a month. Already the time loomed ahead like a prison sentence. He wouldn't get in till well past midnight—that would kill one day. Only twenty-nine after that. His strong, tanned hands clenched around the leather-covered steering wheel, and once more the large foot in the well-worn Nikes pressed down on the accelerator. The sooner he got there, the sooner he could be gone. And the Lotus sped along the Pennsylvania highway like an arrow, straight and true to the heart.

ONLY A TRACE of redness marred the cool blue beauty of Jessica's eyes as she slid once more behind the empty desk and waited, waited for God knows what. *It must simply be stress,* she told herself firmly. Understandable stress, caused by the upcoming merger that depended so much on her initiative and her ability to charm X. Rickford Lincoln during the upcoming weekend. Not to mention the changes her expected success would wreak in her life. The vice-presidency was everything she had worked for, everything she had longed for. Peter Kinsey, charming, passive, clever, would propose marriage. It would be a good match for her, a sensible, advantageous mating of brains and blue blood and ruthless ambitions. They would both supply the brains—her determination would more than make up for her Scandinavian blood, which wasn't quite WASP-ish enough. In the past few months Peter had been devoted, charming and diffident enough to allow her to keep the relationship on a platonic level. But once the merger went through, the engagement formalized, she'd have no more excuses. None that he would believe, anyway.

It was going to be a busy weekend, no doubt of that, and she'd have felt a lot better able to face it if she'd had more than a few hours of sleep every night during the past week, if she'd managed to eat more than a mouthful or two at her irregular meals. Rickford Lincoln was a recently divorced man in his late sixties, a big, powerful bull of a man eager to celebrate his new freedom. And Jessica had the distinctly uneasy impression that he wanted to celebrate that freedom with her. What had started out as sly glances and lubricious looks during the early part of the negotiations several months ago had quickly graduated to semiserious propositions, seemingly innocent touches that always managed to graze her flat buttocks or the gentle swell of her breasts. And Jessica had used that attraction, played with it with masterly cleverness, stringing him along to the point of agreeing to the merger with no more than a promising smile, just the right amount of reluctance in moving out of the way of his damp, clutching fingers, and the hint of wonders to come in her cool blue eyes.

It had worked, as it had worked so often in the past

during her climb up the corporate ladder. A smile here, a word there, always stopping just short of cementing it with an affair. Not that anyone had realized she did stop there—she had the reputation of being a cool customer, ready to sleep her way discreetly to the top. So far she had managed to avoid it with practiced skill, but she wasn't sure how much longer she could do so.

Her priorities were clear, and sooner or later she'd have to pay the price. Her ambitions and talents had stood her in good stead, leading her to Jasper Kinsey's table, Peter Kinsey's side, a vice-presidency in Kinsey Enterprises, Inc., and a future as part of that wealthy, safe family. And if that future included trading her body for Peter's practiced caresses, then it could have been far worse. He was never rough, never inconsiderate in their restrained petting, and she was very skilled in simulating responses that left him convinced she would be a mass of passion when they finally made love, and that he would be capable of satisfying her as no man had ever had. And in a way, he would. She loved the holding part of sex, the gentle stroking that preceded and followed the act, the feeling of safety cradled in his arms. If her limited experience in making love had left her cold and removed, she knew well enough how to disguise that fact, could always disguise that fact with her actress's ability.

Or at least she had been up till now. Her one experience a few years earlier had been unpleasant and undignified, but her partner, a self-satisfied lawyer named Philip Mercer, had been convinced of his prowess. She could convince Peter just as easily. But X. Rickford Lincoln might prove to be a different matter.

"Jessica, are you in there?" Jasper Kinsey's bluff tones were unmistakable, and for a brief, mad moment Jessica considered diving under the desk. Jilly was long gone, no longer able to run interference for her, and Peter must have failed in his bid to distract his father's attention.

Quickly she ran a nervous hand across her dry face. Just what she needed—a confrontation with old Jasper's far-too-observant eyes.

Of course she had no time to duck. She dropped her hand, raised her head and presented her cool, Snow Queen smile to her future father-in-law and current boss as he strode into her office.

"There you are, Jessica," he said in an accusing voice. "Peter was trying to tell me some nonsense about you being tied up. This is an important weekend; I don't need to tell you that."

"No, Jasper, you don't need to tell me that," she said evenly. "I'll be coming out to the Hamptons tomorrow morning, definitely before noon. I have a few things to clear up...."

"Rick Lincoln is coming out tonight."

A small shiver of distaste ran across her backbone, but her face was impassive as always. "I know, Jasper. And he'll be there for the entire weekend. I'm sure I won't be missed for the first night."

"I wouldn't be sure of any such thing, Jessica. You've handled this merger very nicely, very nicely indeed. Lincoln is ready to be landed like a fish on a line, and we need to be certain you don't let him wriggle off."

Jasper gave her what passed for a benevolent smile,

but Jessica wasn't fooled, even for a moment. No one had said a word, not even the slightest hint had escaped that anything more than corporate wheeling and dealing was expected of her. But somehow, somewhere she had gotten the uneasy feeling that she was the sacrificial lamb to be offered to Lincoln's aging libido, with Jasper and Peter Kinsey the benevolent bystanders. And the idea was destroying her almost nonexistent appetite, robbing her of her sleep, and stringing her nerves out until she was ready to scream.

But damn it, it wasn't their decision. It was her body, it had always been her choice how she used it. And it still would be. She wasn't going out to the Hamptons until she decided how she was going to handle things if push came to shove. After all, what did one night mean when balanced with millions of dollars' profit, security and power for the rest of her life? She was more than adept at turning her mind into a peaceful blank when the situation called for it.

"I know what's expected of me, Jasper," she said in the cool, tranquil voice that was one of her greatest assets, not sure of any such thing. "And you can trust me to handle this. Have I ever let you down?"

"No." He granted her that. "But what the hell's keeping you from coming out to the house tonight?"

Jessica's thin fingers clenched around the paperback book, and sudden inspiration struck. "I promised Elyssa I'd see her," she improvised quickly, always a gifted liar when the situation called for it. "Of course, I can always call her and cancel...."

Jasper Kinsey had two ambitions in life. One, to found a financial empire beyond his most avaricious dreams. The realization of that ambition was tantamount to impossible, given the scope of his greedy fantasies, and his second goal was just as farfetched. He wanted to marry Elyssa MacDowell, a woman he'd coveted for almost thirty years. He was no closer to her bed than he had been when he first met her, when she was the child-bride of Hamilton MacDowell, but he never gave up hope. His almost doglike devotion hadn't interfered with his voracious sex life, but Elyssa was still a weak point in Jasper Kinsey's stalwart defenses.

"No, no." It was an immediate about-face. "You go see Elyssa. But be with us in time for lunch, Jessica. I'm going to have a hard enough time making excuses to Lincoln about tonight."

"Have Peter make them for me," she suggested.

Jasper gave her a sharp, suspicious look, but she merely continued her distant composure. "I'll do that," he said finally. "By eleven tomorrow, Jessica. I'm depending on you."

"You know that you can."

Jasper specialized in abrupt departures. Jessica sat there, watching the empty doorway, listening to the sound of his footsteps echoing down the deserted hallways of Kinsey Enterprises on a late Friday afternoon.

The reprieve made her almost dizzy with relief. She leaned back in her chair, weakly grateful that fate had allowed her that last-minute inspiration. Elyssa had already told her she was spending the weekend at her ex-husband's town house. Her calm, good sense and undemanding warmth would soothe away Jessica's rough edges, and Hamilton's acerbic wit would brighten her up again. And she could continue out to the

Kinseys tomorrow morning feeling far more able to face the decisions the coming night might or might not bring.

She picked up *The Slaughterer* again, smiling fondly at Hamilton MacDowell's bearded photograph on the back cover. Matt Decker's creator would provide the perfect haven of rest and reflection that she so badly needed. Tossing the novel in her purse, she pushed away from the desk and headed out into the dubious freedom of the weekend.

## Chapter Two

Hamilton MacDowell was a big, bluff, hearty bear of a
man, with a mane of thick gray hair, a full beard, a
stomach that attested to a life of enjoying good food
and the wit and soul of a bon vivant. He greeted Jessica
with an exuberant hug, crushing her against his body,
which towered over her Nordic height, held her away
and clucked his tongue.

"You looked starved, my girl. Doesn't Kinsey let
you get anything to eat? I'm all for pleasures of the
flesh, but food is one of them. Woman cannot live by
sex alone." He released her, long enough to turn to his
ex-wife with the same welcome, tinged with a melancholy sadness that always seemed to edge his dealings
with Elyssa MacDowell. "Elyssa, my love. You look
absolutely ravishing, as always."

Elyssa smiled faintly, used to Ham's hyperbole, returned his kiss and settled comfortably against him as he
flung one beefy arm around her narrow shoulders to lead
her into the compact little town house they had shared
for more than fifteen years. Though in this case, Hamilton's words were no exaggeration. Elyssa MacDowell
was quite simply stunning, her fifty-three years sitting

on her with a grace and beauty that magically seemed to increase with time. She was small, fine-boned and slender, with silver-gray hair, cropped close to her head, that had once been silky black. Her eyes were a dark, liquid brown, her faintly lined brow serene, her mouth gentle, her nature solid as a rock. She smiled up at her ex-husband with real, uncomplicated love.

"I hope we didn't disrupt any plans, Ham," she said in the low, well-modulated voice that was part and parcel of her charm. "But Jessica has a case of terminal gloom, and I decided it was our duty to try to cheer her up."

"My pleasure, darling, but how will young David feel about losing your company?"

"He'll survive," Elyssa replied dryly, pulling out of his embrace with a grimace. "As long as old Johnson doesn't mind."

"Touché," Hamilton said lightly. "It's your business if you choose to become involved with a man not much older than your son."

"Yes, it is," she replied, matching his lightness. "Just as it's your business if you choose to become involved with a man old enough to be your father."

Ham let out a short bark of laughter. "Don't let Johnson hear you say that. He prides himself on his youthful appearance."

"Is he here?" Elyssa looked about her with distant curiosity.

"Heavens, no. Have you forgotten that Springer is due sometime in the next few days? I have no intention of rubbing salt into old wounds."

Jessica looked up, startled, from her perusal of the Picasso that adorned one wide, white wall of the eclectic town house. "Your son is coming? I had no idea,

Elyssa, or I never would have intruded. I know how seldom you see him."

"Hush, hush, little one," Hamilton murmured, the only human being who could call her that and get away with it. "If he does happen to show up an added presence will only ease matters. Springer and I have never gotten along, despite Elyssa's best efforts, and he's only here under duress. I don't really expect him for another day or two, anyway. In the meantime, your presence this evening will be a delightful respite. But you must promise to eat. When Elyssa called to tell me you were coming along, I became positively inspired, and I won't have you insulting my *bœuf en daube*."

"You know perfectly well I don't eat *bœuf* in any language," Jessica replied tartly, her first real smile of the day taking the sting out of her words. "I'll have to settle for cottage cheese and canned peaches."

Hamilton shuddered theatrically. "Try it and I'll force-feed you, and I have little doubt Elyssa will help. Have you ever heard of anorexia nervosa, darling? It's looming on the horizon if you don't watch yourself."

"Yes, I would love a drink," Jessica said firmly, flinging her exhausted body down on the white sofa that somehow never seemed to show a mark.

"Dubonnet Blonde?" At her nod Hamilton bustled off in the direction of the kitchen. He already knew Elyssa's taste from their years of marriage. "And I've made a nice little mustard chicken for you, darling. Nothing to compromise your high morals." With a little wave his burly figure disappeared into the kitchen.

"Why the stricken face?" Elyssa questioned softly, ever observant.

"Just Ham's choice of words," Jessica replied, giving herself a tiny shake. "My morals don't feel very uncompromised right now."

Elyssa nodded, used to Jessica's frank speaking, knowing full well that she spoke so openly to no one else. They had become friends when Jessica had first arrived at Kinsey Enterprises, a cool, determined Snow Queen, just out of college and ready to conquer the world. Elyssa was a major stockholder and one of Jasper Kinsey's oldest friends, a warm, bright lady with capabilities far exceeding her limited social duties as the token woman on the board of trustees. For some reason Jessica's coolness and Elyssa's warmth had blended, and their unlikely friendship was the one real relationship Jessica could count on.

"Some problem with the Lincoln merger?" Elyssa probed gently.

"Not necessarily. Perhaps I'm just being paranoid," Jessica said morosely, then swiveled in her seat to look beseechingly up at her friend. "You don't suppose Peter and his father are planning to have me sleep with old Lincoln just to cement the deal, do you?"

Elyssa hesitated, clearly torn between honesty and a desire to reassure her. That hesitation was answer enough, and her words did little to improve matters. "I don't really know. I think Jasper's capable of turning a blind eye if it helps business, but I don't know about Peter. I do think he really loves you, and I can't believe he'd want anyone to hurt you. But my opinion isn't the point. What do you think?"

Jessica shrugged, the familiar black gloom and indecisiveness settling down around her. "I don't know. I suppose I'll find out soon enough. We're all going to be out at the summer house this weekend; things should be pretty obvious by the time we get back to the city. I don't suppose I could talk you into coming with me." It was a forlorn hope, and reluctantly Elyssa shook her head.

"David's got all sorts of plans for this weekend, and you know how possessive he can be," she said apologetically.

Jessica knew full well how possessive David Linnell could be, and not for the first time she wondered how Elyssa could stand his petulant displays of temper. Of course, David Linnell was thirty-nine years old, arrogant and extremely attractive. And after Hamilton's dereliction Elyssa somehow needed that demanding possessiveness that Jessica found infuriating. She managed a tight smile. "Of course. But what about your son, if and when he shows up?"

A small frown wrinkled Elyssa's wide, usually serene brow. "We'll work it out," she said vaguely, and Jessica repressed a disbelieving snort. If David had his way, Elyssa would sever all her relationships with friends and family, existing only for his selfish wants. He and Jessica frankly and quietly detested each other, he recognizing her as a major threat to his control, and she despising his petty demands. How the introduction of Elyssa's adored son into the ten-month-long relationship would change, it remained to be seen.

Hamilton bustled in, his imposing paunch swathed in a white apron, bearing a tray of drinks with a silver frame tucked under one arm. Serving the drinks with a flourish, he whipped out the framed picture, setting it on the polished cherry end table with a fond swipe at an imaginary speck of dust. "Have you ever seen my son, Jessica?" he inquired with intense paternal pride.

Jessica stared at the silver-framed photograph, her mouth hanging open. "That's Springer?" she inquired faintly. He was laughing at the photographer, the black hair ruffled by a brazen wind, the eyes crinkled against the bright sunlight, a warmth and light love in those immensely dark eyes. You could fall into those eyes, she thought dazedly, fall into those arms, get lost in that beautiful mouth. . . .

She quickly summoned forth her coolest smile. "He's very good-looking," she said distantly. "How come you don't keep his picture around?"

Hamilton laughed. "Are you kidding? If any of my friends took a look at that picture, they'd be showing up at any hour of the day or night, and somehow I don't think Springer would take to that too well. He only comes here under duress as it is—I doubt he'd care for the kind of attention my friends would give him."

"I take it he doesn't approve of your life-style," she said delicately.

Hamilton shrugged. "You could say so, indeed." Immediately he changed the subject. "That's a great photograph, isn't it? Elyssa took it a couple of years ago when she went out to visit him. That's why he looks so loving." There was no bitterness in Ham's voice, only a deep sadness, and Elyssa reached out a slender, ringless hand to touch his arm in silent, loving sympathy.

"Don't, darling," she said softly, and Ham smiled, his ruddy face accepting. "You'll make peace with him. Sooner or later," she added.

He nodded, placing one meaty hand over her slender one. "Ever the trusting, loving one, eh, Elyssa? I'll have to believe you're right in this case. I just hope it's sooner, rather than later." He gave himself a shake, rather like a massive Saint Bernard shedding water, and beamed at Jessica. "We're doing a fine job of cheering Jessica up. What do you say the three of us kill a couple of bottles of champagne? We need to celebrate your upcoming engagement, at the very least, and my upcoming rapprochement with my son. And what do we have to celebrate for you, Elyssa?"

"I'm thinking of moving in with David," she said, her calm, even voice unruffled.

Ham winced, and even Jessica was hard put to look properly enthusiastic. "Champagne sounds like a wonderful idea," she said finally.

"And you'll sleep over, Jessica? Elyssa was planning on spending tonight anyway, and you know there's always room for you. I don't want a drunken lady wandering around town unescorted."

She had done it often enough, with the entertaining addition of Hamilton's current lover, the elderly and charming malicious Johnson Endicott, and Jessica nodded her agreement. "But we'll have to send out for more champagne, Ham," Elyssa warned. "It'll take more than that to put a dent in the sobriety of two hard-boiled women like us."

"Hard-boiled," Ham scoffed. "Maybe you are, Elyssa, but Jessica's a frail lamb beneath her disguise." His voice was absolutely serious, and Jessica stared at him sharply, her eyes narrowed. But all Ham did was smile back at her blandly. "Don't give me that icy look, my

Norse goddess. You don't fool me for a moment. And when you get back from cavorting with your soulless fiancé, I want you to come over and meet my son. Maybe he can put some color in your cheeks and some meat on your bones. Of course, I'm not saying whose meat...."

"Ham!" Elyssa reproved on a muffled laugh. "Besides, I think you'll find Springer's changed."

"What, he's no longer bedding every female in sight?" his father scoffed. "I thought he'd still be trying to prove he's not the man his father is."

"I think, I hope, I pray he's coming to terms with who and what you and he are," Elyssa said slowly.

"He's had more than enough time," Hamilton grumbled. "I'll order more champagne. Moët or Piper?"

"Royalties still as good as ever, Ham?" Jessica inquired lazily from her perch on the comfortable sofa.

Ham shrugged self-deprecatingly. "What can I say? The world seems to be enamored of the Slaughterer and his bloodthirsty adventures. As long as I turn out one every two months I can safely keep us all in imported champagne."

Jessica lifted her glass. "Here's to the Slaughterer."

Ham responded. "And here's to my favorite ladies."

Elyssa raised her white wine. "And here's to happy endings."

"Unrealistic, my dear," said her ex-husband.

"Wishful thinking," said her friend. And they both drank.

## Chapter Three

Hamilton MacDowell's town house was dark and silent as Springer bounded up the broad front steps, his sneakered feet noiseless on the worn stone. It was after two in the morning—the welcoming committee would be sound asleep. Which was just the way Springer wanted it. The last thing he was in the mood for was the strained effort of his uncomfortable father, never sure whether he should attempt to embrace his son or not.

Sliding a large hand into the pocket of his jeans, he fished around until he came up with the set of keys needed to keep the world at bay in New York City. He never could remember which order they came in, and it took ten minutes of mild cursing to finally accomplish unlocking the fortress. Damn, he was too tired to have to deal with Hamilton's paranoia, he thought, resisting the impulse to slam the door shut behind him. The familiar smell came back to him as he paused in the hallway. The smell of his childhood—polished wood, potpourri, the faint, teasing tang of French cooking redolent of tarragon and thyme. And unexpectedly a sharp knot of grief hit him, leaving him suddenly as alone and vulnerable as a fifteen-year-old boy can be.

He swore then, a short, obscene word spoken out loud that quickly banished the ghosts. He was twenty years away from that time—and yet whenever he stepped back into this house those years fell away for a brief, devastating moment.

Moving on silent feet, he made a swift tour of the first floor, like a blind man familiarizing himself with possible pitfalls. The couch was the same one that had been there for a dozen years, though Hamilton had had it recovered in some nubby white cotton. The Wyeth still hung over the mantel, the Chippendale highboy that he used to hide his toy trucks in still presided with stately elegance in the corner. And there was that damned picture of him that Hamilton doubtless resurrected each time he was due for a visit, grinning as if he hadn't a care in the world. He remembered the day Elyssa had taken that picture—a clear, sunny day on Puget Sound with a stiff, warm breeze that swept away cobwebs and regrets with an impartial hand. He'd give five years of his life to be back there right now, not prowling around his father's living room, dreading the morning.

There was even the heavy silver ashtray that had held his first smoking attempts. It was Mexican, in the shape of a large sombrero, and when he was sixteen he'd stub out half-smoked cigarette after half-smoked cigarette in a ring around the silver hat brim.

Springer shook his head at youthful folly, feeling the remembered need for cigarettes that hit him in moments of stress. The next month would be filled with stress—cigarettes wouldn't help matters.

But a shower and a drink would. The town house was cool but not air-conditioned, and the long summer drive had left him hot and sticky, the shirt clinging to his back. Grabbing his suitcase, he bounded silently up the two flights of stairs to the solitary third-floor studio he had claimed for his own on his last visit. He even had his own private entrance—the once-used servants' stairway down to the kitchen and out the back. If he worked it just right, he wouldn't have to see much of Hamilton at all.

The room was just as he had remembered it—its sprawling proportions taking over all of the third floor, leaving just enough space for a Spartan bathroom. The bed was new—he'd fit in its king-sized proportions better than in the narrow single bed that had been there last time.

"A bribe, Hamilton?" he questioned wryly, his voice a husky drawl in the still, warm air. The windows were left open to the cooler night air, and Springer dumped his suitcase on the bed before heading for the shower. At least the bed would make the next thirty days more comfortable. He'd had to sleep diagonally in the single bed, and even then his feet had hung over the edge—and God knows what would have happened if he'd been fool enough to bring a woman home. They would have had to make do on the floor. Or on Hamilton's couch. There would have been a certain ironic satisfaction to that.

Coming out of the shower, he rubbed his thick black hair with a towel, eyeing the bed longingly. He could almost believe he might sleep, if it weren't for the telltale tension in his wrists, the silent tick-tick of his heartbeat. Pulling on a faded pair of jeans, he padded, barefoot, down the back stairway to the kitchen. He knew where Ham kept his brandy, and very fine brandy it was. It would do the trick. . . .

Springer stopped dead still in the doorway of the kitchen, a numbness washing over him, quickly replaced by a sick fury that left him shaking with rage. This time Hamilton hadn't gotten rid of his current protégé. His newest was standing at the kitchen stove, heating some milk, the brandy on the counter beside him. In the dim light Springer could see the tall, skinny body of the boy, wrapped in a florid silk kimono that flapped around his shapely bare, shaved legs. The face was thin, delicate beneath the close-cropped blond hair, the expression set and preoccupied.

With a great effort Springer willed himself to relax. He had to admit, his father's taste had improved in the past few years. This skinny, androgynous creature was at least more appealing than Johnson Endicott's raddled excesses. Well, he could be pleasant—he'd had more than twenty years to accept his father's preferences. He still found it easier to accept them in other people, but he wasn't about to cause a scene.

Nevertheless, some devil was prompting him, no doubt due to his nervous exhaustion. "Aren't you a little young for my father?" His husky voice broke the stillness in a studied drawl. "He usually prefers his boyfriends a little long in the tooth."

IT WAS UPON HER AGAIN. The screaming, clawing, smothering panic that spread over her, leaving her muscles paralyzed, her mouth open but no scream issuing forth. Her throat tightened, a clammy film of sweat covered

her skin, and somewhere in the distance she could hear
voices, shouting at her, screaming at her, calling her
filthy names....

She sat bolt upright, instantly wide awake. It took her
a moment to remember where she was. The lofty proportions of the town-house bedroom mocked her
panic. There was no need to check the glowing clock
beside the comfortable bed. It would be two forty-five.
It always was, each time the dream hit her, each time
she woke up. Sometimes the dream would be so deeply
embedded she'd remember nothing, only the remain-
ing tremors and the cold sweat covering her reminding
her that it had happened again.

Nothing had ever stopped them. Not sleeping pills,
alcohol, hypnotism, psychotherapy, deep relaxation or
yoga. And it had happened every damned night for the
past two weeks.

Wearily she sat there, her head in her hands, waiting
for the tremors to subside. She knew they would, knew
almost to the minute when the shudders would stop.
She pulled herself from the bed, wrapping Johnson's
silk kimono around her slender body. Chances were
she wouldn't sleep till dawn. Hot milk and brandy had
sometimes been able to fool her resistant body into
drifting off before then, and it was worth a chance.
Ham's kitchen would be deserted at this hour—she
could make her potion and pray that this would be one
of the lucky times. She didn't know how she could face
the decisions the weekend would bring if she didn't
have just a tiny bit more sleep.

There was definitely a feeling of unreality to the
sound of that husky drawl in the dimly lit kitchen. "My

father's boyfriends," he'd said. Slowly she turned, with majestic calm, to look at Elyssa's son.

He was quite a sight in the flesh. And a great deal of flesh there was. He was wearing nothing more than an old pair of jeans hugging the long legs that Hamilton had assured her could eat up a basketball court in seconds. The long, narrow feet were bare; he wore no belt and no shirt; his chest, dark with a summer tan, was wiry, muscled and lean, the flesh warm-looking to Jessica's jaded eyes. And he was standing there with that beautiful, aloof Indian face of his, branding her as one of his father's lovers. Male lovers at that. He obviously hadn't come to terms with his father, she thought absently, still staring at him.

Springer was leaning against the doorjamb, watching her out of hooded eyes that were clearly filled with contempt. "I'm Springer MacDowell," he added. "Hamilton obviously didn't expect me tonight, or you would have had your walking papers. When you go back to bed you might tell him I'm here." His voice was cold and cynical as he straightened up, prepared to head back upstairs.

Jessica later wondered what had come over her. She was usually the most deliberate of people, but something about Springer MacDowell's contempt, both for her and for a man she loved dearly, coupled with the almost brazen good looks, wiped out her usual care. She started toward him then, and the movement of her lithe, thin body halted him. She knew if she spoke her light, clear voice would give her away, just as the stronger light from the hallway would illuminate the very feminine lines of her face and eyes.

Without a word she came up to him, and his eyes were like chunks of black marble staring down at her. She wasn't used to looking up at men that much taller than her five feet eight—and it took her a moment to quell her reaction. But he had gauged it already, seen the flicker in her eyes in the darkened kitchen, and his mouth curled in disgust.

"Sorry, boy," he snapped. "I'm not your type." Before he could turn away she reached out one slender hand—the rings lay discarded on her bedside table—and came in contact with that warm smooth skin. She touched his arm, and of its own volition her hand slid across the smoothly muscled flesh, across his shoulder and down his chest. He stood very still, but she could feel his tension beneath her hands as he watched her.

Now that she had started she didn't quite know how to stop. It was also a fairly dangerous activity—from Springer's words she could guess that he wouldn't take very well to a strange man making a pass at him. She might get one of those strong, well-shaped hands driven into her empty stomach.

Jessica started to pull her hand away, and just as quickly his hand shot out, catching her wrist in an iron grip. "Don't stop now," he whispered, pulling her slowly forward. She tried to pull back, but her puny strength was useless against him. A moment later her slender, shaking frame was up against his hard, strong body. Staring up at him mutely, she tried to break his hold on her, but it was useless. She stood there, held against him, and waited.

Her breath was coming rapidly beneath the thin silk kimono, while his was even, steady, unmoved by her struggle. "You'll find I'm a hell of a lot more man than my father ever could be," he drawled. "If that's what you're looking for." And then to her horror one large hand came up and cupped the very definite swell of breast through the silk. "Unless, of course, you prefer other women. You look as if you might." And his mouth moved down toward hers.

Without hesitation she brought her knee up, but he was too fast for her. Before she knew what was happening she was released, a safe two feet away from him, her mouth untouched as her breast still tingled from his casual caress.

"What are you doing here?" he questioned evenly enough, not moving any closer.

For the first time Jessica spoke, her voice tight with tension in the still night kitchen. "Visiting," she snapped. "Not that it's any of your damned business."

He smiled then, a slow, wicked smile that on another man, at another time, might have penetrated her icy resolve. "Now I've placed you. You're Elyssa's friend Jessica, aren't you?" He cocked his head to one side. "You're not at all the way she described you."

Jessica knew exactly what she looked like. Pulling the thin silk closer around her narrow body, she could imagine how her small, pale face looked, the short hair standing in spikes all around. "Neither are you," she shot back. "Would you mind moving away from the door? I'd like to go to bed."

With a great show of insolent grace he moved, exaggeratedly careful not to touch her. "My visit might end up being more interesting than I thought."

"Don't expect me to provide entertainment," Jessica said in her cold, clipped voice. "I'm leaving first thing tomorrow morning to spend the weekend with my fiancé." There, that ought to slow him down.

The smile stayed damnably fixed. "Fiancé?" he said softly. "Bully for you. Anyone I know?"

"I doubt it. He's the head of the corporation I work for." Now why was she trying to impress him?

"Peter or Jasper Kinsey? Must be Jasper—you don't strike me as a woman who'd settle for second place on your climb to the top."

That was quite enough for one night. She withdrew even more, pulling the robe more tightly around her body. "Good night," she said coldly. 'I don't expect you'll be awake when I leave tomorrow, so I'll say good-bye, too." She moved past him, down the darkened hallway, without a backward glance. The overhead light silhouetted her slender body for a moment.

"I wouldn't count on it," he said softly. She was far too skinny, far too angry, far too ambitious for him to expend any energy on. Still, there was something about her that called to him. Maybe it was those blue eyes, cold and lost and angry. Or the stubborn set to her chin as she stared up at him. Or the vulnerable, unsmiling mouth that had first tipped him off to her sex. Not to mention that undeniable swell of breast that remained despite her skinniness. "No, Jessica, I wouldn't count on it at all."

# Chapter Four

***The Slaughterer, vol. 72: The Wrath of Decker***

*Matt Decker surveyed the carnage around him. He always forgot how much damage a machine gun could inflict in such a short period of time. The streets of Miami were spattered with blood, the blood of the enemy, and he saw it with satisfaction. If only he'd managed to find that amazon.*

*Her large blue eyes haunted him. Ilse, someone had called her. Probably part of the Baader-Meinhof gang. She'd taste his vengeance before long. No one was safe from the mighty justice of the Slaughterer for long. But how those wide blue eyes of hers haunted him.*

"YOU DON'T LOOK any more rested, Jessica," Ham said sternly. "And that's your third cup of coffee this morning. I'll have you know my coffee is very strong. You'd better cut it with some food or you'll be climbing the walls."

Jessica kept to her perch on the wooden stool in the big old kitchen, the same kitchen that had witnessed her disturbing, unlikely confrontation with Hamilton MacDowell's son. "If I have any food I'll fall asleep at the wheel halfway out to Long Island. I didn't get much sleep." That was an understatement. She had spent the hours from three to somewhere after seven staring into the darkness, her ears attuned to sounds from above her, sounds that never came. After another hour or two of fitful sleep she had dragged herself downstairs to face Hamilton and Elyssa's sympathetic company. She yawned hugely, then managed a stiff smile that fooled no one. "I think the sooner I get off the better."

"You can't, Jessica," Elyssa protested from her station by the coffeepot. "Springer came in sometime last night and I don't want you to take off without finally getting a chance to meet him."

Jessica hesitated only a moment. "Some other time, Elyssa. I really have to get an early start—you know how I hate driving on the expressways, and the longer I put it off the worse it will be."

"I'm ready when you are."

Considering that she had only heard that voice once before, the familiar way it slid down her spine was surprising. She didn't bother to turn, to give him the benefit of her attention, but then, there was no need. With a glad cry Elyssa threw down the linen towel and rushed into her son's arms.

"You're up early, darling," she murmured. "I thought you'd sleep till at least noon."

"Normally I would have, but I had a previous engagement," he said, smiling down fondly at her. A gloomy foreboding filled Jessica, and she watched the cool nod he exchanged with his father with a feeling of extreme wariness.

"You're not going off right away, are you?" Elyssa

cried. "You just got here, Springer, and I haven't seen you in months."

"Sorry, Ma," he said, slinging an arm around her slender shoulders and casting a speculative glance at Jessica's still form. "But I'm spending the weekend at Peter Kinsey's out on the island. He suggested I drive Jessica, since she apparently hates city driving."

Elyssa cast a confused glance between the two of them, taking in the wary stance of one, the mocking smile of the other. "You two somehow managed to meet?" she questioned carefully.

"Somehow," her son said. "We ran into each other looking for a midnight snack." He looked at his father then, the distant, cool look back in his eyes. "For a moment I thought you might have developed better taste in your old age."

"Springer," Elyssa reproved gently, but Hamilton took it in stride.

"Still your same winning ways, I see," Ham said softly. "Welcome to the East Coast, my boy. I'm glad you could make it." He held out one beefy hand, and Jessica found herself silently praying he would take it.

Springer waited just long enough for the tension to stretch to the breaking point, and then he reached out and took his father's hand. To Jessica's eyes it wasn't much of a concession, but to the others it was clearly a start, and nervous smiles broke some of the strain.

"I didn't know you and Peter still kept in touch," Ham said, handing him a cup of coffee. "I thought after Princeton you two drifted apart."

"We did." He took a long, appreciative sip, the shadows beneath his dark, fathomless eyes attesting to his exhaustion. "But when Jessie mentioned him last night I decided it was time to renew my acquaintance."

"Jessie?" Elyssa echoed, as Jessica choked on her coffee. "I've never heard you called a nickname before. I thought you didn't like them."

"I don't!" she snapped, setting her coffee cup down on the butcher-block table. She noticed with distant dismay that her hand trembled slightly, from both the caffeine and the presence of that infuriating man.

"Well, don't even bother trying to change Springer," Hamilton advised. "He'll call you any damn thing he wants, and there's nothing you can do about it."

"I can refuse to answer." She slipped off the stool. "And I'd better get going. Thanks again, Ham. I appreciate your shelter from the storm." She gave him a swift kiss on his raddled skin. Jessica wasn't the type to touch people, and when she did, it was for a very good reason. She wanted to show that cool, mocking creature that some people loved and cared about his father, didn't make arbitrary judgments and nasty cracks.

"I'm ready," Springer said blithely, draining his coffee.

Jessica plastered her Snow Queen smile to her tired facial muscles. "I'm not going with you."

His damnable grin widened, so that he looked like a huge Cheshire cat smiling down at her. One that just swallowed a canary. "Of course you are, Jessie," he said mildly enough. "You're a calm, sensible woman—you aren't going to be unreasonable about it. Peter was very pleased that I'd be able to drive you out there—apparently he worries about you in city traffic. Are you that bad a driver?"

"She's very good," Elyssa defended her, if not with perfect truthfulness. "She just doesn't like it."

"So if she doesn't like it, she can drive with me. Don't worry, Jessie, you'll come back with Peter. All you have to put up with is a couple of hours of my company. Surely you're tough enough to take it."

She shouldn't let him goad her, shouldn't let him challenge her like that. Her head snapped up; her eyes met his for a long, silent moment. "I'm tough enough," she said lightly.

He nodded—approvingly, she thought. "Where are your things?"

"Already at Peter's. I keep a change of clothes there." Was that defiance she heard in her own voice? What had happened to the Snow Queen?

"That's why you were prancing around in Johnson's hand-me-downs," he said, half to himself. "Then let's go."

"When do you think you'll be back?" Ham broke in. His voice sounded studiedly casual, but any fool could see the trace of desperation, the caring beneath the facade.

Any fool who cared to look. Springer didn't. "Late Sunday, probably. Don't change your plans for me." Jessica noticed he deliberately refrained from calling his father by name or title. "I'll be in and out during the next few weeks—I can look after myself."

Even he couldn't miss Elyssa's face falling in sudden dismay. Leaning down, he kissed her cheek lightly. "See you, Ma. Say hi to David for me."

His gaze turned to Jessica, and she told herself if he did anything disgustingly macho like take her arm to usher her out of the room she would kick him, and this time she wouldn't miss. But he didn't touch her, just waited patiently, and she had no choice but to precede him out of the kitchen.

"You like David?" she questioned on her way out the front door.

"What I've seen of him, yes. Don't you?"

"No," she said. And wondered why, for the first time in weeks, she was hungry.

HE DROVE FAST, and well, most of his attention on the crowded highway around him, only a small portion of his mind tuned to the tense, thin figure of the woman sitting beside him, her hands clenched in her lap beneath the loose-fitting linen suit. He wondered what devil had made him call Peter Kinsey that morning and cadge an invitation. He could tell himself that he was grabbing at any excuse to escape his father's town house, but he knew better. And it wasn't Peter Kinsey's undemanding charm that drew him, or the thought of a few days on the ocean. He lived on the ocean, in sight of the crashing Pacific, and the tame New York shoreline of the Atlantic held no great charm for him.

But he knew what had made him call Peter Kinsey; he just wasn't quite sure why. It was the cool, composed Ice Princess sitting beside him who had teased him, tickled him, edged him into an uncharacteristic whim. And he didn't even like her, or anything about her. He had had his share of cold, overly ambitious women, with no heart or soul, just a driven need for power. He didn't need another one. He told himself last winter that he was tired of athletic performances and no emotion. For thirty-five years he had avoided commitment like the plague. Whether he deserved it or not, he wasn't about to turn around and get involved with a woman just as incapable of it.

Besides, she'd already committed herself to Peter Kinsey. His mouth curved in a mocking smile. She certainly had her priorities straight.

"What's so funny?" she demanded testily. His smile broadened. She'd been more aware of him than she'd been pretending, which suited him just fine. It might provide an entertaining diversion to see just how uptight Miss Jessica Hansen who didn't like nicknames was. Could he get beneath the frosty exterior, make her chilly eyes warm with wanting? Could he have her, writhing and twisting beneath him, above him, warm and pliant and loving? Somehow he doubted even Peter Kinsey saw her that way. He never could resist a challenge, and she definitely was one, with her icy demeanor and long, lean limbs. He did like a tall woman.

"Funny?" he echoed finally, contemplating what would get the fastest reaction from her. "I was just wondering how long it was going to take me to get you in bed." He waited for her reaction to his opening salvo.

It took him completely by surprise. Her eyes widened in momentary shock, then drooped seductively. She put one slender hand on his forearm, the manicured fingertips lightly kneading the skin with just the right amount of pressure. Not too light, not too hard— it was completely sensual and made him think suddenly of how that expert touch would feel on other, more sensitive parts of his body. He'd obviously underestimated her sexual capabilities. She leaned forward, her face very close to his, and he could smell the coffee on her breath, warm and sweet and almost unbearably enticing. Her lips were close to his, so that they almost grazed him, and her voice was soft, breathless and low. "It'll be a cold day in hell," she murmured.

Jessica pulled back into her seat, a satisfied smirk adorning her pale face. Obviously she thought she had put him in his place. He quickly disabused her of the notion. "That's quite good, you know," he remarked in a conversational tone. "Just the right amount of come-hither. Is that how you made it to vice-president in such a short time? By being the ultimate tease?"

If he didn't know better he would have thought that was an unbidden pain that clouded her clear blue eyes. "Of course," she said in a brittle voice. "Except that I usually deliver."

For some reason he didn't believe her. And then he cursed himself for being a romantic fool. Jessica Hansen fascinated him, as she doubtless meant to. It had to be part of her power, like a black widow spider's. She'd probably slept with everyone from the stockboy on up, and he had lost his taste for shopworn relationships, hadn't he? Casting a furtive glance at her self-contained profile, he was no longer so sure.

"Do you want to stop for something to eat?" he said suddenly, wanting to get away from the car, wanting to sit across from her at a table and talk like rational human beings, not unexpected enemies. He could see her hesitate for a moment, then shake her head resolutely. "Anorexia isn't in anymore," he added as a little jab.

It bounced off. "It was your decision to forgo breakfast," she said serenely. "You'll just have to wait till we get to the Kinseys. I'm sure there'll be mountains of food to keep you occupied."

"I can think of better ways to keep occupied," he drawled. "Do you think there'll be any unattached women around, or will I have to share you with Peter?"

Strangely enough, she took his question seriously. "There'll be other women. You'll be able to take your pick."

Springer couldn't help himself, and afterward he wondered why he said it. And meant it. "I pick you, then."

She shut her eyes in sudden pain. "Stop it, Springer," she said wearily, and he liked the sound of his name on her pale mouth. "Stop playing with me and stop watching me."

His eyes moved from her set face, dropping to the hands curved palm upward—loose, for a change—in her lap. And he saw the scars across her wrists, old and faded, but inexorably there. They must have been deep once, long ago. And then he raised his eyes to meet her stricken ones, and she slowly turned her hands palm downward on her lap.

He didn't even hesitate. All teasing had vanished, and he moved his hand from the steering wheel and placed it over one of her still ones. His hand was large, strong and warm, and it enveloped hers. He waited for her to pull away, but she made no move. Keeping her face averted, she leaned back against the worn leather seat and closed her weary eyes. Leaving her hand in his warm, oddly comforting grip.

WHEN JESSICA HAD COME HOME that afternoon her sister Sunny was at track practice and wasn't due back till six. Her mother was working, volunteer work at the hospital. She worked there every Tuesday, as Uncle Bob knew. Jessica had stood there inside the door, staring at her father's comatose figure, the heavy snores that should have been comical wafting through the room, her eyes filled with panic as Uncle Bob had loomed over her.

They hadn't believed her, of course. Her father had slapped her face and called her a tramp. Her mother had looked her up and down with that cool, disapproving look she had perfected long ago and smiled a disbelieving smile. And Sunny had continued to run, shutting herself away from the family hysteria. And everyone apologized to Uncle Ben, who'd looked abashed and said that's all right, he understood. Jessica was prone to fantasy and exaggeration.

That was the first time she'd slashed her wrists.

Jessica kept her eyes on the expressway, away from Springer, letting her hand rest in his strong soothing hold. She was remembering far too much, far too often, and the man beside her only made those memories more painful. She ought to pull away from him, withdraw farther in the narrow confines of the small foreign car. But she knew she wasn't going to. And she knew she was making a mistake. Springer MacDowell was only going to add to the unbearable burdens weighing her down. With a sigh she leaned back, closing her eyes. And left her hand in his.

## Chapter Five

Eight hours later Jessica surveyed her reflection in the mirror, looking for signs of strain beneath the iron control. Her lips were a luscious dusky red, her ice-blue eyes large and cool and luminous, her wheat-blond hair a neat cap to her delicate skull. It would have taken someone with uncommon perception to see past the coolly amused half smile, the impression of wealth and control the clinging black Halston sheath presented. She doubted that anyone milling around the Kinsey living room would be perceptive enough, or sober enough, to see more than what he or she wanted to see.

Except for Springer. And she refused to grant him that perception. He was a stud, on the make for whatever was available, and right now she was a challenge. So what if Elyssa thought he'd given up his absorption with quantity, not quality. Jessica could hardly count herself as suddenly irresistible. She knew as well as he did that she was definitely not his type. His animosity was clear, as was the kindling light of desire that brightened those dark, fathomless eyes of his. And that light made her very, very nervous.

She had been unconscionably stupid to let him take her hand like that. She should have pulled away with a light joke and a condescending laugh. But she hadn't. She had sat in his tiny, cramped car, staring out at the traffic, and let him hold her hand in that way. And in doing so, she had let him in closer than anyone had been in years. Never had she felt so open, so exposed, so vulnerable. It had been a much more intimate act than sex, and her guilt and dismay was far greater than if he had pulled off the expressway and taken her to a motel.

So much for common sense, she told herself, shrugging her shoulders. Perhaps the Halston wasn't the right choice, she thought belatedly. Not with her current weight. Her shoulders looked just a tiny bit too bony beneath the halter top, and interested onlookers could probably count her ribs above the backless dress. Maybe that would be enough to drive away Springer MacDowell and X. Rickford Lincoln, leaving her to the undemanding comfort of Peter Kinsey.

The noise of the cocktail party filtered through the open terrace windows of her bedroom. Just a small party, Jasper had assured her on their arrival. No more than fifty of their closest, most important friends. And she wouldn't even have to act as hostess. Jasper's current inamorata, an elegant but spectacularly talentless actress, would do the honors.

Jessica had smiled, keeping her eyes averted from a steadily amused Springer. She had understood the politics of it well enough. Rickford Lincoln needed to be reminded that the Kinseys had wealthy and powerful friends, that they could entertain with not the slightest concern that the all-important merger would go through. Image was everything, and the Kinseys were adept at preserving that image. Was it only her imagination that her own had begun to crack a bit around the edges?

She had put off making her reappearance for as long as she could. She'd given them time enough. By now Springer would probably be off on the long stretch of private beach with one of the neighbor's wives, and if fate was extraordinarily kind, so would Rickford Lincoln. Somewhere in the long quiet of the afternoon, when a nap eluded her, she had come to her decision. She would do what had to be done. She could only hope that luck would keep Lincoln far away, at least until she got a decent night's sleep and could cope with him.

Luck wasn't with her. Heading down the almost deserted hallway, Jessica recognized his burly figure coming toward her. She contemplated wheeling around and heading back in the opposite direction, then chided herself for her cowardice. She had told Springer Mac-Dowell she was tough enough—now was her chance to prove it.

"There you are, Jessica," Lincoln boomed, moving in on her. "I wondered where you'd gotten to."

Forcing herself to look at him objectively, she had to admit that he wasn't a bad-looking man. The years sat well on him, with his crowning mane of silver hair, the bushy gray eyebrows, the big, husky body that couldn't be called fat. He exuded an aura of power that should have a powerful aphrodisiac to any right-thinking young executive on the rise. She gave him that distant smile that held faint, unmistakable promises, the smile she had perfected years ago and that had kept Rickford Lincoln malleable over the bargaining table.

He moved closer then, pressing against her slender body. He was a man who invaded other people's space, pressing against them, all the while smiling affably. He did it to intimidate people, and it usually worked quite well. Jessica's cool smile didn't waver, her feet didn't falter, and she stood her ground. "I wondered if you were trying to avoid me, Jessica," he continued plaintively.

She raised an eyebrow artfully. "Paranoid, Mr. Lincoln? If I wanted to avoid you, I wouldn't have come. This weekend was planned for your benefit." He had been drinking Scotch, she noticed with an inward shudder of distaste. She hated Scotch drinkers.

"But you weren't here last night," he reminded her with a trace of petulance in his voice. A petulance just slightly laced with threat.

"I'm here tonight."

He pressed closer then, his belly leaning into her slender frame, and one big hand caught her unresisting one. "So you are, Jessica," he said lightly, meaningfully, "I need to talk with you."

"Of course."

"About the merger. The contracts... There are several points that I think could use some more discussion."

*Here it comes,* she thought, dropping her eyes for a moment to see his hand fondling hers in what he doubtless thought was a sensuous gesture. His hands were old, puffy, with silver hair sprinkled across the backs of his fingers. She raised her eyes back up to his and summoned her limpid smile.

"I'm at your disposal."

His smile broadened. "After the party. I think my room is the best choice—that way we're unlikely to be disturbed."

She nodded, feeling curiously numb. Why should it matter? It wasn't as if she was a virgin—surely she could trade one night for a secure and powerful future. Why was she balking? It was nothing more than her smiles and her subtle flattery had promised for the past three months. "I don't think I'll have any trouble getting away from Peter..." she began, experienced enough to leave herself an escape hatch.

"No, I don't think you will," Lincoln said smugly. "He knows how important this merger is."

Jessica looked up sharply. The threat was out in the open then, and she didn't like it. She needed the polite veneer that it was still her choice. "I'll speak to him," she said coolly, putting Lincoln in his place.

"You do that. But I don't think you'll hear any objections to a late-night bargaining session." One of his heavy hands reached behind her head then, holding her still as his face descended. His lips were thick, wet and demanding on her cold, unresponsive ones. She stood still for the assault, not moving, and a moment later he pulled back.

"You're a cool one, aren't you?" he queried, not the slightest bit discouraged.

"I don't like being pawed in hallways," she replied, unmoved.

Lincoln laughed, moving away. "Sounds like you need a little discipline, Jessica. And I'm the man to do it. My room, no later than one o'clock. I'll have some Scotch waiting."

"Not Scotch," she said hurriedly. "I hate Scotch."

His grin broadened. "Champagne, then. I'll be wait-ing." He was moving back toward her again, his wet lips open, when they heard someone moving down the hall. He broke away with unaccustomed nervousness and tugged at his pants. "Later," he said, and without turning, continued on down the hall, leaving Jessica to face the late arrivals.

Springer MacDowell and Peter Kinsey were an ill-matched pair, she thought distantly, watching them advance on her. Peter was so quintessentially Prince-ton, from his sandy-colored hair, perfect features, Ivy League clothes that were a step above preppy, and that way he carried himself, certain of his welcome and his cleverness, yet charmingly free from arrogance or self-importance. In comparison, Springer looked like a large, dark, dangerous savage, and the light in his fath-omless eyes was directed with unwavering steadiness at Jessica. She met that look, her chin raised in uncon-scious defiance.

"Who was that?" he queried, mildly enough. Jessica waited for Peter to answer. He looked uncharacteristi-cally nervous.

"Rickford Lincoln," he replied with an uneasy laugh. "Jessica's been overseeing a merger with the Lincoln Corporation these past few months. It's just about to go through, knock wood." The look he cast Jessica could definitely be described as beseeching, and for a moment she wondered if Kinsey Enterprises was in even worse shape than she realized.

"Could I talk with you, Peter?" she said suddenly.

Peter shied away like a nervous colt. "Not right now,

darling. I'm afraid I'm on an errand for Father, and I haven't a moment to spare. I'll catch up with you later, all right? In the meantime, why doesn't Springer escort you back to the party? I'd like you two to get to know each other. I may not have mentioned it, but Springer and I were very close when we were in school."

"No, you didn't mention it," she said coolly, meeting Springer's lightly amused gaze with her usual reserve.

"Well, you two become friends, and I'll find you." He was moving down the hall at a rapid pace, and Jessica watched him go with a curious sense of defeat.

"Well, Jessie, I don't think you're going to get any help from him," Springer murmured, his voice a husky drawl.

She turned back to him. "What do you mean?" Her voice wasn't encouraging. She shouldn't even be talking to him, she should turn her naked back on him and head back to the noise and the crowds. She stayed where she was.

"I mean Peter *darling* is going to turn a blind eye to Lincoln's advances. It looks like you're the virgin sacrifice on the altar of business survival, and he isn't going to offer more than a token objection."

He was fast, she had to grant him that. "Hardly a virgin," she said coolly. "And no sacrifice, nor Peter's possession to be offered. I make my own decisions."

"Sure you do," he mocked lightly. "I could see your face when Lincoln was touching you. You didn't look very happy."

"I do what needs to be done," she snapped, nettled. "Not that it's any of your business."

To her surprise, he nodded. "You're right, of course. It has nothing to do with me if you chose to screw up your life. And I can't even tell you to take it easy on Peter, since he's obviously willing and eager for you to cement the merger in a charmingly old-fashioned way. As long as you don't mind the Kinseys pimping for you...."

Jessica found she had raised her hand to hit him. He stood there impassively, waiting for her hand to connect with his dark, arrogant face, and slowly she dropped it, amazed at the rush of emotion that had swept over her. She never lost her temper, never allowed people to get to her. A sudden feeling of nausea assailed her, and it took all her control to swallow the bile that rose. She managed a shaky smile. "You are good," she said meditatively. "But not good enough. Leave me alone." She wouldn't call him by name. Mr. MacDowell was too absurdly old-fashioned, Springer too intimate.

He hesitated for a moment, something like regret in his eyes. "If you want to change your mind, I'll drive you back to the city," he said suddenly. "You don't have to do anything you don't want to do."

Her control was back, completely, and she bestowed a faint, wondering smile on him. "Of course I don't. And I'll leave at the end of the weekend, when I'm ready to go. I'm sure I can persuade Rickford Lincoln to give me a ride back if Peter's not ready to go."

He stared at her for a long moment further. She could feel the tension in his body, matching hers, and she looked up at him fearlessly, her eyes wide and deceptively uncaring, willing his anger to spill forth.

But it didn't. He swallowed it, almost as if he found her too pathetic to hate, and once more she wanted to slap him. "You're worth more than an executive hooker," he said suddenly. "Don't you realize that?"

The cool smile was getting a little stiff by now, but she refused to let it waver. "Of course I realize it," she mocked. "I'm worth an executive vice-presidency and the boss's son."

She couldn't get through that damnable, unreasoning concern that seemed to underlay his mockery. "If you change your mind..." he said again, unwilling to let her go.

"I won't." She held out one slender arm. "And now I think we ought to rejoin the guests. I have some circulating to do."

"I'm sure you do. Ever the little hustler." He eyed her coolly, making no effort to take her arm. "You go on ahead. I think I need some fresh air." And he walked past her, his face shuttered with contempt and something else even more disconcerting.

Jessica watched him leave, watched that tall, animal grace of his. He was still wearing jeans and a light cotton shirt with the sleeves rolled up—at a formal party, no less. And damn him, he got away with making his own rules.

Just as she was going to, she told herself grimly. It would be a real test of her abilities, to meet Lincoln in his room at one o'clock and escape unscathed. But she could do it, she knew she could. And laugh at all of them while she did.

# Chapter Six

The cocktail party, which had started sometime after five, was just breaking up at one o'clock. There was no way Jessica was going to roam the halls in the floor-length white silk caftan with the row of tiny buttons up the front, looking for Lincoln's room. With her luck she'd either run into Peter, who'd stammer and look miserable and be forced into taking a stand, or, even worse, wander into Springer MacDowell's bedroom. Not that the caftan was particularly seductive. She had chosen it with care, the long, flowing lines giving her an indefinably untouched air. She rather fancied herself as a vestal virgin, cool and powerful and removed. But it had been a long time since she'd been a virgin, she thought, and a sudden, incomprehensibly fresh grief swept over her.

The house was slowly getting quieter, settling down for the night. She wandered over to the French doors, staring out at the wide sweep of beach that fronted the Kinsey's rambling house. It was a fortunate thing that her relationship with Peter hadn't yet progressed to bed, though the time was definitely looming closer.

He'd made a few halfhearted attempts, but he hadn't pushed it, a forebearance Jessica attributed to a combination of gentlemanly instincts, an innate lack of passion and an unwillingness to interfere with Lincoln's plans for her. She could only be grateful for the first two reasons and detest the third with a frighteningly healthy anger usually absent from her icily calm demeanor.

But it certainly made things easier tonight—there would be no awkward questions, or the awkward lack thereof. Peter knew what she was doing, she was sure of it. And had chosen to turn a blind eye. And she was no longer certain she could live with that.

Squares of light on the beach illuminated each pair of French doors—one by one they slowly went dark. She opened hers a crack, breathing in the smell of the sea, the sharp salt tang of it. She didn't have to do it, of course. Instead, she could step out onto that fine silver sand, walk down to the water and dive in. The cool, cleansing surf would put everything in perspective. And then she could come back out, lock herself in her room, and go to bed, blessedly alone. Slowly she closed the door again.

They would have put Lincoln in the suite of rooms just off the central courtyard, she realized as she stepped out into the hallway. And Springer would be in the opposite direction, farther down the end of her wing, with French doors leading out onto the beach like hers. No one would see her.

Her bare feet were noiseless on the thick beige carpeting that covered the rambling modern house. It was almost two—with any luck Lincoln would have passed out by now, and she would have another night's reprieve. There was still a good chance she could manage to escape unscathed, but the memory of Lincoln's leering eyes, the eyes that had responded to her subtle but too effective come-ons during the past three months of negotiations, warned her that she shouldn't put too much hope in it. Lincoln had every intention of collecting on her promises tonight, and it was more than probable that this time she'd have to pay the piper.

Jessica knocked very, very softly on his door, ready to turn and run if he didn't answer in five seconds. He answered in three.

The monogrammed navy silk robe with the white ascot was very attractive, she told herself, stepping wordlessly into his room. It minimized his bulk, made him look elegant, strong and powerful. So why did she feel like a virgin sacrifice?

*Damn it, those were Springer's words.* How would it feel if he could see her now, slender and waiting, alone in the candlelit room with that lusting old man drooling over her? *He'd hate it,* she thought, and smiled her first real smile.

Rickford Lincoln knew excitement when he saw it. Through his Scotch-fuzzed brain he saw that smile curve her face, saw the slender, boyish body through the shimmering silk, and lunged.

Jessica had seen that narrowing in his glazed eyes and prepared herself. His lips were slobbering over her collarbone, his hands grabbing at the silk, and with her usual efficiency she turned her mind off. Turned it to a merciful blank filled with rolling green meadows, a blue, blue sky, the smell of clear lake water and the distant sound of birds wheeling through that almost cloudless sky. She could lie back in the grass, feel it tickling her skin, and the noisy gruntings and moanings were a distant irritation. The hands on her skin melted away, and she was gone, floating with the puffs of clouds. *Doesn't the sky look green today,* she thought dreamily, staring down.

And then it was gone, ripped away from her with a sudden, shocking violence, as his bleary, raddled, lecherous face hovered over her, breathing heavily. Wave after wave of Scotch-laden fumes covered her face, choking her. She opened her eyes, staring up at him, and began to scream.

"Dammit to hell!" Lincoln swore, scrambling off her in panicked haste and retying his robe with nerveless fingers. "Stop it, for God's sake! Shut up!"

She could see it from a distance, from her perch up among the clouds. Jessica was lying there, her caftan half off her slender body, her blue eyes glazed and blank, her mouth open in a scream that kept coming. And there was nothing she could do to stop it.

And then the room was filled with people. Lots of people. Peter Kinsey, his fair hair rumpled, standing helplessly by, Jasper Kinsey, rage and something akin to fear darkening his distinguished face. The talentless actress was by his side, a negligee pulled around her, unaware that the hastily donned robe was completely transparent. They all stood there by Lincoln's embarrassed, infuriated figure and watched her as she screamed.

And then she was back, pulled into someone's strong arms, her face pressed against a warm, hard chest, and the screams were gone, leaving the room deafening in its silence.

"What the hell happened?" She could hear Springer's voice through his chest, feel his hands on her back, stroking, soothing, gentle hands. Her breath was still coming in shuddering gasps, her face and hands were tingling, her mind ripped free from that merciful blank. She knew where she was, and what she had done.

No one had bothered to answer Springer's question. She could hear Jasper Kinsey's voice, low and soothing, murmuring hurried apologies to X. Rickford Lincoln. She could feel Peter standing there helplessly, afraid to risk his father's displeasure by coming to her, afraid to alienate her by adding his excuses to his father's.

Springer's short, obscene expletive brought them all up short. "Don't let us bother you," he snapped, scooping up Jessica's trembling form in his arms. She barely weighed more than a kitten, he thought absently, his arms tightening their hold. She turned her face against his shoulder, hiding from those wondering, condemning faces.

"Is... is she all right?" Peter had the decency to ask, putting a tentative hand on one limp arm. She flinched as if burned, keeping her face averted, and Springer shifted her closer against him.

"She'll be fine," he said, not particularly certain of that fact. "I'll take care of her."

"Would you, Springer?" There was real gratitude in Peter's voice as he accompanied them to the door. "I'd come with you, but I think I'd better help Dad try to smooth a few ruffled feathers."

Springer looked down at him over the limp figure cradled in his arms, and his eyes darkened in contempt. "You do that," he said lightly, no sound of his disapproval filtering through his voice. "I'll take care of her," he said again.

THE NIGHT AIR WAS COOL and salty on her skin. Jessica could feel the shift in the rhythm of his footsteps as he moved from the terrace to the soft white sand, but she was still unwilling to raise her head from its hiding place against his strong shoulder. Slowly she became more aware of him as the tingling lessened in her limbs. He had taken off his belt, and his shirt was open and untucked. The soft white cotton cushioned her head, but warm, smooth flesh pressed against her arm and the open caftan that he had pulled hastily back around her trembling body. She wondered when he'd done it but knew that it had been his hands and no one else's who had touched her. And with distant despair she could feel the strands wrap tighter around her, that tenuous, torturous, spider's-web stickiness tying her to him. She was a fat, juicy butterfly, caught in his trap, and he was a tarantula, keeping her captive, waiting till his hunger grew and he could feast on her when her struggles grew too weak.

Or was she the spider? The black widow, mesmerizing him, pulling him closer while telling him to go away, and the moment he came within reach, her touch would poison him, whether she wanted to or not.

"Relax," his voice rumbled as he felt her body tense in his arms. "No one's going to hurt you."

At the sound of the patent lie she began to struggle,

but his arms only tightened. "Stop fighting me, Jessie," he whispered.

"Let me down." Her voice was muffled against his shoulder, hoarse and rusty and raw with pain. For a moment it seemed as if he was going to ignore her, and she added the final, ignominious concession. "Please, Springer."

Slowly, slowly his body came to a halt; slowly, slowly he loosened his hold to let her slide down the length of his body. Her bare feet touched the sand, and she tried to move away from the protection of his hands. The lights of the house were far away, and then suddenly they seemed much farther—bright, glistening little pinpricks glaring at her. A moment later she found herself sitting in the sand, her head pushed between her knees, a strong hand kneading the back of her neck.

"Take slow, deep breaths," he ordered, and she dutifully complied, breathing in the ocean's smell and the faint, tantalizing scent of Springer. The spinning gradually faded, reality began to intrude with a sickening rush, and Jessica shuddered.

"Oh no, what did I do?" she moaned, lifting her head to stare sightlessly at the moon-silvered ocean.

"That's what I was wondering," Springer drawled, removing that marvelously soothing hand from the back of her neck. "What happened in there?"

Wrapping her arms around her long legs, she rested her chin on her knees with a weary gesture, still refusing to look at her rescuer. "I don't really know. I think it was the Scotch."

"The Scotch?"

She did turn to him then, her face composed, belying

the continued trembling in her limbs. "He was breathing Scotch fumes on me. I don't like Scotch drinkers," she said simply.

Springer was watching her out of those unreadable eyes. "What were you doing in his room at two in the morning?" he questioned suddenly.

A mocking smile curved her mouth. "Don't be naive, Springer—you know as well as I do what I was doing there. Cementing a business merger."

"Well, I think you may have botched it up," he replied mildly enough, not rising to her bait. "Lincoln didn't look very happy. Nor, for that matter, did your future father-in-law. Tell me, do you do this sort of thing often?"

She considered lying to him, but the trembling in her body, instead of lessening, was unaccountably increasing. She wished he'd put his hand back on her neck, soothing the strained muscles, that he'd put his arms around her again and press her against that soft white shirt. She shook her head, to banish such demoralizing thoughts, and answered honestly enough. "No." Her voice was low. "No, I don't."

"Then why did you tonight?" His voice sounded no more than distantly curious, for which she was glad. If she'd caught a note of pity in that deep, husky drawl, it would have been the final straw.

"It didn't appear that I had any choice," she replied faintly. Light shivers were rippling over her body, and surreptitiously she pulled the caftan closer around her shoulders. The silk offered her no warmth at all, not when she needed the warmth of a human touch.

And it wasn't human touch she wanted, she realized .

belatedly. She had no desire at all to track down Peter and seek the comfort she knew he would offer. She wanted Springer's warmth, Springer's comfort. Damn him.

"Why the Scotch?" he said suddenly. He must have seen her shivering, for suddenly his large strong hands reached out and caught her trembling shoulders, kneading them with a light, sure touch that sapped some of the tension from her.

Raising her head, she closed her eyes, arching into his touch like a starving kitten. "I suppose because my parents were alcoholics," she said distantly. "Though I don't remember either of them drinking Scotch. It was bourbon when they were younger, and then vodka to hide the smell, and then pills so they could pretend they were straight, and then vodka again." Why didn't he slide those large, beautiful hands down over her shoulders, she wondered, and pull her back against him? She needed more warmth than his hands were providing.

"I suppose that might explain it," Springer agreed, watching her out of narrowed eyes as his hands continued their steady kneading. He found he wanted to slide his hands down and pull her closer, against him. He wanted to protect her from whatever had terrified her enough to scream like that, her ice-blue eyes a blank of horror; he wanted her to warm up, body and soul. And he wanted her to warm up to him.

That was the last thing she needed right now, though. He should take her back to Peter, and let him do the comforting, the warming. Jessica Hansen was nothing but trouble, and she was someone else's trouble, not his. He'd take her back to the house and go find Peter.

He didn't move, couldn't move. She smelled of hyacinths, sweet and musky, and tinged with innocence, and the unexpectedness of it startled him. He would have thought she'd prefer something cool and sophisticated, something modern. Not the delicate, old-fashioned scent that brought to mind summer dresses and hillside picnics.

She was cold, so cold, and she needed his warmth. Without further wavering she leaned back, coming up against his solid body, his warm chest. She could feel his surprise, his momentary hesitation, and then his hands slid down from her shoulders, his arms circling her frail body, pulling her back against him. Jessica let out a long, shuddering sigh, closing her eyes once more. She was safe at last.

At least, until he chose to leave her. The sudden thought that he could, would do exactly that, sooner or later, panicked her.

"What is it now?" he murmured behind her, apparently entirely at ease in this strange situation. "Relax, Jessie."

But that was just what she couldn't do. She needed him, needed the warmth and comfort his body could give her, and she knew from experience that she'd have to pay for it, pay for the holding and soothing. At that point no price would have been too high.

Turning slowly in his arms, she slid her hands up around his neck. He was looking down at her, an arrested expression on his dark face. And there on the windswept, deserted beach, she reached up and pressed her mouth against his unsuspecting one.

Deliberately she kept her mouth soft, pliant, waiting for him to make the next move. She could feel his hesitation, indecision, and she increased the pressure, reaching out with the tip of her tongue to lightly touch his lower lip. She heard a low, muffled groan, and then his hands were cupping her close-cropped head, holding her gently as he deepened the kiss, his mouth warm and wet and hungry on hers.

Jessica accepted her success complaisantly as she felt her body wrapped closer to his protective bulk, and tilted her head back under his onslaught, willing the clouds to return, the clear, sailing blue sky, the birds . . .

And then suddenly she was alone, released unceremoniously from his embrace as if she were contaminated. Scrambling to her knees in the sand, she stared at him with a mixture of shock and confusion. He was sitting there staring at her, his breathing a little heavy, his eyes angry and opaque, his mouth thinned in contempt.

"Is that how you usually do it, Jessie?" he demanded.

"What are you talking about?"

"Close your eyes and dream yourself away? I don't need performances, in bed or out of it. I prefer flesh-and-blood companions whose mind and emotions are involved along with their bodies. You're not really capable of that, are you?"

Denials, protests, insults flooded her mind but stopped short of her mouth. She just knelt there, her caftan still pulled loosely around her, staring at him in numb surprise. "I...I..."

The anger left him as swiftly as it had come, and he reached out his hand, that large, gentle hand that held such warmth, stroking the side of her face, and his voice was very sad. "You really wouldn't have known the difference between me and Lincoln, would you? If he hadn't been drinking Scotch you'd be doing your little act right now, writhing underneath him while your mind was a thousand miles away...."

"Don't!" She thought it would come out in a scream, but instead it was barely audible. "Please, leave me alone. Go away."

He continued to stare at her, and then he rose to his feet. For a moment Jessica thought he really would leave her, abandon her on this empty stretch of midnight beach. But as his words ripped her apart, his hands healed her as they reached down and pulled her gently to her feet.

"Come back to the house, Jessie," he said softly. "I won't let the demons get you. Not tonight."

She looked way, way up at him, the beginnings of a question in her haunted eyes. But she could read no answers. Letting her slight hand rest in his large, capable one, she followed him into the house.

## Chapter Seven

The house had once more regained its silent stillness, almost as if Jessica's hysteria had never ripped apart the thick velvet texture of the night. No lights had been left burning to guide them back—even Peter's bedroom light was extinguished. The hand that enveloped her slighter, trembling one led her past Peter's closed door, past her own darkened room, down the silent, carpeted hallway. She made a token effort at pulling away, just slight enough to tell herself she tried, but his grip only tightened. And then they were in his room, the sliding glass doors open onto the windy beach, the salty air filling the darkened confines of the back guest bedroom. Springer didn't turn on the light, just pulled her in and shut the door behind them, but Jessica knew the room very well. They had put her in it the first time she'd visited the Kinseys, long before she and Peter became involved, when old Jasper was still having occasional lustful thoughts in her direction. It had been sheer luck that nothing had come of it, nothing that would interfere with her plans for Jasper's son.

At the sudden memory of her almost-fiancé she looked up at the dark, silent figure standing motionless beside her. She was slowly regaining her equilibrium, and this time when she pulled her hand away he let it go, leaning back against the door with a lazy grace accentuated by the darkness of the room.

"So what do we do now?" she queried, and was pleased to hear her voice come out brittle and composed.

He said nothing, leaning against that door as if he had all the time in the world, and Jessica could feel her regained composure begin to slip once more.

"I should thank you for rescuing me," she managed with a bright laugh. "I really don't know what got into me—probably just a little too much to drink tonight."

"You didn't drink anything." His slow, deep voice broke the darkness.

"What?" The interruption unnerved her.

"I said you didn't drink anything tonight but Perrier and lime. I was watching you."

Somehow the thought of those dark, unreadable eyes following her every move was even more unnerving. "Why?" she asked abruptly, the brittle composure shattering.

She could see his teeth flash in the moonlit bedroom, and his eyes glittered. He was so close, yet not close enough. His warmth was tantalizing, his scent intoxicating—of warm flesh and the ocean and the faint, pleasant smell of brandy, not Scotch, on his breath. "Why do you think?" he countered, raising a hand to gently stroke the side of her face.

Before his flesh could touch hers she flinched, trying to pull away from him. But she was backed into a corner, with no way to get past him, and he followed her, holding her still with his imprisoning body, forcing her to accept his gentling hand on the chilled skin of her face. "What are you afraid of, Jessie?" Springer whispered against her skin.

The trembling began in her ankles, sweeping upward over her chilled body, racking her with shivers so tiny as to be imperceptible if the man hadn't been standing so close. *I'm afraid of you,* she thought desperately. *I don't want to be alone in the darkness with you—I'm afraid you'll steal my soul. And even worse, I'm afraid you'll leave me, alone in the darkness without you. I'm afraid of everything about you.*

But she couldn't tell him that. She struggled for a reasonable excuse and came up with it. "I don't want to be another notch in your thighbone," she murmured, still imprisoned by the heat and force of his body. The only part touching her was his hand, gently caressing the side of her averted face.

"And I don't want to be one on yours," he countered softly, and Jessica flinched. "That's the danger when you use sex for more than recreational purposes. When you use it to advance your career, or to convince yourself you're a man, or to blot out unpleasant memories. You forget you can make love just for the pure pleasure of it."

Jessica couldn't help it; she laughed in his face, the bitterness raw in the calm night air. His hand stilled on her flesh, and she could feel the tension in his tall, wiry body. "Oh, Jessie," he said finally, his voice a weary rush of sadness. "It doesn't have to be that way."

The sadness was almost more demoralizing than his nearness, the gentle, undemanding stroke of his strong, slightly callused hand. "Tell me about it," she said in a light, mocking voice. "You ought to know. Your mother says you've had every available female on both coasts in the past fifteen years."

She waited for his withdrawal, but it didn't come. "Then you can trust my experience," he murmured. "Come to bed with me, Jessie."

She didn't move. She could have pushed him away, and he would have let her. She could have strode past him, out of his room, out of his life, and he would have let her. She didn't move.

A thousand protests screamed through her mind, a thousand drawling insults to put him in his place. She didn't say a word.

A hundred misgivings filled her mind. Peter and Jasper and Kinsey Enterprises. And X. Rickford Lincoln, his heavy face masked with lust and then anger. She needed Springer MacDowell like she needed a hole in the head.

"I'm going back to my room."

"No, you're not."

"Are you going to try to stop me?"

"No." The word was low and beguiling, and his other hand slid up her arm, lightly touching, tantalizing, but in no way restraining. "You can go if you want to. But you don't want to. Do you?" His head moved closer, blotting out the light, his other hand holding her still for his kiss. The lips were warm, flesh on her flesh, a gentle exploration, a question, a soothing balm for her lacerated soul. "Do you?" he whispered again against her lips.

She would have shaken her head in denial, but it would have broken the tantalizing bond. "No," she said silently against his mouth. And liking the way her lips moved against his as she formed the word, she tried it again. "No."

It seemed to be all the permission he needed. His arm slid around her slender body, pulling her up against him, and the warmth began to seep into her chilled flesh once more. His mouth moved on hers, soft, damp and tantalizing, his tongue deftly tracing the soft contours of her lips before slipping inside. Jessica told herself she could remain passive, stand there in the comforting circle of his arms, with his mouth on hers, and be unmoved. It would be easy enough to view it as a performance, she told herself. After all of Springer's practice he must be rather deft—she could watch him with interest, see how he managed to move her from the corner of the bedroom to the wide queen-sized bed several feet away. Would he carry her? She'd rather liked it when he carried her out on the beach— what she could remember of it, that is. Men didn't usually attempt to carry her. Despite her current birdlike weight, her five-foot-eight-inch proportions made her an unwieldly package, unwieldly enough to discourage even closet romantics like Peter.

But Springer was tall enough and strong enough to do the thing with grace. He might even—

Suddenly she jumped, startled, and stared up at him in amazement. Springer had just bitten her on the nose.

"When I kiss a woman I like her complete attention," he observed politely. He still had her tightly wrapped against his body, and she recognized belatedly the feel of his hardened flesh against hers.

"I was just wondering how you were going to get me

over to the bed," she said, hoping to puncture that imperturbable calm of his.

"Who said anything about a bed?" he drawled, nudging her hips with his blatantly aroused pelvis. "I thought we could make love right here."

She knew he was goading here deliberately, making her angry enough to shatter the dreamworld she built up every time he kissed her, but it didn't halt her rage. Shoving him back with a sudden surge of strength, she caught him off-balance. He fell back against the door, and she was free, racing across the room toward the sliding glass door and an unwanted freedom.

She didn't get very far. A large foot stuck out, catching her ankle, and she tripped, sprawling sideways across the rumpled bed, with Springer beside her, half on top of her, his hands catching her pale shoulders and pressing her against the sheets.

"That's how I'm planning to get you on the bed," he said, his voice breathless with suppressed laughter and something else. Jessica looked up at him then, recognizing that laughter, and to her amazement, released a small, rusty laugh of her own.

"Very adept," she said dryly, ignoring the unfamiliar tightening in her loins. Even with him supporting the majority of his weight on his elbows he was still heavy, his hips pressing against hers, one long leg flung carelessly over hers, imprisoning her. And yet it wasn't a prison, she thought. It was safety, protection from the outside world. And very dangerous protection it was.

"Well, well," Springer said softly, his breath warm and damp and sweet on her suddenly vulnerable face beneath him. "I've done very well with you tonight,

Jessie, love. I've made you laugh—" his mouth gently brushed her temple "—and I've made you angry—" he kissed her nose "—I've frightened you—" he kissed her ear "—and I've turned you on." He pulled back to eye her speculatively. She could feel the warmth of his flesh through the open shirt, feel the rigidity of his desire through the heavy denim jeans. "That's quite a torrent of emotion from a Snow Queen."

The room grew suddenly still as Jessie lay beneath him. She could hear the distant sound of the Long Island surf, the quiet rustle of the sheets around them and the springs beneath them. Everything else was silent.

"I wonder," Springer murmured with a vague, almost clinical interest, "if I could make you cry?"

"Would you want to?" she whispered back.

"Very much. Not from sadness," he said, moving closer to kiss each fluttering eyelid. "I want to make you moan and weep from pleasure. And I want you to cry when you need to, and something tells me you need to a lot."

"I don't cry," she said, ignoring the strange emptiness in the pit of her stomach. "And I hate to disappoint you, but I make love in total silence."

She could see the grin slashing across his face in the midnight room. "Liar. I'm sure you make all the appropriate noises at the appropriate times. You're a professional actress, poor Jessie. You know your part and you play it to the hilt."

"Then what am I doing here?" She wanted the words to come out stubborn and challenging; instead, they merely sounded plaintive and just a tiny bit lost.

"Stepping out of character," he whispered. "And to-

night when you moan and cry you're going to mean it."
Springer's mouth feathered hers, softly, his tongue
delving past her parted lips. "Aren't you, Jessie?" he
taunted, returning again and again to her mouth like a
hummingbird drawn to a flower. "Aren't you?"

"Yes," she found herself saying, not quite believing
it.

With clever, knowing hands he pulled the caftan the
rest of the way off her shoulders, down to her waist.
She lay there passively beneath his touch, a slight smile
on her face, as his mouth moved to follow his hands.
"Your skin is like silk, Jessie," he whispered against
her. "Smooth and creamy and untouched. Are you
cold, Jessie?" He slid the rest of the caftan off her hips,
the strong, callused hands warming her cool flesh. His
mouth was at her breasts now, capturing one small
peak, his tongue swift and sure and suddenly arousing,
and his hands trailed back up her legs to her narrow
hips. She could feel the emptiness in her belly sink
lower, and the hollow began to fill with a slow burning
that frightened her. She trembled in his arms, suddenly
frightened, but his hands drew no closer, even as his
mouth turned to her other breast.

She was vaguely aware of him shrugging out of that
loose white shirt, knew when his hand left hers to
fumble with the clasp of his jeans. But she had lost her
interest in practical matters. Technicalities no longer
had the ability to distract her—instead of wondering
how he was going to peel out of those faded jeans of
his, she found she needed all her scattered concentration to deal with the unexpected longings that seemed
to have taken over her body.

He was warm and strong and hard against her as his hands and mouth once more claimed her. Her brain seemed to be melting in the heat of the moment, all practicalities fading away beneath the delicious, practiced onslaught. She could feel those strong, hard hands of his sweeping down her hips, and for a moment she panicked. She had no protection, but then, that was no real problem. She had played baby roulette once before and she figured she was safe—one more curse from an angry god. And she had no cream with her—Springer would find out soon enough that sex with an Ice Princess would come fraught with all sorts of discomforts.

And then his hands slipped down between her legs, finding her with a sure touch that sent the coals in her loins into a burning blaze.

She tried to pull away but he held her fast, one arm pinning her down as his mouth trailed damp, demoralizing kisses across her flat stomach, while his fingers stroked her into a quivering submission that was gradually turning into something else. She could hear small, whimpering sounds, tiny cries of pleasure and frustration, and she realized with a distant shock that the sounds came from her. She had meant to make the requisite noises to soothe Springer's male ego. Never had she thought that he could actually elicit that burning, seeking response from her.

"That's right," he murmured against the gentle fullness of her breast. "Talk to me, Jessie. Tell me about it."

She was fighting it. Fighting the spreading languor, fighting the bewitching heat of his body. Desperately she struggled to regain that part of herself that seemed in danger of being lost forever, but the effort was proving to be too much. Against her will her hips were arching against his hand, even with her strong white teeth clamped down on her lower lip the small cries were escaping from the back of her throat. And still he played with her, patient, determined to wrest the response from her that she didn't want to give.

His large, strong hands were under her arms, pulling her up across the bed until her head rested on the pillows. The hands left her, trailing down her fevered body to her legs, parting them with inexorable gentleness. And then he was above her, dark and strong and menacing, like a fallen angel, and she knew he would take her, and she knew she would be lost.

She made one last, hopeless effort to summon up the green pasture, the clear blue sky, floating, floating...

Until the slow, steady invasion began to rip through the cloudlike veil, and her eyes flew open, staring up into his intent ones, as he slowly filled her, the smooth fluidity of his movement telling her that even if her soul wasn't ready, her body was.

"Stay with me, Jessie," he whispered thickly. "Don't leave me alone while you go off to never-never land. Feel me, feel this." He slowly withdrew, then arched up to fill her again. "It's real, it's good. Stay with me, Jessie."

She had no answer for him. She was lost forever, trapped, not by his strong, hard body, but by the long-dormant desires that had risen beneath his skillful handling. She could feel the tension knotting her muscles—from her toes, which dug into the rumpled sheets, to her fingers, digging into his strong shoulders. She could feel the quivers that were shaking her body beneath his. She was lost, out of control, with no place to hide.

"Don't," she gasped in a weak cry. "Don't do this to me." The clear blue sky faded forever beyond reach, leaving only the midnight darkness.

"I can't stop, Jessie," he murmured. "I have to." And his hands reached down to cup her slender buttocks as he thrust deeper, deeper, his muscles bunching under her clinging hands as he drove her onward, further and further, their skin wet and clinging, their breathing rapid, their hearts pounding.

*No,* she wept inside. *No, I won't. I won't let him....*

And then suddenly, in the midst of her protests, it shattered, the one inviolate part of her, and the midnight darkness split apart as her body arched up against his. She could hear her voice in the distance, weeping "no" to the angry heavens, and the rain of her tears washed over them.

She was still crying, still mumbling "no" like a hopeless litany when he withdrew from her body, rolling onto his side and pulling her into his arms. One strong hand brushed the tears from her swollen face as he pressed her head against his sweat-slicked shoulder. "Yes, Jessie," he said softly, gently mocking. "Yes." And reaching down with infinite care, he caught one trembling hand as it rested numbly against the sheet. Bringing it to his mouth, he kissed the faint, spidery tracing of scars on the wrist. "Yes, Jessie," he said again. Her sobs were slowly, slowly dying away. "Go to sleep, love."

"No," she whispered one last time. And slept.

# *Chapter Eight*

The nightmare of memory was on her again, and there was no way she could fight her way out of it. She shivered in her sleep, pulling her hands closer to her body, protectively, and tried to fight the past. But it was useless, a vain struggle, as she lay there entwined in Springer MacDowell's arms and the mists of sleep, and remembered.

The second time Jessica slashed her wrists was when Sunny had dropped out of high school, pregnant, and married her seventeen-year-old boyfriend. And the third time was when her parents wrapped their car around a tree out on Route One. The ironic part of it was that neither of them had been drinking. They'd both been going through a period of peaceful sobriety and relative sanity. It was another drunken driver who'd forced them off the road by pulling directly in front of them at a red light.

To everyone's horror, Jessica had laughed when they told her, a short, sharp laugh. And then she'd calmly arranged for the funeral, every last little detail, from what they would wear, decked out in their twin bronze

coffins, to what would be lovingly chiseled on the head-
stone, to who would baby-sit for Sunny's three-year-
old and one-year-old during the service. And two
weeks later, when everyone was gone, she went up to
her solitary bedroom and slashed her wrists again.

She did a better job of it that time. The cuts were
deep, and she lost a lot of blood. They sent her to ther-
apists, and she played mind games with them. They
sent her to her stern Lutheran pastor, and she prayed
with him. They sent her to her sisters, and she baby-sat
for one and listened to the other's triumphant social
life with glazed boredom.

She joined Maren at the university for lack of anything better to do, and it was there she discovered her
ability to make unpleasantness disappear. She kept cool
and aloof from Maren's harem of jocks and scholars,
and it was there that she acquired the nickname "Ice
Princess." She was so completely different from Mar-
en, who pursued an almost desperate quest for love
and approval. Jessica needed no love, no approval, no
hasty fumblings and fevered couplings. All she needed
were her brains and her blind ambition.

She became adept at manipulating people by the time
she finished graduate school, with the reputation for
sleeping with her professors to get good grades. In fact,
she slept with no one. She knew just how to play an
ardent suitor along, without ever having to deliver the
goods.

The only time she'd ever been caught short had been
three years earlier, just after she'd joined Kinsey Enterprises. For a brief period Philip Mercer had been able to
charm his way into her armored heart, into her life,

into her bed. And she had withstood it, with her mind sailing in the blue, blue skies, until Philip had given up attempting anything more than a physical penetration of her icy reserve and left her. And she was relieved.

Everyone at Kinsey Enterprises assumed she was sleeping her way to power. And she was happy to have them believe it. It kept her peers at arm's length, convinced that she wouldn't bother with the lower orders. And it kept Peter Kinsey at bay, waiting for Rickford Lincoln to finish with her. But it hadn't kept Springer MacDowell away, and now she was lost.

JESSICA COULD FEEL the wetness of tears on her face, but she didn't dare move. Her cheek was pressed against a warm male chest; the even rhythm of his breathing told her he was asleep.

For a moment she forgot where she was, the memories of her childhood crowding in around her. She had thought those were tucked far away in the past, where they couldn't get to her anymore. The last thing she needed was to have them crop up in her sleep, so that she lay crying in Peter's arms....

Except they weren't Peter's arms, were they? She had never slept with Peter. The tears dried on her face as she lay there, motionless, willing her body to stay relaxed in the stranger's arms, so as not to wake him and invite all sorts of uncomfortable questions. And he wasn't a stranger. He was Springer MacDowell, and he already proved himself to be the most dangerous man in her life.

Slowly, carefully, she began to inch away from him, cursing herself for her inexplicable reluctance. He slept heavily, his face buried in the pillow, the silky black hair, which was longer than hers, tousled across his high forehead. She wanted to reach out and smooth that hair back, she wanted to crawl back into the bed and press her body against his. And the very thought horrified her.

He didn't stir as she let herself out the sliding glass door. The sun was rising out across the Atlantic, sending peach-colored tendrils across the dark green water breaking on the sand. She hoped her own door had been left unlocked, that no well-meaning soul had gone to check on her during the night. The caftan hung loosely around her slender frame, her long bare feet made distinct prints in the wet sand, walking from Springer's room to her own. And she hoped no budding Hercule Poirot would be out early to check on her, to tot up the clues and come to an embarrassing conclusion.

She would ignore it, she decided as she reached her door. She would simply pretend it never happened. Without question that was the most effective way to deal with it, with him. Last night was an aberration, never to be repeated. If she simply refused to accept it, it would go away, and things would be the same as they were.

But they wouldn't. She knew that far too well. That blessed anesthesia was gone, and she had the forlorn feeling she would never get it back. Damn his soul to hell.

The door slid back noiselessly, and Jessica stepped into her room. Lying in the middle of her neatly made bed was Peter, his pale blue eyes watching her with something akin to guilt.

Carefully Jessica pushed a hand through her close-cropped hair, then managed a cool, not unwelcoming smile. "Good morning, Peter. Have you been waiting long?"

"Most of the night," he said gently. "Are you all right, Jessica?"

"Of course," she said politely. "I'm sorry about the scene last night...."

Peter dismissed it with a wave of one aristocratic hand. "Don't mention it, darling. I'm only sorry that you had to be involved in something so distasteful. I had no idea that Lincoln was quite so taken with you. Not that I don't admire his taste..."

So that's the way he was going to play it, she thought, stalling for time. She moved with her usual grace, seating herself at the dressing table, her back to him, his reflection clear in the mirror. She sent out a tentative feeler. "I only hope I didn't jeopardize the merger."

"Don't worry about it. Lincoln wouldn't want any word of last night's little scene to get out. It doesn't reflect too well on him, you know, trying to seduce his host's girl friend. And the merger's too far along for him to back out without a damned good reason. No, everything should be fine. As long as..." He hesitated.

Jessica frowned at her reflection. Here came the pay-off. "As long as what, Peter?"

"As long as you...we...can keep him reasonably hopeful. You know just how to do it, darling. A smile here, a touch there and just the hint of a promise. I've seen you do it time and time again, and strong men weep." He smiled his engaging, affable grin at her.

"It's one of your greatest assets to the company, that charm of yours. I can't tell you how much I admire it."

Her lips were swollen, she noticed absently, and the fair skin beneath her chin was scraped from someone's beard. Her eyes were swollen, too, from crying, and there was a flush to her usually pale cheekbones. She turned and managed a cool smile to her fiancé. "I'm glad it's useful," she murmured, with just a hint of dryness. "And I know just how to handle Lincoln. I think you can tell your father that he can rely on me to retrieve the situation."

Peter's relief was painfully evident as he hopped off the bed. "I knew I could count on you. I told Father that, but he wanted to make sure...that is..."

"I understand," she said gently, and indeed, she did.

Peter smiled again, his charming, Ivy League grin, which ill-became a procurer, she thought distantly. He leaned down and kissed her cheek—warmly, approvingly, she noticed. "You're looking very pretty this morning, darling," he murmured. "Different somehow."

"Am I?" she questioned idly, toying with the silver-handled brush in front of her.

"More approachable." Their eyes met, icy blue ones looking up into paler ones, and there was an uncomfortable moment of understanding. Peter was not a stupid man, and he knew very well what he was asking of her.

She stood up then, looking directly into his eyes. They were the same height, a fact that had never bothered Peter, and his smile was warm, approving and only slightly anxious. She shouldn't do it, she told herself. She shouldn't come from one man's bed and go directly to another's. But she had to find out.

Sliding her arms up around his neck, she brought her mouth to his, gently, questioningly, pressing her slight body against his silk-robed one.

He responded instantly, ever the gentleman, she thought vaguely. He deepened the kiss with his usual suave expertise as his hands caught her narrow hips and held her against him. And she stood there beneath the onslaught of his embrace, a deep sorrow filling her. The clouds were gone, as she had feared, totally and completely banished. But with Peter, no desire replaced them. It was just a man's mouth on hers, a man's body pressed to hers, and it meant nothing. It could have been a doctor's touch, the feel of him was so impersonal. And yet she could feel his arousal against her, feel the wanting in his arms. It left her unmoved, and the realization devastated her.

Slowly, carefully, she pulled out of his arms, managing a sad smile. Peter looked at her for a long moment, trying to read her reaction. But she had always been too adept at hiding her feelings, and he was no closer to understanding her.

"Well, get some sleep, darling," he said finally, looking away. "Maybe we'll go sailing later. It looks as if it will be a lovely day." He moved toward the door, pausing there for a moment to look at her. "I love you very much, you know," he said suddenly.

"I know," she said wearily, and she did. She roused herself to give her stock response. "And I love you,

Peter." And as the words left her mouth she watched with no reaction at all as she saw Springer's tall figure in the doorway, directly behind Peter's rumpled figure.

Peter didn't even see him, didn't see that mobile mouth slashed in contempt, the dark eyes ablaze. A moment later Springer was gone, leaving the two of them alone once more.

*Ask me,* Jessica begged silently. *Ask me where I was all night, ask me who I was with. If you do love me, Peter, show me.*

But Peter merely smiled a foolish smile, blew her a kiss and walked down the hallway, closing the door quietly behind his graceful figure. Leaving Jessica to stare back at her reflection in the mirror, hopelessly, eternally alone.

## Chapter Nine

**The Slaughterer, vol. 81: Pearls of Pain**

*Matt Decker surveyed the carnage around him. Much as he hated to admit it, he bungled the last job. There were too many complications—the girl with the big eyes and the long legs. The lone kamikaze terrorist with the hand grenades. And his own sudden needs.*

*With impartial care he stitched a row of bullets around the crowded Nicaraguan street. He had to remember he was the lone wolf on a quest for justice. There was no room for amazons in his game plan.*

"WHAT HAPPENED between you and Jessica?" Elyssa's voice was diffident, hesitant, as she accepted the glass of Dubonnet from her son's strong, tanned hand. She did her best not to interfere in his life—she had learned from long and bitter experience that he had to make his own mistakes, and learn from them without his mother hovering over his shoulder, pointing out where he went wrong. But when her closest friend was involved....

"What makes you think anything happened?" Springer countered lazily, collapsing into Hamilton's sofa with the same tangled grace he'd had when he was fifteen. "I haven't seen her since the weekend out at the Kinseys's. That was...let's see—" he took a deliberately casual sip of his drink "—two or three weeks ago, wasn't it?"

His mother wasn't fooled. "Two weeks ago. I thought you'd be driving her back to town. Instead, you showed up a day early, looking like a thundercloud, and Jessica's been more and more elusive."

"She had Peter to drive her back," he said repressively. "And I doubt that I had anything to do with Jessica being elusive. It strikes me that that's an art she perfected long ago."

"True enough. But she was never that way with me."

"Well, don't blame me. There was a lot going on that weekend that might have affected her," Springer drawled, stretching his long legs out in front of him.

"You mean Rickford Lincoln," Elyssa murmured, not missing Springer's barely restrained curiosity. "I'm worried about that situation."

"What's to worry about? Jessica strikes me as a woman who has her priorities straight. If getting to the top of the corporate ladder means sleeping her way there, I'm sure she's capable of doing just that." He drained his drink in one tense gulp.

"Perhaps," Elyssa said in a noncommittal voice. "She's certainly very adept at leading men on. She's got Lincoln drooling all over her, and those damned Kinsey men are egging her on."

"I wouldn't think she'd need encouraging." Springer was mixing himself another drink, one even darker amber than the previous one. Elyssa noted it with curiosity—he usually stopped at one mild one, especially when they were going out for dinner.

"I don't know. Jessica's a complicated person—not at all what she appears to be. She's not very happy with her life right now. Not that she's ever been a serene person, but things seem to be getting worse for her, and she no longer confides in me. I just wondered if you knew anything about it."

Springer turned from the bar set up on an antique butler's table, and his eyes were dark and cynical. "She may not feel like confiding in my mother."

"What would that have to do with anything? I was her friend long before she met you."

He hesitated for a moment. "Maybe the fact that she went to bed with me that weekend might account for her elusiveness," he said finally. "And don't give me that disapproving look, Mother. We're both consenting adults."

"I thought you had gotten over that sort of behavior," she said mildly enough, her eyes dark with disappointment and a distant pain.

"What sort of behavior?"

"Sleeping with every attractive woman you can get your hands on. Haven't you come to terms with life yet?" The tone was mild, the words deeply cutting.

"All right, I deserve that," he said grimly. "And as a matter of fact, you're right. I hadn't slept with anyone in months when I came here."

"Then why Jessica?"

"Maybe I have a masochistic streak."

"Maybe you have a sadistic streak. Jessica doesn't need any more complications in her life, and she doesn't need hit-and-run weekends to destroy the security she's worked so hard to build up. How could you, Springer?" Elyssa's voice was shaking with anger.

"What makes you think I'm responsible?" he countered curiously. "How do you know she didn't seduce me?"

"Don't play games with me, Springer," she snapped. "I know both of you far too well. Jessica's sex life is, as far as I know, nonexistent, despite what everyone believes. I'm very disappointed in you."

"Whose mother are you, anyway?" he murmured. "For pity's sake, it was just a roll in the hay. You don't need to make a federal case out of it. Next thing I know you'll be dragging out a shotgun and telling me to make an honest woman of her."

"I doubt she'd have you," Elyssa said coolly. "I think, if she had her choice, Jessica wouldn't marry anyone. Her opinion of men isn't very high. And when you behave like this I don't think I blame her."

"Let's not fight," he said suddenly, squatting down in front of her and giving her what she cynically recognized as his most endearing smile. "This is our only night without my respected father around, and I want us to enjoy ourselves. Tell me what I can do to make it up to you about Jessica. Should I call and apologize?"

"You can leave her alone," Elyssa said firmly. "And you could also make more of an effort with your father. He loves you very much, Springer, and you keep him at arm's length. Can't you see how much you're hurting him?''

Springer's face had shuttered closed once more. "I'm working on it," he said repressively, and she knew it was hopeless. She loved them both so much, but fate had conspired to bring too much pain to their small, tortured family.

She smiled then, her warm, forgiving smile. "All right, let's drop all unpleasant subjects. I thought you were taking me out to dinner?"

"I am. I thought Cassin's would be a good choice. You approve?"

A tiny frown flitted over her forehead, then vanished. "Cassin's would be fine. It's one of my favorites." She finished her Dubonnet with a flourish, smiling up at his loving face. "Let's go."

JESSICA HAD ALWAYS LIKED Cassin's, ever since Elyssa had taken her there several months ago. She liked the subdued gray walls, the Palladian windows, the hushed murmur of voices and even, on rare occasions, the food. She had lost another two pounds, none of her clothes fit her, and even Peter was beginning to suggest gently that a woman could be too thin.

But there was nothing she could do about it. Her nonexistent appetite had taken a turn for the worse. In the past two weeks she could barely keep down anything more than dried toast and gingerale. She was hoping that Cassin's delectable French food would be able to tempt her appetite and trick her stomach into accepting nourishment. The merger was coming down to the wire, Lincoln was becoming more and more difficult to put off, and Peter was only an added note of confusion to the whole mess. He had finally formally proposed, suggesting they wait till after the merger for an official announcement. Jessica could recognize Jasper Kinsey's fine hand in that—he wanted to make sure his son would have an out if the deal fell through. She should have a lovely time tonight, she thought cynically, seated between Lincoln and Peter, their hands on either knee. Damn them all, anyway.

She had no intention of sleeping with Rickford Lincoln. She had come to that irrevocable decision when she woke up late the next morning two weeks ago and found that Springer MacDowell had decamped. Not that his abrupt departure had anything to do with it, she told herself righteously. She had merely come to the belated realization that yes, she was worth more than a corporate hustler. She was more than capable of leading one lecherous old man along without getting caught.

Peter, however, was another matter. Without examining her motives, Jessica had done everything she could to avoid sleeping with her finacé. She had never been enthusiastic about the idea, and the night she spent with Springer somehow put the seal on it. She hadn't told him about it, as Peter had made it more than clear that he didn't want to know. And he hadn't pushed her into bed—he'd been, as always, a complete gentleman, willing to accede to her needs and demands. If his high, aristocratic brow wrinkled in confusion more often, Jessica ignored it with an unaccustomed cowardice. He had waited months to sleep with her, he could certainly wait a little while longer.

With the grace that she had taught herself and was now second nature, she weaved her tall, slender body between the tables at Cassin's, following Elberto's military bearing as he led her. She knew she was looking her best. The simple gray silk sheath had been taken in that afternoon to fit her diminishing contours, her wheat-colored hair hugged her beautifully shaped head, the mauve shadows around her fine eyes only made them bluer.

The warm strains of music accompanied her journey, and inwardly Jessica flinched. That was the one drawback with Cassin's: the small, intimate dance floor. She had no doubt that Lincoln loved to dance, and she resigned herself to a period of groping later that evening. She would have to be very careful to be just encouraging enough to keep him on the fine edge of bewitched, without pushing him over into impatience and near-assault. Peter could be counted on to help in that matter—his emotions were clearly tangled every time he chaperoned Lustful Lincoln, as Jessica privately termed him. On the one hand he was quite unaccountably, endearingly jealous of the old man. On the other, he was obviously terrified that something might jeopardize the merger. He hadn't come right out and asked Jessica to bed Lincoln, but she had the melancholy suspicion that the moment might come.

"There you are, darling!" Peter rose with his usual fluid grace, and Lincoln lumbered up beside him. "I was worried about you. I can't imagine why you wouldn't let me pick you up."

"Because I like my independence at times," she replied lightly, giving Lincoln her perfect smile, cool, with just a promise of banked fires. Fires that would fizzle out, she realized with cynical amusement, the moment he breathed that Scotch-laden breath on her. "How are you, Mr. Lincoln?"

"How many times have I asked you to call me Linc?" he said plaintively, his eyes gleaming beneath the bushy gray eyebrows. It was a game they played, and she positioned the appropriate simper on her face.

"How are you, Linc?" she said. Honestly, at times it was like taking candy from a baby. Men were so damnably transparent, most of them. Maybe that's why the chase had lost its savor. They were all the same, she thought as she slid between the two men while Elberto held her chair. They—

"Hello, Elyssa, Springer," Peter said, his preoccupied expression brightening. "I didn't know you were coming tonight. Why don't you join us?"

Jessica knocked over her water glass. Afterward she would curse herself for being so obvious, but she couldn't help it. The sight of those dark, unreadable eyes staring down at her, that mouth a thin, mocking line, and all her self-assurance shriveled away. Only for a moment, however. Throwing back her shoulders, she gave the two newcomers a dazzling smile, so dazzling that she had the pleasure of seeing Springer momentarily taken aback.

"Yes, how lovely to see you," she murmured in her low, pleasant voice. "You should have told me, Elyssa, and we could have gotten a larger table. I can still talk to Elberto—"

"No need," Elyssa said hurriedly. "Springer and I were looking forward to a dinner à deux, and—"

"And the last thing you need is a great meal ruined by business discussions," Peter finished for her, smiling. "I don't blame you at all, just have pity on us poor working stiffs while you enjoy your meal. And save me a dance later, Lyss."

Very few peoople were immune to Peter Kinsey's considerable charm when he chose to exert it, and Elyssa MacDowell wasn't one of their small number. "I will, Peter. Enjoy yourselves."

Springer hadn't said a single word during that light interchange. Jessica could still feel his eyes upon her, but she refused to meet their steady gaze. *Go away,* she said under her breath. *Go away and leave me alone.*

"Yes," he said finally, that husky, sexy voice tickling her backbone. "Enjoy yourselves." She watched his tall, straight back follow Elyssa's slender, tiny figure, and there was a curious look of longing in their icy blue depths.

"You don't like each other very much, do you?" Lincoln observed, pressing his wool-covered knee against her silk-clad thigh. "Anyone can see it. Can't say as I blame you—he's an arrogant young man. It does seem a shame, though—his mother is such a charming woman." He licked his thick pink lips.

"Anyone can see it," Peter echoed hollowly, his eyes on her immobile face. "Shall we order?"

Even Cassin's venerable French chef couldn't tempt Jessica's appetite that night. To be sure, the dark eyes watching her from across the room might have had something to do with it, not to mention the expected gropings under the table from at least one pair of hot hands. Peter was curiously subdued, smiling, charming, but making no effort to stroke her leg, take her hand under the table, rub against her hip. Maybe he was afraid he'd run into Linc, she thought distantly. For whatever reason, he was leaving her entirely in Lincoln's hot little paws, and Lincoln was enjoying his freedom.

"I hope you both will excuse me," Jessica said after the waiter cleared away her barely touched plate. I'm really tired and think I'll go home now."

"One dance, Jessica," Lincoln demanded, draining his Chivas Regal with unappreciative haste. "You can't leave yet, the night is still young."

Jessica controlled her instinctive wince. "I'm exhausted, Linc. Peter can tell you that my schedule recently has been murderous—I really do need my beauty sleep."

"This merger's taking a lot out of you, isn't it?" Linc said craftily, and Jessica waited for what was to come, contenting herself with a nod. "What you need, my girl, is a good long vacation, away from work, away from everything. Don't you agree, Kinsey?"

Peter nodded absently, his eyes alert. *He knows as well as I do what's coming,* Jessica realized. "But there's nothing we can do about it until the merger's completed," he said reasonably.

He'd baited the hook, Jessica thought. Now all he had to do is wait for Linc to snap it up, and then he can reel him in.

"Well, we haven't too much longer to wait, have we? My lawyers and your lawyers are wading through the papers right now—it shouldn't be more than a couple of weeks. I tell you what—why doesn't Jessica come with me on a cruise around the Mediterranean when this is all over? I have a yacht that gets far too little use just waiting for me, with a full crew. You won't have to do a thing but lie in the sun and relax. What do you say?"

Jessica smiled faintly. "I don't think Peter can get away," she replied, deliberately reminding him that she was ostensibly Peter's date.

Linc's face took on an even rosier glow. "Even better," he said gruffly. "You need to be away from everyone. And I'm sure young Kinsey here won't mind if a harmless old man keeps you company."

Jessica controlled an inelegant snort. "I wouldn't call you a harmless old man, Linc," she purred, and he preened like a rooster.

"Think you can trust me to take care of your fiancée, Kinsey?" he inquired, leaning past Jessica, his thick hand kneading her thigh. She'd have bruises tomorrow, she thought distantly, and smiled sweetly.

"Oh, I trust you, Linc." Peter's expression was bland, charming and suddenly as impregnable as Springer Mac-Dowell's.

"But I still need to go home, Linc," she reminded him.

"No problem...I'll run you home," he said expansively, his eyes glistening in anticipation.

She shook her head. "No, thank you, anyway. I only live a few blocks away, and I'd rather walk."

"But—"

"Better take no for an answer, Linc," Peter broke in easily. "I've learned that when Jessica makes up her mind there's no changing it."

A sullen expression deepened the flushed face of the businessman opposite her. "Then you'll have to dance with me to make up for it," he said, the sulky tone holding just a trace of a threat.

For just one moment she considered refusing. No one was going to threaten her, no one was going to order her around. She raised her head to sweetly tell him no when she saw Springer watching her, that cynical look on his dark face. "I'd love to," she said abruptly. "Just one, though."

Linc practically leaped out of his seat, his hamlike hand heavy on her thin arm. So intent was he on getting her out on the postage-stamp-sized dance floor that he was oblivious as they passed Springer and Elyssa MacDowell. Jessica flashed him a small, sweet smile as she passed, telling him quite effectively to go to hell. Springer returned the smile and leaned back in his chair, that delectable mouth of his curving in malicious enjoyment. And then he was out of sight, hidden as Linc yanked her against his bulky frame, and all Jessica could do was savor the memory of his initial anger.

# Chapter Ten

The band was playing a sophisticated blues, something slow and just slightly defiant. It suited Jessica's mood perfectly as she allowed Lincoln to press his large frame against hers. She could only be glad he'd pushed her head against his shoulder, out of the line of fire from his Scotch-laden breath. She refused to think about why she hated Scotch. She knew full well, but it made life a great deal easier simply to accept her dislike without delving into its reasons.

His light wool suit was scratchy against her skin, and her legs were pressed so tightly against his that she could barely move. He had taken advantage of the darkness of the dance floor to breathe heavily in her small, delicate ear. She accepted with stoic forebearance when he decided slobbering with his tongue might excite her, she accepted with irritation the steady jarring of his pelvis against hers. He obviously wanted to make certain she knew how aroused he was and perhaps hoped that pressure of hardened flesh would in turn arouse her. He was in for a disappointment, she thought to herself, sighing.

Lincoln took that sigh for a sound of excitement, and he began to slobber across her cheekbone. She could smell the Scotch, but grimly she withstood the fear. She was safe, surrounded by people, nothing could happen to her. The revulsion was beginning to wash over her, combined with a sudden panic that she might push him away and destroy everything she'd worked for.

He'd taken her arms and twined them around his neck, draping his own around her slender hips. His hands were playing around her lower back, dropping lower to press her buttocks against him, his fingers kneading. She tried to step on his foot, but like most of his generation he was a very good dancer—he managed to sidestep her quite adeptly without realizing her intent. The panic was building, and she couldn't even flash a call for help to the waiting Peter. Lincoln had her face pressed hard against his shoulder, and there were too many people around, in between her and their table. There was no one to turn to for rescue, she'd simply have to tough it out, but then he'd moved his hand to her chin, and he was going to try to kiss her in the middle of this crowded dance floor! She could see his face move closer, see the tiny broken blood vessels in his aging skin, and in sudden despair she closed her eyes, unable to fight him.

The mouth never connected, the hands fell away and her eyes flew open again. Springer was standing there, an unreadable expression on his dark, beautiful face, ignoring Lincoln's glare of frustrated rage.

"I'm sure you don't mind if I cut in," he said smoothly, and there was nothing Lincoln could do but acquiesce sullenly as Springer took her gently into his arms.

"I'll wait for you at the table," Lincoln managed. She watched for a moment as he walked back across the room, his physical condition making him awkward.

"You are a witch, aren't you?" Springer said lightly. His hands were gentle on her, not pulling at her, and the song changed, to something low and sweet and sad. "Getting an old man like that into such a condition. You ought to be ashamed of yourself."

"He did it to himself," she said, looking up at him, wondering if he had chosen to forgive her. He had rescued her—he knew that as well as she did. She could only wonder why. It was more than possible he had his own revenge in mind.

"I think you ought to be restricted for people of uncertain health, like cigarettes and booze and salt. Dangerous for the blood pressure." There was a good three inches between them: not enough to be noticeable to anyone watching them but enough to be oddly frustrating. He was wearing a suit tonight, the first time she'd seen him in such a thing. The clean, European lines suited him, she thought absently, almost as much as that sexy white shirt he'd worn when she last saw him.

But those were dangerous thoughts. "I hope your mother doesn't mind you abandoning her," she said lightly. He felt so good. That height gave her a feeling of security she seldom had, and the strong shoulder beneath her hand seemed made for her head.

"She's the one who sent me to rescue you."

She knew she was overreacting. She knew she should laugh lightly, thank him for his good services and finish the dance. But she was coming to realize that he had the uncanny ability to destroy all her polite defenses, to rip through the convenient social veneer.

Without a word she pulled herself out of his arms, telling herself the devastating disappointment she felt was simple irritation. Without looking at him she strode back across the restaurant, skirting the dance floor so that she wouldn't have to come face to face with Elyssa's concern. Peter was alone at the table when she got there.

"Lincoln had to leave—apparently he wasn't feeling well. Some stomach thing, he said. Are you going to let me see you home, darling?" Peter's pale blue eyes were diffident and far too knowing as he politely rose, ever the gentleman.

She scooped up the tiny leather clutch purse. "No, thanks, Peter." She was pleased to hear that her voice sounded entirely normal, albeit just slightly breathless. "I'll see you in the morning." She pretended not to see him lean toward her for a good-night kiss, and a moment later she was out on the sidewalk, moving past the leisurely crowds at a speedy daytime Manhattan pace.

A summer night in the city was usually one of her favorite times, but tonight she paid no attention. She moved swiftly, her high heels clicking on the sidewalk, ignoring the well-dressed couples, the curious glances, the occasional leer of a passing taxi driver. She needed to get back behind the pure white walls of her apartment, hidden away from other people's demands, other people's hurting. It was all she could do to keep from breaking into a run, but her long legs ate up the distance at a rapid rate.

She was almost at her apartment building when Springer caught up with her, one of those strong, large hands catching her arm and spinning her around.

The spiked heel snapped underneath her, her ankle twisted and she fell against him. His arms went around her, holding her close, and her close-cropped head rested on the shoulder that she'd longed for just minutes ago. "You move pretty fast when you set your mind to it," he said, a hint of laughter in the voice above her head.

Damn, his arms felt good, Jessica thought helplessly, knowing she should break out of them and push him away, knowing that she wasn't going to. She was going to leave it up to him to release her, which he did, far too quickly. Squatting down beside her on the sidewalk, he took her long, slender leg in his hand, running his fingers over her ankle. She could barely control the unbidden shiver of delight that washed over her.

"Do you think you can walk?" he queried, standing up again, one arm holding her balanced against him. "Your apartment isn't far, is it? I can carry you."

"I can walk." Gingerly she set her foot down. It was painful, but she could make it. With his help. The thought was disturbing. "Why were you following me? And what's happened to Elyssa? Shouldn't you be seeing to her?"

"Peter's taking Elyssa home," he replied blandly as they moved slowly down the street.

"Oh, great," she said sarcastically. "What did Peter say to that?"

"Nothing, of course. Doesn't he always turn a blind eye to whatever you do?"

"You still didn't tell me why you followed me." They had reached her apartment building by then. The doorman made all sorts of concerned noises, but Springer very efficiently escorted her past him, up the elevator and into the hushed, airy confines of her sparsely furnished apartment before he bothered to answer her.

She was leaning against the heavy door, keys dangling from one limp hand as she stared up at him. She hadn't bothered to turn on the light—the dim glow of the one living-room lamp she'd left on was the only source of light in the place. Reaching past her, he carefully locked each of the three locks, still without answering her question.

"Why?" she asked again, her voice hushed in the stillness.

He had both hands on either side of her, braced against the door, and she felt imprisoned by his long arms. The sheer size of him played havoc with her emotions—she felt both sheltered and trapped by him. "I could tell you we had to talk, but I don't think that would do any good, would it?"

"Would it?"

"I could tell you you're playing a dangerous game with Lincoln, but you'd only tell me you know what you're doing." His voice was low and husky and irresistibly beguiling. "I could tell you that Peter Kinsey, charming though he is, will never give you what you need, and you'll tell me that it's up to you to know what you need. I could tell you you're destroying your life and you'd just say it's your life to destroy."

"Lovely conversation we're having," Jessica murmured. "And do you have anything to offer me in place of Peter and my career?"

"No." It was said without hesitation, without regret, it seemed. And she accepted it.

"Then why are you here?" She looked up into those dark, dark eyes of his, so unlike any she had ever known. She hadn't needed to ask that question; she knew. He had come for her, and yet the thought didn't give her its customary satisfaction, its feeling of power. It left her completely vulnerable, powerless and frightened.

He could read that powerlessness and fear in her eyes, in the slight trembling of her mouth. "You know why," he said gently, and lowered his mouth to hers.

The keys dropped onto the carpeted floor as her hands pressed against the solid wood of the door, seeking some sort of reality to combat the insidious assault on her senses. But the door was cold, unyielding wood, and the body in front of her was warm, strong and seeking. She used her hands to propel her forward, into his arms, as her mouth opened beneath his.

How could there be such a difference between bodies, she wondered dazedly. Lincoln's arousal disgusted her, Peter's left her cold. The feel of Springer's desire sent waves of longing through her veins, a longing that frightened her. She wanted to pull away from him, but she couldn't. All she could do was twine her arms around his neck, threading her hands through that silky black hair, and hold him closer, closer. She needed him, needed his warmth and strength and power, needed to believe that he cared. It no longer mattered that his mother had probably sent him once more; it no longer mattered that Peter would have a very good idea what they were doing and didn't care enough to face it. Nothing mattered but the mouth on hers, the hands cradling her body against his, stroking, soothing, holding, as his mouth seduced her.

His mouth broke away to trail warm, lingering kisses down the side of her neck. "Where's the bedroom?" he murmured against her skin.

She stiffened, an unwelcome reality intruding when she least wanted it. She didn't want to take Springer into the carefully designed confines of her bedroom that was part and parcel of the formal, distant apartment, with its white walls and stark, modern furniture, its mirrors and white rugs and lack of welcome. "No."

He didn't stop the demoralizing little path his mouth was blazing, and the hands on her body tightened just slightly. "Don't lie to me, Jessie," he murmured. "You want me just as much as I want you. And you know it, even if you want to deny it." His hands slid up her back to the neckline of her gray silk dress, and with the dexterity she'd noticed and hated before he began to undo the long zipper.

She tried to protest, but the words wouldn't form in her mind, much less make it to her mouth. Besides, her mouth was too caught up in tasting the warm skin of his neck to answer. Even his prompting failed to penetrate.

"The bedroom, Jessie. Where is it?" The dress was loose around her shoulders, only held up by his encompassing arms. A moment later it dropped to the floor around her silk-clad ankles, covering the discarded keys, leaving her wearing only a wisp of a slip and her panty hose.

He had pulled away just slightly enough to let the dress fall, and she could look up into his intent, passion-clouded eyes, and for a moment her usual sanity intruded. Was he going to carry her off to the bedroom? Would he continue to undress her, and how was he going to deal with something so prosaically unromantic as panty hose? She had little doubt he'd do it with his customary deftness.

A small, knowing smile danced around his mouth, as if he read her thoughts. "Stalling for time, Jess?" he murmured, his mouth dipping forward to lightly tease her lips. "It's a waste, when we both know what's going to happen. Whether I like it or not, I haven't been able to think about anything but you and that night two long weeks ago. I need you, Jessie. And you need me even more than I need you."

If he only moved back a few feet, she might be able to regain some sense of equilibrium. It was impossible with the sheer, warm bulk of him mere inches away, waiting for her. "What makes you think I need you?" She put up one last fight.

"Because as far as I can tell you haven't been loved very well at all. You need all the good loving you can get—your body's starved for it."

She could feel a hot, angry flush suffuse that starved body. "Are we talking about love or sex?" she countered.

"We're talking about bedrooms, Jessie. Where is it?" There was a decided edge beneath the mocking drawl, and then a look of belated enlightenment crossed his shadowed face, and she felt herself enfolded in his arms, one large hand spanning her slender neck and slowly caressing. "You don't want me in your bedroom, is that it?" he murmured. "All right, I'm flexible. The living-room couch, the bathtub, the kitchen? Just point me in the right direction." His mouth was teasing her pale, soft skin as his other hand molded her hips against his.

She could feel the trembling begin in her knees, traveling up her thighs and settling deep in her belly. Her hands were at his chest, fumbling with the buttons, and she knew if she didn't feel that warm, sleek hide of him beneath her desperate hands before long she'd go mad. "The back bedroom," she whispered, so low she hoped he wouldn't hear. "On the right."

But he heard, his mouth catching hers as a reward, before scooping her up in his arms with all the romance she could have wanted.

He didn't turn on the lights before he lay her down on the narrow little bed in the study that served as her escape when things grew too overwhelming. It was her haven, her solace, the only place she felt safe and free to be whoever she wanted to be. And she had absolutely no idea why she had wanted Springer to take her here, to a room she'd allowed no one else in.

He kicked the door shut behind them, standing over her as he fumbled with his tie. The streetlights were the only illumination as she lay on the faded patchwork quilt, looking up at him out of shadowed, wary eyes. His usual expertise seemed to have escaped him, for the tie knotted, and he had to yank it over his head, the buttons on his shirt caught, and he sent it spinning.

He was yanking at his belt when he caught her eyes.

"God, Jessie, you make me so crazy," he muttered, sinking on one knee on the narrow bed beside her. His hands were shaking and not at all deft as he stripped the panty hose off her, and he almost strangled her with the slip as he pulled it over her head. And then she was lying there, naked, vulnerable, the soft cotton of the quilt under her back, looking up at him out of longing eyes.

There was nothing she could say, nothing she would do, to protect herself from his invasion of her mind and soul and body. And there was nothing she wanted to do. She had brought him back to her private room, and it was a secret measure of trust and faith that he would never even be aware of.

It only took Springer a moment to strip off his trousers, and for a moment Jessica looked at him, in all his uncompromisingly aroused glory. She hadn't really seen him the other night, had done her best to avoid looking directly at Philip Mercer on the few occasions they'd been to bed together. But tonight she wanted to look at Springer, wanted to see him. But she wanted to feel him even more.

She held up her arms to him, beseechingly. And with a groan he covered her, spread her, filled her with that strong, masculine beauty of his. Her body arched beneath his on the quilt, drawing him in even deeper as her legs wrapped around his narrow hips, and the arms clinging to his broad back were desperate. *Don't leave me,* her mind cried, as shadows and sensations beat like the wings of a thousand birds against her consciousness. And then, unexpectedly, before he had more than set up the age-old rhythm that had once disgusted her, the familiar-unfamiliar tightening gripped her, arching her up against him, as wave after wave swept over her. It was mysterious, overwhelming, indefinable, and she wept against him, her tears hot on their damp skin.

He cradled her against him until the last spasm passed, and in sudden shyness she tried to pull away. "Not so fast," he whispered in her ear, his teeth capturing her sensitive lobe and nipping lightly. Another ripple of pleasure shook her body, and he laughed breathlessly. "Do that again," he murmured, biting her again. Her body trembled once more, and he pushed against her. "I'm afraid I'm not quite finished," he added politely, his tongue lightly tracing her tremulous lips. "And I don't think you are, either."

She opened her mouth, to question, to protest, when he deepened the kiss, his tongue a warm, wet, powerful intruder, reminding her of his other intrusion. Slowly he rocked against her, drawing her with him, his hands firm and strong on her hips, holding her tightly. For a moment she wanted to pull away, to protest, her body weary and reluctant. And then the trembling began again, deep inside, with an even greater force. It was happening again, she thought with amazement, her fingers digging into the warm, muscled shoulders above her. It couldn't be, but it was. He couldn't . . . she couldn't . . .

It hit her with the shock of a tidal wave, drowning her. She could feel him against her, within her, rigid with the suddenness of his release, could hear his voice, the rasping breath against her shoulder, the barely discernible words, love words, sex words, praise and pleasure tumbling from him. It took far longer to die away this time, and she smiled in exhaustion against his chest, holding him close against her. She didn't want him to leave her, ever; she wanted to stay beneath the warmth and strength of his body. She could hear the steady rhythm of his breathing slow, and she kept very still, willing him to fall asleep.

How many times had she dreaded the thought of being trapped under Peter's body while he slept, blissfully sated? What had happened to her in the past two weeks, that she would want to lie here, crushed by a much larger body? She didn't want to examine her motives, didn't want to think about it. She recognized when his breathing slowed into the steady sound of sleep. Moving with infinite care, she arranged herself more comfortably beneath him. And placing an odd, irrational kiss against his shoulder, she closed her eyes and prepared to join him in sleep.

## Chapter Eleven

She knew he was watching her. Sometime during the night they must have shifted around. Right now she was lying curled up against him, the old quilt wrapped around their naked bodies, and her eyes were still closed. Through her eyelids she could sense the slow breaking of dawn over the gray city, through her skin she could sense the curiosity of the man beside her. And for the first time in her life she wanted to snuggle closer, not pull away. For now, maybe she could fake it. How was he to know whether she slept or not? Maybe she really was sleeping. Otherwise, why would she want to move closer to the alien body in her bed? With a muffled sigh she stretched out her long legs, rubbing them against the even longer legs behind her, and wished she never had to wake up.

Springer wasn't fooled. He'd slept with too many women, too many times, not to know when someone was pretending to be asleep. He knew when a woman was faking, before, during or after making love. And what still astonished him was her response. A response that seemed to surprise her even more than it surprised him. Someone must have handled her very, very badly when she was younger, that she'd come to expect so little out of making love. Not that he didn't do his damnedest to make it pleasurable for her, but he was, even with his experience, not as miraculous as she appeared to think he was. And her response still embarrassed her. He could see the faint flush stain her high, Nordic cheekbones, the cheekbones with not enough flesh on them, and a slow smile lit his face.

Springer could very easily get used to the idea of showing her just how pleasurable it could be. Each time they made love she loosened up a little more, opened up to him. And for some reason that mattered to him, even knowing she was someone else's fiancée, heading to be someone else's mistress. A cold, ambitious lady, lying in his arms, pretending to be asleep, all the while her trim bottom was pressed up against him enticingly. He must be going through a midlife crisis at thirty-five.

He slid an arm around her, drawing her closer against him, smiling as she nestled closer, still feigning sleep. This room didn't look at all like her. The rest of the apartment was all pure white walls with a splash or two of color from carefully selected, exquisitely tasteful modern paintings. Everything had seemed ruthlessly up-to-date, though he had to admit his attention wasn't on her interior decor last night.

But this room was lined with bookshelves, filled with books. Old leather-bound sets, sleazy paperbacks and everything in between jostled for room on the overflowing shelves. The quilt spread over them was old and beautiful, the one painting was a Watteau. Romantic, innocent, very unlike the lady lying in his arms. Or was it?

One hand reached up to cup her small breast, and he noticed with approval its immediate response. Damn, he wanted her again, wanted her more than he had wanted anyone for a long time. He couldn't seem to get enough of that too-skinny body, that nasty tongue of hers, that lost, hungry look in her ice-blue eyes when he filled her. He could feel himself hardening against her at the thought, and he wondered if she'd ignore it, still pretending to be asleep. How far would she let him go, her eyes tightly shut, her muscles not quite relaxed enough for it to be believable. He had just begun to turn her over in the narrow confines of the single bed when the phone rang.

Jessica's eyes flew open, wide with shock and dismay. There was no room for pretending any longer, but he tried to put off the inevitable. "Don't answer," he whispered, kissing her lightly on her soft, parted lips.

He would have given anything for her to respond, and for a moment it seemed as if she might, her lips clinging, her tongue reaching out to lightly, shyly skirt his lower lip. And then her eyes darkened, and she pulled away, out of his arms, out of the bed, stumbling away from him.

Springer watched her as she tried vainly to pull her skimpy little slip on. Reaching down he plucked his shirt from the floor and tossed it to her. It reached halfway down to her knees, and her mumbled thanks were interrupted by the regular shrilling of the phone above their heads.

She dived for it at the same time he was reaching out. Of course he was the victor, pulling her back down on the bed at the same moment he uncradled the phone. She opened her mouth to yell at him, but he only smiled silently and handed her the phone, his other hand holding her down beside him on the bed.

She had no choice but to answer. "Hello?" Her voice was strained, slightly hoarse. "Yes, Peter, it's me." She glared at Springer, willing him to go away, struggling against his inexorable hold. He merely smiled, trapping her legs with his. "No, Peter, that's quite all right. I usually get up around six anyway. No, I don't think so. No, I can't. Peter..."

Springer could hear the rumble of Peter Kinsey's voice on the other end of the line, could see the frustration in Jessica's pale face as she struggled vainly against his light but implacable hold. Finally she lay back in his arms, panting slightly. "No, I'm all right, Peter," she said breathlessly. "I was just trying to get dressed while you called."

Springer put his head down beside hers, hoping to decipher Peter's agitated rumble, but she jerked away from him, frowning fiercely. "What was that, Peter? I didn't quite hear you."

Suddenly her body went very still, and a fleeting, stricken look danced across her face. Springer could feel her withdrawal, feel her moving away from him, and he knew that no matter how hard he held on, she was gone.

He dropped his arms, and slowly, like a sleepwalker, she rose from the bed. "Yes, Peter," she said dully, that stricken look gone now, replaced with an unreadable expression. "Certainly, I can manage that. If you think it necessary." She moved back across the room, the telephone in her hand, her mind elsewhere. "I don't know if my passport's up to date. I probably need some shots. Maybe you could do something about that.... All right. Yes, later." Slowly she replaced the phone on the cradle, leaning over Springer's watchful figure to do it.

"What's up?" he said softly, not wanting to startle her.

She roused herself from her abstraction. "What? Oh, I gather I'm going to the Mediterranean in a few weeks." Without another glance in his direction she headed for the door.

"Part of your honeymoon?" he inquired coolly, unable to help himself.

She paused by the door, bestowing a singularly sweet smile on him. "No, Springer. Part of my business deal. I'll be going with Lincoln." And she closed the door silently behind her.

Her hands were shaking by the time she made it to her bathroom, and the tears pouring down her face mingled with the hot water of the shower. Peter and Lincoln had made the arrangements—a month-long cruise of the Mediterranean, to help them wind down from the intensive negotiations of the past few months. The joining of two massive corporations like Kinsey Enterprises and Lincoln Incorporated had to be handled like the mating of porcupines—very carefully. Any wrong move could result in disaster, and they had all been very circumspect. Peter would accompany them, as would Jasper and whoever was enjoying his attentions at the moment. But they would go back after the first week. Only Jessica was deemed worn down enough to merit the entire month-long cruise. With only her host to keep her company.

She could still hear the barely controlled panic in Peter's voice over the telephone. Things must be desperate indeed for him to have to come so close to asking her to whore for him. She had said all the right things; as far as Peter was concerned the merger and the vacation were assured.

And what was Springer thinking right now? What had gotten into her last night, to have gone to bed with him like that? And why was she standing in her shower, crying, and wishing she were still back there with him, weeping against his broad shoulder and having him tell her everything would be all right?

Because everything wouldn't be all right, she told herself feverishly. Not unless she made it so. And she still wasn't quite sure how she could manage it. But relying on a man like Springer MacDowell would only get her deeper into trouble.

The slam of the front door echoed through the apartment reverberating through her body, and she flinched beneath the hot, steady stream of the shower. Well, at least there wouldn't be the need for stilted morning-after conversation. And she leaned her forehead against the marble tile and wept some more.

SPRINGER USED TO LOVE the empty early-morning streets of Manhattan and the Upper East Side. But not this morning. His impossibly long legs ate up the distance between Jessica's austere apartment at Park and Seventy-second and Hamilton's town house in the sixties, all the time his brain was in ferment.

Damn her, damn her, damn her, he cursed. And damn him. What the hell was he doing, being jealous of a woman he scarcely knew? He hadn't even been jealous of his wife during the short miserable time they'd been married. Why should he suddenly discover that unpleasant emotion for a woman he had no right to feel jealous over, no reason to even like?

But there was no denying it, he thought ruefully, ducking into a small hole-in-the-wall café for a cup of wretched coffee. He was overwhelmingly, insanely jealous, and there was nothing he wanted to do more than hit something or someone. Preferably X. Rickford Lincoln.

Hamilton's house was dark and silent when Springer let himself in just after seven. Tossing his jacket onto a nearby chair, he lowered himself onto the rough cotton sofa with a weary sigh. He was too tired to do anything, too wired to go back to sleep. Stretching his long legs out in front of him, he leaned back, wishing he had another cup of coffee to nurse, while he figured out what he was going to do about Jessica Hansen.

In the end that decision was taken from him. He heard the phone ring, once, twice, and had every intention of ignoring it. He knew Hamilton turned off the phone in his bedroom until eleven, and whoever it was could damn well wait. He had already had his day spoiled by one damned phone call.

But the ringing was insistent, nerve-racking, and suddenly ominous. And Elyssa's panic-blurred voice on the other end was even more frightening.

"Thank God I've found you, Springer. I've been calling everywhere—I even tried Jessica a few minutes ago, but there was no answer. Where have you been?"

Springer was immediately, completely alert. "It doesn't matter—I'm here now. What is it, Mother?"

Elyssa took a deep, shuddering breath. "It's Katherine."

## Chapter Twelve

**The Slaughterer, vol. 54: Decker's Drop**

*Matt Decker surveyed the carnage around him. Things were too quiet, he didn't trust it when things were so quiet. The calm before the storm, and only the Slaughterer knew how bad the storm could be. A hail of bullets, a wind of firepower and devastation would rain on this little side street in the Himalayas.*

*Decker shoved the gun in the ankle pocket of his combat jump suit before heading out into the snow. Ilse would like it here, he thought suddenly. Maybe he'd find her holed up somewhere. Maybe finally they'd have their showdown.*

*In the meantime, he couldn't let himself be distracted. Terrorists had been masquerading as abominable snowmen, and he had to melt their cover with a blaze of bullets. A lean, determined smile cracked his face as he moved out. The calm before the storm never lasted long.*

THINGS WERE GOING VERY WELL INDEED. If she had any sense at all, Jessica could lean back and view her life with a justifiable amount of satisfaction. But then, when had she ever had enough sense, she wondered.

*Count your blessings,* she instructed herself, leaning back in the cushioned desk chair and staring blankly out at the heat-hazed Manhattan skyline. First, she seemed to be regaining her health. During the past two weeks she'd not only been able to keep food down but had actually developed an appetite. If she kept eating the way she had been, it wouldn't be too long before she had to go on a diet. Her hollow cheeks had begun to fill, her stomach was no longer concave, and that concentration-camp look was fading rapidly. It wouldn't be long before her semi-irregular periods would become regular again, and the peaceful lethargy would soon translate itself into her usual high energy.

Then there was the problem of Peter. He, thank God, had kept his distance, accurately gauging her reluctance with no more than a questioning look. Despite the fact that she was unofficially engaged to Peter, she had no intention of sleeping with him until things became a little clearer in her own mind. He was probably too caught up in the intricacies of the merger and Rickford Lincoln's polite blackmail to worry about his fiancée's sexual skittishness. She doubted that he was highly sexually motivated in the first place. If he was, he would hardly have been satisfied with her manufactured, tepid responses, and she would have been unable to hold him off for so long.

Lincoln, secure in the belief that she was going to be his property for fun and games on board the yacht, had also backed off, contenting himself with a pinch here and there, a fumbled grope when he thought no one was looking.

And best of all, Springer was gone.

Two weeks ago, immediately after the night he'd spent in her apartment, he'd taken off, without a word. Not that she deserved a word, she realized fairly. And she couldn't bring herself to question Elyssa. Too often she saw the curiosity in her friend's liquid dark eyes that were too much like her son's, but Elyssa didn't bring up the subject, and Jessica refused to. No, she was grateful, immeasurably so, that Springer had disappeared. He was simply one more complication in an already convoluted life, a complication she could gladly do without.

Especially when things were coming down to the wire. Jasper had phoned her a few moments ago—the papers had been drawn up, the time of signing arranged with all the flourish the Kinseys relished. They would meet tomorrow afternoon to sign the agreements, continue on to the Tavern on the Green to seal the bargain with a proper celebration, and then depart on Friday for the Mediterranean. It was unfortunate that something had come up, and neither Jasper nor Peter could accompany them for that first week, but then, that was business. And Jessica wasn't to even consider not going herself—she had earned her vacation, and Lincoln's yacht, away from everything, would be just the place.

A cynical smile twisted Jessica's pale mouth. Part of the agreement would be a very fat bonus for her efforts on the Kinseys' behalf. More than enough to get her far away, if that's what she chose to do. As the time was getting closer, she was still undecided, and this time she couldn't even turn to Elyssa and Hamilton for help and advice. Not with the memory of Springer hovering in the background. No, it was more than time for her to make up her own mind.

The telephone buzzed discreetly by her left shoulder, and she eyed it with marked hostility. There was no way she was going to come to a decision with all these interruptions. She reached out, hesitated, then grabbed the receiver with a sense of weary acceptance.

"Jessica? I know you said not to bother you but it's Dr. Brochu, and I figured it might be important." Her secretary's voice was filled with the concern that was far too prevalent nowadays. It seemed as if Jessica could pull the wool over everyone's eyes but Jilly's.

"Thanks, Jilly. Put her through." Leaning back in her chair, she picked up one of the number two pencils she preferred and began to tap it idly against the teak desk. No doubt Morgan Brochu would be prescribing multivitamins and B-12 shots and all sorts of other nasty things. Jessica had seen her reluctantly, only the necessity of updating her shots and Peter's constant carping overcoming her resistance. She had known what to expect, and Morgan Brochu's shocked exclamations rolled off her back.

"Hello, Morgan," she said wearily. "No more lectures, please. I had more than enough from you yesterday. I promise to take whatever nasty vitamins you prescribe for me, but you have to promise not to be so disapproving. I assure you, I'm much better than I was three weeks ago."

"I'm sure you are," Morgan Brochu said dryly. "I had them rush your blood tests because I was concerned, Jessica."

"And?" she prompted, tapping the pencil. "Am I

anemic? I wouldn't be surprised—I've been absolutely exhausted lately."

"Yes, you're anemic. Edging toward anorexic but not there yet. You're also in the early stages of pregnancy."

The pencil broke. Jessica stared unseeing out at the heat-glazed cityscape as a thousand thoughts and voices crashed inside her head.

"Did you hear what I said, Jessica? Are you there?" Morgan's brittle voice couldn't hide the concern that filtered over the telephone line.

"Yes, I'm here. And I heard you. I don't suppose there's any chance—

"I'm certain. The blood test is very accurate, and it only confirmed the physical evidence I found yesterday when I examined you. You're definitely pregnant, though not very far along. I'd guess maybe three to six weeks."

"Three to six weeks," Jessica echoed. Her brain couldn't even begin to take it in, to make the obvious calculations.

"Now would be the time to do something about it," Morgan continued briskly, very businesslike. "It's a simple enough matter so early on—an outpatient procedure. I can refer you to a colleague of mine if you wish."

"No, thank you, Morgan."

"You shouldn't wait too long to do something about it, Jessica," Morgan cautioned. "You know as well as I do the dangers in a late abortion."

A sudden, dreamy smile lit Jessica's face, with only the picture window to view it. Morgan was leaning over backward to be diffident, but Jessica knew her too well to be fooled. An ardent feminist, Morgan had campaigned for a woman's right to legalized abortion. She also hated abortions with a passion, and refused to perform them, referring her patients with nonjudgmental concern. She would never believe what she was about to hear.

"What sort of prenatal vitamins should I take?" Jessica murmured, leaning back in her chair.

The screech on the opposite end of the phone made her smile broaden. "Do you mean you intend to keep the pregnancy?"

"There wouldn't be much reason to take prenatal vitamins otherwise, would there? I am healthy enough to carry a pregnancy, aren't I?" There was latent concern in her voice.

"Oh, you're healthy enough, despite having gotten too damned close to starvation. It surprises me that you managed to conceive, but I guess it's that good Scandinavian stock. If you take your vitamins and eat properly you shouldn't have any trouble."

"That's good," she said dreamily.

"Jessica, if you're going through with the pregnancy I'll need you back in here. We need a complete workup, records of the father as well as you. I assume Peter will be cooperative?"

"I'm sure he would be. The problem is, I don't think he's the father." Best not to be too certain, she thought.

The sudden hissing of breath from the opposite line was all the comment Morgan would make. "Would it be impolite of me to ask who it is, then?"

"Not impolite but useless. I don't know the father."
It wasn't really a lie. She knew very very little about
Springer MacDowell, so little, in fact, that it wouldn't
take much to simply ignore the fact that he happened,
by sheer accident, to help her conceive a baby in her
underfed body. She was very adept at ignoring things
she wished to blank out in her past.

"Are you certain, Jessica? Couldn't you make a
guess? There are things that need checking on—RH
factor, inherited diseases and the like."

"I'm afraid not," Jessica replied cheerfully. "Why
don't we assume it was an immaculate conception?"

Morgan's sharp bark of laughter was her only response. "Do you want me to recommend an obstetri-
cian?"

"If you can. But I won't be in New York." That
easily made the decision that had eluded her for
months.

"Where will you be?"

"I'm not sure yet. Someplace away from the city,
away from business and people like the Kinseys. People
like Jessica Hansen," she said lightly.

"So you and Peter aren't going to get married?"

Another decision, easily made. "No."

"But what if it's his child?" Morgan persisted.

"I'll deal with that when the time comes. I'm not
really sure if I owe him anything."

"You may owe him a child."

"Perhaps," she said distantly. "Vitamins, Morgan?"

"I'll call in a prescription to your pharmacy. No
drugs, no alcohol, all right? If you're going to keep the
pregnancy you may as well do it right."

"I may as well," she agreed tranquilly. "I'll talk to you tomorrow when I've made my plans."

"Do that."

Softly, silently, Jessica replaced the phone. She stared at the pristine confines of her corner office, the broken pencil on the immaculate teak desk. She looked at her hands, thin and strong and well-shaped, and she dropped them lightly on her still-flat stomach. The sudden bubbling of joy, like champagne flowing in her veins, threatened to spill over. And all she could think was, at last she had done something right.

SPRINGER SLID DOWN in the chair, careful to keep his long legs out of the path. He'd already tripped one nurse—he had no desire to repeat the experience. With the way his life was going right now, it would only be fitting if the next one he tripped was carrying a loaded bedpan.

Sliding around, he tried to cram his six-foot-four frame into the metal-and-plastic chair made for a much smaller, much more padded human being. Did hospital administrators take a certain pleasure in seeking out the most uncomfortable chairs for the waiting rooms? Maybe they figured the physical discomfort would take people's minds off their medical worries.

With a sigh he pushed himself out of the chair, wandering down the hallway for the twentieth time in the past hour. For that matter, why did surgery always seem to take twice as long as it was supposed to? Damn, he wished he'd have let Elyssa accompany him back to the Coast. He'd been so caught up in worry and guilt and panic that he hadn't anticipated what hell it would be, sitting in the waiting room, waiting, waiting, waiting. With no one for company but the sullen brunette with the too-youthful clothes clinging to her perfect figure. He didn't want to go back, share that cubicle of space, never meeting her accusing eyes. But there was no place else to go.

He'd have to go back to New York to get his car. Hamilton had it garaged somewhere—he could only hope vandals hadn't stripped its venerable beauty. As soon as he knew everything was going to be all right he'd fly back, maybe stay a few days before the long drive....

Hell, was he trying to kid himself? After all these years? He was going to see Jessica. They were completely mismatched—she was everything he disliked in women. Cold, ambitious, shut off from human emotion.

And yet he'd seen emotion in those lost blue eyes of hers, emotions like fear, anger, even a surprised desire. And once or twice he'd heard her laugh, and the sound still haunted him with its rusty, rippling charm. And she wasn't cold at all, once he had gotten past that armor-plated efficiency. She was warm, and trembling, and so shiveringly responsive that he felt himself harden just remembering.

A familiar figure in green scrubs hurried by, and Springer was pulled out of his reverie in sudden alertness. But no, it wasn't anyone he knew. The operation was supposed to take an hour—it hadn't been much more than an hour and a quarter. There was nothing he could do but wait.

Elyssa hadn't been much help. During the endless

ride to the airport, when all the unanswered questions about Katherine were threatening to drive him crazy, he'd tried to distract himself by asking about Jessica.

Elyssa had hesitated, obviously loath to interfere. "Is that where you were last night when I was trying to find you?"

"Yes."

"I wish you wouldn't, Springer," she had said plaintively. "You don't need to add another scalp to your belt. Just because you can't resist a challenge—"

"Is Jessica a challenge?" he'd drawled. "I got the impression that she might be far too easy with her favors."

"She's not cheap, Springer," Elyssa had snapped.

"I didn't think so. I imagine she'd be a very expensive habit to acquire."

"I wouldn't have thought a man with your experience with women would be so easily deceived," Elyssa had snapped, rising to the bait quite nicely. "Jessica doesn't happen to be an executive hooker."

"Then what is she?"

There was a slight softening in Elyssa's dark eyes. "A confused, unhappy young woman. And she doesn't need you to add to her confusion. Not for some sexual whim on your part. Oh, Springer, I thought you'd gotten past all that. I can't stand the thought of your hurting Jessica more than she's been hurt already."

"I'm not going to hurt her," he'd replied. "And you're right, I have gotten past sexual whims."

"Then why did you do it?"

He met her gaze with his customary honesty, the

honesty he reserved for those he loved. "I don't really know," he admitted.

Elyssa shook her head sadly. "Keep away from her, Springer. You may not want to hurt her, but I think you already have. She's a lot more vulnerable than she looks."

Leaning against the hospital window, Springer remembered that vulnerability, just as he remembered that mask she'd pull over herself. But which was the real Jessica? The efficient, manipulative vice-president of Kinsey Enterprises? Or the shivering, clinging woman who ran from him and then reluctantly, completely, fell into his arms? Retrieving his car was only an excuse. Far more important to his peace of mind was finding out who Jessica Hansen really was.

"John." His ex-wife had never called him Springer. Probably figured that if she had her own name for him she'd own him. That pinched, sour voice broke through his reveries, and he pivoted on his heel to face the approaching figure of Katherine's doctor.

# Chapter Thirteen

Jessica stepped out into the cooler night air outside the Tavern on the Green, greeting its soft breezes with an unconstrained smile. She could feel the curious eyes of the man beside her and considered hiding her unexpected pleasure with the night and life in general. She dismissed the thought, turning to encompass Peter in her sense of well-being.

"You're looking quite pleased with yourself," he observed.

"Why shouldn't I? We've just been celebrating an extremely successful merger; I'm about to go on a long vacation. I'm very pleased with my life right now."

Peter's high forehead was creased in disbelief. "Somehow I hadn't gotten the impression you were looking forward to your trip with Lincoln. Particularly since I'm not able to join you." He sounded faintly aggrieved, and Jessica didn't bother to hide the wave of irritation that swept over her.

"I never expected you'd be able to join us, Peter," she said, her voice deceptively gentle. "After all, that was an unwritten part of the bargain, wasn't it?"

A dull red suffused Peter's face. "I don't know what you're talking about, Jessica. I would never—"

"Then I'm not part of the deal?" she queried gently. "A month of unrestricted fun and games with Jessica Hansen isn't included in the terms of the merger? Shall I go back in and tell Lincoln that I won't be going with him tomorrow?"

"No!" Peter's voice was strangled, and Jessica almost felt sorry for him. Almost. A light film of sweat had broken out on Peter's tanned, aristocratic face, and the panic she'd only guessed at was in full evidence. "Jessica, even you don't know what kind of shape we've been in. This merger was our last chance—if it hadn't gone through we would have been looking at receivership by the end of the year."

"But the merger did go through, Peter. The company will have a nice infusion of fresh money, and Lincoln will have the possibility of substantial profits. And he'll have me as a lagniappe."

"Damn it, Jessica, it's not as if we're asking for something you've never done before," he cried, shoving a rough hand through his blond hair. "You're not a virgin sacrifice, for heaven's sake."

Springer's term, she thought distantly. And Springer who had told her she was worth more than executive prostitution.

"You are asking me to do it, then?" she questioned serenely. "I just want to be sure I have this straight."

"Jessica!" he pleaded.

"You and your father want me to sleep with Rickford Lincoln to cement the merger, is that right? Is it?" Her voice was still tranquil. "I need an answer, Peter."

"Yes."

A small, resigned smile lit her face. "I see."

"You needn't act as if it's a surprise," he said defensively. "You're a savvy person—you know the score. This has been in the cards for months now."

"Yes, it has."

Still Peter watched her, his face awash in misery. Poor Peter, she thought absently. Immorality didn't sit well on his patrician soul—he hadn't the killer instinct his father possessed in abundance.

"Father's transferred your bonus to your account. I think he's planning to give you an extra little something..." The words trailed off as he realized how they sounded.

Jessica laughed in genuine astonished amusement. "How tacky of you, Peter," she murmured. "You're going to have to learn more finesse if you plan to keep this up."

"I didn't mean it that way."

"Of course you didn't." She had surreptitiously slipped off the huge diamond ring that had hung loosely on her left hand, and she tucked it into her palm. Moving closer, she slid her arms around his waist. "Kiss me good-bye, Peter. Lincoln's picking me up around nine tomorrow, so I won't have another chance to see you."

"Jessica, you don't have to go," he said miserably. "The merger's signed, there's nothing he could do...."

"Hush, darling." She slid her hands back, casually dropping the ring into his pocket. He wouldn't discover it for days. Reaching up, she kissed him lightly.

"Let me come home with you, Jessica. We need to talk about this."

"No, Peter." She pulled away from his suddenly clutching embrace. "I have a lot of last-minute packing to do. Good-bye, Peter."

There was nothing he could do as she made her way to the nearest waiting taxi but follow her, opening the door and helping her in, the misery still stamped on his face.

Leaning back, Jessica breathed in the myriad smells of a New York City taxi on a summer night. Sweat, cigarettes, exhaust and onions. Part of her would miss New York. And part of her would miss Peter Kinsey and think of him with gratitude. He couldn't have given her a better going-away present. By asking her to sleep with Lincoln, he had destroyed any responsibility she felt toward him. If somehow word got back to him that she'd had a baby, he would know better than anyone else that it couldn't be his. But no one would believe him if he denied it, and the thought gave her a certain tranquil satisfaction.

Now there were just the two of them, she thought, placing a thin hand on her flat, silk-covered belly. And that was exactly the way she wanted it.

Of course, there were problems, she thought as she entered her darkened apartment. Moving through the hall at her rapid pace, she avoided the memory of that night with Springer with single-minded determination. But none of the problems were too large to be overcome.

She had lied to Peter, of course. All her clothes were packed, waiting in the hall, all her few belongings were locked up and stored in the once precious back room that she now avoided like the plague. She was going to impose on Elyssa, who little expected it. She was counting on her to arrange a sublet for this huge place while Jessica found someplace to settle. The bonus money wouldn't go very far if she had to pay the extraordinary rent on this apartment, but she didn't have time to see to it herself. She had to be gone and fast.

Kicking off her high-heeled sandals, she wandered into the kitchen to peer into the almost empty refrigerator. Dutifully she poured herself a glass of milk, for once wishing she could have a drink to calm the trepidation that threatened to overwhelm her. It was typical of fate, she thought, swallowing the milk with a grimace of distaste. She, who seldom drank alcohol, would suddenly develop the urge when it was strictly forbidden. Just as well. She had an absolute horror of ending up like her parents.

There was still the question of where she was going to go the following day. At first she thought she'd just drive, but she couldn't even decide in which direction. Her sisters would always welcome her. Sunny, newly divorced in northern Minnesota, would be glad to have help with the three children driving her to the edge of distraction. Or Maren, with her pretty suburban Chicago house, her pretty suburban family and her delicate little suburban drinking problem. No, she couldn't stay with Maren.

Perhaps she should head south. Though with the summer humidity at an all-time high—

The doorbell slashed across her rambling thoughts, and she jumped, spilling the last bit of milk across the silk front of her black dress. The kitchen was still and dark, echoing the shrill intrusion of the doorbell as it sounded again.

She moved slowly toward the hall, wary and on edge. It had to be someone she knew. Her building had very good security and an excellent night doorman—no one would get past him unless the visitor was well-known. He'd never met Lincoln—she was safe at least from that. Logic told her it should be Peter, with one more excuse, one more argument, but for some reason she didn't think it was. Would Henry remember Springer from two weeks before?

Squashing down the sudden surge of panic, she reached the door as the bell rang again. *Don't be absurd,* she told herself. Springer was long gone, and if he did reappear it would hardly be at her door at eleven o'clock at night. Dear Lord, don't let it be Springer.

It was Springer's parents on the other side of her peephole. It took her a few moments to fumble with the three locks, long enough for her to regain a portion of her equilibrium. "What in the world are you two doing here?" she greeted them lightly as she swung open the door. "Not that I'm not delighted to see you at any hour. What brings you to town, Elyssa?" A sudden, horrifying thought came to her, stripping her of her smile and her banter. "Nothing's wrong, is it?"

"You tell me, darling," Elyssa retorted sternly, pressing her cheek against Jessica's for a moment. "I got your note."

"Hello, Ham," she murmured as she was enveloped in a bear hug. "Elyssa drag you along?"

"I dragged myself. What's going on, lambkin? Running out?"

"You weren't supposed to get my note till Monday," Jessica accused lightly. "No fair."

"The U.S. mail was for once quite efficient. So you're not going off with Lincoln?" Elyssa questioned.

"No."

"I'm glad. I can't imagine that Peter really expected you to. He must not have realized—"

"Oh, he realized all right," Jessica said, throwing her slender body into the uncomfortable sofa. "He came right out and asked me tonight."

"But you'd already decided to leave. Does he know?"

"Not yet. He'll find out soon enough. I expect Lincoln will call him when he comes to collect his door prize and I'm not here." She kept her voice light. "I hope you're not here to talk me out of it."

"Not at all, Jessica," Elyssa said firmly. "I think you're doing the right thing."

"But we're worried about where you're planning to go, what you're planning to do," Ham added seriously.

*I'll be having your grandchild,* she thought, but said nothing. "I haven't decided."

Ham heaved a sigh, exchanged glances with Elyssa, and then plunged in. "In that case, we have a proposition for you."

"I don't want to have anything to do with Springer," she said abruptly, betraying herself.

Ham looked surprised, obviously having missed those developments. "It has nothing to do with Springer, Jessica. He wouldn't have to know anything about it."

"About what?"

"We have a house, Jessica. It's been in the family for generations—an old, rambling Victorian summer cottage on one of the Champlain islands in Vermont. It's been empty for years; since the divorce, as a matter of fact. We've rented it out a few times, kept it up, but neither of us has had the time or the inclination to go back. We thought you might like to go up there for a while. It's very secluded, but I don't think you'd mind that."

Jessica eyes had lit up. "Hamilton, you angel!"

"And you could consider doing me a little favor while you're there rusticating."

"Anything," she promised rashly.

"You might think about honing your writing skills. I'll never forget that parody of the Slaughterer you wrote for me last Christmas. It was marvelous."

"But Ham, that's all I can do, I assure you," she protested, confused. "I'm completely uncreative. I can only do parodies and satires. God knows, I've tried, in college and later, but I just don't have it."

"I'm not asking you to force anything," Ham said mysteriously. "Just keep it in mind and we'll talk about it later. So, do you want to go?"

"More than anything. You two have saved my life."

"I hope it's not that bad," Elyssa said gently. "And the house has been winterized, after a fashion, though no brave soul has ever attempted to survive the rigors of Vermont weather there. If you're bold enough you can stay as long as you want. As Ham said, it's a little remote and lonely, but I know you prefer it that way."

"I would. Elyssa, it sounds like heaven."

A wry smile lit Elyssa's concerned face. "Wait till you've experienced a Vermont winter before you say that."

"I've already experienced Minnesota winters—I doubt it's worse."

"Then it's settled. Come by for breakfast tomorrow, and we'll give you keys, maps, instructions, the works," Ham said expansively. "Not to mention coffee and croissants. Elyssa brought fresh beans and pastry when she arrived tonight. We spent most of the evening trying to figure out what to do with you, and I think we've contrived quite well."

"I'm used to taking care of myself."

"Of course you are, lambkin," he soothed. "And aren't you getting a little tired of it? Let those who love you take over for a short while. You need peace and quiet to sort out your life. We both can recognize when someone's on the fine edge."

The tears that neither of her friends had ever seen filled her blue eyes, and she went into Ham's arms like a frightened child. "Bless you both," she whispered. "But I'll be fine."

"I know you will, Jessica," Ham rumbled. "I know you will."

*Part Two*

## Chapter Fourteen

Marianne Trainor pushed the thick mane of chestnut hair back from her broad forehead, streaking her sweat-damp skin with mud from the garden. She knelt there among the potatoes, picking off the brown striped beetles one by one and dropping them in the kerosene solution, shuddering each time one bit the dust. Every time her resolve began to fail her she looked at the stripped leaves and remembered the sparse potato crop from last year, and her determination hardened. It would be so much easier if she could just dust the whole damned thing with insecticide and forget about it. But Tom had wanted an organic garden, so she dutifully pulled the beetles off by hand, planted marigolds to discourage cabbage bugs, planted matches with her broccoli to keep the cutworms away, and still ended up with those little green creatures steaming with her cauliflower. She could pick them off before she added butter, of course, but she was never sure if she got them all. And the kids wouldn't touch it.

"Ma!" Eric's piping, seven-year-old voice carried on

the cool Vermont breeze. "Someone just drove up to the MacDowell house."

Marianne sat back on her ankles, running a broad, work-roughened hand through her hair and adding a healthy dollop of mud to the chestnut length. "No one's been there for years except Ephraim," she mused, eyeing her son's sturdy little figure. He'd already outgrown his pants, and where she'd find the money for more... He'd just have to make do with ankle-high jeans until school started.

"It wasn't Ephraim, Ma. And he only goes up there every other week to check, and he went up yesterday. It was a new car, with a lady driving."

Gratefully Marianne rose to her feet, capping the jar of kerosened beetle corpses and consigning the rest of the potato crop to temporary perdition. "I guess we'd better go see, hadn't we? We promised Ephraim we'd help him keep an eye on the place, and besides, we might have new neighbors. That would be nice, wouldn't it?"

"It didn't look like she had any kids with her," Eric said doubtfully.

"Maybe they were asleep in the back," Marianne suggested, picking her way through the carrots in need of thinning, the wormy broccoli, the spinach that had already bolted. She wasn't really cut out for gardening.

"Without a car seat?" Eric was shocked to the depths of his seven-year-old soul.

"Not everybody is as careful as we are, darling." Reaching his side, she ruffled his thick crop of sandy hair, adding his share of the garden to his scalp. With a luxurious yawn she stretched her arms to the sky.

"Let's go wake Shannon and find out what's going on down at the lake."

Marianne Trainor could never look at her tumble-down farmhouse without a clutching of despair and pride. The roof was a patchwork of shingles and tin, badly in need of repair, the windows needed glazing, the porch sagged and the clapboards were cracked and split, letting in the chilly Vermont air come September. The barn was even worse, with its gentle list to the left, the holes in the roof letting in the rain and snow and stars to keep Billy and Lilly, their cantankerous Nubian goats, company. It always amazed her that a good strong wind didn't topple it, crushing the goats and the chickens in a welter of splintered wood. But it had remained strong and sturdy despite its appearance, and the goats and chickens remained.

She hated those animals, almost as much as she hated her husband. Tom was a lawyer, an overachiever, ambitious, idealistic and completely impractical. This had been his back-to-the-land kick, the last-ditch effort to save a faltering marriage that wasn't strong enough to survive the passing of years and Tom's mindless egoism. He'd come home to their small eighteenth-century gatehouse in Connecticut and announced he'd left the prestigious law firm in New York, bought a minifarm in Vermont, and they were going to start a new life. Eric was four and a half then, Shannon just born, and Marianne had stared at her handsome husband in numb astonishment.

Tom's infatuation with farm life lasted a few months. He enjoyed splitting firewood, but he was afraid of chain saws. He liked working on the old house that was little more than a hovel but he was hopelessly inept, always ending up hiring hippie labor that was overpriced and almost as inept as he was. He bought chickens and goats and a cow, bought an outrageously expensive tractor and plowed a huge garden. But the chickens pecked each other to death, leaving five—of the original two dozen—that produced one egg every four or five days but still had to be watered and fed. The goats had to be milked, but everyone hated goat's milk, and they left olivelike pellets all over the porch, making going barefoot more than hazardous. Tom decided the garden was women's work, leaving the planting, the weeding, the harvesting to the more and more harassed Marianne while he sketched elaborate designs for improving the ramshackle house and drove into Burlington to buy more and more impractical toys.

Their marriage went from bad to worse to nonexistent. They had been in Vermont for ten months when he left, in the midst of a March blizzard, to go back to New York, to his law firm and the elegant lady lawyer who was waiting for him.

That had been two years ago, and Marianne was still mad. Shakingly, furiously angry, and expected to be for the rest of her life. Tom had been generous with his support—too generous. The mortgage was paid off, the children had enough to eat, and the aging Toyota four-wheel drive was at least reliable. Marianne had renewed her nurse's license and augmented the family income by working every other weekend in Burlington. But the checks had become less frequent, missing a month now and then, sometimes two. And there was no way she could get in touch with her ex-husband—he wouldn't return her calls and he always seemed to be out when she called his firm. Barbara, the new Mrs. Trainor, insisted on an unlisted number.

At the thought of that tiny, exquisite, sophisticated creature, Marianne's strong, dirt-caked hands curved in fists. Marianne was what could be called a fine figure of a woman, large, robust, well built. Not at all like the demure second Mrs. Trainor. Marianne was six feet tall, raw-boned, wide-hipped, deep-bosomed, with a broad, freckled face, thick chestnut hair and an infectious laugh. She hadn't felt much like laughing the past few years, but for her children's sake she still did. But it was a lonely life on this tiny, remote part of the Champlain islands, with only upper-class seasonal neighbors who thought anyone who wintered in Vermont must be lacking in common sense, not to mention social acceptability. It would have helped if she had had a friend or two. But the nurses she worked with were in general much younger than her thirty-five years, and the only neighbors near her age were smug young housewives whose lives revolved around shopping and their husbands. Marianne was too old, too involved, too different to be accepted.

No one had rented the MacDowell place in several years. It was probably some writing friend of the old man's, here to hole up for several weeks to complete a manuscript. Eric had said it was a woman driving the car—at least that was an improvement over the lust-driven adventure writer of two summers ago who couldn't fathom how Marianne could spurn his heavy-handed advances. The last thing Marianne needed or wanted at this juncture in her life was another damned man, just when she was starting to make it on her own. But it would be nice if the woman at the MacDowell place could be a friend.

JESSICA SAT SLUMPED in the uncomfortable front seat of her Subaru station wagon and stared at the rambling house in front of her, the clear blue of the lake shimmering just beyond it. The house was a late-Victorian cottage, with a wraparound porch that cried out for wicker rockers, weathered shingles and cedar shakes on the roof. The place was absolutely beautiful, spotless and quite deserted, with a curiously expectant look. As if it were just waiting for Jessica to move in.

She must have been reading too many bad romances. *Houses don't wait for people,* she thought, pulling her cramped muscles out of the driver's seat and onto the curving dirt driveway, the keys clutched in her hand. There was a soft glow from the late-afternoon sun, softening the aging contours of the house, and for a moment Jessica let herself dream. Dream that there were people in the house, awaiting her, longing for her. A man in the kitchen, a baby at his feet, both looking up at her with a welcoming smile....

She shook her head. The shadowy man of her momentary fantasy looked far too much like Springer Mac-Dowell, and the child at his feet had the same dark eyes and silky black hair. Fantasies like that were far too dangerous. Springer MacDowell was gone, and the tiny mite inside her had nothing to do with him. Nothing at all.

She heard the noise of the ancient automobile from a distance, chugging up the road, and for a moment a sudden panic washed over her. She could close her eyes and see Springer, his long body folded behind the compact seat of his Lotus, chasing after her. But the Lotus growled, purred, hummed; it didn't chug and buck and grumble. Her icy blue eyes opened in time to see the disreputable Jeeplike vehicle pull to a stop behind her Subaru, and she watched with mingled despair and amusement as an earth mother tumbled out, followed by two grinning urchins.

"Hi, I'm Marianne Trainor," the earth mother said, advancing on the waiting Jessica. She found herself looking up into warm brown eyes, a wide, smiling mouth, and she found herself smiling back.

"Jessica Hansen," she replied, holding out her thin, well-shaped hand, only to have it swallowed up in Marianne's large, dirt-stained paw. She waited patiently, unused to small-town ways.

"We're your neighbors down the road." Belatedly Marianne noticed the garden still clinging and quickly brushed it off against her faded jeans. "My son, Eric, saw you driving down to the lake, so we thought we'd visit and make sure everything's okay. Uh, are you friends of the MacDowells?"

This was done with an embarrassed lack of delicacy, and Jessica belatedly caught on. This amazon had come to check on the house for Hamilton and Elyssa. "Yes, I am. I'll be staying here for a while."

"A while?" Marianne questioned.

"Quite a while. If I can take the winters. Ham doesn't think I can, but I intend to prove he's wrong."

That wide, enchanting smile lit Marianne's face again, warming everyone in her vicinity, even Jessica.

"You'll be able to take it all right," she said firmly. "And we'll help you out. You're the first woman I've seen in the past three years that doesn't make me feel like the Incredible Hulk. I'd do anything to keep you around, if just to convince the locals that I'm not the only tall woman in the world."

Jessica laughed, a rusty-sounding chuckle. "Aren't you a local?"

Marianne shook her head. "Not me. I'm a transplant from Connecticut." A loud screech from the disreputable car caught her attention, and she dived back in, emerging with a towheaded daughter on her hip. "This is Shannon, and that suddenly quiet young gentleman is Eric, who's quite desperate to know whether you have any children. We're sort of remote out here."

"No children." Jessica turned to the boy, giving him a tentative smile. "Not till mid-April, that is."

"Just in time for a spring snowstorm." Marianne groaned. "That is, if you're planning to still be here."

"Oh, I'll still be here."

Marianne gave a brief glance around the packed car. "Is your husband with you? I didn't think to ask before."

"No husband," Jessica replied tranquilly.

Marianne was obscurely pleased. "Boyfriend?"

"No boyfriend, either. Just me and junior." She patted her flat stomach.

"You won't find much in the way of male companionship around here," Marianne felt compelled to warn.

"Good. I think I've had enough of male companionship to last me for quite a while," Jessica replied. "Want to join me while I explore the house?"

Marianne grinned. Her hideous day was rapidly improving. "Glad to. We can even show you where things are—my husband and I stayed here for a month before we moved into our house. I miss being so close to the lake, but it's colder in the winter."

Jessica followed Marianne's sturdy frame up the front steps, with the silent Eric taking up the rear. "What do you and your husband do up here?" she questioned idly.

"I homestead, which means I try to keep body and soul together without spending any money and rarely succeed. I also work weekends in Burlington at the hospital. In obstetrics," she added with a grin.

"That's reassuring to hear. And your husband?" The cottage smelled of closed air and mothballs and cedar, and Jessica had the curious feeling she should have been carried over the threshold. By whom, she mocked herself. By Springer?

"My husband," Marianne said carefully, "is a lawyer in New York. We don't see much of him and his new wife."

Jessica heard the slight thread of pain in Marianne's matter-of-fact voice and nodded, filing it away for future reference. "Sounds like we're going to have a matriarchal society on this end of the island," she commented.

"Sounds like. There's Andrew Cameron at the old Hill place, but no one sees much of him except at town meetings, and there's Helene LaPlante still out at her farm. She just sits there and knits and gossips, but she's a good old soul despite her nasty tongue. She has three large, not too bright grandsons who are more than willing to help split firewood, clean chimneys and do anything you'd rather not do, but you have to keep them in line."

"And that's all?"

"That's all on this end of the island. Missing the city already?"

Jessica looked around at the snug confines of the front living room, the multipaned windows looking down over the lake, the old wicker furniture and the fieldstone fireplace, and she gently stroked her belly. "This is heaven," she said with a sigh. "I don't ever want to go back."

"Wait till the first snowfall," Marianne warned. "But I think you've got what it takes. It's a good place to raise kids, even if it is lonely."

Jessica smiled dreamily out at the lake. "It's home," she said. "It's home."

"WHERE THE HELL IS SHE?"

"Don't swear at me, Springer," Elyssa said in a deceptively tranquil tone of voice. "I didn't put up with it when you were a teenager and I won't put up with it now."

Slowly Springer counted to ten, forcing his tightly clenched hands to relax. "Sweet, dear Mother," he said in a deeply sarcastic voice, "would you please tell me where Jessica Hansen has disappeared to? Peter and Jasper haven't the faintest idea, and they're as mad as hell."

"They're not nearly as mad as Rickford Lincoln," Elyssa said, smiling complacently.

"And he's not nearly as mad as I am. Where is she?"

"Why should you be mad, Springer? I don't recall that you have any rights over Jessica."

His hands had clenched again, and slowly he loosened them. He'd forgotten how frustrating his mother could be when she was being reasonable. "No rights at all," he agreed. "Where is she?"

His mother leaned back against Ham's sofa and eyed her son. "If she wanted you to know she would have left word," she said more gently. "I'm afraid I can't tell you."

"But you know where she is?"

"I know. Leave her be, Springer. She's been through too much during the past few months—she needs some time to herself. Maybe later..."

"Later I'll be working," he snapped. "I can't afford to jet back and forth between coasts looking for a neurotic female who has no idea what she wants out of life."

"Give her time to find out."

He glared at his mother, totally out of tune with her for the first time in years. "I don't—"

"I know, you don't want to. But you've got other responsibilities right now. School's about to start, and Katherine needs you. Go back to Washington, Springer. If and when Jessica is ever ready for you she'll let you know. And if she doesn't, I will."

He opened his mouth to protest, to inform her that he didn't give a damn about Jessica Hansen and her high-strung psyche. He snapped it shut again. "I'll have to trust you," he said finally. There was nothing else he could do.

"Yes," said Elyssa, "you will." She reached out a gentle hand. "Be patient, darling."

He grimaced. "I'm afraid that's something I still haven't quite mastered."

"It's about time you did." There was no censure in her voice, only a weary resignation, as if she learned that lesson years ago. "Give Katherine my love."

Springer hesitated. "And give Jessica mine."

## Chapter Fifteen

**The Slaughterer, vol. 71: Jungle Madness**

*Matt Decker surveyed the carnage around him. A flame-thrower could do a hell of a lot of damage in a jungle like this. The tangled underbrush caught at his ankles; the trees closed in around him like demented terrorists. He hacked away at it with a machete that had met more than its share of human flesh. He missed civilization, the gritty feel of the city streets. He didn't belong in the jungle.*

"ARE YOU SURE it's okay to be here?" Jessica's hoarse voice was barely above a whisper as she followed Marianne's lanky figure through the knee-deep snow. Her burgeoning stomach vied with the deep, wet snow to make the going difficult, and she was panting by the time they reached the small clearing in the woods. The air was redolent of balsam and fir and the wet freshness of new-fallen snow, and Jessica drew in a deep appreciative breath.

"Listen, I've cut brush here every Christmas since

we moved up," Marianne replied, letting the pint-sized Shannon slide down her body to land waist-deep in the snow. "Cameron won't mind if we take enough branches to make wreaths—hell, he won't even know. I don't think he comes out of that workshop of his for months at a time once the snow falls." Pulling a pair of pruners from the capacious pocket of her oversized khaki parka, she began cutting. "Of course, I'll have to admit he wasn't best pleased to catch me raiding his raspberry patch last summer, but he was decent enough in the long run, and I sent Eric over with a jar of preserves to make up for it. He would never have bothered with them—he would have eaten a few and let the birds get the rest." Snip, snip, and the pile of green-needled branches began to grow.

"You didn't bother to tell me about the raspberries when you dragged me out here," Jessica replied tartly, wading over to a likely tree and starting in.

"Then you never would have come. I know what a chicken you are, especially when it comes to strangers. If Cameron shows up we'll just offer to make him a wreath, too. If they have wreaths in Scotland," she added doubtfully. "Oh, well, he lives in America now—he'll have to get used to our customs. Mind you get the balsam and not the spruce."

"I can't tell the difference. What does it matter?" She continued cutting indiscriminately.

"The spruce trees have needles that go all the way around the branch and are very bushy, and they drop their needles all over the house in less than a week. Balsam has flatter needles that stay on the branches for months. It also smells a hell of a lot better. That there is cat spruce, and if you smell it you'll understand why."

"In other words I'm to cut balsam."

"Unless you like sweeping up pine needles and having the house smell like a litter box."

"Not particularly." She eyes a branch doubtfully, trying to decide whether it had needles halfway or all the way around the thin branch. And then she raised her eyes a little higher, to meet a pair of very green eyes watching them stonily.

Marianne had her back to them, cutting away with abandon while Shannon played nearby. "Actually Cameron isn't a bad kind of neighbor," she remarked cheerfully as she plundered his trees. "We don't have to see him or have anything to do with him, but the presence of a man in this deserted end of the island discourages some of the rougher elements."

"And he provides you with trees and raspberries to rob," a rich, incredibly Scottish voice came from the still figure watching them, and Marianne whirled around, dropping her pilfered branches and her clippers in the deep snow.

With a curious blend of amusement and guilt Jessica watched the man advance upon them. It was an unpleasant feeling, being caught red-handed, but it appeared that Marianne was prepared to shoulder the burden of the responsibility. Indeed, after a cursory glance all the Scot's attention was focused on her tall friend.

"So you've taken to robbing my poor trees, Mrs. Trainor," he said, fixing those sparkling eyes on her. "For shame, woman. And dragging this poor pregnant lady with you while you do the dirty deed. She looks half frozen, not to mention the wee bairn at your feet."

He was a small man, staring up so fiercely at Marianne, not much more than five feet six or seven. Thin and wiry, he had bright green eyes, an angular, not unattractive face with just a trace too much stubbornness, and a thick shock of curly brown hair shot through with streaks of red in the early-winter sunshine. He was dressed in ancient corduroys, a thick wool sweater and galoshes, with a brightly colored scarf around his neck, and his glower heated the air around them. Jessica felt like an Eskimo in her heavy layers.

"Now, Andrew," Marianne began placatingly, part of her attention on the snow as she tried to find where her expensive clippers had gone. "You know you don't need every single little branch—I doubt you come here more than once a year."

"If you're going to call me Cameron behind my back you may as well do it to my face," he said sourly. "And I walk this way almost every day, Mrs. Trainor. I don't fancy seeing my trees stripped bare by your greedy fingers. Trees are living creatures; they don't like to have parts of them ripped off by savages."

"Savages!" Marianne snapped, forgetting her search for the clippers. "I'll have you know we were going to make Christmas wreaths and garlands out of your precious branches. And we wouldn't have bothered, except your trees have the straightest branches of any hereabouts. And if you're talking about the souls of trees, I can't think of any better fate for a tree than to celebrate Christmas." Even as she said it she realized how foolish it sounded, and a deep flush suffused her face.

Andrew Cameron stared at her for a long moment, and then, to the women's surprise, a smile lit his dour face. "If you're thinking a tree has a soul, you may not be as great a philistine as I thought you were," he remarked. "But I'll thank you to ask me next time you want to plunder my forest."

"I have no idea how to get to your cabin, and you don't have a telephone," Marianne said with some asperity, bending down to search through the snow for the L. L. Bean clippers that had been one of Tom's expensive toys.

He was watching Marianne with a peculiar expression on his face, and Jessica had a sudden, absurd suspicion that she banished as soon as it entered her mind. "I may get one" was all he said. "The clippers are to your right."

Marianne glared up at him, considered ignoring his directions, and then thought better of it. She couldn't afford to lose an expensive pair of clippers to a pride that might more honestly be called spite. Of course, they were exactly where he pointed, which didn't help her temper.

"Do you suppose you've cut enough," he asked with heavy sarcasm, "or were you needing some more?"

"We've got enough," Marianne snapped. "That is, if you're willing to let us leave with our ill-gotten gains."

"I'm willing. The pregnant lassie has mainly spruce, you know," he pointed out, and Jessica began to share Marianne's annoyance.

Marianne's eyes met hers for a rueful moment. "We like to mix the spruce," she said loyally.

Andrew Cameron shook his head in disgust for the folly of women. "In that case, if you're finished, you may as well come back with me to get warm."

"There's no need—"

"The bairn looks half-frozen, not to mention the pregnant lassie," he interrupted. "And if you're going to keep robbing my forest you'd best learn how to find me. Come along. A cup of tea will do you wonders."

"The poor pregnant lassie," Jessica finally spoke, her voice heavy with sarcasm, "is Jessica Hansen."

The surprisingly friendly green eyes met hers, and she could have sworn there was a trace of a wink in them. "I know that," he replied. "It's a small island. It's a pleasure to meet you, Mrs. Hansen. I'm glad you like my trees."

"Not Mrs. Hansen, Miss," she corrected with the fearlessness that had become second nature to her. "And it's Jessica." A tentative smile lit her face. "And I would love some tea."

"Traitor," Marianne murmured under her breath. "All right, Cameron, we'll come." She scooped up Shannon's sturdy weight and dumped it on Cameron's slighter figure. "You carry Shannon."

If she hoped to intimidate him she was off the mark. "Gladly," he said, adjusting her weight comfortably. Marianne waited for Shannon to squirm and fuss. The child wasn't used to strangers, particularly male ones.

But Cameron seemed to have exerted some sort of magic spell over her recalcitrant daughter. He'd already taken off through the heavy snow, striding through the drifts as if they were no more than soap flakes, Shannon tucked tightly against him.

"I suppose we don't have any choice but to follow the man," Jessica observed. "He's taken your daughter captive."

"You're right," Marianne said glumly. "Think you'll have any trouble?"

"No such luck. You didn't tell me Andrew Cameron was so...so..."

"So feisty?" Marianne supplied. "So disagreeable? So pigheaded? So young? So short?"

Jessica laughed, a low, amused sound. "So handsome, Marianne."

"Handsome?" Marianne gave a disbelieving snort. "You've been away from men too long. He's no more than passable." There was a curiously vulnerable light in her eyes as she watched the figure of the Scot and her daughter tramping farther into the woods. Their voices floated back to them, a light, lilting song. "Would you listen to that? They're singing Christmas carols, damn it." She started after them. "Wait up, you two."

To Jessica's relief the cottage wasn't too much deeper into the snow-shrouded woods. Definitely not far enough to support Marianne's claim not to know where it was. It was a long, low log building with an attached woodshed, the smoke curling from the chimney like a plume, adding to the puffy white clouds in the blued winter sky. A welcome blast of warmth greeted her, and she sank gratefully down on a narrow bench by the wood stove, stripping off her sodden gloves and rubbing her chilled hands briskly before looking around her.

Marianne had taken the seat across from her, a sour

expression on her face, and Andrew was over by the far wall in what served him as a kitchen, busying himself with the tea fixings with the cheerful hindrance of Shannon. There was a narrow cot in the far corner, neatly made, a closet in the corner and a rough table. The rest of the long, narrow room was a workshop, a maze of wood, machinery and musical instruments in various stages of construction and repair. Jessica took the proffered cup of tea unthinkingly, the rich apple-and-cinnamon smell of it tickling her nostrils.

"I've only herb tea, but in your condition you shouldn't have too much caffeine," Cameron said sternly.

"Why does everyone suddenly become an expert on childbirth and pregnancy?" Marianne said plaintively before Jessica could respond. "Caffeine doesn't do any harm."

"Better to be safe than sorry," Cameron said sternly. "A little less caffeine might improve your temper, woman."

"There's nothing wrong with my temper that a little less of your interference wouldn't cure," Marianne snapped back.

"Do you make musical instruments?" Jessica interrupted. Ever the peacemaker, her father had called her.

"I do." He seemed loath to drag his attention away from the battle with Marianne. "I wouldn't be interfering if you didn't traipse all over my land, helping yourself to my trees and my raspberries at will, without so much as a by-your-leave."

"Listen, you sawed-off Scottish runt, those berries were on the edge of rotting when I got to them."

"What kind of instruments?" Jessica said somewhat desperately as Shannon climbed onto the bench beside her.

"What?" Cameron demanded irritably. "Oh, anything I'm in the mood for. Mostly stringed instruments—guitars, dulcimers, mandolins, banjos."

"Can you make a living at it?" Jessica persevered, her business interests cropping up.

"Yes."

"Of course he does," Marianne interrupted before he could sail into her again. "He makes more money than the rest of this island combined—this rustic workshop is only an affectation. His instruments aren't just that, they're works of art, collector's items, and he gets obscene prices for them."

Cameron's temper seemed to have abated somewhat. "I wouldn't have thought you'd be that conversant with my business, woman."

"Stop calling me woman, damn it!" Marianne snapped.

"Stop swearing, damn it!" Cameron shot back. "I don't like to hear a woman swear."

"Then shut your ears. If I weren't around you I wouldn't need to swear."

"How long have you two known each other?" Jessica inquired, wrapping her arms around Shannon's sleeping figure. "You sound like you grew up together."

"Too long," Marianne stated.

"Not long enough," Cameron said obscurely, earning him an odd look from his nemesis. And then, suddenly tiring of the battle, he turned to Jessica. "Do you play any instruments, Jessica?"

"A little piano," she admitted with a shrug. "Nothing more portable."

"You need music. Your bairn needs to hear music. These early stages are important to his development. If he hears music while he's in the womb, he'll grow up to be a music lover."

"I told you, everyone's an expert on prenatal care," Marianne announced to the world in general. "Besides, it's a girl."

"How do you know, woman?" he shot back. "Is it your bairn she's carrying?" That shut Marianne up, if only for a moment. "So would you like to learn an instrument? Something you can hold against your belly while the baby grows, listening to the sweet sounds?"

"Cameron, you don't need to make any more sales," Marianne said nastily.

"I'm warning you, woman...." And he was. Marianne wisely shut up. "If you want to learn," he continued with an odd gentleness, "I'd be honored to lend you an instrument and even give you lessons."

"Why?" Jessica asked abruptly.

"Because I have a fondness for bairns and mothers," he said simply. "And even though I'd be doomed to spending more time with your sour friend there, I'd be willing to endure it to stand as your friend also."

The light in his green eyes completed the message, and Jessica grinned back. She should know better than to be a matchmaker, especially for such an incredibly mismatched couple, but she couldn't resist. She had the curious conviction that the feisty little Scot was just what Marianne Trainor needed. "I'd be honored, Andrew." And their handshake was a bargain that had little to do with music.

It was going to be a cool, rainy autumn, Springer thought, tipping back his chair and staring out the wide picture window into the misty Washington afternoon. Like every other autumn and winter in the ten years he'd lived there. Sooner or later he was going to get tired of that constant rain, and that moment seemed to be looming closer and closer.

The mug of coffee cradled in his large hand was lukewarm and bitter, and he drained it with a grimace of distaste and dissatisfaction. Dissatisfaction with his coffee, with the West Coast rain, with his life. And he knew perfectly well it had nothing to do with coffee or Washington. It had to do with missing someone he still barely knew, someone who had managed to become entangled in his soul in a damnably short period of time.

It was only because the whole situation was so unresolved, he told himself, setting the empty mug on the floor beside him. If he'd just had one more chance to see her, to talk to her, he wouldn't have been left with this gnawing feeling in his gut—the feeling of unfinished business, of a wanting that never seemed to go away, months after he should have forgotten all about her.

Elyssa had been right. Now in this winter of his discontent he was going to have to learn patience. For Katherine's sake, and for his own. He just wished it were an easier thing to learn.

## Chapter Sixteen

It was early morning on Christmas Eve. Jessica ran a nervous hand through her thick tangle of wheat-blond curls, chewing the pale lipstick off her lips for the third time. She was no longer used to wearing makeup, and twice she'd rubbed her eyes, smearing the mascara. Who was to say that one had to wear makeup in the big city at Christmastime? Fumbling in her outsized purse, she pulled out the lip gloss and tried again. It was an armor against the outside world, she decided, pulling her loose-fitting wool dress to hang more evenly over her five-month belly. And she'd need all the armor she could get, leaving her little nest and braving the bold, bad world of New York once more.

She would never have gone, nothing would have convinced her but the tears in Elyssa's voice the week before, as she'd added a final plea. Hamilton MacDowell, bluff, macho, indestructible Hamilton MacDowell, had a particularly virulent form of cancer. He wouldn't last another year.

Where was Marianne when she needed her? There was a light snow falling, already sticking to the bare

roads and covering the gray, melted-down snow. Surely
the venerable Toyota couldn't have failed her again.
Once more she paced across the shiny wood floors,
once more she checked the wood stove. Marianne had
promised she would keep the fires going while she was
in the city to make sure the pipes didn't freeze. Andrew
would have been more than willing to help her, Jessica
was certain, but Marianne was determined to do it herself. So far she had managed to make herself scarce the
three times Cameron had tooled his aging Valiant to
their end of the island, and the great romance appeared
to have foundered before it even began. Marianne was
able to avoid him as long as she wanted—he had to pass
her house to reach the MacDowell place and she could
steer clear until the ancient, rusty car rattled its way
back down the road.

It was a source of great frustration for Jessica, but
there was nothing she could do about it. In the meantime, the lessons were becoming more and more important to her. Cameron was right—she loved the feel
of the banjo against her expanding belly, loved to feel
the music flowing through the beautiful instrument
and her burgeoning body. Moving across the room, she
ran a caressing hand down the neck of the banjo and its
firebird inlay, plucking a string and letting the pure,
crystal sound echo in the room. She only wished that
she dared to take it with her to New York. It soothed
her better than the most powerful tranquilizers.

There was nothing to be nervous about, she reminded herself. Elyssa had said Springer would be at
the opposite end of the country. He never came East if
he could help it, and Christmas had particularly bad

memories for him. He had no idea of his father's illness—Hamilton had been adamant. The closest Springer MacDowell would come would be via the telephone, and he wouldn't ask to speak to her. He wouldn't even know she was there, much less five months pregnant.

And that was another problem. Elyssa had no notion of her condition, and Jessica could think of no tactful way to broach it. In the end, she decided to let her stomach announce itself. With luck, the MacDowells would be too discreet to question her. If their concern outdistanced their discretion, she would place the blame on Peter, on some Vermonter, perhaps Cameron. She had effectively blanked out her child's parentage, and nothing was going to force her to think about it.

Elyssa and Hamilton would be godparents—she had long ago decided that, perhaps as a sop to her conscience. That would be their tie, and it would be enough. The baby was hers, her immaculate conception, and she would only share it with those she wanted. This baby wasn't going to belong to anyone else by virtue of blood or an accident of birth.

It was a mistake going to New York and Jessica knew it was. Everything would have been so much easier if she could have just let them know sometime in the summer that she was a mother, with no embarrassing way to pinpoint dates. But with Hamilton sick, there was no question but that she would go. She would simply have to count on a not very beneficial fate to carry her through the visit relatively unscathed. For the first time in her pregnancy she could be grateful that she had gained so much weight early on. She looked a bit more than five months pregnant, which could only work as a blessing.

She could hear the telltale sound of the Valiant from far down the road, and she dashed to the window, peering through the frosted pane. It was Cameron, all right, the Valiant chugging and puffing and moving valiantly along as befit its name, with a miserable-looking Marianne by his side. A small, secret smile lit Jessica's worried face as she watched the odd couple approach.

"The Toyota bit the dust once more," Marianne announced as she scrambled from the front seat before Cameron could move. "I was hiking up the road when he came by." There was a distinct lack of gratitude in her voice, but Cameron only smiled sardonically.

"A happy Christmas to you, Jessica," he greeted her. "I wanted to wish you Godspeed before you left, and it looks like I've come in handy. Not that your friend will admit it."

"You have your uses," Marianne said sourly. "I left the kids with Mrs. LaPlante. I figured Burlington on Christmas Eve will be a complete zoo, but this way I can buy some last-minute things without interference." She tossed her head at Cameron dismissingly. "Thanks again."

"Uh, Marianne..." Jessica began, amusement ripening inside her as she pulled her down coat around her chilled body. "I'm afraid we have a problem."

"Which is?"

"I took the Subaru in for repairs. The four-wheel drive is sticking on. I thought we'd be able to drive in the Toyota."

Cameron's sardonic grin widened, and he made a

sweeping gesture toward the venerable old wreck. "Ladies, my chariot awaits you."

"Damn." Marianne's reaction was heartfelt if tactless. "I don't really need to go in. Why don't the two of you...?"

"Don't be silly, Marianne. You need to finish your shopping, and this is a perfect chance. That is, if Cameron doesn't mind."

"Not at all," he said politely, barely hiding his air of satisfaction. "I have a few things to do myself."

"I don't think—"

"Don't be ridiculous, you silly woman," Andrew snapped. "I'm not going to compromise you in the space of a busy afternoon. Help me get Jessica's bags and try to be sensible for a change."

Marianne stood there, obviously torn, and her broad, pretty face was set with stubbornness. Jessica tipped the scales. "Please, Marianne. I need you for moral support. I'm not very happy about going to New York. For one thing, I'm worried about Ham, and for another, they don't know I'm pregnant. You can help me keep my mind off what I'm going to face when I get there."

Jessica could have almost felt guilty at the way Marianne capitulated if she hadn't known that Marianne wanted a good excuse for being in the intoxicating, dangerous presence of the irascible Scot.

"Do you think you'll see Peter?" Marianne asked anxiously.

"I don't know," Jessica said, her voice diffident. "He's married now—I don't really expect to run into him." She smiled, holding up her overnight bag. "And this is all I'm taking. We may as well go." She moved past her friend to climb into the backseat before Marianne could open her mouth in protest. "You take the front seat. I still have to get my purse rearranged."

There was nothing Marianne could do but glare impotently at both of them. Jessica busied herself with her overstuffed purse, to avoid both Marianne's accusing eyes and her uncomfortable questions. She'd told her as little as possible about her child's conception, contenting herself with relating her broken engagement and nothing more. Marianne assumed Peter was the father, as Jessica hoped everyone would, and she had no intention of enlightening her.

"Get in, woman," Andrew growled. "The snow's getting heavier, and we don't want Jessica to miss her plane."

"No, we wouldn't want that," Jessica murmured, unconvinced, staring at the ticket in her lap with a sinking feeling. "We wouldn't want that at all."

She'd been deliberately vague about her time of arrival, preferring to arrive at the charming little town house on her own. Elyssa would be there—it had sounded as if she'd moved back in when Jessica had last spoken with her. She'd forgotten to ask about David—indeed, would have gladly continued to forget about David, if only Elyssa would. But maybe he'd be there, after all, along with old Johnson, whose oversolicitiousness had always set her teeth on edge. But no Springer. Elyssa had promised no Springer.

She stood for a moment outside on the steps in the chilly winter air, hesitating. The branches were bare on the tree-lined street in the East Sixties, and the small, discreet signs of Christmas abounded. A season of joy and cheer, celebrated by an unwed mother and a dying man. It would make a good TV movie, she thought with a wry smile, raising her gloved hand to ring the bell before she could change her mind. But they'd need a handsome hero.

"Darling!" The door was flung open, and Jessica felt herself pulled into Elyssa's scented embrace, the slender arms clinging like a lifeline. "Thank heavens you're here! I was afraid you'd change your mind, stay in Vermont. I can't tell you how happy I am to see you."

To Jessica's surprise she felt her own eyes fill with tears, and she hugged Elyssa back, suddenly very glad she had risked everything to come. "I had to," she said with a watery smile. "You and Ham are my family—I couldn't have Christmas without you." She let herself be pulled into the warm hallway redolent of pine needles and spice, still keeping the down coat close over her expanding body. "How is Ham doing?"

As Elyssa shut the door behind them she took a moment to compose herself, and Jessica could see the lines of strain, the circles under her dark, liquid eyes. She had always looked so youthful and vibrant, so young and alive, but today Elyssa MacDowell looked every one of her fifty-three years. "Not good, Jessica," she said with a deep sigh. "They're pumping him full of painkillers, blasting him with cobalt, but it just keeps growing. He's lost a lot of weight—don't mention it, okay? I just wish he'd let me tell Springer."

"Springer still doesn't know?" Jessica questioned carefully. "He's not here?"

"He has no idea. He's spending Christmas with some friends on Puget Sound—I don't know if he'll even remember to call. It's not fair of Hamilton, not to give Springer the chance—" her voice cracked "—the chance to say good-bye."

The momentary, suicidally irrational disappointment that Springer really wasn't going to turn up vanished. "He's that bad?"

"He's not good. Part of the problem is that he's lost interest. He doesn't seem to feel he has any reason to hold on, and part of me can't blame him. I know it's selfish of me, but I'm not ready to have him die yet. If he could just hold out, go into remission, it could last indefinitely. If not—the doctors can't be very specific—it could be a matter of weeks, it could be six months. His white count is low, and—" She broke off suddenly. "I'll fill you in on all that later. He knows you're here—he can't wait to see you. Let me take your coat and you can go on in. He's sitting up today. Just be prepared for a change." She held out her hands for Jessica's coat.

There was nothing she could really do to put off the inevitable. The house was sinfully warm, as befitted a place of sickness, and the down coat was turning into a sauna. With an effort at nonchalance she undid the buttons with one only slightly trembling hand and shrugged out of her coat. "Here you go. In the living room, you said?"

Steeled for a reaction, she felt absurdly relieved and deflated when the distraught Elyssa didn't even bother to look at her very evident belly but simply nodded, turning to hang up the coat. "Go on in," she said again. "I'll give you two some time alone before I bring in the drinks. Dubonnet?"

A small smile lit Jessica's face at her friend's understandable abstraction. "Perrier, please. I'm not drinking right now." Patiently she waited for a reaction, but none was forthcoming.

"That's probably not a bad idea," Elyssa said vaguely, making a little shooing motion with her hands. "I'll be in shortly."

Jessica paused outside the living room, smoothing the rough woolen dress over her rounded stomach, her booted feet quiet on the marble foyer floor. She wasn't quite sure what she expected from her old friend, but she held her breath, pasting a dazzling smile on her face before stepping into the room.

The smile faded quickly as Hamilton looked up at her. He'd lost his noble paunch, his rosy cheeks, his vigor. The man that looked up at her still had twinkling eyes, the only sign of life in that pale face, but even his gray beard seemed to have lost its liveliness. The blue eyes smiled at her, meeting her worried eyes, then traveled down directly to her pregnant stomach.

"How are you, Ham?" she queried softly just inside the doorway.

"The better for seeing you, little one. Though if my eyes don't deceive me you aren't so little anymore. Come here and kiss me, darling. It's not catching," he said lightly.

With a sudden rush Jessica ran across the room and threw her arms around his slight, suddenly fragile figure. "You look like hell, Ham," she said gruffly, her voice filled with tears.

"Well, thank heavens someone has the nerve to say that to me," he replied, his voice equally gruff, as he stroked her shining length of hair, which had grown at a quick rate. "You, on the other hand, look magnificent." He held her away for a moment, and there were tears in both their eyes. "Sultry and fecund and delicious. Is it Springer's?"

She only blinked. "Of course not."

"Well, don't bother trying to convince me it was that wimp of a fiancé. Peter Kinsey couldn't father anything. So who's the father?"

She stalled for time by pulling up a chair beside his. "No one you know," she replied tranquilly. "Besides, he's ancient history. This is my baby and no one else's."

"I always thought you were clever but I didn't think you could manage to pull off an immaculate conception," Ham shot back. "So this isn't my grandchild?"

Jessica smiled at him. "Your godchild," she said gently. "Yours and Elyssa's. Will that do?"

He shrugged, but she could see the pleased look in his bright eyes. "I don't know if it's a good thing to saddle a kid with a godfather who's about to kick the bucket. Why don't we have Springer serve as backup?"

"No!" The word came out with unexpected anguish, but it took only a moment for her to regain her calm. "No, Ham. You're her godfather, no one else."

"Her, eh? How do you know it won't be a boy?" Ham snorted. "I can tell by the way you're carrying that it's a boy."

Jessica laughed. "Marianne says everyone becomes

an expert on babies when they're around a pregnant woman. What makes you think it's a boy?"

"You're carrying the same way Elyssa did, with Springer. All in front." Tactfully he ignored her stricken expression. "So I'm going to be a grandfather," he mused, pleased.

"Godfather," she corrected.

"Oh, yes, godfather. I always get those two mixed up." There was a devilish grin on his pale face. "You'll have to keep reminding me."

"Damn you, Ham," Jessica said lightly.

"Why are you damning my husband?" Elyssa queried as she backed into the room, a small tray of drinks in one slender hand.

"Come here and meet your new grand—that is, god-child, Elyssa," Ham invited her, then watched with delight as the tray crashed to the parquet floor. "It's going to be a boy."

"Girl," Jessica corrected, rising from her chair with ponderous grace and helping the shocked Elyssa with the broken glass. "I'll bet you."

"When's it due?" Hamilton asked desultorily, but Jessica wasn't fooled.

"In the spring," she said firmly. "And that's as specific as I care to get."

"All right, I'll bet you a case of Moët that it's a boy. And I guess I'm going to have to live long enough to find out whether I win or lose, won't I, Elyssa?"

"Certainly," Elyssa said briskly. "I've never known you to welch on a bet, no matter what the cause."

"No," Hamilton said with relish, "I never have. I'm certainly not about to start now."

CHRISTMAS HAD NEVER BEEN Springer MacDowell's favorite time of year. It always reminded him of other families, that mystical, fairy-tale world that normal families seemed to be and his family never was. For Katherine's sake he always made an effort, and this year it was more important than ever.

But this year he felt even less like celebrating. Something was wrong, something he couldn't put his finger on. For a week he'd been tempted to take Katherine back East for her first Christmas with her paternal grandparents. He'd thought better of it, of course. But here it was Christmas Eve, and they were condemned to one more weary round of forced festivities at his upwardly mobile ex-wife's town house. And he knew Katherine wouldn't like it much better than he did.

Maybe after Christmas they could go East. And maybe Jessica Hansen might possibly have surfaced. Though why such a thought should cheer him was a mystery. But it did. He looked out into the Seattle drizzle with a tiny bit more holiday spirit. Maybe New York for the New Year.

## Chapter Seventeen

"I hope you don't mind, but I've put you in Springer's room," Elyssa said, leading the way up the staircase that had narrowed by the time they got to the third floor. "I'm in the bedroom you usually use, and Johnson's been staying in the other bedroom."

"Where is Johnson?"

Elyssa shrugged her narrow shoulders. "Who knows? He tells Ham that he can't bear to be around death and suffering—he's too sensitive for it. So we don't see much of him, which is just as well, I suppose."

"And David?"

Elyssa sighed. "I don't know about David. He'll have to accept that Ham is a prior responsibility. I can't just abandon him, leave him to die alone in pain and misery."

"But David thinks you should?" Jessica drawled, letting her tone of voice carry just a trace of censure.

"Let's just say he thinks our relationship should come first," she temporized.

"You mean he thinks his relationship should come first."

"Don't, Jessica! I'm having a difficult enough time as it is. I haven't seen him in days, it's Christmas Eve, and I miss him."

Relenting, Jessica put a soothing hand on her friend's arm. "Then why don't you go to him?"

"I can't leave Ham."

"Of course you can. I'm here; I'll take care of him if he needs anything. He isn't in any medical danger right now—there's nothing you can do that I couldn't do just as well. Why don't you grab a bottle of Moët, stop by a delicatessen and show up on his doorstep with a midnight feast?" Much as it galled her to encourage Elyssa's relationship with that pig, she couldn't stand her friend's unhappiness. First Marianne and Andrew, now Elyssa and the detested David. She certainly seemed to be becoming a sentimental matchmaker in her old age.

Doubt and excitement played over Elyssa's expressive face, and she suddenly looked ten years younger again. "Would you mind terribly, Jessica?" she breathed. "You just arrived, and I was looking forward to sitting around catching up on what's been happening to you. And if you think you're going to avoid telling me all about my godchild you have another think coming."

"I'll tell you all about her—we'll have plenty of time. In the meantime, why don't you go put on something pretty and sexy, and fix your makeup while I call you a cab? You can make it up to his place by midnight if your hurry."

"Are you sure?"

"I'm sure. Hurry up, Elyssa. And Merry Christmas."

Elyssa paused long enough to give Jessica an exuberant hug, then sped down the stairs like a teenager. "Merry Christmas, darling," she called back.

With a distant, satisfied smile on her face, Jessica steeled herself to enter Springer's room. The reality was a relief and a disappointment. It was a large room, with lots of windows looking out at the taller buildings and the bright Christmas lights, and very little furniture, no pictures, nothing to signify that anyone in particular called this room his own. Elyssa had tried to personalize it with a small, delicate Christmas tree to welcome her, the tiny white lights glowing in the cavernous room. The huge bed was the only thing that made her think of Springer, both because of its size and for other, less comfortable reasons.

There was a telephone on the bedside table, and she quickly called a taxi for Elyssa before she headed in for a long, relaxing shower in the adjoining bathroom. It was past midnight by the time she emerged, shoulder-length hair wet, face scrubbed, her rounded body wrapped in a thick flannel nightgown. For a moment she considered going back down to the kitchen and warming some milk, then thought better of it. She had finally developed a taste for milk during the past five months, but the thought of Ham's kitchen at midnight brought back too many memories, memories that were safely buried in the back of her subconscious. At that point she didn't even remember what Springer Mac-Dowell looked like.

Curling up in the oversized bed, she pulled the down quilt around her, turning off the bedside light to stare at the twinkling Christmas tree in the corner. How were Cameron and Marianne progressing, she wondered. Had Marianne conquered her distrust enough to ask

him to share their Christmas dinner? Or were the two
of them alone, miserable, wanting to be with the
other? Except that Marianne was too stubborn to ever
admit it, Jessica thought with a sigh. And Cameron too
cagey to push things. No, they were probably alone,
and sound asleep on Christmas Eve. As she soon
would be. Punching up the pillows behind her, she
pulled the comforter closer, placing a soothing hand
over the sleeping baby inside her. "Merry Christmas,
precious," she said softly.

The harsh ring of the telephone shot through her
nerves like lightning, and she jumped for the telephone
before it could wake Ham from his fitful night's sleep.
"Hello?" Her voice sounded breathless, startled, sleepy.
There was a long hesitation on the other end of the
line. "MacDowell residence," she prompted. There
was a faint crackle of long distance on the line, just
enough to give her a moment's warning.

"Jessica?" Springer's voice was deep, disbelieving,
from across the continent, and the baby kicked, sharply. She had forgotten how deliciously deep and sexy
that voice was, how seductive. Damn him.

"Hello, Springer," she said, her voice a miracle of
calm self-control. "Merry Christmas."

"What are you doing there?" It was abrupt, definitely lacking any qualities of seasonal cheer, and Jessica responded in kind.

"Spending Christmas."

"Is my mother there?"

"She's out for the night with David. Do you want
me to wake your father?"

"He's in bed already?" Springer's voice was disbelieving. "He must be slowing down in his old age. No, I don't want to talk with him. You can tell him I wished him a merry Christmas. So does Katherine."

It was like a sharp blow in the solar plexus, and if her voice was a trifle breathless from the pain he wouldn't be able to tell from so far away. "Katherine?" she couldn't help but echo.

"Katherine," he verified, giving away nothing. "We'll call next week sometime, when all the holiday bustle is over." There was a long, uncomfortable pause. "How have you been, Jessie?" His diffident voice sounded less than interested. "I expected you'd still be around when I came back to pick up my car, but my mother said you'd moved. Where've you been?"

"Oh, here and there," she said vaguely. "And I've been fine. Thriving, actually. And you?"

"I'm fine, the weather's fine, everything's fine," he shot back, clearly tiring of the polite conversation. "Why did you run away, Jessie?" His voice had dropped lower, and the seductive strings wrapped around her heart once more. Suddenly she could see him all too clearly—the dark, fathomless eyes, the silky black hair, the long, clean limbs of his beautiful body.

A thousand calm, polite excuses came to mind. Peter, Lincoln, any number of things that Springer would remember and believe. And they had a great deal to do with why she left. But they weren't the major reason; the major reason was now kicking up a storm, and Jessica had gotten out of the habit of lying in the past few months.

"I...it seemed..." The words trailed off, and her eyes filled with the tears that pregnancy seemed to make part and parcel of her daily life. "Merry Christmas, Springer," she said, and quietly placed the phone back on the hook.

He didn't call again. Cradling her arms around her shivering body, she huddled down farther into the covers, closed here tear-filled eyes and willed herself to sleep.

MARIANNE SAT BY HER WOOD STOVE, eyes firmly fixed on the dull black iron, on the wood floor that needed refinishing, on the figures of Eric and Shannon, sound asleep on the lumpy old sofa. She had lit the room with candles, a tradition she couldn't change, even though it softened the light, made the room damnably romantic. The glow from the Christmas tree didn't help, the smell of fir and wood smoke and mulled cider teased her nostrils, and she wished Cameron would leave.

She had no more polite conversation left, no more food to feed him; he'd had three cups of coffee and the rest of the bottle of very fine brandy that Tom had left behind. The sound of his voice, with its soft, teasing burr, was melting her resistance, sneaking its way past her rigid refusal to get involved ever again. He was such a damnable man. What in the world was she doing, sitting here staring at the wood stove, wishing he'd leave, wishing he'd kiss her?

Well, there was nothing so strange in that, she reasoned. It was a soft, romantic night, filled with memories of Christmases past, it was no wonder she was feeling vulnerable. And it had been so long since she'd been kissed.

"Don't you think it's getting late?" she said sourly.

Cameron was leaning back in the rocking chair she'd spent last winter recaning, puffing away on an evil-looking meerschaum pipe, the rich tobacco scent mingling with the smells of Christmas.

"Are you telling me I've overstayed my welcome?" he inquired serenely, not the slightest bit put out.

"I didn't mean that..." she said hastily, guilt and something else washing over her.

"Of course you did, Marianne. Don't disappoint me by becoming all sweetness and light. You'll only turn mean and nasty the moment Christmas is over, and my illusions will be shattered."

"If I'm so mean and nasty why did you bother to come?" she shot back, sliding more comfortably into her usual argumentative state. As long as they fought she wouldn't have this demoralizing need to have him kiss her.

He smiled, a smile of peculiar sweetness. "How could I resist, when I knew how much it galled you to ask me?"

"It did not!" she fired back.

"You mean you wanted my company on Christmas Eve?"

"No. That is..."

"Marianne, you asked me to have Christmas Eve with your family because beneath your cold exterior there beats a heart of oatmeal mush, and you couldn't stand the thought of some poor soul, even your nemesis, being alone on Christmas Eve." He had knocked the dottle out of the pipe and had risen, stretching his wiry body with an indolent yawn.

She was glad of the romantic candlelight—it hid the

uncontrollably mournful look in her wide brown eyes. She watched him in silence as he pulled the lightweight sweater over his lean body, followed it with a much heavier one, and wound a scarf around his neck. "Fat lot you know," she murmured under her breath as he headed for the door.

He stopped dead in his tracks, turning slowly to look at her, huddled miserably by the fire. "What did you say?" There was a sudden look in his narrow, clever face, one she might almost have called hope. But what could he be hoping for?

"Nothing," she said, turning coward again.

"Woman," he said with a sigh, "you are the most frustrating female it has ever been my misfortune to meet."

"Sorry," she said, unrepentant. "And don't call me woman."

He stood there, staring at her. "Woman," he said again, his rich Scottish accent caressing the word, "you're not sorry at all."

She had to turn her face to hide her sudden smile, and she missed his swift movement. One moment he was standing in the middle of the room, eyeing her with his usual irritation, and the next moment he was beside her, one strong, beautiful hand sliding behind her neck, under the heavy mane of chestnut hair, tilting her head up to look at him.

She did so easily, too surprised to resist. "Woman," he whispered, "you'll drive me mad." And his mouth caught hers, in a brief, deep kiss that tasted of brandy and pipe tobacco and of an intense longing that left her shaken. She raised her hands to touch him, but he had already moved away, not even aware of her incipient response. "Happy Christmas, Marianne," he said, and was gone.

She stared after him, at the closed door that shut out the wind and snow and Andrew Cameron. She raised a trembling hand to her mouth, to wipe away the feel of him. But instead, her fingers gently caressed the lips that he'd kissed so briefly, and her sigh woke the sleeping children.

SPRINGER LEANED BACK against the kitchen wall and began to curse, low, inventive swear words from all over the world, colorful, obscene, incredibly imaginative. Just the sound of her voice, that soft, slightly husky voice had managed to knock the supports from underneath him. He never would have imagined she'd be there tonight. If he'd thought, he might have changed his ironclad policy and taken Katherine East for Christmas. She would have been delighted to see Elyssa and Ham.

But what the hell good would it have done him? It had taken months to get her out of his mind, months to forget those vulnerable blue eyes, that tremulous mouth, that shattering response that seemed to shock her. But it was useless—she'd locked herself away from any kind of involvement, closed herself up, and he couldn't keep battering away at the door. He had no desire to play sweet Sir Galahad, or amateur psychologist, or even family friend. Jessica Hansen was danger, pure and simple, and he needed to keep as far from her as possible.

So why was he standing alone in the kitchen of his ex-wife's home on Christmas Eve, leaning against the wall and aching for a skinny, complicated New York lady who was nothing but trouble?

With a last effort he roused himself, pushing against the wall and plastering a bright holiday smile on his face as he moved back to join the others. Maybe he could look up one of his old girl friends—he certainly had enough of them. Maybe one of them could make him forget about Jessica Hansen for a while.

THE TOWN HOUSE WAS DEADLY SILENT as Elyssa let herself in. She'd extinguished the Christmas-tree lights when she'd left, turned off everything, knowing she wouldn't be back till daylight. Slipping off her shoes, she moved on stocking feet into the pitch-black living room.

Ham and Jessica would be sound asleep. Not a creature was stirring, not even a mouse, she told herself with the raw edge of hysteria. Slowly she moved across the inky-dark room, felt around under the fragrant blue spruce for the electric cord, and plugged it in. The tiny colored lights sprang to life, and Elyssa stared at them. Moving on leaden limbs, she sank down into the sofa, curling her feet up underneath her. The rage and misery began to build, started to bubble over, and she quickly caught up a pillow and held it to her mouth, to muffle the sounds of animal agony. Curling in upon herself, she wept into the pillow, howled and cried and screamed, until her tears had run dry, and she was a dry, lifeless hulk. *Damn David, damn his shallow soul to hell.* Still gripping the sodden pillow to her chest, she leaned back to stare out of aching, red-rimmed eyes at the shimmering lights of the Christmas tree. Maybe later she would sleep.

## Chapter Eighteen

**The Slaughterer, vol. 62: Pearls of Doom**

*Matt Decker surveyed the carnage around him. It always surprised him, the way innocent lives intertwined. Their bodies littered the sidewalk, victims of the war with terrorism. He stepped over the old lady's body with no regret. He'd learned long ago in his righteous crusade against the powers of evil that innocent people sometimes got in the way. And if they did, he didn't hesitate to blow them away. It was more important to get his man, or men, than to worry about some bleeding-heart liberal whining about human rights.*

*He blew the smoke from his Beretta, tucking the hot steel back in his belt without a flinch. Glancing back at the lifeless old lady, he shrugged. One more victim of the terrorist conspiracy to rule the world, he told himself and moved onward on his lonely way down the Beirut sidewalk.*

JESSICA MOVED SLOWLY in the shadowy living room. The sparkling lights of the Christmas tree, combined with the muffled glow of dawn, illuminated Elyssa's huddled figure on the sofa. Her silk dress was a bright splash of blue against the white cotton. Jessica hesitated, wondering if this feeling of unease wasn't merely pregnancy-induced heartburn.

"Merry Christmas, Jessica." Elyssa roused herself, and Jessica could hear the hoarseness in her voice, the ragged edge of tears still lingering. "What are you doing up so early?"

Jessica moved into the room with her peculiar pregnant grace, sinking down into the sofa beside her friend. "I've gotten psychic in my old age. Something's wrong, isn't it?"

"Everything's fine," Elyssa said mournfully, not making much of an effort.

"Sure it is. Then why are you home? Last time I saw you, you were off to spend Christmas Eve with David. Why did you come back? Wasn't David there?"

"He was there all right. He just wasn't alone," Elyssa said numbly.

"That bastard," Jessica said softly.

"Don't blame him. I wasn't there when he needed me—haven't been there for a long time. Ham's been too sick for me to leave him, and David needs—"

"David needs a kick in the ass. How could you swallow that crap he fed you? Don't you realize that anyone so mean-spirited and selfish as to deny a dying man some love and comfort can't be worth anything? He's just too insecure to last long without some adoring female by his side. The man's a worthless piece of crud, Elyssa. He always was."

"But I could have tried harder..." she said weakly.

"Your only mistake was getting involved with him in

the first place," Jessica fought back. "And I wouldn't be surprised if you didn't always know that."

"I loved him," Elyssa defended herself.

Jessica smiled then. "Past tense already. He's a jerk, Elyssa. Let him go and wait for a better man to come around. They're not all worthless."

A weak, watery smile lit Elyssa's face. "Thanks, mom," she said wryly. "Since when have you become such a staunch defender of men? I never heard you have much good to say for the species, and I wouldn't have thought your opinion would improve, given Peter's abdication."

"But Peter—" Jessica swallowed her sudden protest. "I left Peter first, remember," she said finally.

"But your situation can hardly be comfortable. Especially now that he's married to the Kerr girl. Is he going to help you with financial support?"

"I don't want financial support from Peter," she said truthfully enough. "And don't change the subject. You need to stop throwing yourself away on worthless men."

"I haven't made a habit of it, Jessica," Elyssa protested. "David was my first mistake."

"He was a big-enough one to last you for a while." Jessica leaned back, clasping her hands loosely over her rounded tummy.

"I suppose you're right. You, of course, don't make mistakes." Elyssa's faintly aggrieved note was belied by her rueful expression.

Jessica laughed. "Of course I don't. Can't you tell?" She gestured to her stomach. "You should aim for faultlessness, Elyssa."

"God protect me," she said devoutly with a laugh. It was a weak laugh, slightly forced, but a laugh all the same, and Jessica was reassured.

For a moment, when she'd seen Elyssa curled in a fetal ball of misery, she had been afraid that the pain had gone too deep. She had underestimated Elyssa's resilience, as she tended to underestimate most people's. Few people, she had come to realize, were as easily destroyed as she feared.

Elyssa put her slender hand on Jessica's. "I'll be all right, Jessie," she said softly. "It hurts, but I'll survive. Don't worry about me, worry about yourself."

"I don't need to worry about myself. I'm doing better than I ever have in my life," she said, and was surprised to realize it was true.

"Are you? Even carrying Peter's baby and not being married to him? You forget, I know you pretty well. You've got too much of that conventional Midwestern morality to go around having babies by yourself without feeling guilty."

"Whenever I feel guilty I squash it down," she said firmly. "My daughter and I will be just fine up in Vermont. That is, if it's all right for us to stay there," she added, suddenly anxious. "Ham said he wanted to talk to me about something...it wasn't the house, was it?"

"No, it wasn't the house. We're very happy to have you there, even happier knowing that you're content to be there. It's about *The Slaughterer*."

"*The Slaughterer*?" she echoed. "What does Ham's male adventure series have to do with me?"

Elyssa hesitated. "Ham would kill me if he knew I talked to you before he did, but I'm just as glad to have the chance. It means so much to him, and I'm afraid he might not broach it the right way...."

"Broach what?" Jessica was mystified.

"He wants you to ghostwrite *The Slaughterer* for him."

"But what about Johnson? I thought he'd been Ham's ghostwriter for ages."

Elyssa laughed. "Heavens, don't say that to Ham. He thought no one knew that he didn't write them himself anymore. He has his image to protect, you know."

"But what happened to Johnson? Did they have a fight?"

"You might say so. Johnson has been more than scarce since Ham's been sick. He's been acting like it's AIDS or something, which has been hard for Ham, after all the years they've been together. And then he found out that Johnson hasn't even been writing them, either—he's been farming them out to various young male friends of his."

"Oh."

"Oh, indeed. So my poor Ham has had to deal with betrayal on three levels from Johnson—as a friend, as a business associate and as a lover. It hasn't made things any easier."

"But why in the world would he want me to ghostwrite them? Surely he could find someone much more qualified."

"You don't have to be very qualified to do *The Slaughterer*. Just get the names of the guns right, have lots of killing and a tiny bit of sex, and you'll do fine. Your best qualification is that you're a natural parodist. Ham's always kept that thing you did for Christmas."

"But..."

"He wants you to do it, Jessica. He wants to ensure that *The Slaughterer* keeps on for a while, to show Johnson that he doesn't need him. And he wants to do something for you. *The Slaughterer* brings in quite a comfortable sum of money, you realize. It could give you a nice start on a nest egg for you and your daughter."

"Elyssa, it's a ridiculous idea."

"Perhaps. But it means a great deal to him. He's been thinking about it ever since you left, and he's got his heart set on it. Even if you won't do it, lie to him, Jessica. Tell him you will. It would set his mind at ease about both of you."

"Me and the baby?" she queried, confused.

"No. You and Matt Decker. Ham's very sentimental under all his cynical bluff—he loves *The Slaughterer*."

"Then why doesn't he write it anymore?"

"Everything just dried up on him about four years ago. He tried everything—drugs, therapy, hypnosis, but it wouldn't come back. That's when Johnson took over, and sales, unfortunately, increased. That set the seal on Ham's writing block."

"I don't think that had anything to do with Johnson's dubious talents—I think the market improved for male macho fantasies."

"Of course, I agree with you, but Ham still took it hard. He won't if sales improve after you write one; as a matter of fact, he's counting on it. Unfortunately, he won't know. They've got *Slaughterer*s scheduled till the summer—he'll probably be dead before yours would get released."

They were both silent for a moment in the slowly lightening living room, the cheerful lights of the Christmas tree a counterpart to their dark thoughts. "I'll do it for him, Elyssa," she said suddenly. "At least, I'll try."

Elyssa's relief came in a breathy sigh. "That's all he can ask. Thank you, darling. It will mean a great deal to him." She hesitated a moment. "Uh...he won't want you to tell anyone, you realize. Apart from someone like Marianne Trainor."

"I wouldn't think of it."

"Not even Springer," she added, and the name hit Jessica like a blow.

"I can't imagine that I'd even have the chance, much less the inclination," she said lightly. "Speaking of which, he called just after you left."

"He did? Damn it—I was sure he wouldn't. Was he surprised to hear your voice?"

"A bit," Jessica said dryly. "He said he'd call back in a few days. He just wanted to wish you and Ham a merry Christmas. Do you really think it fair that he doesn't know?"

"No, I don't think it's fair at all. But there's nothing I can do about it—Ham's adamant. I've given up arguing—maybe you can make him see reason."

"I don't want to have anything to do with it," Jessica shot back, trying to squash down the panicky feeling that came over her at the thought of Elyssa's son. "Springer's problems have nothing to do with me—I'm much better off not involved."

"I suppose you're right," Elyssa said doubtfully. "Did he have anything to say?"

"Just that he and Katherine wished you both a merry Christmas." She kept her voice diffident.

"How nice," Elyssa said vaguely, her mind wandering.

*Who's Katherine,* Jessica wanted to scream. *For heaven's sake, tell me who Katherine is.* But she said nothing, merely bit her lip and told herself it didn't matter. Katherine was just another in a long, endless line of Springer's ladies, and she could thank God she wasn't a part of it, had never been a part of it. And the baby gave her a swift kick beneath the ribs.

Elyssa had turned to view the tree with its gaily wrapped packages piled beneath it, missing Jessica's expression. "We'll have a good Christmas," she said fiercely. "Despite everything, we're going to make this a wonderful Christmas for Ham. Won't we, Jessie?"

No one called her Jessie but Springer. Inwardly, she cringed at the sudden memory, but she smiled at Springer's mother. "Yes, we will, Elyssa. A wonderful Christmas."

# Chapter Nineteen

April in Vermont was a godless month. For every warm, wet spring day, with the smell of the damp earth and the sap in the trees, came a heavy, blanketing snowstorm that paralyzed any vehicle that managed to navigate the mud. After getting stuck for the third time in two weeks, when even her four-wheel-drive Subaru couldn't get her out, Jessica decided to wait it out. Winter couldn't last forever in Vermont, could it? Marianne assured her it could.

This was the fifth snowstorm of the month, she thought, staring out into the swirling white. And it was only April fifteenth. The Ides of April, the taxpayers' bane and her due date. Thank God babies never get born on their due date—she'd be in big trouble if she had to try to make it to the hospital in this stuff.

She put a hand on her aching back, rubbing with an absent touch. During these past few weeks it had been particularly painful, but not quite so bad as it was that morning. She must have slept on it the wrong way. It wasn't surprising—at this stage in the game she had to get out of bed to change positions, and it took a great deal of discomfort for her to move. She must have slept too heavily to notice.

She was still tired and sleepy. Her daughter had a habit of kicking her into wakefulness two or three times a night, and then a silly childish fear would enter her mind at the thought of her upcoming labor. Marianne would be with her, she'd promised. But during those first dark moments she would suddenly, unreasonably, long for her mother. The mother who had never been there for her, and never would be again.

Jessica moved to the east window to check the thermometer, but the wind had plastered snow against it, and she couldn't read it. It could be thirty degrees or it could be ten. *When the wind blew, there was no way you could warm this drafty old barn of a house,* she thought with wry affection.

On such a miserable day she didn't have much choice. Matt Decker had just finished his first incarnation, the rapidly weakening Ham loved him, and there was nothing to do for the time being. She could sit huddled by the wood stove, staring out at the storm, or she could climb back into bed, turn up the electric blanket, and read a nice, juicy female fantasy. Matt Decker's violence had gotten a bit tedious after a while, and Jessica found she needed the respite of a scented and flowery romance.

Or she could read her baby books over again, checking for the twenty-third time how to deal with problems in breast-feeding, how to bathe a baby, what comprised a basic layette. Not that she'd learn anything new—by this time she'd memorized Penelope Leach. The lovely maternal fantasies were only causing her frustration.

*No, maybe Jane Austen on a day like today,* she thought, giving a small anguished groan as she leaned down to load the stove. *And then a nap,* and maybe, if fate had any sense of fairness, it would make up for the hideousness of the weather and take away her backache.

She loved this house, she thought for the hundredth time as she glanced around the living room, the solid cherry walls, the random-width pine floors, the rough but comfortable country furniture. She loved the casement windows, even when they looked out onto a blizzard; she loved the huge country kitchen with the iron sink, the ancient refrigerator and the well-scrubbed oak table. And she loved the bedrooms, the two downstairs, with their neat, narrow iron beds and their marble-topped dressers. But most of all she loved her bedroom, up under the eaves, with its fading flowered wallpaper, its sagging iron bed, the antique trunk full of old quilts and the dresser with its wavering mirror. Even the rag rugs that provided little protection for bare feet in the middle of the night charmed her. If she'd had any sense at all, she would have moved to one of the downstairs bedrooms and shut off the upstairs entirely. It was foolish to heat the whole house for only one person.

But she had fallen in love with her bedroom when she'd arrived in early September, and even forty below in January hadn't evicted her. Granted, she'd had to turn the electric blanket up to ten, the electric heater to high, and then had lain awake all night worrying about whether she was going to end up with a fried baby, but they'd both survived. Even with the damp chill of a spring snowstorm she wasn't going to abdicate now.

Jane was as soothing as ever and though the lumpy, sagging bed probably did her back more harm than good, she snuggled down deeper anyway. There was something to be said for spring storms.

It was hours later when she woke up, and for a moment she couldn't remember where she was. She was cold, bone-chillingly cold, and wet, and the pain in her back had moved around to her stomach, ripping her apart with a sudden shaft of pain that sent her rigid, then collapsing in relief. It was dark, yet she was sure she'd left the light on. And the bed was cold and—God help her—wet.

Sudden, blinding panic swept over her as the full realization hit. The power was off, her water had broken and she was in labor.

With a small whimper of fear she pulled herself off the bed. She had to get to the telephone, to call Marianne and get some help. Thank God another pain hadn't come yet—she'd have to remember to time them. As long as they were ten minutes apart—maybe it was just gas again. But no, there was no denying her soaked clothing. She shivered in the chilly air as she started down the narrow staircase. *Please, not another pain,* she prayed to an impassive God. Let them be at least twenty—

Her prayer wasn't answered as another pain ripped across her stomach, and she nearly fell. How long had it been? More than five, surely. But less than ten. How long did she have? Long enough to make it into Burlington in a blizzard? Long enough for Marianne to get there? Long enough for her to even get to a telephone?

She leaned against the wall, panting, as the pain let

up. Why the hell was the telephone so far away? At least it was near the wood stove—she was freezing.

The wood stove was still kicking out the heat, and waves of it washed over her, adding to her dizziness, as she kept up her silent litany with fate and her baby. *Just hold on,* she prayed. *Just stay put for a few more hours, long enough for me to get to the hospital. Please, darling, hold on.*

Picking up the phone in chilled fingers, she dialed Marianne's number before putting the receiver to her ear. When she did listen she dropped the phone in numb horror. The phone line was completely, absolutely dead.

"No!" she cried out loud, tears streaming down her face. "No, please, no."

But the phone was silent and still and the snow piling up at a rapid rate around the old house.

It took her a moment to stifle the sudden panic. "Calm down, Jessie," she ordered herself sternly, the sound of her voice in the quiet house soothing her. "Getting hysterical won't help matters. First you've got to check outside and see whether you dare try to make it to Marianne's."

The blur of white answered that first question, and with a trembling hand she let the curtain fall again. "All right, second, you have to make sure you have enough wood to keep it warm in here. Some candles for light, a couple of quilts to spread on the floor." She was mumbling, wandering around, when the next pain hit her, and she sank into a chair, doubled over with the suddenness of it. When it passed she pulled herself upright. How long had it been? Was it shorter between the last two, or longer? Where the hell was the clock?

With a sudden moan of despair she realized that every single damned clock in the damned house was electric. She didn't even have a watch. There was no way she could time her contractions, there was no way she could get help. There was nothing she could do but lie there in the darkened house and have the baby that wasn't listening to her pleas to hold off.

One of her baby books had instructions on what to do if you went into labor when you were alone. But the books were upstairs by her bed, and nothing could get her to traverse the dark, narrow stairs again to get it. She had read it at least five times, surely she could remember it well enough. Put the baby on your stomach afterward, she remembered. Don't try to cut the cord—wait for help. Someone will get there eventually. Won't they? Keep the baby warm. Keep warm yourself. *God help me, is this punishment for all my sins? Have they been so very many that I deserve this?*

Even a pile of quilts on the pine floor would be too uncomfortable—she had to try to drag a mattress from one of the downstairs bedrooms and bring it into the living room. It would be all right—God wasn't punishing her. If she just took it slow and easy, she'd be all right, she and her baby. Her daughter, she thought wistfully. *Please, darling, take your time.*

At first Jessica thought it was just the howling of the wind. She was tugging away at the mattress on the old iron bed, her ungainly body and exhausted condition making it slow work, when the muffled thudding came again. With a disbelieving cry she stumbled out of the room toward the front door when another contraction hit her, knocking her to her knees. *Don't go away,* she whimpered beneath her breath. *Don't go.*

She didn't even wait for the pain to subside. She staggered to the door, fumbling with the latch. Thank God she never bothered to lock the door in the safe Vermont countryside—she doubted she'd be able to manage it. "Don't go," she whispered, "don't go." A moment later the door opened and she fell into Andrew Cameron's arms.

He didn't waste time with foolish words or questions. She felt herself lifted in his surprisingly strong arms and carried back to the stove. He'd kicked the door shut behind him, and a moment later he had her bundled in one of the quilts she'd dropped on her trip to the front door. The small glow of candlelight further dispelled some of the gloom and panic, and for the first time Jessica began to relax. She wouldn't have to go through it alone.

"How close are the pains, Jessica?" Andrew had come to kneel in front of her, his narrow face dark with concern.

"I—I don't know," she replied faintly, huddling in the quilt. "I don't have a watch, and the clocks are all electric." She caught her breath in a shuddering sigh. "If we leave right now, I'm sure we can make it to Burlington." Actually, she was sure of no such thing. She only knew she had to try.

Andrew shook his head. "We can't, Jessie," he said softly. "I skied up here, and I could barely see two feet in front of my face. Even the snowplows aren't out right now—nothing's moving. You're going to have to stay put."

"Oh, no," Jessie moaned, as another pain started its inexorable build.

"Have you called Marianne? You should thank your lucky stars she's your closest neighbor, lassie. She's helped deliver hundreds of babies—she's an old hand. Your son will pop out with no trouble at all with her by your side."

"Daughter," Jessie croaked. "Can't . . . can't call her." *Breathe,* she told herself. *Remember your breathing.* "The telephone's out," she gasped.

Andrew swore an effective Gaelic curse. "I'll have to go for her, then. I promise, Jessie, I won't be long. Let me make you comfortable before I leave."

She clasped his arm in sudden desperation. "Don't leave me, Andrew. I'm frightened."

"I've got to, lassie. You need Marianne more than you need a helpless Scot. As they said in the movie, 'I don't know nothin' 'bout birthin' babies.' Marianne does." The quote sounded utterly ridiculous coming out in his rich Scottish brogue, and through her tears Jessica laughed. "Trust me, Jessie. I won't abandon you, and neither will Marianne."

"Will she even come with you? She's been avoiding you since I came back from New York."

"Since Christmas Eve, to be exact. Don't worry yourself, Jessie. Her caring for you far outweighs her fear of me. She'll come with me—probably even beat me back here." He pulled the comforter closer around her shivering body, then bent to load the stove. "Is there anything I can get you before I leave? Anything to make you more comfortable?"

"You could get me a clean nightgown. My clothes are soaked." she admitted.

"Good idea. You can change while I'm gone, but don't go far from the stove. I don't want to find you've birthed your baby in the kitchen."

"I wouldn't do that. I—" A new pain began to ripple across her, and she stared up at him in renewed panic. "Hurry, Andrew," she whispered urgently. "They're getting closer."

IT WAS A LONG AFTERNOON, a longer evening and an endless night. It was almost an hour before Marianne could make her way through the waist-high drifts to the isolated house, and in the meantime Jessica was absolutely convinced she was going to die. Marianne and Andrew would arrive back and find her dead.... What was that hideous line from Macbeth's three witches? Something about a birth-strangled babe, ditch-delivered by a drab.... Why did she always have to remember things like that when she least wanted to?

But Marianne fought her way into the house, and Jessica's labor had slowed its headlong pace. Andrew arrived an hour later, after having delivered Eric and Shannon to Mrs. LaPlante's for the night. And then the hard part began.

Hours and hours of breathing and panting, hours of holding back, hours of pushing. Andrew was stationed at her head, holding her hand and helping her breathe, while Marianne cosseted and threatened, cajoled and cursed her baby into the world. It was hard, exhausting work, and Jessica lay there with sweat pouring down her pale face.

"Why d'you think they call it labor?" Marianne had snapped. "Hold her head, Andrew, damn it. Try to relax, if you can, Jessie. We've got hours to go."

Jessica burst into tears for the twentieth time, and even Andrew groaned. "Bunch of pansies," Marianne muttered unsympathetically. "Get her mind off the pain, Cameron. What made you decide to show up tonight, anyhow? It isn't exactly the weather for a pleasure ski."

A wry grin twisted his mobile face. "You've forgotten, you heartless woman, that I'm a Scot. Blessed with the second sight, I am. I knew something was happening. It was probably the bairn calling to me. He knew it was time to make an appearance and he was calling to the only available male in this matriarchal society."

"It's a girl," Marianne said wearily, pushing a hand through her straggling brown hair. So far she had avoided looking him in the eye, as she had avoided his very presence for the past four months. She had the unpleasant feeling her isolation was about to end, and she didn't know whether to be relieved or panicked. Maybe she was a little bit of both, she decided.

"Thank you, Andrew," Jessica whispered. "I haven't thanked you yet, have I?"

"At least three dozen times, lass."

"I'm sorry to be so boring," she said tearfully.

"Don't worry about it lass. Believe me, this is far too lively an evening for the likes of me."

"I'm sorry," she whimpered again. "I—"

"Breathe, damn it," Marianne swore as Jessica whitened in pain again. "Come on, Jessie. We have to get this little girl born." She cast a defiant glance at Andrew.

"Boy," he said silkily, unmoved.

AT 11:45 P.M. ON FRIDAY, April fifteenth, Jessica Katrina Hansen gave birth to a healthy, seven-pound baby boy. He had very dark brown eyes for such a little thing, and silky black hair like an Indian's. Jessica, Marianne and Andrew viewed their tiny accomplishment with complete fatuousness as he let out an ear-piercing yell.

'We're going to need a father's name for the birth certificate, Jessie," Marianne warned, touching the tiny little hand with a wonder that never ceased no matter how many times she experienced it.

"Matt Decker," Jessica murmured, smiling dreamily at her son.

"Come on, Jessie, be serious."

"I am. His father's Matt Decker. I don't know what type his blood is, but I know there's always a lot of it." With a weak chuckle she leaned back.

Marianne shook her head in disgust. "Do you want me to put him down for you?"

"Not right now. You'd think that after nine months I would have gotten tired of holding him, wouldn't you? Just give me a few minutes."

"All right. You're warm enough?" They'd turned the downstairs bedroom into a makeshift delivery room, with Andrew building up the fire in the stove to epic proportions to ensure proper warmth.

"Just fine." Jessica sighed happily.

"Do you want to go to the hospital when the plows come through? Just to check everything out."

"I don't think so. The baby's fine, I'm fine. I think we should stay here, all snug and cozy." She smiled up at her friend. "Go and rest, Marianne. I think you've worked harder than I have."

"I'll be glad to keep you company...."

"Go, Marianne. You'll have to face him sooner or later," Jessica said gently.

There was no sign of Andrew in the candlelit living room. Slowly, like a zombie, Marianne moved to the dining-room table, sinking into a straight-back chair and dropping her head into her arms. She heard his footsteps a moment later, and reluctantly she lifted her head.

"You look like hell," he said roughly, and she managed a weak grin.

"Ever the flatterer," she murmured.

"You look like you've been kicked by a horse," he continued ruthlessly, watching her out of those Celtic green eyes of his. "You look like you could sleep for days."

"I could," she admitted.

"You're also the prettiest woman I've ever seen," he said, and his voice was strained.

Marianne just continued to stare at him, too tired and too wary to respond.

"You're not going to make this easy, are you, Marianne?" he said suddenly.

"Make what easy?" Her voice was as hoarse as his was.

"You and me."

"There isn't any you and me, Cameron. And there never will be."

"Why?"

"For one, because you're five years too young and five inches too short."

"Women tend to outlive the men in this country," he responded. "This way I can keep up with you."

"You intend to be around that long?" She couldn't keep herself from asking.

"That long," he verified. "As for being too short, you'll find, woman, that you'll have nothing to complain about when it comes to my size." There was a devilish light in his eyes, and Marianne couldn't help herself; she laughed.

"Don't bother me now, Cameron, I'm too tired to fight off your advances," she murmured. "Catch me later when my defenses are up. You wouldn't want to take unfair advantage of a poor woman, would you?"

"I would. I've been waiting a long time for you, Marianne Trainor, and I'm not in the mood to wait a hell of a lot longer. You'd better get accustomed to the fact, woman. I'm going to win in the end."

"Don't call me woman," she murmured sleepily, putting her head down on her arms again. "I'm too tired to argue with you." She closed her eyes, just for a moment, just to rest them, and a moment later she was sound asleep.

He just stood there, watching her for a long time. She couldn't sleep like that; she'd end up even more stiff and sore than the night had already made her. On the other hand, she'd jump like a frightend rabbit if he put a hand on her. He knew he had a little more time to wait—he'd almost wrecked the whole thing by moving too fast at Christmas. No, he'd have to leave her there and hope she'd wake up shortly and move to the couch. In the meantime he had to get back to his house and stoke the fire. He didn't dare spend the night here, much as he wanted to. He didn't dare touch her. But the time would come, and soon. For now he'd have to bide his time.

"Good night, woman," he whispered, his rich Scottish voice caressing the word. "Sleep well, you nasty-tongued viper."

Marianne smiled in her sleep.


IT HAD BEEN a hell of a day. Springer had started out the day snapping at Katherine, had gotten a speeding ticket driving to work, the muffler had fallen off the Lotus and who knew where he was going to get another muffler for a 1963 Lotus. Work had been a nightmare, the rain was a constant downpour, and by the time he arrived home he was in such a tearing, uncontrollable rage that he put his fist through the flimsy plywood door of his closet.

Which hadn't helped matters. It had come and gone during the past few months, that nagging sense of something being wrong, something happening beyond his knowledge and control, but it had never been as strong as it was that day.

Maybe it was just a built-in reaction to April fifteenth. He never liked to pay taxes on the comfortable trust fund Elyssa's father had left him, but it didn't usually precipitate his current foul mood. And it certainly wouldn't be responsible for the gnawing sense of anxiety that had no basis.

An exhausting session of handball hadn't helped.

Driving too fast in his mufflerless car hadn't helped. He could only be grateful that tonight was Katherine's night to spend at Maureen's. At least he wouldn't have to subject her to his moods.

The weather report only deepened his gloom. The entire country was in a mid-April mess, from spring blizzards in Vermont to downpours and flooding in the Northwest. And no letup in sight.

Well, there was nothing he could do about his current mood, when he didn't even know what was wrong. He could always go out, find some friendly little yuppie bar awash with ferns and drown his sorrows. But he'd spent too much time in this town—he doubted there was a bar around where he wouldn't run into someone he knew. And he wasn't in the mood to see anyone at all.

He turned off the television as the rest of the local news started, and the knob broke off in his hand. With a short obscene word he threw it across the room.

Tonight was a fitting night to drown his sorrows, whatever the hell they were. Maybe good old Jack Daniel's would begin to blur the edges enough to let him get a good night's sleep. And if it didn't, at least he wouldn't mind being awake as much.

Damn, he thought, tossing his long body down on the couch without managing to spill a drop of the dark amber drink. Jessica Hansen picked the oddest times to invade his memories. He took a deep gulp, savoring the smooth, burning taste of it, and closed his eyes, remembering.

# Chapter Twenty

**The Slaughterer, vol. 39: The Wrath of Decker**

*Matt Decker surveyed the carnage around him. There was nothing bloodier than a back street in Paris when the Slaughterer had been called to his noble task. Shoving the snub-nosed Walther in his jacket pocket, he picked his way through the bodies. The young woman had escaped, taking her baby with her. He couldn't worry about it—she was only a minor cog in the wheel of international terrorism. He'd mete out his justice eventually. And the kid was another one of them—probably fathered by some member of the Baader-Meinhof gang, a terrorist in the cradle. His time would come, too.*

*In the meantime, Decker had to see the old man. He didn't have too much time left—cancer was accomplishing what Decker had so far failed to do. It was killing Maurice Rocco, kingpin of the Paris underground and friend to terrorists everywhere. Decker planned to go see him, to laugh in his face and then maybe speed him on his way to hell. Decker smiled his chilly smile as he crossed the narrow back street and headed south.*

"YOU SURE you'll be all right?" Marianne queried anxiously. It was late June, and Matthew Decker Hansen was two and a half months old. He was lying in his honorary Aunt Marianne's arms, blissfully asleep, unaware that his mother was about to leave him for the first time in his short life.

"I don't know," Jessica admitted, shoving a nervous hand through her shoulder-length curtain of wheat-blond hair. "But I don't have any choice in the matter. Ham wants me, Elyssa needs me. It's going to be harder for him to die than for me to watch it, and they need me there. It's the least I can do after all they've done for me."

"This boy is going to miss you, you realize?" She nodded toward the sleeping child.

"He probably won't even know I'm gone," Jessica said fondly. "I guess there are advantages in not being able to breast-feed. I'd hate to have to take him with me. It's going to be tough enough as it is, without worrying about Matthew. I know you'll take perfect care of him." She touched his soft cheek with a gentle finger. "I'll miss him."

"How long do you think you'll be gone?"

"I can't say for sure. Elyssa said Ham's in and out of consciousness, but he wanted to see me before he died. I don't imagine it will be more than a couple of days. I'll try to bring Elyssa back with me—getting away from everything should do her good."

"So will the sight of her godson. Listen, don't worry about us, just take care of yourself. If it makes you feel better, you can call us every night just to make sure we're fine."

Jessica laughed ruefully. "Don't worry. I expect I'll be calling twice a day. Take care of my darling, please." Leaning closer, she brushed her lips against his sweet-smelling baby skin. He stirred in Marianne's arms for a moment, opening those dark, fathomless eyes that never failed to amaze her for a brief moment before drifting back to sleep.

"I will, I will," Marianne promised. "Now hurry up before you miss your plane. Give Elyssa my love."

"YOU LOOK MARVELOUS, darling," Elyssa greeted her warmly, enveloping her in her warm, scented embrace. "No one would ever know you just had a baby."

"I'm fifteen pounds heavier than when I lived in New York, Elyssa," Jessica said wryly.

"You were fifteen pounds underweight back then. Come along in and see Ham. He's awake right now. He's having a good day—he's a lot more alert than he has been." She led the way, her reed slimness having moved on to nervous gauntness.

"I'm glad to hear that."

"Yes, I think having you and Springer here will be just the thing," Elyssa continued with deliberate art-lessness.

Jessica was already halfway into the downstairs din-ing room that had been transformed into a sickroom before the words penetrated. It had never occurred to her that Elyssa wouldn't be alone with Hamilton. That they would have had to finally, eventually tell Springer that his father was dying, and that Springer, despite his eternal anger, would be there.

She stopped dead still, but it was too late. Ham was

lying propped up in a hospital bed, his eyes the only sign of life in his sunken face. But what eyes they were, twinkling with merriment and just the faintest trace of devilry as they met hers. She kept her attention firmly fixed on him, a warm smile on her face, as she ignored the tall figure that unwound itself from the chair beside the bed.

"Hello, darling," Ham breathed on the mere trace of sound.

"Hi, Ham," she said gently, moving across the room because she had to, moving closer to that watching figure by Hamilton's side. "You still look like hell."

His laugh was a painful wheeze. "I can't say the same for you, little one. You're still a damn pretty woman. Almost as pretty as Elyssa."

"No one's as pretty as Elyssa, I've come to accept it as a whim of cruel fate," she said lightly as she reached the side of his bed and took one wasted hand in hers. The bones stood out against the thin covering of skin, and it was cold and lifeless to the touch. Slowly, deliberately she turned her head to the side, to look directly into a pair of unreadable dark brown eyes. The twin to her son's eyes.

"Hello, Springer," she said evenly, wiping that unacceptable thought from her brain with ruthless speed. "How have you been?"

Such idiotic words, she chided herself. But there wasn't much else she could say to the man who stood so close to her, with such a closed expression on his face. She could stare at him covertly, drink in all the deliberately forgotten beauty of his face with those high, arrogant cheekbones, the hawklike nose, the deep, knowing eyes and that mouth that had changed her life. He was wearing a chambray shirt, his shoulders broad and slightly bony through the pale blue material, and the faded jeans hugged the narrow curve of his hips, traced the length of his long legs, ended at a pair of disreputable old sneakers. He looked lean and fit and dangerous, the light in his eyes holding not one trace of warmth as they swept over her. She knew what he would see.

The added fifteen pounds suited her, filling out the concave lines of her face but not obliterating her distinctive Nordic cheekbones. Jessica had dressed in a Liz Claiborne suit from her New York days that still managed to fit, and if one didn't look too closely one would think she was the same woman. If one didn't look into her blue eyes and see the faint trace of warmth that had melted the ice. If one didn't notice her mouth, which was far too used to smiling down at her son. If one didn't see the air of pleasure and confidence with which she faced the undemanding Vermont world.

Of course, it wouldn't have mattered if Springer did look closely. His very presence had wiped out her sense of well-being, chilled her heart, made her a stranger to smiling. She was suddenly very frightened, and there was nothing she could do about it, with Ham's thin, skeletal hand in hers, clinging to her. She couldn't run away, back to her baby. She had to see this through.

Springer took his time. Those dark, judging eyes swept over her, once, twice, in a leisurely, measuring fashion that gave no clue to his final judgment. "Jessie" was all he said, acknowledging her presence and her greeting.

Of course, he'd had the advantage of knowing she

was coming, of being prepared. She, like a perfect fool, had not even considered the possibility. If she had, nothing, not her emotional and spiritual debts to Elyssa and Ham, not her own conscience, would have gotten her to leave Vermont and Matthew.

She looked down at Ham, a teasing question on her lips, one that died away at the sight of him. He'd drifted into sleep, his chest rising and falling with rapid, difficult breathing. Slowly she disengaged her hand, letting his fall back on the mattress.

"He does that a lot nowadays. Really, Jessica, he's perked up since Springer arrived."

"I'm not surprised," Jessica said politely. Springer sent her a slashing, cynical look before he walked out of the room, without another word spoken in that drawling, caressing voice of his. The two women watched him go.

"He's not doing well," Elyssa said in a whisper.

"You said it was near the end, Elyssa," Jessica reminded her.

"I mean Springer. We only told him this week. He got here yesterday and he's barely said a word to either of us the whole time. He's sat by Ham's bed hour after hour being scrupulously polite, but I'm afraid of what's going to happen."

"Why should anything happen? He's been estranged from Ham for decades—he probably just doesn't care all that much." Jessica said.

A small sad smile lit Elyssa's pale face. "You don't think that any more than I do."

"I don't know what I think. I don't really know Springer all that well."

"No, I suppose you don't," Elyssa said with a sigh. "So tell me, how's that marvelous baby of yours? It must have broken your heart to leave him, even for just a few days."

"It was," she said with a wry smile.

"What does he look like? He must have blond hair and blue eyes like you and Peter. Does he smile yet?"

"Of course. He's been smiling since he was two weeks old. Didn't Ham show you the picture I sent him?" She carefully avoided any confirmation of her son's appearance.

"You sent him a picture of Matthew? How sweet of you, darling. He must have forgotten about it—he wanders a great deal, I'm afraid." She sighed. "We haven't said anything about Matthew to Springer. Ham's probably forgotten, and I decided that should be up to you."

"I appreciate that. I... I don't see any reason to mention it. It's not really any of his business, is it?"

And Elyssa, whom Jessica had always thought she'd fooled, looked her clearly in the eye and said, "Is it?"

Ham, bless his heart, moved then, and Jessica looked away, not answering the question. "Hi, there, you old reprobate. Did you like my Matt Decker?"

He managed a travesty of his old grin. "Which one? Volume ninety-six, ninety-seven, or the baby? I like all three, but I prefer the baby most of all."

"You didn't tell me Jessie sent you a picture of him, Ham," Elyssa chided softly. "I would have liked to have seen my godchild."

"Didn't I? Must have slipped my mind. Are you going to tell my son about him, Jessie?"

"No. What business is it of his?" The question came out more sharply than she would have wished, but Ham looked pleased.

"You tell me, little one." Before she could retort he moved his sunken eyes to his ex-wife's worried face. "Where is Springer now, Lyss?"

"Gone somewhere. I heard the front door slam just after you fell asleep."

"Did I fall asleep? I seem to do that far too often." He sighed, and Jessica could hear the faint, imperceptible struggle for breath. "Come back later, Jessie. I promise I won't tease you about Matthew. Sometime when I'm feeling better and Springer isn't in the house." He winked, as if sharing some great, naughty secret, just the two of them. "Go along, you two. You must have some gossip to catch up on. And I have some sleep..." His voice faded away, and without another word Elyssa caught her sleeve and motioned her out of the room.

"He doesn't look that bad, Elyssa," Jessica said, aware of the hollow lie of her words. "Surely he's got some time left. I didn't see any machines, any medicines. He can't be that bad."

"He won't have the machines, Jessie, and he stopped the medicine last week. He stopped eating this week, and he'd been in a light coma until Springer arrived."

"Oh, no."

"Don't fool yourself, he's dying, Jessie. It won't do any good to deny it, and he won't let you. I wouldn't have asked you to come down if he had any time left. He doesn't." She smiled, a distant, sad smile. "He's in a lot of pain, Jessie. Don't hold him back."

Springer was back, charging through the front door and giving them only a cursory glance. "He's asleep again?" he questioned. The words weren't precisely terse—just short and to the point, either missing or ignoring the pleading pain in his mother's eyes.

"He just drifted off. Where did you go, darling?"

"Around the corner for cigarettes," he replied, his eyes glancing over Jessica and then skittering away.

"I thought you gave them up."

"I did."

"When did you start again?" Elyssa persisted, and Jessica wanted to tell her to stop, to leave him be.

"Five minutes ago," Springer drawled, and moved past the two women to his father's sickroom.

## Chapter Twenty-one

Hamilton MacDowell died two days later, at three o'clock in the afternoon. He'd been slipping in and out of a coma for the past twenty-four hours, barely aware of his family and friends around him. His breathing became sporadic, shallow and then deep, and he moved restlessly on the bed, as if eager to rid himself of his pain-racked, skeletal body. The shuddering breaths grew farther apart, and then they stopped altogether, and the silence of the room was deafening.

Jessica didn't dare move from her spot by the door. Springer and Elyssa were on either side of the bed, watching intently, until finally Elyssa raised her head, tears streaming down her calm, almost relieved face. "I think he's gone, Springer."

Springer met her gaze with a distant, remote calm. "Yes." He rose then, moving away from the bed, from his father, from Elyssa. "I guess that's that," he drawled, his dark, unfathomable eyes sweeping over Jessica's stunned figure. "Do you want me to call Dr. Marlin?"

Elyssa was watching him with confusion and concern and the beginning of anger stirring in her eyes. "I'd rather take care of it," she said, the trace of anger coming through her clipped voice.

"In that case, I think I'll go out. I'm not used to sitting still for so long." He stretched, a graceful, unconcerned gesture. Jessica continued to look at him out of wondering eyes. "I'll be at the club if you need me. Don't expect me for dinner—I'll just get something out." He walked out of the room without a backward glance, either at the two women or at his father.

Elyssa rose from her chair, slowly, painfully, as if every muscle in her body had been pummeled, as if she were a hundred years old. "I didn't think he still hated him that much," she said in a muffled tone of voice.

Jessica moved then, putting a supporting arm under Elyssa's suddenly frail frame. "Come into the living room and I'll get you some tea."

"I'd like a drink, I think," she said in a muffled tone of voice. "Something very strong and dark. Could you do that for me, darling, while I call Dr. Marlin?"

"Certainly. Are you sure you wouldn't rather have me call him?"

"No, I want to do it." For a brief moment the perfect serene beauty of her face crumpled in an ugly mask of pain. A moment later it was gone, and she was as placidly beautiful as always. "Did he really not care, Jessie?"

Jessica wasn't quite sure how to answer her plaintive question. "You know him far better than I do. What do you think?"

"I can't believe a child of mine could still be so unforgiving," she whispered. "But at this point I don't know. I just don't know."

THE OLD TOWN HOUSE seemed very quiet for a place in the heart of New York City's Upper East Side. Jessica could hear the sound of the traffic, the intermittent honking of horns, the occasional sirens slicing through the thick night air. She could hear the hum of the central air conditioning, the distant ring of someone else's telephone. But at a little past midnight it was very, very still in Hamilton MacDowell's town house, the house bought and supported by *The Slaughterer.*

Jessica had developed more than an affection for Matt Decker, despite his self-righteous attitudes and his stridently right-wing politics. She'd given him a bit more humanity in volumes ninety-six and ninety-seven, and a lot more sex. In some ways she thought of this house as Decker's, now that Hamilton was gone.

And he was gone. Jessica knew full well that accounted for most of the feeling of emptiness about the place, the feeling of silence. Elyssa was bedded down for the night with a heavy tranquilizer and a good book and Springer was still out. She'd called Marianne, to tell her about Ham. She didn't know whether she could leave Elyssa quite so soon, but hoped she could catch the late afternoon plane back to Vermont the following day. She missed her home and friends, but most of all she missed her baby.

Not that it was her home any more, she thought, taking a sip of the Benedictine that was one of the few liqueurs she could stomach. If he'd left the house to Elyssa, she would have no problem. If it was left to

Johnson Endicott or, even worse, to Springer, she may as well kiss Vermont good-bye. Or at least that house.

Now wasn't the time to worry about such things, she told herself sternly, draining the Benedictine and rising on slightly unsteady feet. It had been a long, painful day, but her nerves were still strung up tightly despite the advanced stage of exhaustion her body was in. She wouldn't sleep, she knew it, despite the aid of the Benedictine. She could always wake Elyssa up and avail herself of her offer of a sleeping pill, but that would only be a last resort. Elyssa needed her sleep more than Jessica did.

Maybe a hot shower. Maybe some long, boring book to wipe out the thoughts and memories and worries. Maybe some food. No, that wouldn't help. For the first time in a year her appetite had disappeared, aggravated by Springer's distant presence. She had always thought it a marvelous joke of nature, that pregnancy had cured her nausea, not caused it. But it had been all she could do to keep her dinner down last night as she avoided Springer's dark, troubled eyes.

And that was her problem tonight. She might as well admit it—she had seen, or thought she'd seen, past the mask of calm on Springer MacDowell's dark, aloof face. There was no way she was going to get to sleep tonight until she heard Springer's footsteps going past her second-floor bedroom door as they had for two nights now, heard his sneakered feet bounding up the third-floor flight of stairs. And then maybe she'd rest, secure in the knowledge that he was all right.

Jessica didn't bother to ask herself why it mattered. She only knew it did and was too weary of fighting to deny it. But there was no guarantee that he would come back at all tonight. And if she was going to be in any kind of shape tomorrow she'd better try to get some sleep.

She moved silently through the house, turning off lights, leaving one small lamp burning in the hall to guide Springer's way. She stopped for a moment in the kitchen, remembering with a surprising smile the night she first saw Springer. She shook her head in disbelief. She wouldn't have thought she'd have such fond memories for the start of an essentially painful relationship. But it had been the start of a change for her, a change that had saved her life, and she couldn't resent it or him any longer.

Flicking off the overhead light, she opened the door to the back stairway, then stopped dead still. There was a noise up there, a soft, muffled sound that she couldn't place. She moved her hand to the light switch, when his voice floated down to her, husky, almost unrecognizable. Except that, of course, she recognized him on that midnight-dark stairway.

"Don't turn on the light," he ordered, and the sound was choked. She waited for him to tell her to go away, but he said nothing more, and she could hear the heavy, strangled sound of his breathing.

Slowly she moved up the stairs, feeling her way in the darkness. He was halfway up, his head buried in his arms, his big body racked with sobs. And the last traces of ice around Jessica's heart melted.

"Oh, Springer," she whispered brokenly, putting her arms around his shaking body. "Don't cry, darling."

But she didn't mean it, and he didn't listen. He needed to cry. He put his shaking arms around her slender figure, holding her so tightly she thought her ribs might break, and he wept harsh, racking tears into her cloud of hair. His tears were wet on her face, wet on her shoulder, and his body shook in her arms as she soothed him with mumbled, meaningless words.

She knew immediately when it all changed. She could feel the tension in his arms increase, feel the hands that were loose on her back begin a subtle caress. And then he broke free of her comforting embrace, standing up so swiftly she nearly lost her balance. But he caught her deftly, his hand like a band of iron around her wrist, and a moment later he was dragging her up the stairs. She tripped once, skinning her knee, but he didn't even pause, just jerked her onward. And then they were in his darkened bedroom, the door slammed shut behind them, and he had pushed her up against the wall and was kissing her with an angry fierceness that brought her to a state of arousal and panic.

"Springer," she whispered against his mouth, a plea, a sanction. But he ignored it, his mouth plundering hers with a fierce violence that momentarily panicked her. She struggled in his arms, but he only used his larger body to press her back against the wall, pinning her there while his mouth plundered hers.

"Don't fight me," he murmured against the side of her neck, and his voice was raw. "Jessie, please don't fight me. I need you; I need you more than I've ever needed anyone in my life. Please, Jessie."

The last of her panic vanished. She had needed him

so long and so much that she hadn't been able to admit it even to herself. And now, suddenly, miracle of miracles he needed her, needed the solace her body and her love could offer him. And she opened to him willingly, gladly taking the excuse he offered her.

Not another word was spoken as he stripped off her clothing, the jeans, the loose cotton tunic, the wispy bra and panties landing in a pile on the floor. She could be glad the wall supported her, otherwise there was a good chance her knees might give way. His mouth and hands were everywhere on her, feverish, demanding, arousing her and arousing him to a level past thoughts and memories. He was rough in his need, rough in his haste, but the thoughtlessly delivered pain only made her love him more. He was lost in mute anguish, and she could soothe him, bring him sweet forgetfulness if only for a night. She reached out her hands, tentative hands that slowly became more sure as she gave herself up to his overwhelming need.

He half carried, half pulled her over to the bed, that huge bed she'd slept in at Christmastime, alone except for the baby in her belly. She tumbled with him onto the rumpled blue sheets, her hands eager on his warm, smooth skin as he quickly shed his clothes. And then he was on her, in her, surrounding and encompassing her as she welcomed him into her arms, her body, her heart and soul. She shivered and trembled beneath him, her hands clinging desperately to his damp body. It was all heat and darkness, the salty taste of sweat and love and sorrow wrapped up into a heated ball of passion. Jessica could feel it coiling like a snake in her belly, building, climbing, ready to strike. Her fingers clutched his shoulders, slipping on the wet skin, her mouth was buried against his shoulder, and still she could feel his tears on her face.

His hands slid under her hips, cupping her rounded buttocks, pulling her closer against him. She heard a soft moan in the stillness of the room, mingling with the soft rustle of the sheets, and she knew it was her voice, her moan of pleasure and despair against him. She brought her knees up around him, cradling him, holding him tightly as he strained against her, with no thought for her own pleasure, only his surcease from the pain that was driving him. She held him, her voice whispering against the silky black hair that was plastered to his skull, soft gentle words, meaningless, loving words, that were suddenly strangled in her throat when the first shocking wave of pleasure hit her. She was dimly aware of the arms tightening around her, holding her as the second wave hit, and then everything receded into the blackness of the hot velvet night. In the distance she could hear him, feel the sudden rigidity in his body as he joined her in that subliminal release, and a small distant part of her called out to him. But he was too caught up in his race for forgetting, and there was no way she could reach him, except in his bed.

Her breathing was slowly returning to normal, her senses reacting to the room around her, the darkness and heat of the third-floor bedroom, the warmth of the body beside her. She could tell from his breathing that he was asleep, and she turned her head an imperceptible bit to stare at him, lying facedown in exhausted sleep. His eyes were swollen, his face gentle in sleep and looking younger than the thirty-six years Elyssa had attributed to him. The silky black hair was damp with sweat and plastered against his forehead, his strong back was rising and falling with the rhythm of his breathing. She could smell the brandy that she had tasted on his mouth—he would sleep very soundly for a good long time.

Slowly, carefully she rose on one elbow. She should go back to her room, escape from this monumental error in a line of endless stupid mistakes. But he'd told her he needed her, he'd begged her to stay with him. And she, poor fool, took the excuse with an open heart just waiting to be smashed.

Might as well be hanged for a sheep as well as a lamb, she thought sleepily. It was bad enough she had gone to bed with him so readily—it could hardly matter that she stayed. Leaning over, she gently kissed the strand of silky dark hair away from his forehead. She had a curious sense of déjà vu—how many times had she kissed Matthew's forehead with the silky dark strands? She moved her mouth down to kiss his, lightly tasting his lips. He stirred for a moment, and she told herself he didn't know where he was, who he was with. Nevertheless, when he reached out a strong arm and pulled her next to his sleeping body, she went with no resistance at all.

## Chapter Twenty-two

Jessica could hear him in the shower, the steady pounding of the water on his body, the muffled thump and knock as he moved in the enclosed stall that was far too small for his lanky body. She opened her eyes cautiously, staring about her with a kind of reluctant curiosity. The sun was up, but just barely, and she was lying in a huddle beneath a pile of blankets, her body aching in places she hadn't even known existed. She could see the mute testimony of the night before, the trail of clothes from the door to the bed, the bed covers half on the floor and half covering her, the pillows every which way. She should sneak back to her bedroom while she had the chance. What in hell was she going to say to Springer when he came back in?

She had just pushed the bedclothes back when she heard the shower stop, and quickly she dived back under the tangle of sheets, pulling them over her head and feigning sleep. A moment later she heard his footsteps in the room, felt his eyes watching her rumpled form. She held her breath, waiting for him to leave. The bed sank beneath his weight, and she had no choice. She opened her eyes again, to meet his steady gaze.

He was sitting at the edge of the bed, dressed in an old pair of jeans and nothing else, and his silky black hair was still wet from the shower. He hadn't shaved yet, and the dark eyes looked bloodshot and slightly swollen. He watched her gravely, no smile on his face, no clue in those dark eyes as to what he was thinking.

He reached out a hand, gently brushing her exposed arm, and she flinched. "You've got a hell of a bruise," he said, and his voice came out slightly rusty.

The purplish mark wasn't the only sign of the night's ceaseless activities. Springer had been like a man possessed—insatiable, determined to lose himself again and again in her welcoming body, equally determined to bring her with him. Jessica no longer knew how many times they had made love, how many ways. It was all a welter of dreamlike pleasure that didn't seem quite real in the shadowy prelight of dawn. Not with him watching her so somberly.

"I've got pale skin," she said, matching his soft tone, as she pulled herself into a sitting position, the sheet still covering the multitude of her post-pregnancy body. "I bruise very easily. All you have to do is breathe on me and I turn purple."

He couldn't resist it. Slowly he leaned forward, so that his face was barely an inch away from her startled one, slowly he let his breath out, the soft, moist air bating her lips, tasting of peppermint toothpaste. And then his lips brushed hers, gently, wonderingly, for far too brief a moment before he pulled back to survey her with a clinical air. "Not purple," he said. "But a delicious shade of pink."

She'd caught her breath at his sudden kiss, and she sat there, the sheet pulled up to her neck, staring at him bemusedly. A tiny smile pulled at the corners of his mouth. "You don't really need that sheet," he murmured. "Not after last night." He reached out to give it a tiny tug, but she held fast, still staring at him wonderingly.

"I'm cold," she said stubbornly, drawing her knees up.

"It's at least seventy-five already, Jessie. It's going to be a very hot day," he said gently. A shadow crossed his already haunted face. "I didn't hurt you, did I?"

*Yes, you hurt me,* she thought. *You've torn out my heart, trampled all over it, and I don't think I'm ever going to feel whole again.* Smiling slightly, she shook her head. "I'm fine."

He didn't look convinced. "We need to talk, Jessie."

"If you want." It was an irresistibly dangerous idea, but then, when had she been cautious where Springer was concerned? She could always run away if things got too close for comfort.

"Look, I've got a million things to do. I have to talk to...to my father's lawyer about his will. I'm executor, and I don't have the slightest idea what's in it. Probably bequests to all his boyfriends." There was a mocking note to his voice, but a light one, no longer condemning. "That'll keep me busy this morning, and I really need to talk to my mother. I've been so angry with her, for keeping his condition from me, that I haven't been able to give her any of the comfort she needs. You've done all that, and I'm grateful, but it's about time I faced up to things."

"She'd like that," Jessica said gently, still holding on to her knees.

His hands caught hers, prying them from their clinging grip and holding them, his long fingers kneading the rigid muscles. "And then we could go out for dinner. Some place quiet, and small, where we could talk. Would you do that for me?" That voice of his was seducing her all over again. With most of her New York defenses gone, she was helpless to resist him, and she found herself smiling dazedly up at him.

"Yes," she promised rashly, and meant it. "Yes."

It was a strange morning for her. For the first time in years, in decades, perhaps, Jessica allowed herself to hope. She was going to risk it tonight, she was going to open herself up to Springer MacDowell and see what happened. They needed to talk, he said, and he was right. If they could even begin to communicate as well with words as they did with their bodies, then there was more than a chance that they might . . . they might . . .

She didn't allow her fantasies to go any further. Half of her wanted to run away back to Vermont before her world could come crashing down around her, half of her wanted to push him away before he could reject her. But she stayed, keeping Elyssa company, talking with gentle fondness about Ham and his foibles, while they waited for Springer to return from the lawyer's office.

"Springer looked better this morning," Elyssa observed from her perch on the sofa. She herself looked a marvel of calm acceptance. But then, she'd had more than enough time to prepare herself for the inevitable—she'd spent the past six months grieving.

"You saw him before he went out?"

"He stopped in on his way downtown," Elyssa replied. "We talked for just a bit—I think he might find it possible to forgive me not telling him about Ham sooner. I wanted to, but it was terribly important to Ham not to play on Springer's guilt."

"And instead he added to it," Jessica said in a low voice.

Elyssa's fine dark eyes met hers for a pregnant moment. "I'm afraid he did." She sighed. "But I think Springer can handle it. He looked like holy hell this morning: bloodshot eyes, shaking hands, circles under his eyes. He looked like he'd been on a three-day drunk."

"And you think that was looking better?" Jessie questioned curiously.

"I do. Yesterday and the days before he had everything bottled up inside. Somehow he was able to release it last night, and once he starts to let it out he'll be able to deal with it. He always had trouble accepting the fact that he still loved Ham, despite everything."

"What was everything?"

Elyssa hesitated. "I suppose you may as well know. We never talked much about it, and perhaps that was wrong. Springer came home from school one day when he was fifteen and found his father on the couch with one of his friends."

"Oh, no." A sudden, horrifying flash of memory streaked through Jessica's mind like a bolt of lightning—a couch in a middle-class living room in Minnesota, rough, horrible hands pawing, pawing... "No," she said again, banishing the image.

"Yes. He knew about his friend. But he didn't know about his father."

"Did you?"

"Hamilton had always been completely honest with me. I was only seventeen when I married him, naive and very much in love. He told me about himself, and he tried very hard to change. But he simply couldn't, no matter how much he loved both me and Springer. I could accept that, Springer couldn't. But I couldn't accept how much he'd hurt Springer. I think subconsciously he knew Springer would come home that day and find them, had set it up on purpose. He just couldn't cope with living a lie anymore. But it couldn't have happened at a worse time for Springer, just when he was becoming a man."

"What happened?"

"Oh, I left Hamilton, of course. I really had no choice. In the sixties, arrangements such as Ham's and mine only worked if they were kept secret. And Springer was completely out of control. He had worshiped his father, you see, and he felt betrayed in the most elemental way." Elyssa leaned back, her eyes distant. "We tried sharing custody for a while, but that didn't work. At first Springer would refuse to go, and then every time he had to spend the weekend he'd bring a girl and make love to her on that damned sofa, making sure Ham would know what he was doing. I hated that sofa."

"You aren't sitting on it, are you?" Jessica couldn't help but ask, and Elyssa managed a wry smile.

"Thank goodness, no. I talked Ham into throwing it out years ago. I have no idea whether this one has seen any illicit sex, and I don't really care. Nor, do I think, does Springer anymore." She sighed. "Maybe now he'll finally learn to let go of the pain and grief his father caused him. If he can admit he loved him, even as he hated him, then there's hope for him. If he can't, I don't know if he'll ever be able to make any kind of commitment to anybody. And that's such a lonely, wasted life."

"Yes, it can be," Jessica said noncommittally.

Elyssa looked up sharply. "Did you love your father, Jessie? How did you deal with your parents' deaths?"

"Of course I loved my father," she said instinctively. "And I don't remember much about their deaths—it was so long ago."

"How long?" Elyssa persisted.

"Many years ago. I don't really want to talk about it, Elyssa. I've dealt with it, it's over."

"How long did it take you to come to terms with it?"

Jessica closed her eyes as the tension washed over her. Slowly she unclenched her hands, opening her blue eyes to meet Elyssa's troubled dark ones. "I'd say about thirty-two years," she said roughly.

Elyssa was very still. "I'm sorry, Jessie."

Jessica was proud of herself; she managed a shaky smile. "I'm sorry, too. Don't worry about Springer, Elyssa. He'll make it. He's tough, and he doesn't hide from things the way I do. He's going to be fine."

"So are you, you know," Elyssa said gently.

"I know," she said. She stretched, barely swallowing

the exhausted yawn that convulsed her body. "I'm tired."

"You look it. You don't look as if you got any more sleep than Springer did." Elyssa watched with complete fascination as Jessica turned a deep crimson. "That's the curse of pale skin," she observed. "You blush so easily."

"I wasn't blushing, Lyss, I was just..."

Her words trailed off as they heard the slam of the front door. He didn't bother with the myriad of locks and double locks, didn't pause as he headed unerringly for the living room. Jessica sat motionless in her chair, watching him out of stricken eyes.

She had hoped he'd never look like that again. His eyes were black with rage, his face pale, his entire body vibrating in barely controlled fury. He threw down the blue-backed sheaves of paper that had to be Hamilton's will, ignoring his mother's shocked witness.

"Who the hell," he demanded thickly, "is Matthew Decker Hansen?"

# Chapter Twenty-three

**The Slaughterer, vol. 90: The Death of Rocco**

*Matt Decker surveyed the carnage around him. The great Rocco had finally been brought down in a spray of bullets from his trusty Lambretta. Decker had stitched a row of blood around the room, impartial in his justice-dealing. The two lovers were entwined in the corner, rigid in death, and Decker casually slipped the still smoking Lambretta into his sharkskin pants, flinching as the hot metal touched his skin. His job was done for the day. Rocco dead, the two lovers following him to the hell where Decker decided he belonged.*

*It felt good to have the job finished, he thought, picking his way over the corpse-littered Brasilia street. He wondered where he'd be called next.*

JESSICA COULD NEVER THINK BACK to that moment without a shudder of pure horror. She had sat there, motionless, dumb, staring up at Springer out of stricken eyes, unable to say a word.

It had been Elyssa who'd saved the situation, if saving it was. "That's Jessie's son," she'd said calmly. "And I'd like to know what's put you in such a temper? Sit down and have some tea and tell us about the will. And how did you happen to hear about Matthew?"

Springer didn't move from his stance by the door, and Jessica couldn't bring herself to look anywhere but just beyond his left shoulder. "I came across Matthew in the will, of course," he snapped, "Who's his father?"

Still Jessica said nothing. Elyssa cast her a sympathetic look before answering for her. "Peter Kinsey, of course. Though what right do you have, cross-examining Jessie about her life?"

"Why didn't you marry him, then?" The words came out like Matt Decker's bullets, and Jessica flinched.

This was one Elyssa couldn't answer. "I didn't want to," Jessica said finally. "And he didn't want to marry me."

"Does he support his son?"

"None of your damned business." She did look at him then, anger banishing the last of her panic. "It doesn't have a thing to do with you."

"No? I was just curious why my father would leave the Vermont house and a trust fund of a hundred thousand dollars to Peter Kinsey's son when the Kinseys have more money than *The Slaughterer* ever brought in."

Jessica just looked at him, speechless with shock.

"I wouldn't be so sure— *The Slaughterer* has been very profitable," Elyssa murmured. "But how marvelous for you, Jessica. I'm so glad Hamilton did that. He mentioned he was going to do something, but I hadn't realized—

"Why the Vermont house?" Springer intruded.

"Because that's where Jessica and Matthew have been living during the past year. Surely you don't begrudge them the Vermont house—you haven't been back since you were in your early twenties."

"I had my reasons," Springer snapped, still staring at Jessica as if she were a slimy thing just crawled out from under a rock, she thought. "Would you leave us alone, Mother? I think Jessie and I need to talk."

Elyssa caught the small, imperceptible shake of Jessica's head. "I don't think so, darling. Jessie doesn't need to be subjected to your temper without some protection. Anything you have to say to her you can say in front of me."

He cast his mother an exasperated look before turning the full force of that black glare on the unflinching Jessica. "Are you sure it's Peter Kinsey's child?" he demanded harshly. "And not mine?"

Elyssa sucked in her breath sharply but said nothing, waiting for Jessica's reply. She took her time, opening her blue eyes wide, staring up at him in complete earnestness. "It's not your child, Springer," she said. "It's Peter's." And the wonder of it was, she had even managed to half-convince herself. Enough so that she could look at him quite fearlessly.

He stared at her for a long, searching moment. "All right," he said finally, the rage draining away from him, leaving only a cool, exhausted calm as he crossed the room and sank into a chair, as far away from Jessica as possible. "I believe you."

*So easy,* she thought distantly. And so quickly did everything come tumbling down. She was so caught up in trying to assimilate those two facts that she didn't hear what he said next.

"I beg your pardon?"

"I said I want you to sell me the Vermont house. You can name your price, as long as it's reasonably close to fair market value."

"I don't want to sell it. And if it's left to Matthew I don't know if I could, legally."

"You're his mother, aren't you? His parents have legal ownership in trust for him—they can do what they please." His attractive mouth curled in an unattractive sneer. "I don't fancy Peter Kinsey having half ownership of the Vermont house, even in trust for his son."

"Listen, Springer, Jessie's in no shape to argue about that, nor am I, for that matter. Your father's scarcely been dead twenty-four hours, and even if you don't give a damn, the two of us are having a difficult time adjusting." Elyssa's voice was low and very angry.

Slowly Springer turned to her, all that naked pain in his dark face terrible to look at. "I gave a damn," he said, and without another word he rose and left the room.

"Dear God in heaven," said Elyssa, stricken. "Why did I say that? How could I have thought that?"

Jessica moved then, putting a comforting arm around her slender shoulders. "He won't hold it against you, Lyss. He's hurting just as much as you are; maybe more. You'll both just have to give it time."

"I know." Elyssa sighed, leaning her silver head against Jessica. "Jessie, Matthew isn't Springer's, is he? You would tell him, wouldn't you?"

"Of course," Jessica said, meaning every word of it. "He'd have the right to know."

"But Peter's never said anything—"

"You didn't ask him, did you?" The slight edge of panic in her voice was indiscernible.

"Of course not. But we've talked about you several times, and he's mentioned how he and his wife hope to start a family right away. I'm just surprised he's never mentioned Matthew."

"It's part...part of our arrangement, Elyssa." She stumbled over the lie, part of her self-imposed fantasy shredding beneath the weight of her falsehoods. "Elyssa, I've got to go."

"Back to Vermont?" At Jessica's urgent nod she sighed. "I understand, darling. Springer hasn't been at his most charming, I'm afraid. I've been so glad to have you with me, but I realize you have to get back to Matthew. I'll miss you, though."

"You will be all right?"

"Of course. I've been dealing with this for a long time—it's nothing new or unexpected. It will take time. As soon as Springer calms down I'll let you know what's going on with the will."

"Are you certain you don't mind about the house?"

"Not a bit. I couldn't be happier. I just hope Springer can be more reasonable—you don't need any added unpleasantness. I'd forgotten how attached he was to that old place." She shook her head. "And you've got a *Slaughterer* to finish, haven't you?"

"But—"

"Don't worry about it, darling—the public won't know whether it was completed before or after Ham's death. At some point we need to have a talk with Ham's publisher about the future. He's suggested *The Slaughterer* might continue anyway. But that would depend on you, I think. I wouldn't want Johnson to take it over." She gave a little shudder of dislike.

"We'll see. Why don't you come back with me, Elyssa? Vermont is so beautiful in July—no mud, no black flies, no snow. It would do you a world of good, and you could meet your godchild."

"Not yet, Jessica. But soon. Very soon."

"I'll hold you to it," she said firmly, ignoring her son's silky black hair and dark brown eyes that bore no resemblance at all to Peter Kinsey's blue-eyed, brown-haired charm.

"I'll be there."


NEWARK AIRPORT WAS OLD and seedy and depressing, almost as bad as the Port Authority Bus Terminal, Jessica thought as she slumped back in the curved orange plastic chair. Having the plane be an hour and ten minutes late didn't help matters, nor did the sticky seat of the chair. Some enterprising munchkin must have spilled soda all over it. She could always stand, but there were too many shifty-eyed weirdos ready to accost her. Pananoia came back instantly the moment she left Vermont, she thought ruefully, and compounded with interest each day she was away.

There'd been no sign of Springer when she'd left the town house. She hated leaving Elyssa alone in the house so soon after Ham's death, but her sanity depended on it. One more dark, accusing look from Springer and her determination would sink. One more touch and she'd be lost. She had to get as far away from him, as fast as she could. She knew that full well. So why was it so damned hard?

Things would have been so much easier if it hadn't been for last night. Springer had been distant, removed, a perfect stranger, and Jessica could easily forget the slender, steellike strands that bound them. But he had touched her, and she had emerged from the dark steamy night changed in some imperceptible but life-shaking way. And there was nothing she could do about it but sit here and wait for her plane and mourn for what should have been.


"WHERE'S JESSIE?" Springer was standing in the hallway, dressed in a jacket that had seen better days, his overnight bag at his feet.

"You're leaving?" Elyssa's pale face crumpled in sudden vulnerability, and some of his anger faded. After all, he wasn't really angry at her, he reasoned. She couldn't help it if Ham had decreed he wasn't to be told about his condition, she couldn't help it if Jessie was a cold, lying, scheming bitch.

Moving across the hall, he put his arms around his mother's slender figure, holding her carefully, as if she might break. "I'm just flying out to get Katherine," he said gently. "I'll be back tomorrow morning at the latest. I've already called Maureen and told her to have her ready."

"Springer, are you sure?" Elyssa questioned against the warm comfort of his ancient tweed sport jacket. "There's nothing that would make me happier—it's been so long since I've seen her. But this isn't a happy time—"

"I think she should be at her grandfather's funeral," he said somberly, his tone of voice not leaving it open for discussion.

"If you really think so," she murmured. "I would dearly love to see her, you know that. Springer, you weren't angry about Matthew because Ham didn't provide for his own grandchild, were you?"

Slowly he detached himself, giving her a reassuring little squeeze. "Ham's provided very handsomely for Katherine, Mother. Everything in the will is as you expected, with the exception of Jessie's son." Why did it cause him so much trouble to say that? Why did he resent some poor, distant child with an almost white-hot hatred? He shook himself. "I left a copy of the will in your bedroom. You and Jessie can go over it tonight while I'm gone, and if you have any questions we can ask Dad's—" his voice cracked slightly "—lawyer about it."

"That's the first time you haven't called him Ham in twenty years," Elyssa said softly.

His eyes met hers, matching dark, sorrow-filled eyes, for a long, understanding moment. "So it is. You'll be all right? Jessie will keep you company."

"Jessie's gone, Springer."

"Gone? Where?"

"Back to Vermont."

"Why the hell did she do that?"

"She has a son, Springer, and a life to live. And after your behavior—"

"Screw my behavior," he said savagely. "She ran away again. I'll call Maureen and see if she can put Katherine on a plane by herself."

"Don't be ridiculous—a twelve-year-old on crutches

can't manage without you. I'll be just fine. Jessie wouldn't have gone if she weren't convinced that I'd be okay."

"She probably thought I'd still be here."

"And she still thought I'd survive," Elyssa said with a wry smile. "I promise you, Springer, I'll be fine. Go and get your daughter."

He couldn't hesitate any longer—he was cutting the time close as it was. "All right. But when I get back, when everything's taken care of, I'm going after Miss Jessica Hansen and find out exactly what's going on."

Elyssa smiled. "I think that might be a very good idea."

THE DISTANT VOICE finally called her plane. Slowly Jessica rose, her muscles cramping, her fingers sticking to the edges of the orange plastic seat. In less than two hours she'd be home, back with Matthew, back in the secure fastness of the house by the lake. The house that now belonged to Matthew, according to Springer's terse words. The thought of that security should have made her smile.

But nothing could make her smile right then. Her body ached with the memory of Springer's, her heart ached with the memory of his anger. She had to put him out of her mind, out of her life. He'd certainly looked as if he never wanted to see her again. If she could count on that, maybe she could get on with her life. And maybe pigs could fly.

## Chapter Twenty-four

"I wish you'd cheer up," Marianne said, irritation almost hiding her real concern. "I don't think you've laughed more than once in the past month."

"You're wrong. I laugh every time I see you ducking out of Andrew Cameron's way," Jessie shot back lazily. They were stretched out on the floor of the wraparound porch on what Jessica persisted in thinking of as the MacDowell house, Matthew was dozing in his rush basket in the shade, and the hot July sun was beating down. "You can't run forever."

"Some friend," Marianne responded without a trace of rancor. "Leave my love life alone."

"Love life?" Jessica echoed, sitting up straight and pulling the hot mane of blond hair off her neck. "I didn't know it was a love life. Things must have improved when I wasn't around. When did it become a love life? Last time Andrew came by to give me a banjo lesson you snuck out the back. Have matters improved?"

"It isn't a love life, matters haven't improved, and why don't you mind your own business?"

"When have I ever? There isn't much to do up here but gossip. *The Slaughterer* isn't going at all well, Matthew takes too many naps, the garden hasn't got a single weed in it, and my fingers are raw from playing. I'm ready for you to pour out your heart to me."

"Aunt Jessie's advice to the lovelorn."

"There's that word again."

"Love has nothing to do with it," Marianne said with a sigh. "Andrew Cameron is a very charming, very short, very young man, and I am not in the mood for any man at all."

"That's an improvement. When did you decide he was very charming?"

"You know, you'll look back on the day when Matthew napped so much with nostalgia," Marianne firmly changed the subject. "Just because you're bored right now and want to play with him... You wait till he's teething and nothing will make him take a nap."

"I'm looking forward to it. When did you decide Andrew was charming?"

"What's wrong with the Slaughterer? I thought he was blazing his bloody way through South American jungles right now."

A wry smile lit Jessica's lightly tanned face. "That's what he was doing. Unfortunately he keeps getting sidetracked by his lady friend."

"I didn't know he had a lady friend," Marianne said lazily, taking a deep swig of the Coke beside her.

"He didn't pay much attention to her in earlier volumes, but I built her up. She's a Swedish Valkyrie working for law and order and she has almost as many guns as he has. He calls her his warrior woman."

"Oh, barf."

Jessica laughed. "I enjoy writing the sex a lot more than the killing. There are only so many ways you can describe someone getting his head blown off."

"I don't know, you've been pretty inventive so far. Anyway, I think there's room for more sex in the new one. I liked what you gave me to read so far. What a luscious man. Those long, long legs, that silky black hair and dark, fathomless eyes. You could just drown in them. I wouldn't kick him out of bed for eating crackers."

Jessica was looking at her friend with an expression of absolute horror on her face. "Is that the way I described him?"

"Sure. He sounded heavenly. Now if he were to show up I might not run as hard as I have been from Cameron."

"Oh, yes, you would," Jessica said grimly. "Damn."

"What's wrong?"

"Matt Decker is less than six feet tall, has short brown hair and gunmetal gray eyes."

"Then who did you describe?" A sudden grin lit Marianne's face. "Sounds like it could have been Matthew's father. No wonder you want him to have more sex with his Scandinavian cutie."

"I'll tell you what, Marianne. I won't hassle you about Andrew and you can drop this subject immediately."

"I don't know." Marianne giggled. "I like seeing you so flustered. What's the real Matt Decker like?"

"You know I'm capable of revenge. After Andrew leaves today I'll tell him you want to see him."

Marianne jumped up like a shot. "Andrew's coming today. Why didn't you warn me?"

"I agree with you, I need more laughs in my life," Jessica said lazily. "And I think I hear him coming now."

Marianne looked like a trapped rabbit, her tall, robust body vibrating in sudden panic. And then her shoulders relaxed beneath the thin cotton shirt. "Not unless he suddenly parted with some of his hard-earned cash. That's no aging Valiant tooling up the road. I'd guess it was a Peugot or a BMW."

"Mercedes," Jessie hazarded, before a sudden panic filled her that more than equaled Marianne's earlier tension. Before she could move, the car purred into view, and she leaned back against the house in sudden relief. It was a Mercedes, but the dark-haired man driving bore no resemblance at all to Springer MacDowell, or to the most recent incarnation of the Slaughterer.

"Oh, God." Marianne's voice was numb with pain as she watched the car. It pulled to a stop in front of the house, and a man climbed out. One of the handsomest men Jessica had ever seen, she thought distantly. A little too handsome, with clothes just a bit too perfect. He was smiling, a dazzling smile showing far too many teeth, eyes flashing, sure of his welcome.

"Marianne," he breathed, his voice just a little too high-pitched, and he enveloped Marianne's unyielding figure in his arms.

Jessica watched with unabashed fascination as her friend withstood the embrace of the handsome man, waited until he finally released her. "Marianne, you look magnificent," he said, smiling down at her with every ounce of his not-inconsiderable charm. "I remember that old shirt of mine."

Marianne looked as if she might explode, though whether from anger or something else Jessica couldn't quite fathom. She did, however, decide it was time for her to make her move.

Rising from the porch, she moved forward with her usual unconscious grace. The flashing eyes shifted to her, warming with a casual come-on that she hadn't seen since she'd lived in New York. She set a smile on her face with great effort, coming to stand beside the silent Marianne.

"I'm Jessica Hansen," she greeted him, holding out her slim, strong hand. He caught it, his thumb caressing her palm slightly, and it was all she could do not to snatch her hand away.

"Tom Trainor," he replied, widening that smile of his. "Marianne must have told you about me."

"No," Jessica said. "She didn't." She felt rather than saw Marianne smile at that, and felt relieved. If Marianne was glad to have this lightweight back, she was not the woman she thought her.

"What do you want, Tom?" Her voice banished any lingering doubts. It was more than obvious that Tom Trainor was the last person Marianne wanted to see.

"Why, to see you and the kids, of course." He cast a last, lingering glance at Jessica's reserved countenance, and she could see why Marianne disliked him.

"That's all?" Marianne's voice was cold and suspicious. "Would you like to talk about child support payments that you've missed? Not to mention alimony."

"Yes, let's not mention alimony," he said with a

feeble attempt at a joke. "Look, Marianne, we don't need to air our dirty linen in front of an audience. Why don't we go back to the house and discuss this amicably?"

"Discuss what?"

He hesitated, and the too-handsome face was shifty. "Custody," he said finally, when Marianne made no effort to move.

"Custody!" The word was a shriek. "Who the hell do you think you are, coming here—"

"Now, Marianne, don't get all emotional. We have to deal with this logically. Surely you can't believe your children are having the best possible upbringing in this cultural backwater? If they lived with Barbara and me in Connecticut, they could go to the best schools, have a thousand opportunities—"

"You brought us to this cultural backwater, Thomas," she said icily. "And we're doing just fine, thank you. We don't need Connecticut, we don't need Barbara, and we don't need you."

"I hate to mention this, darling, but I'm a lawyer. I don't think, if this comes to court, that you're going to have much luck. There's no need to make this unpleasant. Be reasonable, Marianne, the children need a father."

"Why are you doing this?" she whispered, her fine brown eyes stricken.

"We want children. The house in Connecticut is too big for the both of us, and we want to start a family."

"Then let Barbara get pregnant."

"She can't." The brief words struck horror into

Marianne's heart. There was no escape. When Tom wanted something, he could be devious, dishonest and impossibly stubborn. And sooner or later, by hook or most probably by crook, he would get his own way, and she would be helpless to stop him.

"You can't have them, Tom."

He took a deep breath, a glint of meanness making his eyes look small and ugly. "We'll talk about it."

"You can go to hell."

"Swearing won't help matters. We need to discuss this like rational human beings—"

"I don't feel like a rational human being!" Marianne cried. "You're trying to steal my babies."

"Oh, for heaven's sake, Marianne." The charm was slipping fast. "At least come back to the house and talk to me."

Marianne shook her head furiously, and Jessica put a restraining hand on her arm. The muscles were knotted in tension beneath the cool cotton shirt. "Why don't you at least talk with him, Marianne? Hear him out, and then tell him to go to hell. I'll watch the kids for you while you do."

"Thank you, Jessica." Tom tried to summon forth his charm once more. "I appreciate your assistance."

"Go to hell," she said calmly.

"I'll keep the kids with me, Jessie," Marianne said quietly, her anger momentarily abated. "They should at least see their father." She moved down the steps. "Come on, Tom. The sooner we get this over with the better. We'll pick up the kids at Mrs. LaPlante's."

"They're not here with you?" he echoed in horror.

"No, they're not," she snapped. "This is Sunday. I just spent the last eight hours in Burlington, working the early shift at the hospital. Mrs. LaPlante takes care of them during that time."

"You see? What kind of life is that for them?" he said plaintively.

"Barbara plans to quit her practice?" Marianne snapped.

"Of course not. But we can provide live-in help, with much better continuity than some local Vermont farm wife—"

"Let's go, Tom, before I strangle you," she snapped. "The kids and I will be back for supper, Jessie. Thanks for asking us."

"Does that invitation include me?" Tom said wistfully, trying out his smile one last time.

"No," said Jessica.

He muttered a curse as he climbed back in the Mercedes. Marianne exchanged a meaningful nod with Jessica before she climbed in beside him, and they roared off down the bumpy road, Tom taking his frustration out in his driving.

Jessica had complete faith in Marianne. Despite the stricken look on her face when he'd first appeared, she'd be more than a match for any man. Especially one like Tom Trainor.

The sudden whimpering snapped her attention back to the porch, and she went to her waking child with a relieved smile. Now she could happily spend the afternoon counting fingers and toes, and try to keep her mind off Marianne's predicament. "I'm coming, angel," she murmured, climbing up the porch steps.

"YOU MEAN TO TELL ME you let her go off with that creature?" Andrew Cameron demanded, his wiry body rigid with anger.

It was just after seven, and there was no sign of Marianne. The two of them were sitting on the front porch of the MacDowell house, the crystal-clear lake shimmering in the early-evening sun. Andrew's presence was a well-planned surprise, but there was no Marianne to be surprised. She hadn't shown up, she hadn't called, and it was only after an hour of nervous chitchat that Jessica finally broke down and confided in Cameron.

"Of course I did. What could I do, tell her no, she couldn't go off with her ex-husband? The man was threatening to take her children away—she had to at least reason with him."

"That bastard. What possible right does he think he has to take the children? She's the best mother I know—present company excluded, of course," he added quickly. "He'll get nowhere with that kind of threat."

"I don't know. He's a lawyer, you know. He'd have more clout if it went to court. And Marianne was looking scared."

"Marianne?" Andrew echoed. "My Marianne, my lioness, looking scared? I don't believe it. A two-ton tank wouldn't scare her."

"Well, Tom's threat did, or I miss my guess." She leaned over to coo at the placidly smiling Matthew. "I'm worried, Andrew."

"So am I, Jessie," he said grimly, setting his gin and tonic down with a snap. "I'm going down there."

"Do you think you should?"

"Do you think I shouldn't? Do you want to wait for hours more, wondering what's happened?" he countered sternly.

"No. But what if they've decided to reconcile, and they're—" The look on Andrew's face cut that particular guess short. "No, they wouldn't do that. Marianne looked too angry and too scared."

"Unless she thought she could save the children by going to bed with him," he said morosely. "I'll kill the bastard."

Marianne and Tom were nowhere near bed, and nowhere near agreement, either. They were sitting at the kitchen table, a table he'd sniffed at disdainfully, just as he'd sneered at the house he'd bought for them two short years ago. After his initial fuss he was ignoring the children, and both Eric and Shannon sat in a corner by the old black-and-white television set, trying to summon forth interest in a rerun game show, every now and then casting worried glances at their arguing parents.

"You can't have them, Tom," she said fiercely. "How many times do I have to tell you that? You just want them for a new toy and I know your attention span. You'll tire of them in a few months, and they'll see no one but your high-priced nanny."

"You always were selfish," Tom shot back. "Never seeing anyone's side but your own. These children need a man around, they need a secure home, not this rural squalor you've subjected them to."

"I've subjected them to?" Her voice rose in a shriek, and Eric's worried eyes, so heartbreakingly like

Tom's, looked over at them, abandoning all pretense of watching "Family Feud." "You were the one who brought us here and left us."

"Well, I don't want to leave them anymore," he said sulkily. "Surely you can't be self-centered enough to deny your children the advantages we can offer them? You say you love them; a good mother is supposed to sacrifice her own needs for the sake of her children. You're doing a pretty poor job of it, let me tell you."

Marianne's shriek of pure rage was magnificent, but Shannon began to cry. She stood there, torn between hitting her ex-husband on the head with the cast-iron skillet that still had the remnants of yesterday's breakfast in it, or rushing to comfort her weeping daughter. Eric's eyes were filling with tears, and Tom glared at her.

"You've made them cry," he said nastily. "Aren't you going to do something about it?" He was sitttng in his chair, no longer the handsome, successful lawyer, looking old and mean and petty.

"Aren't you?" she countered, as Shannon's wails grew louder. "You're the one who wanted to take them away from me. How are you going to deal with their tears?"

"You're the one who's made them cry," he countered smugly, and Marianne reached for the frying pan.

Her hand stopped in midair as a new voice entered the fray, and she watched with amazement and wondering gratitude as Andrew Cameron stepped through her kitchen door, with all the assurance of a man who lived there, his small, wiry body arrogantly sure of his welcome. "What's going on here, woman?" he greeted her, his Scottish accent theatrically deeper as he glared at them impartially. Shannon immediately stopped crying, launching herself at Andrew with a squeal of delight, and Eric followed, clinging to him like a lifesaver in a world where adults had suddenly gone crazy.

Andrew fixed his dark green eyes on Tom's astounded face. "Carrying on behind my back, lassie?" he growled. "Who is this fancy creature, and what's he doing in my house?"

## Chapter Twenty-five

Dead silence reigned for a full minute.

"What the hell do you mean, your house?" Tom blustered, rising to his full six feet in a vain attempt at intimidating the shorter Andrew. "This is my house."

"The hell it is!" Marianne had finally gathered her scattered wits.

"I presume this overblown braggart is your ex-husband," Andrew observed. "What's he doing here?"

Marianne chose the lesser of two evils. "He's trying to steal my babies, Cameron," she cried fiercely. "I don't know why—he's never shown much interest in them before."

Andrew shifted Shannon's clinging body closer, running a casually reassuring hand through Eric's tangled mop of hair. "And why would you be wanting to do that, Trainor?" he inquired in a quiet tone of voice that was all the more intimidating in its subdued quality. Marianne watched with absolute fascination as Tom seemed to shrink a tiny bit.

"They're my children, too," he blustered. "Not that

it's any of your damned business. Who the hell are you and what are you doing in my wife's house?''

"Your ex-wife," Andrew corrected politely. "The name is Andrew Cameron. And since they're going to be my stepchildren, I consider it my business.''

Tom was too angry to notice Marianne's gasp of astonishment. "You and Marianne are getting married? Why wasn't I informed of it?''

"Did you expect to be invited to the wedding, man?" Andrew sneered, enjoying himself immensely.

"What about the alimony payments? Were the two of you just going to pocket them and live off me?''

"Considering that you haven't sent any alimony payments, or child-support payments, in the past three months, we didn't feel we had to be in any hurry to let you know," said Andrew, not missing Marianne's start of surprise at his unexpected knowledge. "On what grounds were you planning to take the children away?''

"He thought they needed a man's influence," Marianne broke in from her stance beside the kitchen counter.

"And you didn't tell him about us? Shame on you, lassie. Can't you see the man's concerned about his offspring?" Cameron's voice was heavy with sarcasm. "Let me promise you, Trainor, that I'll be a better father in a week than you've been their whole lives.''

"I don't like your tone of voice," Tom said, his voice an aggressive whine.

"And I don't like you at all," Andrew returned. "Why don't we go somewhere and discuss this, away from the children? They don't like to hear their parents argue. I think we can come to some sort of agreement." He moved across the room to Marianne's still body, gently detaching the clinging Shannon and placing her in her mother's arms. Eric went as docilely, casting a mistrustful glance up at his father's belligerent figure.

"What the hell do you think you're doing?" Marianne roused herself from her bemused state. "This is my family and my life you two are deciding." Tom was already at the door, just out of earshot, a warlike expression coarsening his handsome face.

Andrew reached a hand up and cradled her face gently, his thumb gently stroking her jaw. Her arms were caught up holding Shannon, and she couldn't push him away. She didn't want to push him away. "Let me do this for you, Marianne," he whispered, those forest-green eyes of his beseeching. Leaning forward, he kissed her full on the mouth, a short, gentle kiss that left her more disturbed than did all her rage at Tom.

She was barely aware of the door slamming shut behind him. She waited a moment for the sound of flesh thudding flesh, the muffled grunts and groans of Tom beating the smaller Andrew to a pulp. But only the sound of quiet, rational voices drifted through the screen door. Marianne sank into the wobbly kitchen chair, still holding Shannon, and pulled Eric against her with her free arm.

"I don't like him, Mama," Eric said quietly.

Marianne couldn't deny the sudden stricken feeling around her heart. "But you barely know Andrew, darling."

"I mean my father," he explained with all the patience of an eight-year-old. "I don't want to live with him, and neither does Shannon. We want to live with you and Andrew."

"Andrew and I don't live together, Eric."

"You should. We both like him a lot. We see him at Aunt Jessie's when you aren't around. He's much nicer than my father."

"Yes, he is," Marianne found herself agreeing. "Much nicer."

She could hear the sound of the light summer breeze in the pine trees overhead, the quiet slap of moths against the screen door as they dived for the light. The sun was setting—it was definitely past the children's bedtime, but Marianne was motionless at the table. They hadn't even eaten dinner, but none of them seemed disposed to move. They sat there, waiting for the victor to return and claim the spoils.

The sudden quiet purr of the Mercedes broke their abstraction. A moment later Andrew walked back in, a quiet determined expression on his narrow, clever face.

"Where's Tom?"

"Gone," he said shortly, taking the dozing Shannon out of her aching arms.

"Gone where?"

"Back to Connecticut. I'd be surprised if he bothered you again."

She pushed a weary hand through her tangled mane of chestnut hair. "How did you manage that? I threatened him with everything I could think of."

"You didn't realize what his problem was. He's short of money. That new wife of his is very expensive, and he can't afford to keep two households going. He

BANISH MISFORTUNE                265

thought he could save money by having the children
live with him."

"Damn his cheap soul to hell," Marianne said bit-
terly.

"I managed to placate him by telling him you didn't
need his money. I don't think you're going to see any
more child support from him, but it's a small enough
price to pay for having him leave you alone."

"A small enough price," she echoed, and to her fury
tears of emotional and physical exhaustion began slipping down her face. She hadn't cried in years, and the
last thing she wanted to do was cry in front of Andrew
Cameron.

"Don't worry, lassie," he said gently. "We'll be all
right."

"We?" she echoed with just a trace of hysteria.
"What's this 'we,' white man?"

"I beg your pardon?"

"Just an old joke." She was suddenly, dangerously,
acutely aware of him standing there, holding her child
in his strong arms, looking down at her with far too
much tenderness. "Do you...do you suppose you
could get Jessica and bring her back here?" she stam-
mered, hating herself for sounding so vulnerable. "I
don't really feel like being alone, and I know you have
things to do."

A trace of a smile lifted the corners of his green eyes.
"That I do. A great many things to do. Why don't you
take a long hot shower and I'll take the children with
me while I go fetch her? Get into something more
comfortable, have something to drink, and by the time
I bring Jessica back you'll feel like a new woman."

She felt perversely disappointed that he gave up so easily. "That would be wonderful," she said, sighing, "but I should feed them and put them down for the night."

"Jessica will take care of it. You go along now." He had withdrawn again, retreated from her. Just what she needed, she told herself dishearteningly. She didn't need some randy little Scot coming on to her after such a hellish day.

Marianne heard his ancient Valiant chug away from the house as she stepped into the claw-footed bathtub with its straggly circular shower curtain. Someday when she was rich she'd have a shower stall again, with a glass door and lots of hot water. In the meantime she had every intention of standing under the streaming jets until the water turned icy cold, washing away the miserable memory of her ex-husband. She scrubbed her long hair, her face, her body with a puritanical violence, knowing it would take Jessica close to an hour to get Matthew and all his accoutrements packed for the night.

When she finally felt clean, she stepped out of the shower and into a threadbare towel that had been one of her wedding presents. She rubbed till her tall, strong body was a bright pink, and for the first time since she was an adolescent she wished she were small and dainty.

"The hell with it," she said aloud, pulling on a faded pair of jeans and a soft, warm flannel shirt. Even in August, most Vermont nights were chilly, and that night was no exception. She'd need an extra blanket tonight. Thank goodness she'd gotten rid of that ostentatious king-sized bed she'd once shared with Tom. The old iron double bed had never held anyone but her and, on occasion, her children. She didn't need to be haunted by memories as she slept that night.

The comfortably ramshackle room that encompassed the kitchen, dining and living areas was looking even messier than usual, she realized as she tried to survey it through Tom's critical eyes. If she had more money she could have the lumpy sofa recovered, maybe buy a new rug instead of the threadbare fake Oriental she'd picked up at a rummage sale last year. Lord knows she tried to keep it clean, but an eight-year-old and a three-year-old were not conducive to neatness, and she had never been much cleaner herself. She should make more of an effort.

But not tonight. Tonight she was going to drink several very large glasses of cheap Italian wine, sit on the lumpy old sofa, and ignore the mess. She was going to sit there and feel sorry for herself while her children slept overhead and Jessica soothed her shattered feelings. And when she had drunk enough, she would stagger up to bed and fall into a deep, dreamless sleep, with no intrusive Scot disturbing her dreams, as he had so often in the past few months. She had been able to keep him out of her life when she was awake, but when she'd been asleep he'd proved damnably stubborn.

But not tonight. Tonight she was going to be alone in her bed without even an erotic dream to disturb her.

She was sitting on top of the kitchen table, already well into her second glass of Bardolino, when she heard the car pull up. It was the noisy rattle of the Valiant, and she sighed. She should have known he wouldn't just pass the message along and let Jessie get there under her own steam. Maybe he'd be perspicacious enough to drop Jessica off and keep on his way.

The sun had set while she was sitting on the sturdy old table, and the porch light glowed yellow against the darkness. She hadn't bothered with more than a couple of lights, and the resulting shadows made her tumbledown house look almost pretty in the dimness. The sweet, Christmassy scent of pine mingled with the smell of the wine, tickling her nostrils. She sat there, swinging her bare feet, trying to look nonchalant.

The sound of the single car door slamming should have warned her. She heard his footsteps on the sagging front porch, saw him silhouetted by the glow of the yellow light bulb. She watched him with a curious sense of fatality as he stepped into the house, his eyes never leaving hers, as he turned out the porch light and closed the warped door behind him.

"Where's Jessica?" Now why would her voice sound so strangled when she was asking such an obvious question? Andrew was moving slowly closer to her with a purposeful walk, and she allowed herself a moment to watch him. For such a small body it certainly was beautiful. His shoulders were just broad enough, his arms wiry with surprising strength, his waist flat and his narrow hips just about the most enticing thing she'd ever seen. His legs were lean and muscled in the old corduroys, and he had a disturbingly intent look on his usually stern face.

"Jessica's at home, where she belongs," he replied, coming up to her in the darkened kitchen, stopping only a foot away. Her perch on the kitchen table brought her even with him, even made her a tiny bit shorter. She should get to her feet, do her best to tower over him. She stayed put, taking another sip of the wine.

"Where are my children?"

"With Jessie. She said she'd be glad to take them for the night," he answered.

She shivered lightly. "No, Cameron."

"Yes, Marianne," he corrected her gently. "I've given you time and space, and you still run like a scared rabbit whenever I'm around. How you can be such a brave amazon with everyone else and be so frightened of me is more than I can fathom."

"I'm not frightened of you," she said defensively.

"You're not?" He moved closer then, his hips touching her knees. "I'm glad to hear it." His hands gently caught her shoulders, the long fingers kneading her strained muscles. His head moved closer, his mouth softly brushing hers with that tantalizing pressure that made her ache for more.

"Don't," she said miserably, and the sound came out in a husky whisper.

"Why not?" He kissed her again, just as lightly, enjoying the taste and feel of her.

"Because you're too young and too short," she cried.

"And you're full of crap," he said sweetly. "But if I don't mind, why should you?"

She sighed, dropping her forehead to his shoulder. "Cameron, I just can't," she tried one more time. "I don't need any more complications in my life."

"Woman," he said, and his arms slid around her, "I

plan to uncomplicate your life. I'm going to take you up to bed and make love to you until you can't come up with any more foolish objections. I never heard such a creature for arguing." Still his mouth teased, tantalized, cajoled.

She made one last attempt. "But I always wanted a man who could carry me up to bed," she wailed, grasping at straws.

A devilish smile lit his dour face. "Well, I could do it if I had to," he allowed, "but I might strain something. It would really make more sense if you carried me."

"You . . ." She opened her mouth in outrage, and he kissed her, deeply, completely, his tongue silencing her as his hands pulled her hips across the table to him.

He was very strong, she noticed distantly. And very aroused. And she began to shiver in his arms. "Take me to bed, my lioness," he whispered.

She smiled up at him through the haze of passion she could no longer fight. "Follow me, shorty."

The big room at the front of the house was dark, lit only by the fitful moonlight shining off the distant waters of the lake. Marianne reached for the light switch, then hesitated, her long fingers trembling in the shadows.

Andrew's warm, strong hand covered hers, stilling the tremors. He brought her fingers to his mouth, kissing them lightly, tasting them with slow, languorous delight. "You taste like wine, my amazon," he murmured against her skin, and she stood motionless, transfixed. "Wine and sunlight and pure, sweet flesh. Let me taste all of you." And slowly, so as not to frighten her, he pulled her into his arms, his mouth meeting hers in the moon-silvered darkness.

Everything had changed, Marianne thought dizzily, trying to cope with the twin rushes of panic and desire that were sweeping over her. This was no longer a stolen kiss in a kitchen, a half-serious flirtation that she could wriggle out of. They were alone, in her house, in her bedroom, with the summer night all around them and the sagging iron bed behind them. And Andrew's tongue was doing things to her mouth that both surprised and dazed her. She could feel the cool night air on her skin, and she realized belatedly that Andrew had unbuttoned the faded flannel shirt. And then his face was buried against her breasts, his breath hot and sweet and arousing against her sensitive skin. And the panic was rapidly fading beneath the determined onslaught of the man in front of her.

She found that her fingers were clutching his strong shoulders, digging in tightly as his tender mouth traveled the circumference of her breast. She should say something, warn him, slow him down....

"Andrew," she gasped, her fingers tightening in sudden fear. "You don't know what you're doing. You don't want..."

He lifted his head and looked at her clearly in the moonlight, and his green eyes were full of tender amusement. "Marianne, my sweet viper, I am twenty-nine years old. I assure you, I know very well what I'm doing, and just how to do it. And I know what I want, have known it since I caught you in my raspberry bushes last summer."

"I'm not the experienced woman you think," she protested.

"You mean you're a virgin?" There was a lilt of

laughter beneath the Scottish burr. "To be sure, after meeting that sorry specimen that used to be your husband, I'm not surprised, but Eric and Shannon are a pretty neat trick."

"That sorry specimen is the sum total of my sexual experience," she said with an attempt at sharpness that sounded far too much like a moan as his hands continued their wicked way with her soft, aching breasts. Andrew was taking this far too frivolously.

"Don't worry, lass," he whispered. "Rely on me to see to your advanced education." Before she realized what he was doing he'd scooped her up effortlessly in his strong arms and was carrying her across the room to the bed.

"Cameron, put me down! I'm too big—" Before the words were out of her mouth the bed was soft and warm against her back, and Andrew Cameron was above her, smiling down. "I thought you said you weren't strong enough to carry me," she said breathlessly. He was leaning above her, one strong hand slowly undoing the buttons of his shirt.

"I lied," he said.

She reached up, pushing his hand out of the way, taking over the task herself. His skin was sleek and hard and strong in the moonlight, and her hands trembled when they reached the waistband of his corduroys.

"You first," he said, slipping her jeans off her rounded hips and tossing them in the corner with his discarded shirt. She lay there naked before him, uncertain whether to blush or preen.

Andrew had no such doubts. "Marianne, you're the

most beautiful creature in God's creation. You're worth all you've put me through and more. I—"

She stopped his mouth with hers. She didn't want to hear the words she knew would come, wasn't ready for them.

And Andrew seemed to understand. He said nothing more to her, using his mouth in far more elemental ways, kissing, biting, arousing, thrusting, until she was arching into the bed with helpless delight as wave after wave of pleasure swept over her. Tom had never used his mouth on her the way Andrew had, though he'd graciously allowed her free rein with his body. But Andrew seemed to take inordinate pleasure in loving her, with his hands, his mouth, until she was writhing and trembling and desperate for more.

He slid up the bed to lie beside her, and she buried her face against his smooth, warm shoulder. "My turn, viper," he whispered, taking her hand and pressing it against him. He was still wearing the soft old corduroys, straining against them, and she undid them with trembling hands, releasing him from his confinement.

He'd warned her, of course. He'd told her women hadn't complained about his lack of size, but she'd thought he'd been teasing her. But he'd been nothing more than truthful. Andrew Cameron was a great deal more man than Tom Trainor, so much so that Marianne suddenly panicked.

He must have felt the tension race through her body. The moment he slipped out of the corduroys he pulled her back into his arms, his strong, rough-textured hands oddly soothing.

"Hush, my brave lioness," he whispered, though she hadn't said a word. "I promise you I won't hurt you. I'll never hurt you."

With gentle hands he rolled her over on her back, leaning over her, a dark, strong shadow in the moonlight. She tensed at the feel of him against her, but his hands and lips and words soothed her, eased her fears, as slowly, carefully, he filled her, coming to rest against her with a strangled sigh that proved his iron control was hard-won indeed.

She lay there beneath him, absorbing the feel, the size, the smell, the warmth of him, reveling in the utter delight of a possession that had no victor and no vanquished. Slowly experimentally, she tightened around him, and his eyelids fluttered open.

She raised her hips, nudging him into action, suddenly desperate for more. His dazed eyes filled with a blazing light, and then her momentary control was gone, shredded beneath the practiced, devilishly glorious heaven of his body.

She hadn't known it could be that way. She was sailing, blissfully awash with the sound and the smell and the feel and the sheer joy of Andrew Cameron pleasuring her body, willing it to go on forever, when suddenly she felt herself fly into a million pieces, shattering into stardust and scattered to the four winds. She heard her voice cry out, a small cry of pleasure so intense that it was pain, and then Andrew was with her, holding her, lost amid the same mystical glories that were beyond comprehension.

It seemed ages before their breathing slowed, before the tumultuous counterpoint of their hearts lessened their calamitous pounding. She felt him lift his head, could feel those dark Celtic eyes of his watching her in the moonlight. The tears would be plain on her face, and slowly, shyly, she opened her eyes.

"Are you all right, lass?" he whispered anxiously. "Did I hurt you?"

It was a faintly tremulous smile that she managed, and she knew her heart was in her eyes with no way of hiding it. "We lionesses are a tough lot," she whispered back. "Didn't you promise that you'd never hurt me? I take you at your word."

He smiled back, and there was no way she could avoid recognizing the look in his eyes—the look of love that no one but her children had ever shown her.

"You can trust me," he said, and it held a thousand different meanings.

"I trust you," she said. And for the moment she believed it.

## Chapter Twenty-six

**The Slaughterer, vol. 99: untitled**

*Matt Decker surveyed the carnage around him. He was back, ready to battle treachery and injustice with his own swift vengeance, determined to let no one stand in his way. Leaning down, he tucked the snub-nosed Model 36 Smith & Wesson into its specially designed ankle holster, then rose to his full height. There was a light breeze blowing, carrying the stench of death and war, and Decker ran a large, well-shaped hand through his silky black hair. His dark, unfathomable eyes narrowed as they looked right, then left, and his tall, wiry body was alert to every*

"DAMN IT!" Jessica ripped the paper out of the Selectric, wadded it in a ball and heaved it across the room to the distant wastebasket. It was a rim shot, dropping into the wicker basket after a tantalizing delay. "Two points," she murmured grumpily. "It figures."

*What the hell was Springer doing turning up as Matt Decker,* she demanded of life in general, leaning back in the uncomfortable dining-room chair and running a weary hand through her mane of wheat-blond hair. How had the macho Slaughterer, with his only average height, his massive shoulders, his marine haircut that disguised its color, and his gunmetal gray eyes turned into a tall, sinuous basketball player? The last thing she needed was Springer MacDowell invading her life, even in such a nebulous way.

Of course, she couldn't really blame herself. The August warmth was beckoning to her, the lake a shimmering blue over her shoulder. Her heart wasn't in the exploits of the Slaughterer right now. She refused to think where her heart really was.

But discipline was discipline, and she had to finish volume ninety-nine soon if she was going to continue to keep Matthew in Huggies and formula. Pushing away from the dining-room table that served as her workspace, she crossed the cavernous living room, keeping her eyes averted from the tantalizing lake, and rummaged through the stack of magazines by the woodbox. *Combat Handguns* was on the bottom, tucked away. With her usual reluctant grin she pulled it out, grimacing at the gun ads. Her subscription must have surprised Arlton down at the post office—she certainly wasn't the type to belong to the NRA. But the magazine had been invaluable in providing fictional guns for the bloodthirsty Decker, whose hardware was half of his charm, according to market surveys.

She wandered back to the table, thumbing through the magazine until she came to a promising picture. An ex-Green Beret, wanted for selling arms and bombs to right-wing terrorists—she couldn't tell whether the magazine approved or disapproved—stared back at her, his flinty gray eyes the color of the machine gun in one beefy hand. He wore a T-shirt with the legend "Kill 'em all, let God sort 'em out." "Matt Decker to the life," she murmured, propping the magazine up against the candlesticks and dropping back into the chair.

Matt Decker's namesake would probably sleep for another hour, maybe two. She had to get another ten pages done or she'd be in real trouble. Her fingers went to the keys, her eyes to the Green Beret's grim countenance, and the words went flying.

At least for two paragraphs—and then ground to a dead halt. She leaned back again, staring at the neat white paper with intense dislike. She never bothered with first drafts—in the case of the Slaughterer it was usually a waste of time. First instincts usually proved the best, no matter how ridiculous they seemed, and each page Jessica labored over was finished copy. She ended up with a lot of wasted twenty-pound bond, but it cost less than her time.

Maybe another cup of coffee. A nice, strong jolt of caffeine might get the old creative juices flowing, even though it would be her third. And food. There was a Sara Lee raspberry coffee cake in the freezer, some cold roast beef in the fridge. She'd eaten frozen coffee cake before—she'd do it again. Why hadn't she appreciated her lack of appetite when she had it, she thought with a sigh, heading for the freezer.

Marianne would be horrified if she saw Jessica devouring frozen coffee cake. But then, Marianne was too preoccupied right now to pay much attention to anyone else's moral lapses. Having come at nine that morning to pick up the children, she had arrived breathless, flushed, happy and nervous. She had chattered on and on, refusing to meet Jessica's eyes as she drank a cup of coffee, not realizing it contained the despised white sugar until she'd almost finished it.

"Where's Andrew?" Jessica had asked lazily, unable to resist the temptation to needle her.

Marianne had almost dropped the thick earthenware mug. "How should I know?" she shot back with a trace of her usual belligerence.

Jessica wasn't to be put off. "Didn't you see him this morning?" she queried gently.

A woebegone look shadowed Marianne's freckled face. "No," she said in a small voice.

"He'd left by the time you woke up?" Jessica persisted, knowing it was none of her business, knowing she should leave it up to Marianne to volunteer the information, knowing she was going to pump her for all she was worth.

"Yes," said Marianne.

"Is that all you're going to say? Yes, no?"

"Yes."

Jessica let out an exasperated sigh. "You're a rotten human being, do you know that, Marianne Trainor?"

"And you're a voyeur," Marianne shot back with some of her old cheer. She still had that slightly off-balance look, almost a mild case of shock, but a relatively happy state of shock for all that. "What do you want, all the details?"

"Yes," Jessica replied promptly. "But I know you're not going to tell me anything. Will you at least tell me how things stand between the two of you?"

"No."

"Marianne..."

Marianne relented. "I won't tell you because I can't. He was gone when I woke up, and he didn't leave a note. I have no idea whether I'll ever see him again." Once more cheerfulness gave way to despair, and she drained the rest of her cold, sweetened coffee with a shudder.

"It's a pretty small island, Marianne," Jessica said caustically. "What makes you think it was a one-night stand? He's certainly waited long enough to get you."

"How do you know it wasn't a spur-of-the-moment thing?"

"Don't be ridiculous. What have you been running from for the past year if he wasn't chasing? In a very low-keyed, determined sort of way, I grant you, but Andrew Cameron was chasing."

"Well, now he's caught me," Marianne said morosely. "And he's probably booked the first flight back to Scotland."

"I don't think so. Despite the fact that you always insulted him, complained about his age and his size—"

A muffled laugh broke through Marianne's confusion, and her freckled, pretty face flushed a deep red. Jessica stared at her in absolute amazement as a reluctant giggle followed.

"What's so funny?" she queried calmly.

"Just your saying I complained about his size." She giggled again.

"I don't think I'll pursue that any further," Jessica said, her voice caustic again. "You had a miserable time last night, you're never going to see Andrew again, and you're sitting there giggling and blushing like a teenager. I don't think I'm going to waste my time worrying about you."

Marianne shook her head. "I think I'm having a mid-life crisis." She sighed, scooping Shannon up in her tired arms and heading for the door. "I'll tell you one thing, though. Either I've hit my sexual peak a little early, which is entirely possible. Or—" she opened the door into the summer sunshine "—Andrew Cameron is simply amazing." She drew the word out on a long, lascivious sigh, giggled again, blushed and left, closing the door quietly behind her.

The very memory of Marianne's addled state brought a smile to Jessica's face. She had no doubt Andrew would return and set all her doubts to rest—she was more worried about Marianne's honorable intentions than Cameron's. She shook her head, staring down at the piece of paper with two short paragraphs leering evilly up at her.

Maybe she should give Matt Decker more time with the estimable Ilse? She was a magnificent, strapping wench along Marianne's lines, capable of holding her own in a firefight or in hand-to-hand combat, the perfect creature to romp amid the sheets in Decker's mobile home-cum-army tank. Maybe they could even get married.

The idea had promise, but it merited more thought. Flicking off the Selectric, she rose happily, a child reprieved from dreaded schoolwork. She'd sit out on the side porch in the sunshine, watch the light sparkle on the lake, and play the banjo while she let Matt Decker and his lady simmer on the back burner.

Matthew was still sleeping soundly, tummy-down, in

the rush Moses basket Marianne had given her as a necessity for Vermont baby rearing. Leaving his door open just a crack, she grabbed Andrew's firebird banjo and stepped out the French doors onto the side porch. It was a glorious day, she thought with a happy sigh, sliding down and stretching her long tanned legs out in front of her. Her cutoffs had seen better days, and her legs were scratched and bruised from a tangle with a raspberry bush. The sleeveless cotton shirt exposed her tanned muscled arms to the beneficent sunlight, and she pushed her hair back from her face, drinking in the warmth. Her hair had grown at a phenomenal rate at first, but it had slowed down during the past few months. It went just below her shoulders, a thick curtain that more often than not got tied in a braid and pushed out of the way. Pregnancy and a hard, physical life had filled her out and toughened her. She was strong and lean and muscled and inordinately proud of her body. She gave herself a satisfied appraisal before propping the banjo in her lap.

She had mastered every fiddle tune and jig Andrew had presented her, from "Came Haste to the Wedding" to "Devil's Dream" to "Flowers of the Forest." She still preferred "Banish Misfortune" best of all, its modal lilt a mantra against all the trouble that sometimes seemed to lurk just out of reach, waiting to pounce. She leaned back against the pillar and began to play.

THE 1963 LOTUS EUROPA ate up the Vermont highways with more than its usual impatience. It was midafternoon, and John Springer MacDowell had been driving since early morning, his simmering rage tempering to a cold, determined fury. It was a damned lucky thing Jessica hadn't stayed in New York—if she'd been in reach he might have hit a woman for the first time in his life.

Not that he should have had any sexist qualms. He'd hit men in anger, more than once. He'd even killed, in Vietnam. But never had he wanted to hurt someone as much as he wanted to hurt ice-blooded, devious, lying Jessica Hansen.

But he wasn't going to hit her, much as a deep-seated part of him wanted to. He'd never hit anyone that much smaller than he was, and he'd never thrown the first punch. And he hadn't hit anyone in almost fifteen years—he wasn't going to start now.

His foot had pressed down harder on the gas pedal as Jessica filtered back into his thoughts, and he forced himself to relax, to pull back on the speed. He'd already had one ticket that morning; he didn't need another. Jessica could wait—she'd still be there. Jessica and his son would still be there.

Vermont hadn't changed in the years since he'd been there. The road at the north end of the island was still as rutted, the maples as tall and sheltering, the lake as clear and shimmeringly blue as he remembered from his childhood. The old Clary place was occupied, he noticed absently as the car purred its quiet way to the lake. The roof looked just as tenuous, the porch even more sagging. The tall woman on the porch was staring after him, he noticed in his rearview mirror, and for a moment he wondered if it was Jessica and he hadn't recognized her.

But the woman's hair was brown, not blond, and the child she'd been holding was closer to four. No, Jessica was at the end of the road, innocently unaware that all hell was about to break loose. If anything about her could be called innocent.

The old house looked no older, he thought as he pulled the car to a stop in front of the circular drive. The shingles were a little more weathered, the flower gardens no longer benefiting from his mother's care. They were blowsy, tangled and overgrown, a riot of color against the bleached gray of the house. For a moment he sat there, strong wrists draped over the steering wheel, as he took in the memories of his childhood.

There was a faint sound on the light breeze, one he couldn't place. With a weary sigh he pulled himself out of the cramped car. Sometime he really ought to invest in a car more his size, he thought ruefully, stretching against the afternoon sunlight.

He could smell the faint scent of raspberries on the breeze, the tang of the towering pines that surrounded the house, and he tried to summon forth that monumental rage that had driven him up here at breakneck speeds.

But it wouldn't come. Other emotions were crowding it out. He was going to see his child, his son, for the first time in his life. And he was going to see Jessica. Jessica, whom he told himself he hated, Jessica of the ice-blue eyes and the lies. He wondered if she'd feel the slightest bit guilty. He doubted it.

He took the steps lightly, two at a time, his ear attuned to the faint thread of music coming from the side porch. He saw her long before she saw him, her long legs stretched out in front of her, her strong hands cradling the banjo as you'd cradle a child.

He realized then that he hadn't really looked at her last

month when his father died. He'd been too caught up in his own anger and misery to notice the changes in her. Motherhood had both softened and toughened her. Her body was stronger looking, fuller, rounder, her face surprisingly tranquil as she leaned against the pillar. The blue eyes that stared dreamily out at the lake were no longer icy, they were soft and dreamy and welcoming. He wondered if they would turn back to ice when he confronted her, whether they'd cloud with guilt. And for a moment a longing, strong and unexpected, swept over him.

He wanted to cross the porch and pull her into his arms; he wanted to crush that soft, smiling mouth with his; he wanted to make love to her on his father's porch beneath the warm Vermont sunshine.

But it was no longer his father's porch; it was his son's. And the woman that he'd felt that astonishing desire for was a cheat and liar, not to be trusted. There were no extenuating circumstances, no room for doubt. She'd known what she was doing, known full well. And it was up to him just how he'd repay her.

His mouth tightened as the remembered anger returned. He took another step toward her, and the porch creaked underneath his Nikes. She looked up, startled, and he had the dubious satisfaction of watching all that warm, sun-kissed color drain from her face, her eyes darken with what could only be called horror, and absolute panic sweep over her features.

He hadn't seen that kind of fear since Vietnam, and he didn't like it. But some small, mean part of him gave her a lazy, menacing smile. "Hi, there, little mother," he drawled.

## Chapter Twenty-seven

She had never fainted in her life, and she wasn't about to start now. The roaring in her ears, the sudden rapid disappearance of the solid porch beneath her, the sickening hollowness in her head and stomach would pass. She reached out and caught the wooden deck in numb hands, letting the banjo slide forward in her lap, and looked up at the apparition with disbelieving eyes. If she blinked, maybe he would go away.

He didn't. He just stood there looking down at her with that bland, threatening smile on a face she once thought devastatingly handsome. She didn't think so now. She thought he was the most horrifying sight she'd ever seen, and she felt her safe, comfortable life slip away from her grasp as the porch seemed to spin away from her.

She had to pull herself together. That thought quickly surfaced through her panic, and with spectacular effort she pulled her backbone straight and even managed to return his smile, albeit stiffly. Her greeting, while lacking in warmth, made up for it in directness.

"What are you doing here, Springer?" *And how soon*

*can I get rid of you,* she added silently. *Dear God in heaven, please let it be before Matthew wakes up.*

He moved closer, and for the first time Jessica felt the threat in that tall, sinuous body of his. He still had that lazy smile on his face, but his dark eyes were almost black with something she didn't care to fathom. All her instincts were set for trouble, but she forced herself to relax.

"I thought I'd visit you and Peter's son," he said amiably. 'And see what's happened to the old homestead. Sort of a sentimental pilgrimage. I haven't been here since I was seventeen." This was all said in a mild voice, but Jessica wasn't lulled.

"Were you planning to stay?" Her voice shook slightly, and she cleared her throat in a vain attempt to cover her fright.

His smile only broadened, and she could see tiny gold flecks in his dark, angry eyes. The man was a sadist, she realized belatedly. He must know.

"I thought I might," he drawled. "That is, if I'm not putting you out any."

"You can't," she said abruptly, no longer caring that the panic showed.

"Why not?"

"Because this is a very small community. How would it look if a strange man stayed with me? My reputation would be ruined and I have to live with these people." She was quite pleased with herself for her instant rationale.

"You don't have to live here at all," he replied. "And I wouldn't think anyone would confuse you with Rebecca of Sunnybrook Farm, given Matthew's indisputable presence. I think you'll have to come up with a better excuse."

"I don't want you here, Springer. Is that a good enough excuse?" she snapped. "Your father left this house to Matthew, in my trust, and neither of us wants you here."

"Speak for yourself, Jessie. You haven't checked with Matthew," he said lazily, unmoved by her anger. "And probate hasn't gone through yet, and most likely won't for at least six months. Until then, this house is still legally part of Ham's estate."

She could hear it now, the beginning snorts and fusses of a wakening baby, and the panic spread. "Go away, Springer," she said, and there was a thread of desperation in her voice. The baby's cries were getting louder and more constant.

Springer just smiled, that disturbing, almost malevolent smile, and reached out to take the banjo from her lap. "I wouldn't think of it. Don't you think you should go get the baby? He's crying quite loudly now."

Matthew had worked himself up to a full-blooded scream, one that usually betokened extreme rage and a very wet diaper. Jessica hesitated for a moment longer, hoping against hope that there was some way she could salvage the situation. If only there was a slim chance that she could get rid of Springer before he actually set eyes on Matthew. There was still a possibility that he didn't know.

Springer's other hand reached down and caught her numb hand, yanking her up to her feet with just enough roughness to banish the last of her doubts.

"Come on, little mother," he murmured, an edge beneath his drawl. "Introduce me to Peter Kinsey's son."

For a moment she found herself hating him with an intensity that frightened her. He was looming over her, seeming taller than ever with her in bare feet, and his lean, strong body was emanating all sorts of hidden threats. He was toying with her, playing with her like a cat with a succulent mouse. He had her trapped in a corner and was batting at her, giving her just enough room to escape and then yanking her back. And once he finished with her, he'd start in on her young.

It seemed as if he could read the frightened thoughts that sped through her mind. "Are you just going to stand there sniveling?" he queried pleasantly.

At that the last of her panicked indecision left her. Her head snapped up, her back straightened and her eyes flashed up into his. And for the first time she recognized the depths of his rage. But now it wasn't any worse than hers. "No, I'm not," she said in an even voice. "I'm going to get my son."

Matthew greeted her arrival with an abrupt cessation of his weeping and a snuffle of watery gratitude. Paying absolutely no attention to the tall figure just behind her shoulder, she cuddled the damp baby against her, in a vain attempt to prolong the inevitable. But Springer's hands, large enough to comfortably cradle the small baby, reached out and took him from her, and there was nothing she could do to hold on to him without hurting him.

"Let me take a look at you, young man." She almost didn't recognize Springer's voice. It was a low, soothing croon, rumbling from deep in his chest, and she watched in amazement as Matthew's little face, already wrinkled in a howl of protest at the strange hands holding him, smoothed out into an expression of wary interest. Father and son surveyed each other, and then Springer moved over to the old dresser that served as a changing table. "The perfect image of Peter Kinsey," he said dryly, his voice still that amazing low note that mesmerized the infant in front of him. "Your mother's managed to let you get quite wet, my boy." He was dispensing with the diaper with startling expertise, replacing it with a new one with a minimum of wasted moves, and all the while Matthew stared up at him, entranced. A moment later he was comfortably ensconced against Springer's shoulder, looking at his mother out of his dark, somewhat startled eyes.

A thousand disparate emotions were sweeping through Jessica. Jealousy and possessiveness were there, combined with the ever-present feeling of panic. But there was also a tiny clutching deep in her heart at the sight of the two of them—the one so tiny, the other so huge—and she had a sudden, inexplicable memory of her fantasy when she'd first seen this house that she'd fallen in love with. She'd pictured a husband and baby waiting for her, filled with love. And the man had been Springer.

But it wasn't love he was feeling now, she thought numbly. He would hurt her if he could, and she was terribly afraid he was going to try to take Matthew away from her. She could feel the panic begin to rise again, threatening to choke her, and she quickly swallowed it. She had to think calmly, clearly, like Matt Decker faced with one of his hordes of crazed terrorists. Even if the odds were overwhelming, she and Matthew could escape. She just had to keep her head.

"He needs his bottle," she said calmly as Matthew began squirming.

"You're not breast-feeding?" The drawled politeness had vanished, at least temporarily, and the question was an attack.

She found she could attack too. "You already know that. It would have made quite a mess of the sheets when we went to bed together last month if I had been."

He didn't even flinch at the deliberate reminder. "We made quite a mess of the sheets as it was. It's much better for a baby to be breast-fed."

It was an old guilt, one she hadn't completely resolved, and hearing it from Springer shattered the last of her calm. "Then you do it!" she snapped. "Maybe you'll have less trouble than I had."

"You tried?" He sounded disbelieving.

"Of course I did! Through anemia, exhaustion, viral pneumonia, and the Vermont version of dysentery. Matthew was starving and hungry, I was starving and getting weaker, and finally the milk dried up entirely. Not that it's any of your damned business."

Springer looked down at the child wriggling cheerfully enough in his arms, into the dark, curious eyes so very much like his own, and then back to Jessica's defiant ones. "Not that it's any of my damned business," he echoed softly, and once more she felt that menace. "Do you feel like getting me a bottle for him or shall I hunt it up myself?"

"I'll feed him." She reached out for the baby, but Springer didn't budge.

"Get the bottle, little mother," he said, his voice brooking no opposition, and there was nothing she could do, short of trying to wrestle the baby out of his surprisingly capable arms. "I'll feed your son."

MARIANNE SLAMMED THE CAST-IRON FRYING PAN down on the old gas stove with a loud clang, fondly picturing Andrew Cameron's head beneath it. She was venting all her anger and uncertainty on the dinner she was hastily pulling together, and she had a sudden, fond wish that their straitened circumstances could have stretched to veal or boned chicken. To something she could pound.

There wasn't much violent satisfaction to be gotten out of tuna-fish casserole. You could be only so hostile opening up the cans without bathing your hands in fish oil, and even chopping onions with a large knife put your fingers at risk. She'd skinned her knuckles grating cheese, scorched the white sauce, and burned herself when she drained the noodles with a trace too much vehemence. Through it all Eric and Shannon sat passively, letting their mother burn off steam while they watched the omnipresent "Family Feud."

She slammed the oven door behind the casserole, then had to go back and check to make sure she hadn't knocked out the flame on the recalcitrant old stove. She remembered the day, not three months after Tom had dragged them up there, when he'd gone off to buy her a new stove. He'd returned late that night with a new stereo system, one he'd taken with him when he vanished back to Connecticut, and she was still risking life and limb cooking on this antique monstrosity.

"Men!" she said in a sneer, roundly condemning the whole species as she glared at the unoffending casserole before slamming the door shut again.

"Hey, Ma." Eric roused himself during a deodorant commercial.

"Hey, what?"

"Billy Goat got into the raspberries today."

"It figures," she replied glumly. "No raspberry jam this year, I guess."

"We can go back to Andrew's and take his," Eric suggested turning back to the television. "He said we could."

"That'll be a cold day in hell," Marianne muttered, pouring herself a tall glass of wine and plopping down at the worn kitchen table. "Damn his little Scottish soul."

The sound of game-show laughter drowned out the rumble of the Valiant. In the back of her mind she heard the car door slam, heard the light footsteps on her sagging porch. She kept her eyes glued to the bleached and scarred top of her kitchen table, not even looking up when she heard the door open.

She ignored the tumult of happy greetings from her children, ignored the sudden pounding of her heart. But she couldn't ignore the slight shadow that fell over her as her children returned to the wonders of Richard Dawson.

"Well, at least the children are glad to see me," he said lightly, his voice quizzical.

"They have no judgment," she mumbled, keeping

her head averted, keeping her heart hardened against the sudden treacherous melting.

There was a long pause, and he tried again. "Something smells wonderful," he said soulfully. "Am I invited for dinner?"

"No."

A gentle hand reached down, caught her chin and turned her unwilling face to meet his. His green eyes were rueful as they scanned her stubborn face. "What have I done to make you so mad at me, woman?" he queried softly. "I thought we'd done with fighting for the time being."

"Where the hell were you?"

A look of relief softened his angular features. "Is that all you're fussing about? I was looking after me and mine."

"What's that supposed to mean?" She had to use all her strength of mind to kep from moving her chin around to kiss that strong hand. She kept her voice sharp, but just barely so.

"I was seeing my lawyer about that ex-husband of yours," Cameron said smugly, releasing her chin with a gentle stroke and seating himself beside her. "He says there should be no problem, provided we get married as soon as possible. Trainor might try to pull a fast one with custody if we put it off too long, and—"

"You did what?" Any softening that had threatened Marianne's state of mind had vanished. "How dare you?"

"You're sounding like a Victorian novel, Marianne," he said caustically. "I was just trying to protect you—"

"Don't you think I might be capable of protecting myself?" she shot back, her rage white-hot. "Or even deserving of being consulted in your high-and-mighty plans? I'm not going to marry you or anyone, Andrew Cameron."

"Don't be ridiculous, woman." He was getting mad now, his temper equaling hers. "You know better than anyone how little you can trust your husband—"

"I know better than anyone how little I can trust any damned man," she shot back. "I am not going from the frying pan into the fire. I did not get rid of one husband telling me what to do just to turn around and marry another overbearing man."

"When have I been overbearing?"

"Since the first day I met you. Today is only a perfect example of your high-handed behavior. The children and I can take care of ourselves, thank you very much. All I have to do with Tom is threaten his pocketbook and he'll leave us completely alone. And I don't need you to do that. I don't need you at all." She didn't raise her voice, not wanting to distress the children, but her tone was low and bitter.

"You don't need me at all," he echoed lightly. "So last night meant nothing to you?"

"Apart from enjoyable exercise, no," she said, lying through her teeth. "And it's not something that I plan to repeat in the near future."

He stared at her for a long moment, and if he hadn't been a damned self-centered, overbearing man, she would have thought that was pain in his green eyes. "No," he said, "I wouldn't think you'd need to. I gave you enough exercise last night to last you for quite a while." He rose then, and she might have imagined that dark, sorrowing look. "I'll leave the papers with you. I made the appointment for you to go and talk with Herbert. He's the best custody lawyer in the state, but you can find someone else if you like. I'd still suggest you see him. I think you might underestimate Trainor."

"As you pointed out, I know him better than you do." *Don't leave,* she wailed inwardly. *Fight with me some more.*

A cynical smile lit his face. "As I also said before, lassie, you're a pigheaded viper. But I'll wait for you, as long as need be."

"Wait for what?" Why did she sound so hostile?

"Wait for you to realize you belong with me."

"I don't belong to anyone!" she shot back furiously.

"As usual you didn't listen. I said you belong *with* me, not to me. There's a difference, woman. And I'm a patient man. I'll wait for you to learn it."

And then he was gone.

Marianne broke the casserole setting it on the table in front of the children, smashing the heavy earthenware into a pile of pottery shards and steaming noodle glop. Eric and Shannon ate peanut-butter sandwiches and went to bed early, while Marianne bustled around, stripping last night's sheets off the bed, rearranging her furniture, whistling determinedly. When she finally got between the cool, clean sheets, all alone in the big old bed, she lay there in the moonlit darkness and missed Andrew.

How had the bed managed to get so wide? How had her life managed to get so empty?

Rolling over, she punched her lumpy pillow, and a cloud of feathers spurted out. She was just drifting off into a trouble sleep when she remembered the stranger in the sports car who had driven past her to Jessica's house. And hadn't driven back down, as far as she knew. She lay there for a moment, wondering what Jessica was doing right then. Probably sound asleep, Marianne thought grumpily. And then she fell asleep herself, hugging the pillow that still smelled faintly of Andrew's pipe.

## Chapter Twenty-eight

At that moment Jessica wasn't sound asleep. She wasn't even in her bedroom. The house was still and silent at eleven-thirty, and she was tiptoeing down the cellar steps to the garage under the house, Matthew's sleeping form cradled in her arms, a bulky bag of diapers, formula and various baby paraphernalia swinging from one shoulder.

It hadn't been the most reassuring afternoon and evening. Springer would barely let her get within touching distance of her son, and his entire conversation seemed to consist of threatening double entendres, all about how Matthew would like the West Coast, how mothers were dispensable, how judges were giving fathers more and more rights. This was accomplished in a gently smiling, casual fashion, and his dark eyes bore down into hers with implacable hatred. Or so she told herself.

She hadn't given it much thought. She'd headed for her bedroom the moment she put Matthew down, and that had precipitated another crisis.

He'd caught her at the head of the stairs, his strong,

callused hand holding her arm in a hard grip just short of bruising. Except that she bruised very easily, with her pale skin and pale hair.

"Where are you going?"

"I told you, to bed. I said good-night," she said, hating the defensive note in her voice.

"I realize that. What room?" He was mockingly patient, and his hand on her arm was inexorable, the skin seeming to burn her flesh.

"My room. The one under the eaves," she clarified. "Do you have any problem with that?"

"As a matter of fact, I do. That's my bedroom—it has been since I was born. I'd like it back."

"No."

"No?" he echoed politely. "I'm not sure that I take no for an answer. That's my bedroom and my bed, and I'm going to sleep in it. Preferably alone."

Now why should that have stung? The last thing in the world she wanted to do was fend off a lust-crazed Springer. But still his words smarted, and she could feel her cheeks flush with color at his insulting drawl.

"Do you expect me to move all my stuff?" she questioned coldly.

"You can leave it in my bedroom if you want to—it won't make any difference to me. I would have thought you'd prefer more privacy when you dress."

"How long are you planning to stay?" she asked for the twenty-fourth time, still not really expecting an answer. "Don't you have a job that you have to get back to?"

He smiled then, that cool, nasty little smile that was

becoming so familiar. "I'm on sabbatical, little mother. All I have to do is relax and make the acquaintance of Peter Kinsey's son."

"Stop it, Springer!" There was the ragged edge of hysteria in her voice, and she swallowed it with difficulty. "Please, just...stop it."

The punishing hand released her arm; he leaned back against the wall and surveyed her, a distant expression on his face. But he said nothing. Evidently he felt he'd said enough for the time being. He just stood there, watching her, waiting for his taunting to take effect.

"I'll take a change of clothes for tonight, and move the rest of the stuff tomorrow morning," she said after a long pause. "If that's all right with you."

"Just peachy," he drawled, unmoved by the look of absolute hatred she shot him then. "Take your time."

*That had been one of many mistakes,* she had realized as she sat fully clothed on her bed, wide awake, as it drew nearer to midnight. There was no way she could sneak back in there and pack enough clothes to see her through the next few weeks. And she didn't have enough money to buy new clothes—all her meager savings account needed to be stretched as far as possible, until she decided what she was going to do.

She hadn't even decided why she had to go, or where. But the threat in Springer MacDowell's presence was palpable, she was a complete nervous wreck, and there was no way she and her son were going to continue on in the same house. Once she got away, had some breathing space, then she could think more clearly.

Matthew, bless his heart, slept soundly as she gathered all the clothes she could stuff into the diaper bag and lifted him into her arms. The house was silent— she could only hope Springer was a heavy sleeper. She really didn't know—the nights she had spent with him hadn't involved much sleeping.

The damned floorboards squeaked as she crept down the hallway, and she halted, breathless, motionless, waiting for the sound of his footsteps above them, the flood of light from the open door. Matthew shifted in her arms, snuffling, and the bag slid down to her elbow, dragging at her.

But there was no sound from above—all was darkness—and she breathed a silent sigh of relief, continuing her flight. Jessica felt like a disgraced daughter fleeing her Victorian father's wrath, and the slightly hysterical giggle that welled up in her at the thought threatened to spill over and betray her. *Just a few more minutes,* she promised herself. *And then I'll be away.*

Matthew still slept that wonderfully heavy sleep he'd been blessed with since he was only three weeks old, and he barely stirred as she fastened him into the car seat. Her hands were shaking with panic and relief as she climbed into the driver's seat, fastened her seat belt, and turned the key.

Nothing happened. Not a whir, not a faint whine, not even a grumble. Just a little tiny click, and then that same, roaring silence.

There was a quiet little whimper, and Jessica realized with some surprise that it had come from her own throat and not her sleeping son. She tried the key again, knowing nothing would happen, and her foresight was rewarded. Another click.

302           BANISH MISFORTUNE

She didn't even hesitate. Springer's pride and joy was parked beside the Subaru in the underground garage. Once, years ago, one of her sister Maren's boyfriends had shown her how to hot-wire her aging VW when she'd lost her keys. With luck she could still remember. How different could a 1963 Lotus Europa be from a 1967 VW Beetle?

She was scrambling around under the dashboard, looking for a lever to release the sleek, low hood, and having very little luck, when a large hand came down on her shoulder, dragging her from the car with a definite absence of gentleness. She was dragged upright before she could do more than shriek, and found herself looking into Springer's mocking face.

"Looking for something, Jessie?"

He wasn't wearing much, and for a moment Jessica wondered if he'd done it on purpose. The faded jeans clung to his mile-long legs, his tanned torso was bare, his arms long and muscled, his hands velvet-covered steel as they held her.

She wasn't going to whimper and squirm; she wasn't going to lie. "There's something wrong with my car," she said evenly meeting his gaze with a certain fearlessness that he might have admired if he hadn't seemed to hate her so much.

"That was my car you were ferreting around in," he observed politely.

"I was going to borrow it."

"And how were you going to do that? I had the only set of keys."

"I was going to hot-wire it. But I couldn't find how to open the hood."

There was no question of it, a faint, reluctant admiration did filter through his eyes for a brief moment. "You do believe in living dangerously, don't you?" His hands released her, and she felt the blood flow back through the cramped muscles. If he didn't watch it, she'd end up looking like an abused wife.

"I don't suppose you could help me find out what's wrong with my car," she suggested boldly. "It just makes a clicking noise when I try to start it. I can't imagine—"

"The distributor cap is disconnected."

She looked at him doubtfully. "You think so? I haven't had any trouble with it before. Will it cost a lot to have it fixed? What if it's something else?"

"It's the distributor cap," he repeated patiently. "I know because I'm the one who disconnected it. I thought you might have a midnight escape in mind, so I figured I'd better be prepared. I'll reconnect it tomorrow, after we talk."

She looked at him then, a slow, steady look that held murder in it. "What are you trying to do to me, Springer?" she asked quietly. "Are you trying to drive me crazy so you can commit me to a nuthouse and take my baby?"

"You've been watching too many old movies." A slow smile lit his face, and if it wasn't filled with the devastating charm she remembered, at least it was missing some of its heretofore lethal quality. "Though now that you mention it, it's not a bad idea."

"It's a lousy idea."

"Perhaps," he allowed. "After all, what would I want with Peter Kinsey's son?"

"Stop it. You knew before you came here whose child he was," she said hoarsely.

"I did. Peter and I happened to run into each other in New York, and we had a long talk. About a great many things, you in particular. He told me he never slept with you."

"Is this the time or place to go into all this?" she demanded, shifting nervously.

"Oh, I don't know." He leaned against his car, crossing his arm across his tanned, smooth chest. "This seems as good a time as any. Matthew's asleep, no one's likely to interrupt us. Why don't we discuss your past love life?"

"Why don't you go to hell?"

"Why didn't you sleep with Peter, Jessica? You were engaged to him."

"Maybe I didn't want to," she shot back. The lone bare light bulb was attacting all sorts of moths from the opened garage doors, and out of the corner of her eye she watched them bat against the light, helplessly attracted to that which would destroy them. She felt a sudden, gloomy kinship.

"Then why did you go to bed with me?" he persisted.

She looked at him squarely in those unfathomable, condemning eyes of his. "I don't remember having much choice in the matter."

It had the desired effect. "Damn your soul to hell, Jessica. I've never forced a woman in my life, and I sure as hell didn't force you. If you were possessed of any honesty at all, you'd know that. But you seem to have an amazing capacity for self-deception. Sometimes I wonder if you even realized that Matthew was mine."

There, it was out in the open. She didn't like hearing it said, didn't like it at all. Somehow hearing the words seemed to make them inescapable, as if, if they'd never been said, it wouldn't have been true. "I knew," she said in a quiet voice. "I just didn't choose to think about it."

"Didn't choose to think about it," he echoed marveling. "How many things does it suit you not to choose to think about? Anything unpleasant, anything not a part of your perfect, self-contained little fantasy world? The Ice Princess and her heir apparent. I don't want a child of mine brought up with so little regard for reality."

"What do you plan to do about it?" Marianne would help her, she thought belatedly. She could borrow the Toyota and drive it till it died. Andrew would help her. Maybe. Men had a nasty habit of sticking together.

He read her far too well, she thought. "I'm not sure yet. I only saw Peter yesterday—up till then I didn't really have any idea. You had me convinced when you were down in New York. I think Mother must have guessed. At least, she didn't seem that surprised."

"You told her?" Jessica was horrified.

"I told her."

"And I suppose she plans to help you take him away from me," she said bitterly.

Springer laughed. "You're paranoid, too. I have no intention of taking Matthew away from you, or even trying. I just don't plan on leaving him entirely to your tender mercies."

"He's mine," she cried.

"Damn you, he's mine, too. You're going to have to face up to that and any other little unpleasantnesses you've been avoiding."

"Why the hell should I? It's my life, and you have absolutely nothing to do with it."

"We happen to share a child," he reminded her grimly. "And that makes your life my business. That also makes this house part mine, too, and I intend to avail myself of it."

"For how long?" It was the twenty-seventh time she'd asked it, and this time she got an answer.

"Until I trust you."

"How long will that take?"

"I have no idea. It may take years. I have the time to waste. You're going to have to accustom yourself to it, little mother. The sooner you do, the sooner I'll be gone."

"I'll accustom myself to it," she said grimly.

A slow grin lit his face, and Jessica felt an unexpected tightening in her stomach. "I knew you'd see reason," he drawled. "In the meantime, why don't you take our son back upstairs and put him to bed? We can continue this conversation tomorrow morning."

"I didn't think you were going to let me carry him again." she mumbled, moving toward the car.

"Sure I will. You've got to realize that I've got three months to catch up on. I'm bound to want to hold him and feed him in the beginning. It will wear off soon enough, and you'll be nagging at me to change the diapers and put him down for a nap."

She didn't like the homey, domesticated sound of

that, any more than she liked that sudden, almost for-gotten warmth in the pit of her stomach. "How long are you planning to stay?" Number twenty-eight.

He finally took pity on her. "A month, perhaps. Maybe two. Maybe three. It all depends. You don't need to worry that I'll put a cramp in your style. I in-tend to have guests up; you won't have to curtail your social life, either."

"How thoughtful," she murmured.

"Yes, I thought so. You want any help with him?"

"No, thank you. Matthew and I will do just fine by ourselves," she said angrily.

"Don't count on it."

Matthew went back down in his crib with not much more than a whimper. Jessica stood there for a long moment, staring down at her sleeping child. "What are we going to do, Matthew?" she whispered. Matthew slept on.

She didn't run into Springer's tall, sparsely dressed figure as she made her way to the front bedroom. She could be grateful for that, she told herself as she stripped off her jeans and sweater and crawled beneath sheets. It was one of the few blessings in a cursed day. And the worse curse of all was the most unexpected. That sudden flash of wanting that had swept over her when he'd smiled his wry, charming smile down in the basement garage. And no matter how hard she tried, she couldn't wipe that memory, that wanting, from her stubborn brain. It was going to be a hellish two months.

## Chapter Twenty-nine

Bright sunlight was streaming in the guest-room window. With a muffled moan Jessica dove beneath the patchwork quilt in a vain quest for darkness and sleep. As long as Matthew was quiet she could sleep; her subconscious had instilled that particular rule, enabling her to grab the miscellaneous moments of sleep offered her.

But no comfort awaited her. The bed was different, lumpy, and there were no sheets on it. The bright sunlight was coming from the wrong side, not the side her windows were on, and Matthew should have been demanding a clean diaper and a bottle hours ago. Flinging back the threadbare quilt, she sat bolt upright and stared at the pretty, anonymous confines of the front bedroom. What the hell had Springer done with her son?

She didn't pause long enough to throw on clothes, didn't hesitate for an instant. She nearly went headfirst down the stairs in her panic, and the sight of his empty crib did nothing for her state of mind. By the time she raced into the kitchen she was practically speechless with fright.

Springer was sitting on the kitchen stool, his faded jeans riding low on his hips, his chest bare beneath the unbuttoned blue flannel shirt. He was holding Matthew with a relaxed, obviously experienced grip while he fed him, and he raised his head slowly, those distant brown eyes of his looking her up and down with a slow, measuring glance. "Something wrong?" he greeted her casually enough.

It was at that moment she realized exactly what she was wearing. She'd been too tired and depressed to put on nightclothes the night before. She'd fallen asleep in a pair of cotton bikini panties and a skimpy French-cut T-shirt, and that's what she was still wearing.

She had two alternatives. She could shriek, blush and race back upstairs, not coming back down until she was properly clothed and some of this ridiculously prudish embarrassment faded. Or she could continue on into the kitchen and act as if nothing was out of the ordinary.

And nothing particularly was. She wasn't overly modest, or ashamed of her body. If it had been a stranger, or someone like Andrew Cameron, she wouldn't have been embarrassed. But it was Springer, who'd seen her in far less, and she was determined to tough it out.

"I guess I overslept," she murmured, moving into the kitchen with an attempt at nonchalance. If only he wouldn't keep looking at her with such obvious amusement, she thought.

"Matthew and I thought we'd let you sleep in. I could hear you tossing and turning for hours last night."

"Sorry if I kept you awake," she said coolly, moving to the open kitchen door in search of a cooling breeze.

"The walls have always been thin, and that bed's springs are pre-Civil War," he murmured lazily, still watching her. "There's coffee on the stove if you want some."

She didn't particularly, not if she had to accept it from him, but it gave her something to do. "Thanks," she murmured ungraciously, moving to the stove. It was still warm, and she poured herself a large mug. Taking a tentative sip, she turned back to find him still eyeing her with that peculiar curve to his mouth.

"What are you staring at?" she demanded finally, irritation beginning to overwhelm her embarrassment.

"I never knew that someone could blush on the stomach and legs," he drawled. "If you're embarrassed, why don't you go put on some more clothes, instead of pretending it doesn't bother you?"

She slammed her coffee down on the counter, slopping half of it over her hand. "I'm perfectly comfortable," she snapped. "If it bothers you, you can go back to New York or Washington or wherever."

His smile widened wickedly. "Oh, I'm just fine, Jessie. You can prance around stark naked for all I care—it doesn't move me in the slightest."

"Thank God for small favors." She refilled her coffee cup, contemplating and then discarding the very real temptation to dump the rest of the coffee on Springer's silky black head. Only the sight of her son resting peacefully in his arms, directly in the line of fire, stopped her. "That should make sharing this house a great deal easier." She took a sip of the coffee, made a face and went delving into the refrigerator in search of cream to take some of the curse off the strong brew.

There was a sharp intake of breath behind her, and she backed out of the refrigerator quickly, turning and standing up again. Springer was looking calm and unruffled, his attention on Matthew, and she wondered if she'd imagined that sudden sound that suggested he wasn't quite as unmoved as he imagined. Or was that wishful thinking on her part?

*Wishful thinking,* her mind echoed in outrage. *Have you gone out of your mind? Why in heaven's name would you want him to still want you? Haven't you got troubles enough?*

*Ego, Jessie,* she said, calming herself. *It has nothing to do with anything more than simple pride.*

"What's going through your devious mind now?" Springer queried, rising from the stool and placing the dozing Matthew in his basket. "I don't trust that look of yours."

"Don't be ridiculous, Springer, you don't trust anything about me, never mind an expression or two," she scoffed, leaning back against the cool white enamel finish of the ancient refrigerator.

"True enough." He was moving closer now, across the room, and in her bare feet and skimpy clothing she felt uncomfortably vulnerable. He stopped by the stove to refill his own coffee mug, and then bore down on her, slowly, menacingly, she thought, his tall, lean body a delicious threat to her suddenly wide eyes.

He was only inches away; she could feel the body heat emanating from all that formidably beautiful flesh, and she wondered if he could hear her heart hammering so loudly beneath the thin T-shirt. His arm reached out, past her waist, and she drew in her breath sharply as his skin grazed her bare flesh. Catching the refrigerator door handle, he pulled it toward him, pulling her unwillingly mesmerized body with it.

It took her a moment longer to come to her senses, and she ducked out of his way seconds before her body would have met his. "I use milk in my coffee," he said blandly, reaching in to the refrigerator without a backward glance. But Jessie knew that no benevolent fate would have kept him unaware of her obvious reaction to that slow, sinuous almost-embrace. And that small, satisfied smile on his face as he turned back to her only increased her murderous thoughts.

"You're a real turkey, you know," she said quietly, standing very still.

"And you're still ridiculously gullible for a woman your age. Why didn't you tell me, Jessie?" His voice was flat, matter-of-fact, so why did she think she heard a trace of vulnerability there? It had to be more wishful thinking.

"I didn't figure it was any of your business. And why should you have cared? I was just one in what I gather is an incredibly long line of one-night stands. You weren't thinking about the possible consequences when we went to bed together. I was just sparing you ever having to think about those consequences. What you didn't know didn't hurt you."

"Cut the crap, little mother," he snarled. "You were too self-centered to even think about my possible reactions; you weren't thinking about sparing me the consequences. I'm just amazed you didn't have a quick abortion and put the whole thing out of your mind. Peter wouldn't have minded.''

Jessica smiled, a small, dangerous smile. "You've just proven my point, Springer. What it all boiled down to is that we don't really know each other. I had no idea what your reaction would be, for the simple reason that I had only met you twice before I found out I was pregnant, and both times we ended in bed together without much conversation. And if you think you know me, you wouldn't wonder why I didn't have an abortion and marry Peter Kinsey. But you don't know me, you don't know anything about me, and you stand there like some damn judge and jury, Cotton Mather to the life, and think you've got me all figured out." Her breath was coming more rapidly in her fury, and her untrammeled breasts were rising and falling beneath the thin cotton top. "Let me tell you, Springer MacDowell, that you don't know anything about me, you never have, and you never will." As her voice rose the sound of it penetrated Matthew's sleep, and he shifted in the basket, whimpering slightly. "Now see what you've done; you woke the baby," she said in a loud whisper, heading toward the basket.

Springer's hands reached out and caught her arms, turning her with a gentleness that nevertheless allowed no possibility for escape, and moved her back toward the kitchen door, out of range of the rush basket. She tried to jerk away, but his hands tightened warningly. "Just relax, little mother," he drawled. "You didn't wake him. He's dry, well fed, and he's been up since six. He's ready for a nap."

"I didn't say I woke him, I said you—"

"I know what you said. I also know more about you than you think." He waited for a moment, then slowly released her, his fingers loosening their iron grip on her arms. "I know that your parents were both alcoholics and they're dead. That you've got two sisters some-where that you don't see unless they want something. I know that you've got the reputation of having slept your way to the vice-presidency of Kinsey Enterprises, and that the only man you've ever slept with is a lawyer named Philip Mercer. Apart from me, that is. I know you've been a good friend to my parents and a lousy friend to yourself." His hand caught one arm again, slid down the silken length of it to catch her wrist, turn-ing it up in his hand to expose the fading tracery of scars. "And I know you've tried to kill yourself, at least once, and did a fairly good job of it."

She didn't pull away from him; she couldn't. "What did you do, hire a private detective?" she accused him in an anguished whisper.

He shook his head. "No, I just did what anyone would do when they needed some information. I asked my mother." His self-deprecating smile failed to pene-trate her glazed anger.

"You've got some of the facts wrong," she said bit-terly. "And you missed one early installment of my scintillating love life."

He shrugged. "I doubt it was important. It seems you've been lacking both quantity and quality. Maybe sometime you'll find someone, maybe you won't. That'll depend on you."

She stared up at him, her mind in turmoil. *I did find*

*someone,* she wanted to scream. "I have no interest in finding a satisfactory love life, Springer," she said icily. "I just want you to leave me and my son alone."

"Don't you realize that..." His words trailed off as they both heard the loud slamming of the front screen door. Jessica knew who it was—only Marianne could slam the door with just that combination of belligerence and energy.

"Jessie, where are you?" she called out, her footsteps coming closer. The kitchen door swung open just as Springer was moving away, across the room. Jessica's wrist still tingled from his touch, and it was with a great effort that she greeted Marianne with a welcoming smile.

"There you are, Jessie. What in the world are you doing still undressed at this hour? Matthew give you a tough night?" Marianne didn't look as if she'd had the best night's sleep herself. Her freckled face was pale in the late-morning sunlight, and her thick chestnut hair was bundled behind her neck in an untidy bun. She had a distracted, exhausted expression to her usually warm eyes, and she didn't even notice the tall, motionless figure by the kitchen sink.

"Not really." Jessica made a deliberate gesture toward Springer. "I have a visitor."

Marianne turned, her eyes widening in shock, first at his presence with her scantily clad friend, and then at his face. And then her face wreathed in a broad smile. "You must be Peter Kinsey," she said brightly. "I'd recognize you anywhere. Matthew looks just like you."

Jessica turned her face against the wall and moaned loudly, her misery complete.

"Actually I'm Springer MacDowell," he said, moving from the sink and bestowing his most charming smile on a surprisingly responsive Marianne. "And yes, he does look like me, doesn't he? Jessie's at a loss to explain it."

"Shut up, Springer." She pushed herself away from the wall. "Give Marianne some coffee while I go upstairs and get dressed. And don't tell Springer all about my love life, Marianne. He won't be interested."

"What love life?" Marianne demanded, bewildered. "You've been Saint Jessica the Divine for as long as I've known you, complete with immaculate conception." She cast an appraising eye at Springer's rangy form. "Though I guess it wasn't so immaculate after all."

At Springer's unrestrained shout of laughter, Jessica contented herself with a resigned sigh. "Thanks, Marianne. Right on top of things, as always. I'll be back."

She was halfway out the door when she heard Marianne's bright voice. "So tell me, how did you and Jessica meet?" She would have given a great deal to hear Springer's answer. He had more than met his match in the determined Marianne, she thought with her first trace of amusement. Maybe she could drive him away.

But she wouldn't count on it. She knew in her heart that Springer MacDowell wasn't going anywhere until he was good and ready to go, and that didn't look to be in the near future. And she still couldn't be sure if she was angry or relieved at that thought. Maybe a little bit of both. And therein lay the danger.

## Chapter Thirty

"You know, Jessie, I like him."

"Traitor," Jessica shot back, albeit with not a great deal of energy. It was hard to summon up the anger that had been dogging her. They were sitting on the side porch facing the clear green-blue of the lake. Jessica was sitting on the steps, knees bent, with Matthew stretched out lengthwise on her thighs, smiling up at her happily. Eric and Shannon were down on the grass in front of them, arguing haphazardly without any interference from their mother, while Marianne drank her coffee, admired Springer's undeniably admirable physique, and tried to look cheerful.

"How long's he going to be here?" She nodded toward Springer's distant figure.

He was wandering down by the lake, poking around the sagging dock, nosing around the tiny semicircle of rocky sand that served as a swimming beach. He was still wearing that faded blue flannel shirt, although he had buttoned the buttons it still boasted and rolled up the tattered sleeves. He'd rolled up his pant legs, too, and for a moment Jessica allowed herself a brief erotic fantasy about those tanned, narrow ankles. She'd never noticed a man's ankles before, never thought of them as a particularly erogenous zone. She thought so now.

She turned to Marianne with a sigh. "I don't know. The most I can get out of him is that he'll be here a month or two. I can't imagine what sort of job would allow him to take summers off."

"You can't?" Marianne's look of determined cheerfulness was replaced with real amazement. "You mean to tell me you don't know what he does for a living?"

She looked up from her son's smiling face. "No, I don't. Do you?"

"Of course."

"How?"

Marianne shook her head. "I asked, dummy. You two must have had some torrid affair, not even taking time to find out what he did for a living."

"Well?"

"Well, what?" Marianne countered.

"Well, what does he do for a living?"

Marianne contemplated her for a moment. "I think I'll let him tell you."

"Marianne..." Jessica's voice held a warning, one Marianne blithely ignored.

"No, Jessica. You ask him; he'll tell you. I'll leave it at that."

"He's probably a member of the Mafia," she said grumpily, her tone of voice at variance with the smile on her face as she bent down toward her son.

"Ask him. We had a nice talk while you were getting dressed, and I promise you, he won't bite."

"He won't bite you, maybe. Me, I'm not so sure

about. How did he manage to win you over so quickly? I thought you were impervious to the male of the species.''

"Maybe Cameron addled my brain," she said glumly. "I like him, Jessica. I really do. And if you gave him half a chance I think..." Her voice trailed off as she caught sight of Jessica's expression.

Her ice-blue eyes were trained on the figure down by the lake with absentminded concentration, and there was a curiously vulnerable look on her face, one that was embarrassingly easy for her friend to read.

"Oh," said Marianne, nonplussed.

"Oh, what?" Jessica tore her eyes away from Springer's lean form.

"I hadn't realized that you were in love with him."

It was close to the last straw. "Don't hand me that crap, Marianne. I'm not in love with anyone, and particularly not Springer MacDowell. If I were going to fall in love I'd pick someone far more...more..." Words failed her.

Marianne nodded. "You're in love with him, all right. You just don't even realize it yourself yet."

"Since when did you become the great expert on affairs of the heart? If I need Dear Abby, I'll write to her. You're right, Andrew must have addled your brains." Her nervous tapping of her feet communicated itself to Matthew, who screwed up his face with a look of intense displeasure.

"I suppose so. Speaking of addled brains, I suppose it would be ridiculous to ask a favor of you," Marianne said disconsolately, putting her empty coffee mug down on the gray-painted porch floorboards.

"Don't you be ridiculous," Jessica said warmly. "Just because your brain's melted doesn't mean I don't love you. Name it."

"I was going to ask you to watch the kids for a few hours, but I hadn't realized you had company."

"Oh, bless you, Marianne. At this point you could rent your kids to me. I need something to keep Springer at a distance. I'm not in the mood for a cross-examination of my history, which he seems determined to do. I was going to try to keep Matthew from taking a nap, but Eric and Shannon will do the trick perfectly. He can hardly ask me about my sex life with Eric listening."

"Is he going to?" Marianne asked, fascinated.

"He has already, and I didn't give him much of an answer. Nor do I intend to. I think he's here to make sure I'm a decent mother for his son."

"And if he decides you're not?" Marianne's broad, pretty face reflected her own tangled situation.

"I won't even consider the possibility." Jessica had to resist the urge to pull Matthew up into her arms. She gave her head a tiny shake. "So, speaking of addled brains, what are you planning to do this afternoon?"

"Go berrying."

"Oh, no."

"Oh, yes. He'll never notice. It was just bad luck that he came across us last year. I'm not going to give up the best raspberries in years because I'm afraid of Andrew Cameron."

"You don't think he'll be glad to have you plundering his bushes?"

"Not after last night. We had a parting of the ways."

"That was fast." Jessica couldn't control the look of

disappointment that shadowed her face. "Don't you think you could have—"

"Do you want advice on your love life, Jessica?" Marianne countered in a dangerous voice. "I have all sorts of opinions on Springer and you."

"No, thank you," she said promptly, only partly subdued. "So if your ways are parted, how come you're going over there to steal his raspberries? Aren't you afraid he'll catch you?"

"I don't think he's going to be anywhere around. And if he does happen to see me, I expect he'll go out of his way to avoid me. Don't look for Freudian motives, Jessica. If I wanted to see him, I'd go over and see him. I wouldn't use raspberries for an excuse. I don't want to see him. I always knew getting involved with him would be a mistake, and I was proved right."

"All right, all right. I won't hassle you anymore. Just answer me one question, will you?"

"You're almost as nosy as I am," Marianne complained to the blue of the lake.

"Just what did Andrew do that was so hideously unforgivable?"

Marianne met her gaze calmly. "He asked me to marry him."

Jessica nodded. "Of course. Inexcusable in a man who loves you. I understand why you don't want to see him again."

"Stay out of it, Jessica."

"Yes, ma'am. Have fun berrying. We'll expect you when we see you."

Marianne relented. "I'll bring you enough for some raspberry shortcake."

"Made with white sugar," Jessica said with a pleased

sigh. "Be careful in the woods. Watch out for marauding Scots."

Marianne's moue of disdain was her only reply as she ran back down the front steps. Jessica watched her stop long enough to say good-bye to her children on her headlong dash to the old Toyota. There was a sudden spring to her step, certainly not inspired by the thought of scrambling through the berry bushes, and Jessica found herself smiling ruefully. What a mess the two of them were.

And she turned her blue eyes down to the lake, to watch Springer. He'd taken his shirt off in the heat of the day, and the sun slid along his tanned back with a caressing hand. Jessica swallowed.

"Time for a walk, Matthew my love," she said briskly, rising from the porch and averting her eyes. "Shannon, Eric," she called. "Stop fighting and come for a walk with us."

"Can we go down to the lake, Jessica?" Eric asked eagerly as he scrambled up the steps, his sister trailing behind him.

"No!" she said, her voice strangled. "No," she repeated in a calmer voice, even managing a smile. "We'll go back toward the woods and see if we can see the baby foxes. We'll go swimming later."

"Okay," Eric agreed. "Do you think Mama might bring Andrew back with her?"

"I don't know. Do you want her to?"

He nodded. "Shannon and I like Andrew. We want him to stay with us."

"I think he'd like that, too. But it's going to be up to your mother." Jessica's voice was doubtful, and Eric shrugged.

"Yeah, I guess. But she doesn't have very good taste in men, does she?"

"What do you mean?"

"Well, she married my dad, didn't she?"

There was no tactful answer to that simple question. "Let's go for our walk, guys. I'm afraid that we're going to have to let your mother sort out her own life."

CAMERON'S RASPBERRIES were incredibly good this year, Marianne thought as she popped another one into her mouth. Despite Jessica's knowing look, Marianne knew she had no ulterior motives in trekking out here. She had come only for the raspberries.

Of course, the raspberries didn't care that she'd stopped to brush out her tangled mane of chestnut hair, or pinched her cheeks to put some color into them, or opened the loose cotton shirt an extra button. And by the time her earthenware bowl was half full, Marianne didn't care much, either. The thorny branches had tangled her hair, scratched her hands and torn her clothes. But it was a beautiful day, with the lazy hum of the bees that were fighting for the raspberries, and the taste of the fruit was seductively sweet in her mouth; for a while she forgot about Andrew Cameron and that gnawing longing that had taken to sitting in the pit of her stomach.

"Woman," his rich Scottish voice filled her ears when she had almost given up hoping, "you have the most incredible gall. First you seduce and abandon me, and then you pilfer my raspberries again. Is there no end to the depths of your depravity?"

She turned, and it was an effort to keep a distant look on her face. "I figured once I had my wicked way with you I could get away with it. That's the only reason I slept with you, you know. To get at your raspberries."

He was very close, and there was a wary light in his green eyes, a hesitant curve to his mouth. He was wearing a loose cotton peasant shirt over his brown corduroys, and moccasins. He looked brown and lean and a little like a woodland elf, and for a moment all Marianne could do was stare at him, her heart in her eyes.

Leaning forward, he kissed her lightly on her parted lips. "You taste of raspberries," he whispered, his voice just a trace louder than the hum of the bees around them.

"They're very good this year," she murmured dazedly.

"Are they? Let me try them again." And his mouth caught hers in a deep, searching kiss, his tongue dipping, tasting, searching out any lingering trace of the fresh, sweet berries in her warm, moist mouth. Dropping her bowl to the ground, she lifted her hands to his shoulders to steady herself, and she was lost. Her fingers slid inside the loose shirt to his warm, smooth skin, and they were sinking to the ground, mouths hungry, touching, tasting, hands eager, fumbling, caressing.

Her hair spilled out around her on the ground as she lay back, her bare skin tickled by the rough grass beneath her. She felt like an ancient Druid priestess, naked and fertile, surrounded by the trees and the woodlands, with the man beside her a priest and a forest spirit, with his eyes the color of the leaves, his golden skin the color of wheat and honey. And then they were one together, with the trees and the sky around them, the lazy buzzing of the bees a distant song that carried them along on the soft summer breeze, with the smell of the crushed raspberries all around them. It was earth and sky, sea and fire, heaven and a sweetly aching sort of hell, and when it was over Marianne lay back in the grass beneath him and fought back the tears that she hadn't wept in years.

It was a long time before she could speak. "If I get stung by one of those bees," she said in a muffled voice, "I'm going to have a hell of a hard time explaining."

"They won't sting you," He moved away from her then, reluctantly, and began gathering the clothes that lay scattered on the ground around them. "And you'll have a harder time explaining the stains in your hair and on your back." He leaned over and picked up a silky lock of hair with a small, caressing gesture. "I've never made love to a woman lying on raspberries before. It's quite an experience."

At that she sat up quickly. "Oh, no," she wailed. The raspberries were scattered on the ground about them, crushed by their recent activity, and the earthenware bowl was shattered.

"Forget the raspberries, Marianne," he said with an urgency that held a rough note. "Why exactly did you come here today?"

Reaching for her shirt, she pulled it around her, shaking her long mane of hair. "That's why I came here," she said stubbornly. "For the raspberries."

"And I can just be thankful that you're in a wanton

mood and I'm the one who happened along?'' he questioned carefully. ''And maybe Buddy LaPlante would have done just a well?''

''Don't!'' It felt like sacrilege, and her brown eyes were open and beseeching as they looked up into his surprisingly stern ones. ''You know that's not true. Don't spoil it, Andrew. It was—'' she drew a shaky breath ''—very beautiful.''

''But you came here for the raspberries.''

''Damn it, no. I came for you,'' she admitted it angrily. ''There, does that make you feel any better?''

He was watching her, his head tilted to one side, and she wanted to reach out and pull that curly brown-haired head back to hers, to taste his mouth again. But he was still looking at her with that dour, Scottish expression of mistrust. ''I'm not sure,'' he said slowly. ''Does that mean you've reconsidered my offer?''

''I can't marry you, Andrew.''

''You mean won't,'' he said calmly, apparently unmoved by her refusal.

''Couldn't we just—'' her voice was very small ''—agree to disagree?''

He laughed then, a sad laugh, but not without humor. ''My lioness is sounding very lamblike all of a sudden. I thought you told me you'd had enough pleasant physical exercise?''

She tried a weak smile. ''A woman's got to keep fit.''

''I'm sorry, lass. I can't do it.'''

''Can't do what?'' It came out as a mournful wail, but Marianne was past worrying about her dignity.

''Can't be your aerobics instructor.'' The strong,

tanned hand that reached out to gently stroke the side of her face should have taken some of the pain away, but it somehow only made it hurt that much more. "I won't have an affair with you, Marianne. I won't bed you with your two little ones in the next room watching their damned game shows. I won't lie abed with you on a Saturday morning and have the kids tiptoe around. I won't do that to them."

"Cameron, they wouldn't mind. They love you."

"But I would mind for them. I'm a traditional man, Marianne. I want to marry the woman I love, I want to help take care of her and her children, I want a reason to belong. A legal reason, a commitment, and I can't settle for less."

She was very still. "You never said you loved me before."

He smiled, a wry, self-deprecating little smile. "Didn't I? Well, you never seemed very conducive to the idea. But I do love you, completely, and it's because of that that I can't settle for an occasional roll in the hay."

"You could live with us," she suggested mournfully. "And we could see how it went."

He shook his head. "I can't do that either, lass. I need you to make that leap of faith for me. For us not to be together would be a terrible waste of the heart and body. But for us to live together without that faith would be a waste of the soul. And I won't do that to either of us."

She stared at him for a long time. "Then I guess we're at a standstill."

"I guess we are," he said, with his endearing smile.

"But don't grieve too much, woman. Standstills have a way of moving. I told you before, I'm a patient man. We'll work it out sooner or later."

"You mean you think I'll come over to your way of thinking and abandon my principles?"

"That's my viper. We'll work it out, lass. In the meantime I'd better help you gather some more raspberries. Fair warning, though—I still expect my tithe of preserves."

She managed a smile. "I would have thought I'd just paid you for your raspberries," she said in a dulcet tone.

"And I figured I just put you even more in my debt. Get up, woman. Time's a-wasting." He reached down and pulled her up, and for a moment she swayed against him, her knees weak.

It was a dangerous moment, and his arms slid around her waist, pulling her closer against him for a brief, tantalizing moment. And then she was released, not without obvious regret on his part.

"None of that, wench," he said. "This is going to be hard enough as it is. Don't tempt me with your wiles."

She smiled at him then, suddenly lighthearted. "I'm a patient woman, laddie," she purred. "We'll see what happens."

He gave her a doubtful glance. "God give me strength," he murmured devoutly. "Raspberries, amazon."

She grinned. "Raspberries, shorty," she agreed.

## Chapter Thirty-one

"You're good with children." The remark came out of the blue, made grudgingly, and Jessica couldn't control the involuntary look of disbelief she cast at Springer.

It was a warm evening. Matthew was dozing peacefully in his seat, Eric and Shannon sat cross-legged on the floor with Jessica, busy building a card house of Frank Lloyd Wright complexity. They were aided in that endeavor by the cracks in the old pine floorboards, just wide enough to hold a card upright. Springer was stretched out on the window seat, the soft summer breeze from outside ruffling his silky black hair. Jessica had thought his attention equally divided between his sleeping son and the paperback novel in his hand. Matt Decker—volume ninety-six—she'd noticed. One of hers.

"What did you say?"

Springer set the book down beside him, looking at her clearly out of those dark dark eyes of his. "I said you're good with children. You have a real feel for them."

A self-mocking smile twisted Jessica's mouth. "Ever

the little mother, I am," she said lightly. "I've had lots of practice."

"Were your sisters older or younger than you were?" He was very careful to make the question casual, as if he weren't really interested.

"I had a younger sister and an older sister. And two parents. All of whom needed to be brought up, and I got elected to the job of doing it." She placed two cards at a careful angle and got an admiring glance from the diligent Eric. "That's the way it usually works out in alcoholic families. Every child has an alloted role. There's the rebel, the scapegoat and the little mother."

He dropped all pretense of reading. "It might have done you some good if you'd rebelled."

"That was Sunny's role." She added another card, all her concentration on the structure in front of her. "Maren was the scapegoat, always causing trouble and diverting attention from the real problem in the family. And I kept trying to hold everything together."

"Is that why you tried to kill yourself? Because you couldn't hold them together?"

The card house collapsed in a flurry. "I'll tell you what, why don't you work on the card house while I put Matthew down?" she said briskly, ignoring his last question. "You're bound to have more luck than I have. Would you like that, Shannon? Springer's very good at card houses."

She rose with one fluid motion and advanced on the drowsy baby. "Wretch," he murmured as she passed him.

Her hands were shaking as she settled Matthew on his stomach and drew the light cotton blanket over him. Wouldn't you know, she thought cynically. To-night of all nights he'd go right to sleep. There was no reason she could delay her return to the living room and to Springer MacDowell's inimical gaze.

But luck, her recent enemy, had chosen to be kind. Marianne had arrived, looking tangled, sunburned and a little shell-shocked, with Andrew in tow. He had Eric hanging over his shoulder, Shannon in his lap, while his fierce eyes were fixed on Springer's lanky form.

"There you are, lassie," he rumbled, a wary look on his narrow face. "I've been meeting your man."

"He's not my man, Andrew," she said with more calm than she felt. "He's just an old—" for a moment her eyes met Springer's expectant ones "—an old friend."

Springer was looking both annoyed and amused at the angry Scottish terrier snapping at his ankles. "And who might you be when you're not defending the flower of womanhood?"

"Andrew Cameron," he shot back, still suspicious. "Have you come to make an honest woman of her?"

"Andrew!" Jessica gasped.

Springer's smile grew cooler. "Not really. But then, I was never given the chance in the first place, was I, Jessica?" His look was a direct challenge, one she wished she could avoid.

But she wasn't a coward, when all was said and done. "No, you weren't," she admitted, and was rewarded by Marianne's and Andrew's looks of shocked disapproval.

"You mean you didn't tell him you were expecting Matthew?" Marianne questioned finally.

"Look, do we need to go into all this right now?" she returned, riled up. "This is neither the time nor the place." She cast a pointed glance at the children, who were paying no attention to anyone but Andrew anyway. She sighed. "No, I didn't tell him. I didn't want to, I didn't think it was any of his business, and I don't think it's any of yours whether I did or not. I'm getting a drink. Do any of you want anything?"

"I'll come with you," Marianne said suddenly. "You want Scotch, Andrew?"

"What else?" he grumbled, still keeping a wary eye on the giant who had invaded Jessica's house.

The small pantry was dimly lit by the low-wattage light bulb overhead, and Jessica busied herself dragging out the various dusty bottles of liquor, hoping to avoid any more cross-examination.

"Do you still have that ancient bottle of Scotch Andrew brought over this spring?" Marianne questioned lightly.

"From Ye Auld Peat Bog Distillery? I do. No one else would drink it." She uncapped it, barely controlling a shudder as the strong fumes wafted through the enclosed space. She thrust it at Marianne. "You pour. I can't stand the smell of the stuff."

"Why not?" It was a simple question, sprung from idle curiosity, but it was all Jessica could do not to snap at her.

"I just don't," she managed calmly enough. "I must have gotten drunk on it when I was a kid. Have you got what you want?"

Marianne nodded. "Just a glass of wine. Are you coming?"

She took a deep breath, and the fumes of the Scotch seemed to press in around her. "I'll be there in a minute."

"Are you all right, Jessica? You look pale."

"Stress," she said with a forced laugh. "I'll be right out."

The swinging door closed behind Marianne's tall figure, and Jessica leaned on the counter, pressing her forehead against the cool glass in the cabinet doors. She could feel the trembling begin, and her fingers gripped the counter, her knuckles white with tension. When the door swung open behind her again she wouldn't, couldn't move. "Tell them I'll be right out, Marianne," she said in a choked voice.

She should have known. Broad, strong hands caught her shoulders from behind, pulling her unresisting body back against his. The fingers were kneading the knotted muscles beneath her yielding skin, and his voice was warm in her ear, stirring the cloud of wheat-blond hair. "What's going on, Jessie?"

It must have been the whisper. She could have sworn there was concern, caring, in that deep rumble of a voice. She could have closed her eyes and told herself he loved her, hated to see her in pain. And she could turn in his embrace, put her arms around his neck and hide her face against the soft, worn blue flannel shirt and tell him of her ghosts.

She clenched the countertop even tighter, her fingers cramping in pain, and she held herself stiffly. "I'm tired," she said in a low, noncommittal voice. "I didn't sleep well last night. I'll be fine once I get some sleep."

The smell of Scotch was clouding her brain, suffocating her. Couldn't he smell it, smell the insidious stuff poisoning the air in the small pantry? Couldn't he know, couldn't he remember?

Slowly the hands released her, the body moved back. "Do you want me to fix you a drink? It would help you sleep. I think Marianne's getting ready to leave—it shouldn't be long now. Plenty of time for you to get a good night's sleep, little mother."

"Damn you, stop calling me that!" Her voice broke. She pushed her way through the swinging door before Springer could reply with one of his sarcastic cracks.

Marianne was already out on the porch, both of her children protesting sleepily at the sudden curtailment of their evening. Andrew had drained his Scotch in one swift gulp and was watching them get ready to leave, an enigmatic expression on his narrow face.

"I want to ride with Andrew," Eric declared loudly, pulling out of his mother's hold.

"Andrew's not coming with us," Marianne said quickly, grabbing his arm again.

"Why not?" Eric demanded.

"Why not?" Shannon echoed.

Marianne looked as if she might cry with frustration and something else. "Because he has other things to do. Important things. He can't spend all his time with us."

Eric looked up at Andrew standing motionless on the porch. "What do you have to do that's more important than us?" he asked with simple curiosity.

"I haven't the faintest idea, laddie. Ask your mother."

"Ma, Andrew says—"

"Into the car, Eric. I don't care what Andrew says, it's late and I'm not in the mood for arguments. Get in." She slammed the door shut behind him before turning her harassed gaze at the couple on the porch. Favoring the unrepentant Andrew with a furious glare, she cast a worried glance at Jessica.

"You look like hell, Jessica," she announced. "I really appreciate your taking the kids today, and I'm going to return the favor tomorrow and take Matthew. You look like you need some time off."

"I can take care of Matthew." Springer had come up silently behind them, and Jessica could barely control her nervous start.

"I'm sure you can," Marianne replied. "But I owe Jessica, and the kids and I really look forward to having Matthew."

"If you like babies so much, you ought to have another one," Andrew suggested out of the blue.

Marianne just stared at him in complete amazement for a moment. And then she climbed into her car and drove off without another word.

"Women," Andrew Cameron announced with a sigh, "are the very devil."

"Yes," said John Springer MacDowell, "they are."

The late August night was very still as they stood on the porch and watched Andrew drive away, the ancient Valiant performing valiantly as always. It was a warm night, with only the faintest whisper of a breeze stirring the thickly growing maple leaves. The warmth of the night, the distant buzz of the kamikaze moths, the smell of the pines and the rich scent of the wild roses stirred Jessica in ways she wanted to forget. She felt weak and tired and very vulnerable, and that was the last way she wanted to feel when she was standing alone with Springer MacDowell. He still seemed to hold a powerful fascination for her, and she had to keep reminding herself just how dangerous he could be.

"Here's your drink, Jessica," he said lightly, his arm reaching around from behind her holding a small amber glass. His other hand had caught her elbow, and he held her there, lightly enough, the glass just beneath her nose, the smell of Scotch wafting upward like a cobra about to strike.

She stood very still, momentarily paralyzed. "I—I don't like Scotch," she managed in a strangled tone of voice.

"I know you don't," he said, his voice flat and inexorable, holding no softness, no compassion. "That's what Rickford Lincoln was drinking the night you freaked out. I want to know why."

"I . . . don't . . . like . . . Scotch." She was trembling violently, her teeth chattering. She couldn't even struggle against that hand holding her captive, the glass of Scotch still held in front of her. His grip wasn't that strong, she could break away if she wanted, but she was caught, trapped, and there was no escape.

"Why, Jessie?" His voice was cold, urgent. "Why?"

And then she did break his hold, pulling away from him. He let her go easily enough, but the Scotch spilled down the front of her loose cotton blouse.

She fell back against the column of the porch, staring stupidly at the growing stain, the smell of it surrounding her. It was like blood washing over her, she thought dazedly. She raised her head to look into Springer's coldly calculating eyes, and another shiver ran through her.

"I was sixteen," she said finally, her voice rusty with pain. "And I was a very young sixteen. I had spent most of my adolescence taking care of my family. I'd never dated, never went to parties, didn't even have any close friends that I could talk with. I thought sex was something that happened in movies, in fields of clover and daisies with pretty people. I didn't know it could be ugly and dirty and painful."

He was standing very still, watching her, the half-empty glass of Scotch in one hand.

"Are you sorry you pushed it, Springer?" she said grimly. "I can make you sorry; I can make you very sorry."

He seemed mesmerized by the husky sound of her pain-filled voice, but with an effort he shook it off. "So you had an unpleasant time with one of your sister's boyfriends," he hazarded. "No one much likes sex the first time. But they don't make a grand opera tragedy out of it; they don't use it as an excuse for the rest of their lives."

"It wasn't one of my sister's boyfriends, Springer," she said, a part of her anticipating his shock, a part of her relishing it. Let someone else share the horror of it for a change, let someone else hurt. "It was my father's drinking buddy. It was a fifty-three-year-old, fat, red-faced drunk who raped me on the kitchen floor while my father was passed out on the couch, who poured Scotch down my throat and did things to me I didn't even know people did to each other. And when my mother came home and my father sobered up, they told me I was lying, they told me I was just trying to get attention, and they told me to apologize to Uncle Bob. And that, Springer, is when I tried to kill myself."

He was standing there, very still, no discernible expression on his dark face. She pushed herself away from the dubious support of the porch and moved close to him, just inches away, and the heat from their bodies made the smell of the Scotch that much stronger. "Do you like hearing about it, Springer?" she questioned, her voice low and hurried. "Does it turn you on to hear just what a victim your son has for a mother?" She reached out and took the glass of Scotch from his hand, draining it defiantly. "I haven't told a living soul about that since my parents accused me of lying. Do you like hearing about it, Springer? I could go into all sorts of details if you'd like. I haven't forgotten it, you know. You accused me of having an incredible capacity for self-deception. But I never deceived myself; I always remembered. Maybe you'd like to hear how he made me help him, made me—"

"Don't, Jessie." His voice was low, hurting for her, and it was the last straw. She had thought she wanted him to hurt, wanted him to feel the pain she'd felt for so long, but she was wrong. The words were said, they were out, and she couldn't call them back, no matter how much she wanted to. And she wanted to very badly.

She looked down at the empty glass she was holding. "You were a piker, you know," she said suddenly in a conversational tone. "You thought you hated your father. It was nothing compared to how much I hated my parents. I hated them so much I would have killed them if I could; I hated them so much I was over-whelmingly, giddily relieved when they died, so relieved I could barely keep from laughing out loud at their funeral.''

"Jessie—''

"But I was smarter than you were, Springer. I knew that I loved them as much as I hated them. And I knew I was going to have to live with that for the rest of my life. And I was doing a damned good job of it, until you showed up. Until you strolled into my life and decided to turn it upside down for some stupid whim. And you're still doing it, still pulling me in a thousand different directions, and I'm not going to spend the rest of my life loving and hating someone so that I'm half crazy with it. Go away, Springer. For God's sake, leave me in peace.''

"Jessie, stop it.'' He moved towards her then, and in a moment she would have been enfolded in those strong arms of his, and she would have been lost forever. The sound of Matthew's sudden wails pierced the night.

She could taste the Scotch in her mouth, and the nausea rose suddenly. "Take care of Matthew,'' she gasped, and turned and ran, stumbling down the front steps and across the lawn.

The woods were still and quiet when she entered them, the only sound the rough rasp of her breath, the crackle of the underbrush beneath her sneakered feet. When she could finally run no more, she sank to her knees in the long grass and threw up the Scotch. She stumbled onward a few more feet, and then she collapsed against a huge boulder, sat there and cried, wept and howled and raged for the child she had been. And she wept away the anger and fear of sixteen years, wept away the shame and the misery and the guilt.

Slowly, gradually the tears died away. She leaned back against the boulder, the granite rough through the thin cotton shirt, and rubbed her sleeve across her wet and swollen face. The moon was almost full, peering at her through the tops of the trees, and Jessica stared up at it, feeling still and peaceful for the first time in years.

The horror was gone. Over. By telling Springer, by letting it out, by crying and raging and storming, she had released it, and the dark cloud that had lodged somewhere beneath her breast had disintegrated, leaving her miraculously alone, somehow fresh and new and clean. Springer had been right about one thing—she needn't make it an excuse for the rest of her life. It was past, over and done with, and it was gone. Wondrously gone.

She had no idea what time it was. She could have been out there for minutes or hours, she had no idea which. It must have been a good long while—the moon had traveled halfway across the sky while she was out there, and it was already making its descent. Stretching out her cramped legs, Jessica stared down at the grass-stained jeans, wrinkled her nose at the lingering smell of the Scotch spilled over her shirt. Slowly she pulled herself to her feet, still trembling slightly, like someone recovering from a long illness. She moved back through the woods toward the house and the lake, silently, ears attuned to any untoward noise.

She knew the sound of the woodland fauna, the little rustle of the squirrels and rabbits, the sudden hush of the litter of foxes down by the edge of the forest, the distant whir of the owl. The raccoons would be out foraging, and the porcupine would doubtless be looking for some inquisitive dog to punish. No one was going to harm her that night.

The house was still and silent, the front light a yellow glow in the moonlit night. She stood for a moment on the front lawn, hesitating. Springer must have settled Matthew back down—he would have gone back to sleep easily enough. He never stayed awake long at night unless he was teething, and Jessica had seen no signs of it that day.

She could go in, take a shower and climb into bed. The moon was shimmering off the lake, the air was fresh and cool and clear, and she didn't even hesitate. She wasn't ready to go back inside, she needed to celebrate her sudden freedom a few moments longer.

The rickety old dock shifted beneath her feet as she stepped onto it, and she could see the darting, swooping forms of the night-flying bats out in the middle of the lake. She kicked off her sneakers and her grass-stained jeans, and pulled the whisky-soaked shirt over her head. And then she dived into the water in one fluid move.

The water was like black satin, warm in the cool night air, gliding over her naked skin like the touch of a lover. She slid through it, cleansing her body as her soul had been cleansed, reveling in the purity of form and feeling and emotion.

She didn't want to leave, but her body was weak from the trauma of the past few hours, and her limbs began to tremble from the exertion. It took the last bit of her energy to pull her body out of the water onto the splintery deck, and she sat there on the wooden planks for a long moment, shivering in the cool night air, too tired and too peaceful to move.

When she finally climbed to her feet, he was waiting. She recognized him without any surprise or embarrassment. Without a word he wrapped the huge beach towel around her chilled body, without a word he began to dry her, his hands gently efficient as they rubbed her icy flesh. And then his deft hands fastened the towel in front, tucking the ends in the cleft between her breasts, with an oddly gentle gesture.

She met his gaze then, fearlessly, not sure what to expect from him. Pity, perhaps. Even reluctant condemnation. But not what she thought she was seeing. It was so unexpected she refused to recognize it, dropping her eyes to the splintered dock.

His hands were on her bare arms, sliding up them with a lover's touch, pulling her gently, inexorably against him. Before she could even guess what he intended, his mouth dropped onto hers, a gentle, searching kiss, devoid of lust, devoid of passion, devoid of that smoking, simmering sex they'd shared. It was a tender meeting of mouths—touching, soothing, loving—and when he pulled back she simply stared at him, too bemused to say a word.

"Come back to the house, Jessie," he murmured. "You need to sleep."

She shook her head, suddenly frightened. She wasn't ready to go to bed with him, she wasn't ready to sleep alone. She wasn't ready to face either of those two possibilities.

"Come back to the house," he said again. "Matthew's sound asleep, but I don't want to leave him for long. I don't want to leave you, either. Come back to the house." A wry smile lit his face, the first she'd seen in hours, days. "I'll even let you have your bedroom back."

She wanted to shake her head again, but she couldn't. One strong arm slid around her shoulders, pulling her against him, and he started back up the lawn to the quiet old house. And leaning her head against his shoulder, she went with him.

And it was only later, lying alone in the narrow bed up under the eaves, that she remembered the words she'd flung at him on the front porch. She'd told him she hated him. That should have come as no surprise. But she'd also told him that she loved him, and the memory astonished her with its rightness. She could only hope that he hadn't heard the damning words. With a quiet groan she turned her face into the pillow and slept, a gloriously free and dreamless sleep.

# Chapter Thirty-two

There was a storm coming. Jessica could feel it in her bones, could smell it on the hot, dry wind, could sense it in the tension of the air.

Of course, it could have been the very real tension between her and Springer. They'd skirted each other— oh, so politely—all day long, without even the buffer of Matthew to protect them. Jessica had slept late, physically and emotionally exhausted, and by the time she managed to drag her weary body out of bed, Marianne was already sharing coffee with Springer in the big old kitchen.

Her sudden, irrational surge of jealousy was a bad way to begin the day, and Marianne's searching look didn't improve matters. But for once her tactless friend held her tongue. Jessica could feel the concern radiating toward her, and she knew it didn't come from Marianne alone. But she refused to meet Springer's gaze, concentrating on Matthew, on her mug of strong coffee, on the hot, sunny day outside the open casement windows.

"We're going to the Discovery Museum," Marianne

announced as she finished her coffee. "The kids love it, and I wouldn't be surprised if Matthew got something out of it. Then McDonald's, and home. We'll be back in the early evening. No, don't get up; Springer already got me enough diapers to float the Russian navy."

"Don't give him any french fries," Jessica warned, trying to control the bereft feeling that had swept over her. They didn't need her, Matthew didn't need her, she was a stranger in a strange land.

"Your ma's a stern taskmaster, kid," Marianne informed Matthew cheerfully. "See you later."

The silence in the kitchen stretched and grew. Jessica kept her attention on her coffee, staring into the black depths as if it held the answer to the questions of the universe. She could feel him watching her, feel those dark, dark eyes trying to read her like a book.

She got up briskly, looking just over his left shoulder. "Well, I've got work to do," she announced cheerfully.

"What sort of work?" It was the first thing he'd said to her all morning, and the sound of his voice sent shivers down her spine. She felt open and vulnerable after the storm of last night, and she kept her gaze on the shimmering lake out the window.

"Writing."

"What sort of writing?" He asked the question lazily enough, but Jessica could feel the real curiosity beneath it.

Steeling herself, she moved her eyes a fraction to the right, looking directly at him. There was no reason to keep it a secret any longer. "*The Slaughterer*," she said, and left the room.

She'd dragged out the Selectric, sorted through her papers, and seated herself at the dining-room table when Springer strolled into the room, a mug of coffee steaming in his hand. He set it down beside her, an enigmatic expression on his face. "You usually drink two or three cups of coffee," he observed. "You've only had one."

She reached out a slightly trembling hand for it. "Maybe I should switch to decaffeinated."

"Maybe you should." He pulled out the chair opposite her and slid into it. "How long have you been doing it?"

"Since Christmastime. The last four novels were mine."

"*Decker's Return*? I thought Johnson had improved."

A smile lit her face. "Your poor father. He thought no one knew that he had ghostwriters."

"Everyone knew," Springer said, tilting back in the chair. "We just let him keep his little fantasy."

"I'm surprised. I think he thought that if you knew you'd somehow use it to harm him."

"There's not much harm a high school English teacher could do to him," he said casually.

"A what!" Jessica shrieked in patent disbelief.

A crooked smile lit his face. "I didn't think that would elicit such a violent reaction."

"You're a high school English teacher?" she demanded, astonished disbelief washing over her.

"Essentially. It's not really a high school, more an experimental educational experience, as they like to call it. But I teach English and American literature and coach their sorry excuse for a basketball team. I thought you knew what I did for a living. I guess I over-estimated my fascination for you."

She shook her head. "I never let Elyssa talk about you. I thought you were a moneyed playboy, what with that car and your jet-setting life-style."

"What jet-setting life-style?" He snorted. "Teachers get summers off, not to mention midterm vacations and the like. It doesn't pay well, but it has its advantages. Sorry to disillusion you—I'm just a working stiff. I have a small trust fund from my grandfather, enough for my needs and a few luxuries, but not much more than that." His eyes seemed to be testing her, but she was still too caught up in the novel idea of his profession to notice.

"I always figured you did something very glamorous and very dangerous," she murmured.

He laughed, a soft, unaffected laugh, the first real sound of pleasure between them in a year. "Glamorous, no; dangerous, yes. You can't imagine what it's like with the kids I teach."

"Are they disadvantaged?"

"You might say so. Their only problem is that they're very, very bright. Gifted, all of them. There are times when it would be a hell of a lot easier if I just taught remedial reading."

"So you spend your time surrounded by budding geniuses?"

"It's demoralizing," he said with a sigh. "At least I manage to get my own back on the basketball court."

"I bet you started the basketball program for the sole purpose of salving your ego." She was enjoying this easy, comfortable banter, and she found herself holding her breath, frightened that something might smash the delicate accord, turn it back into the hostility that ate at her soul.

He smiled, a warm, endearing smile. "I thought you said you didn't know me very well," he drawled. "That's exactly why I did it. That, and to keep them from thinking they had it all over their English teacher. Kids can be ruthless."

"Not Matthew," she said firmly.

"Don't you believe it. That baby has you wrapped around his little finger, and he's going to start testing you sooner than you think. By six months they like to see just how far they can go, and they keep on testing through adolescence."

"You sound like you've had firsthand experience," she said lightly.

He blinked those extraordinary dark eyes of his. "I have," he said. "Didn't you know that, either?"

"Know what?"

"Matthew has a twelve-year-old sister."

She just stared at him, unsure of her reactions. A part of her wanted to rage at him—the depth of her envy was an overwhelming surprise. She also felt an inexplicable longing for a solemn-eyed older sister for her baby.

"Where is she now?" She kept her voice deceptively level as she toyed with her coffee mug.

"With her mother. Maureen has her during the summer; I have her the rest of the time."

"Isn't that a little unusual?" There was no doubt as to her feelings now. They were sheer panic. If he'd already managed to get custody of one child, the second one should prove a piece of cake.

"We didn't fight over it," Springer said after a moment, his observant eyes recognizing her fear and doing his best to assuage it. "Maureen didn't want to be tied down."

"And you did? I thought you'd spent your entire adult life avoiding commitments."

"Just commitments I knew I could never keep. You haven't been going out of your way looking for any sort of commitment, either, as far as I can see."

"Matthew's enough for me," she said staunchly.

"And Katherine was enough for me," he shot back. "Until Matthew was born."

"Katherine?" Jessica echoed softly.

"Katherine," he verified. "Are you sure you never heard her name mentioned? I could have sworn—"

"Oh, her name was mentioned, all right," Jessica said lightly. "But there was never any mention that she was your twelve-year-old daughter. I only knew she was someone important to you."

"And you didn't bother to ask?"

She was too open and vulnerable to lie to him anymore. "I was afraid to."

That stopped him cold for a moment, and she waited to see how he'd respond. "She was in a car accident last summer," he said slowly. "My ex-wife was driving. Katherine's right leg was crushed—she's been through a lot this year." He seemed to hesitate. "She had the accident the night I spent with you at your apartment. That was why I left town without a word."

It was an apology, an explanation, however tentative. One that Jessica wasn't sure she deserved.

"Is she all right now?" she asked delicately.

Springer shrugged. "She's still in a brace. I'll find out when I get back to Seattle."

Jessica didn't even flinch at the reminder. "I'd better get to work," she said distantly.

Springer took the hint. "I'll leave you, then. I'm going to do something about the dock. Part of it's rotten—I'd hate to think of you going through it during one of your midnight swims."

The screen door had slammed shut behind his tall figure, and she found her eyes following him down the wide expanse of lawn to the lake. It took her a long time to turn back to Matt Decker.

THE SHADOWS CAME over the house swiftly. Jessica looked up from Matt Decker's exploits to a gray, windy day, the not-so-distant crack of thunder finally penetrating her abstraction. The hot, sullen, muggy day had turned bad, and it was going to be a hell of a storm.

She flicked off the Selectric with only a small pang. She hated to stop when things were moving along so well, but she also didn't fancy electrocuting herself for the sake of Matt Decker. Another crack of thunder shook the house, and the lights flickered and went off.

Jessica was struck with a strange sense of déjà vu. The power went off often enough around here, once every month or so. But it could never happen without bringing back to her memory the stormy night when Matthew was born by candlelight. And for the first time she found herself wishing that Springer had been with her.

Another crack of thunder, this one close enough to rattle the windows, pulled her out of her reverie, and she raced upstairs to close the windows left open in the early-morning heat.

There was still no rain when she finished with Matthew's downstairs bedroom, and she paused long enough to wonder where Springer was. He must have enough sense to know the lake was dangerous in a thunderstorm. She couldn't allow herself to worry about him—he was old enough to take care of himself.

Stepping out onto the porch, she peered toward the lake. There was no sign of Springer down there, and she perched on the edge of the railing, content to watch the violence of nature from her safe haven. The lake was an angry black, the foam of the whitecaps a delicate lace trimming. The lightning split the roiling dark sky with malevolent regularity, and the pine trees by the shore bent with the wind. It was awesome and frightening in its elemental majesty, and the longer Jessica watched the more peaceful she felt in comparison. The storm outside was storm enough for her—inside, all was still and calm and very clear.

She could see her vegetable garden in the distance, its neat weedless rows a tribute to her compulsiveness if nothing else. The old red barn, all that was left of the farm that had preceded the MacDowell summer house, stood tall and proud against the blackening sky. The Gebbies used it for haying—bales and bales of hay were stored there right now.

The door flapped open in the wind, and Jessica

watched it in dismay. It would have to be the door on the west side, she thought dismally, wincing as the thunder crashed again. The rain always came from that direction, and the bulk of the hay was stored directly in the line of the weather.

In the short time Jessica had lived in Vermont, she'd been inundated with stories of barn fires, usually caused by improperly dried hay. The Gebbies were far too industrious to ever risk storing wet hay, but would baled hay be just as dangerous if it got soaked by the rain?

She could teleiphone the Gebbies and warn them. But she had always been warned to stay away from television sets, the telephone and running water during a thunderstorm. Of course she could close the door herself, race across the narrow field before the rain hit. Did cows ever get hit by lightning? Would a hapless human being?

She was barefoot, dressed in a loose cotton sundress that enveloped her slender body. She could always go up and find her shoes and a rain poncho, but that would take more time. She could ignore the noisy, flapping door and spend the rest of the summer worrying that the barn on her doorstep would burst into flames. Or she could bite the bullet, light out across the field immediately, and if the rain hit, she could always wait out the storm in the cavernous old barn.

It wasn't rain. It was hail, the size of acorns, and it started when she was halfway across the field, bounding off the grass, tapping against the wooden sides of the barn that loomed ahead of her, pelting her with tiny, stinging pellets that made her gasp with pain and temper. The rain came with it, a solid, drenching sheet of it, so that by the time she stumbled into the old barn she was soaked to the skin and feeling very much like an abused pincushion.

The wind was strong enough to fight her for possession of the door, and it took all her strength to pull it shut after her. She was panting from her headlong dash across the field, and her feet hurt from the stubbled grass. But the cavernous old barn with its insulation of hay muffled the fury of the storm, and in the dim light from the octagonal window up by the roofline the place looked surprisingly peaceful. The sweet-smelling hay tickled her as she plopped down on a loose pile of broken bales, and she surveyed her surroundings with, if not outright enthusiasm, at least a sense of safe harbour. *A port in a storm,* she thought, leaning back against the hay and listening with distant satisfaction to the steady thrum of the rain on the tin roof, punctuated by staccato bursts of hail. The thunder was an occasional fanfare in the distance, and Jessica lay there in the soft hay and listened to the symphony, wriggling her bare toes in the misty darkness.

A murky light washed across her as the side door was thrust open. She sat up quickly, and the door slammed shut again, plunging them both back into the shadows.

He moved slowly across the uneven floorboards of the old barn. She should get up and face him, she knew she should, not just lie there in the hay, her eyes wide, waiting, waiting.

The rain had plastered the thin white shirt to his strong torso, and the smell of the storm hung heavy in the air, mixing with the sweet scent of the hay. Someone had once told her that hay was an aphrodisiac. Watching Springer as he moved toward her in the darkness, she could well believe it.

He stopped within a foot of her, his dark eyes black, the raindrops clinging to the smooth planes of his face. She waited for him to say something, knew she should break the silence, but neither of them spoke. Slowly he raised one strong well-shaped hand and undid the first button of his drenched shirt. His eyes never leaving hers, his hand went to the second button, then the third. And then the shirt was loose around him, and he'd pulled it off and sent it sailing into the bed of hay beside her.

Her breath suddenly felt tight in her lungs, and her heart was hammering at a rapid pace. She opened her mouth to say something, then shut it again.

"How scratchy is the hay?" His voice was a low-pitched drawl as he kicked off his Nikes.

Somewhere she found her voice. "It's pretty soft. It's from an early June cutting, and the hay—" her voice choked for a second "—doesn't get coarse until July."

"Good," he said, kneeling down in the hay beside her. He checked the grass with his hands. "Not too bad. We can always put your dress under you."

"Springer..." The beseeching sound of his name was all that came out, and she kept her large, worried blue eyes trained on his face. He looked gentle, amused and very determined.

"Yes?" he said softly, waiting.

She sat there in the sweet-smelling hay with the storm all around her and the man she was afraid she loved kneeling in front of her. "Just Springer," she said on a sigh, reaching her arms up to twine them around his neck and pull him towards her. His mouth met hers, the impetus of his body continuing to push them down into the hay. His mouth was wet and strong on hers, his tongue searching and tasting her, meeting her response with obvious pleasure. His broad, strong hands ran along her sides, up under her dress, pulling it up over her head and tossing it to join his shirt. She lay there in the hay, wearing nothing but a skimpy pair of panties, smiling up at him with unhidden warmth in her blue, blue eyes.

"Some Ice Princess," he murmured, his mouth tasting the corner of hers. "Are you all right? Do you want something underneath you?"

She pulled him down on top of her with a sudden exuberant strength, kissing him deeply. "Just you," she growled sexily.

He laughed then, the sound of his pleasure echoing and wonderful in the empty barn. "That's very easily arranged," he said, rolling on his back and taking her with him. "But you have to do all the work."

She cradled his head in her hands, letting her gently questing mouth trail over his face. "All right," she murmured against his damp, parted lips. "But you'll have to help me. I've only done this once before."

"You were very good at it, as I remember," he said against her lips, and the tingling vibration tickled her. "Use your imagination."

His skin was warm and sleek beneath her hands, and she slid her fingers beneath the waistband of his jeans to unsnap the snap. She pulled the jeans off him, with his help, and stripped off her panties, and then there were just the two of them, lying naked in the soft hay, relearning each other's bodies with slow, delicious fervor; all the while the storm raged outside.

In the end he did have to help her. With his willing cooperation she brought them both to the very pinnacle of desire, with her hands and her mouth and her body telling him how much she loved him while the words stayed unspoken. But at the last moment she hesitated, suddenly unsure, and his strong hands took over, pulling her willing body over his, arching up to fill her before those last-minute doubts could take hold.

They remained very still for a moment, not moving, and Jessica looked down with wonder at the face of the man beneath her and within her, the man who filled her body and her life, and she wanted to weep with the frightening wonder of it.

Springer's eyelids fluttered open, as if aware of her regard, and he smiled up at her, his expression slightly dazed, his breath shuddering in his chest as he tried to control the passion that raged through his body. "We should do this more often," he said in a husky whisper. "It sure beats the hell out of fighting."

She deliberately tightened around him, and was rewarded with a groan of pure delight. She felt deliciously powerful, and yet completely helpless in the face of this wondrous, frightening thing they shared. "I don't know," she said in a tiny, breathless whisper. "We always seem to end up like this before long."

"Thank heaven for that," he breathed fervently. His hands slid up her torso to cup her full breasts, his long fingers wickedly clever. "I like what our son did to your body. Remind me to thank him when he's older." Reaching up, he captured one nipple in his mouth, swirling his tongue over the turgid peak, and this time her reaction was involuntary delight.

His strong, warm hands slid back down to capture her hips, pulling her forward, then rocking her back again. She caught the rhythm, a smile on her face.

"You're in such a hurry," she chided, keeping her voice level with an effort. "What's the rush? We have all afternoon."

He arched up against her, and a slow, unexpected moan of pure pleasure escaped her lips. Her tenuous feeling of control was slipping away, replaced by the sweet-smelling barn and the surging, thrusting passion that threatened to split her body. She should try to slow the pace, she thought dazedly, try to prolong the pleasure.

But there was no staying the inevitable. She could feel her body tremble, feel him tense beneath her, and then all conscious thought left her as wave after wave washed over her, and she could feel him join her, flooding her with love and delight.

She collapsed against him, and his strong arms came around her, cradling her tenderly. She was vaguely aware of his racing heart beneath hers, the tortured rasp of his breathing. Jessica wanted the moment to last forever, the sweet, savoring aftermath of passion strangely precious to her. She wanted to press her mouth against his sweat-damp chest and tell him that she loved him, she loved him.

She bit her lip, stilling the words that threatened to

spill over. She was so very tired. Her body felt drained. She closed her eyes for a brief moment, her ears filled with the steady beat of the rain on the tin roof. There was no telltale click-click—the hail must have passed. The thunder rumbled in the distance, and Springer's heart slowed its tumultuous pounding beneath hers.

She should feel panic, she should try to move away. But she couldn't. Just for now she was going to ignore the danger signals, just for now she was going to rest in the comfort of his big strong body. Later she could run.

WHAT THE HELL was he going to do? She lay there so peacefully, curled up in the hay, with her long, delicate legs like a newborn colt's. Even now he wanted to roll her on her back in the scratchy hay and make love to her all over again.

He was in love with her. He had finally stopped fighting it. At the age of thirty-six he ought to have learned to stop butting his head against a brick wall. He loved and wanted her, not for a one-night stand or a two-year affair. He wanted her for life. They belonged together; he could no longer ignore that simple, essential fact. It only remained for him to convince her.

And she was going to take some convincing. He could still see the wariness, the shadow of distrust in her blue, blue eyes as she looked up at him. But he could also see the vulnerable mouth, feel the longing she tried to disguise, the same longing he felt and had fought against in the year he'd known her.

Most of that year had been spent apart. When it came right down to it, what did they have in common? Apart from Matthew, that is.

And a love of children. A feeling for the old Vermont house. Their struggle to survive shattered childhoods. A fear of loving and being loved. Their love for Elyssa. Amused appreciation for the Slaughterer. Not to mention their incredible sexual bond. Hell, she probably even liked basketball.

He'd have to move slowly and carefully, so as not to startle her. She could learn to trust him, learn to open up to him. He had to be patient with her.

Because she was more than worth it. Somehow with her awkward intensity she moved him more than any woman had ever had. Moved his body, his mind, his soul. And when he'd least expected it he'd entrusted it all to her, along with his love. He was going to have to earn hers in return.

And in the meantime he was going to have to be very careful. He was going to have to suffer the torments of the damned and watch her as she slept that innocent, sated sleep that she so badly needed. And move very, very slowly.

With a sigh he leaned back against the hay. It was scratchier than she'd told him—it felt like a hair shirt on his bare back, but he deliberately refrained from rummaging around for his shirt. Right now he needed all the physical discomfort he could find to keep his mind off the sleeping woman next to him. Pushing deeper into the hay, he closed his eyes.

# Chapter Thirty-three

**The Slaughterer, vol. 99 untitled**

*Matt Decker surveyed the carnage around him. He should have known better; women were nothing but trouble. He'd lived long and hard, he should have known by now that the only thing you can trust is your buddy and your gun. He gave a fond pat to his snub-nosed 45mm enforcer. It was even prettier than that damned interfering female, and it did what it was told to do. When could you say that about a woman?*

*But Ilse was different. She could handle a flamethrower with the best of them, put a bullet neatly between a terrorist's eyes at twenty paces, and her strong, athletic body made him sweat just thinking about it. Running a hand through his silky black hair, he thought back to the afternoon, their bodies mingling, twisting, turning in the Salvadoran sunlight. He could almost taste the sweet-salty perfume of her flesh. . . .*

"DAMNATION!" Jessica pulled the paper out of the typewriter, slashed through the line about his silky black hair and glared at the offending manuscript. If she kept up like this, she'd have to do first drafts, and that would cripple her efficiency. Even now Matthew was sleeping less and less during the days, and there were too many other things to do, besides.

Of course, it was a wonder she could write at all, given the circumstances. When she'd awakened in the barn, she'd been curled up in a fetal ball, with Springer sitting there in his faded jeans, watching her out of fathomless eyes. And the panic she'd managed to squash down earlier washed over her.

She knew he recognized it as the sleepy smile that lit his face faded away beneath the look in his eyes. He managed a tight, tentative smile, watching her with that steady, unreadable regard, and she'd dressed hurriedly in the dress he'd handed her.

*Say something, damn it,* she'd begged silently. *Smile at me, kiss me, tell me anything. Tell me there's nothing to be frightened of, tell me you won't leave me like all the others have.* But he'd said nothing, that distant, preoccupied expression on his face. And together they'd walked back through the rain-spangled fields, not touching, each lost in his own thoughts.

He was sitting across the room from her now, ostensibly reading. But she was acutely aware each time he lifted his head to watch her, and he did it almost constantly. She had no idea what was going through his mind—she would have given ten years of her life and her share of Matt Decker's substantial royalties to know. But she couldn't bring herself to ask him. Those moments of communion and giving in the old barn were a mistake, and she knew that far too well. And Jessica tried very hard not to repeat her mistakes.

Sighing, she inserted another sheet of paper into the

Selectric. The lights had been on for an hour, though they flickered every now and then as if not quite sure they were going to stay. It was past nine, Marianne had brought Matthew back hours ago, and he was already settled for the night. The lights could go out again with impunity, as long as she was safely settled for the night in her bedroom, away from Springer's steady gaze.

And that was another problem. Which bedroom? Springer had let her have her old one, but she had no idea whether he'd continue to be so generous. And while it certainly didn't seem as if he'd want to share a bed with her, he might feel it incumbent on his masculine ego to make the attempt. The front room had a double bed, the one under the eaves was only a single iron bed with a sagging mattress.

There was no way she could tactfully bring up the subject. Except to say that she really needed her sleep. Or she could come right out and ask if she could have the small bedroom to herself. It would make it clear that she was wanting and expecting to sleep alone, and at least the uncertainty would be cleared up.

The lights flickered and dimmed again, brightened, then faded to a distant glow. "Damn," she said lightly, pushing away from the table. Springer hadn't moved, the darkness seeming to have little effect on the book he wasn't reading. "I give up."

Springer looked up politely, seemingly unmoved by the darkness. "Does this happen often?"

"Often enough. There's no way to tell how long it'll be off—it could be minutes or hours." She cleared her throat. "I think I'll go on up to bed."

He didn't move, but she could feel his eyes on her,

even through the darkness. Her palms were damp with sudden nerves, but she managed to keep her voice light. "Where would you like to sleep?" she asked brightly, then realized with growing horror, how that sounded. "I mean, you can have the small bedroom if you like. I'm perfectly comfortable in the front bedroom. Or if you'd rather have the front room, I can take the room under the eaves. It doesn't make any difference to me." She was babbling and she knew it.

He rose then, tossing the book to one side and crossing the room. She stood there unflinching in the face of his steady advance, wishing she could run and hide. But she was through running.

He put his strong, warm hands on her shoulders, the fingers kneading the tight flesh. "We'll sleep wherever you want, Jessie," he said gently. "But we'll sleep together. We've already spent too many nights apart."

"Springer, I don't think..." she began, trying to pull away, but his hands tightened imperceptibly, and in truth, she didn't want to leave him.

"Good," he said, his voice low and approving. "Don't think. If you think too much you'll just get scared all over again. Just feel." And his head dipped down, his mouth caught hers in a deep, searing kiss. "Come to bed with me, Jessie."

It would have taken a stronger woman than she was to resist such a devastating assault. She opened her mouth beneath his kiss, returning it, and when he moved away she nodded, afraid to trust her voice. And his hands tightened on her shoulder in what might almost have been relief, before leading her up the stairs to the narrow bed under the eaves.

IT WAS A RESTLESS NIGHT, her third night without Andrew.
That was how Marianne figured it—she didn't count
her afternoon among the raspberries two days ago. It
was the nights that were the hardest anyway. It was
amazing how fast she could come to need a man in her
bed. And not just any man. She needed Andrew, and
she hated both herself and him for having to admit it.

But admit it she did. She always tried to be honest
with herself, and whether she liked it or not, Andrew
had grown to be immeasurably important to her and
her family. Eric and Shannon constantly barraged her
with questions about him: when was he coming back,
would he live with them, would he teach Eric to play
the guitar? And Marianne had started out noncommittal, traveled to snappish, and finally ended up resigned.
He managed, in an indecently short time, to become
essential to her children as well as to herself, and she
didn't know what she was going to do about it.

It was different from the time that Tom left her. Despite her rage and hurt, the pain had lessened as the
days went on. With Andrew, each night grew harder,
until she was sitting there, staring at the almost full
moon, trying to control the urge to howl out her pain
like a wild dog.

The damned electricity didn't help. She had planned
to stay up late, watching late movies and eating whatever wasn't nailed down. Now she couldn't even read.
Not that she had anything in the house but those
damned romances, she thought irritably. Not what she
needed when she was trying to break herself of her
need for Andrew Cameron.

And Jessica didn't help, either. Marianne had taken

one look at her flushed, slightly dazed face and knew that her half-formed plan had worked. Somehow she and Springer had managed to overcome their differences long enough to give her whisker burns on her neck, and if everything wasn't hearts and flowers they were at least moving in the right direction. And Marianne had had to stifle the pang of envy that had washed over her. Why didn't she have a man like Springer MacDowell?

Except that she did. Granted, he was a hell of a lot shorter—and younger, for that matter. He was also domineering, bad-tempered, cheap and very, very sweet. Worst of all, he had an unfortunate tendency to take no for an answer.

And most amazing of all, Matthew didn't help. Marianne had been convinced that two children were enough for any sensible human being; toward the end of her marriage she had been considering having her tubes tied because of her certainty. But Andrew's careless words, outrageous as they had been, had somehow managed to penetrate her subconscious, so that she had spent the whole day playing with Matthew and suddenly, inexplicably, wanting another baby of her own. One with curly brown hair and green eyes and a stubborn soul.

With a quiet moan of despair she pulled herself away from the window. How in hell had she suddenly become so indecisive? She had always prided herself on knowing what she wanted. What in heaven's name had made her so dithery all of a sudden?

But she knew the answer to that. Andrew Cameron had made her into a helpless, lovesick fool, and there was no cure for it but time. And even that didn't seem like a sure thing.

"Mama?" A small, plaintive voice accompanied the shuffle of pajama-clad feet, and Shannon's rumpled blond head appeared at the door. "The lights are off."

"I know, sweetheart," Marianne said, sighing. "You remember, that happens sometimes. Go back to sleep, and tomorrow it will be all better."

"Couldn't Andrew fix it?" Eric had appeared behind his sister, a studious expression on his freckled face that was so like his mother's.

"I don't think so, darling."

"I bet he could. Why don't you go ask him? I bet he'd come over and try. I betcha," Eric said earnestly, and for a moment Marianne was tempted.

But she resisted the temptation. "The power's off all over the island, Eric. It's the power company, and Andrew can't do anything about that. It's probably even off at his place. We'll just have to sleep through it." A brilliant thought struck her. "We could all snuggle in my bed, like we do when it's real cold." And she wouldn't have to survive another empty night.

Eric shook his head solemnly. "I'm too old for that," he said with great dignity. "That's for when we're sick."

"I could always make an exception."

Eric shook his head determinedly. "I think Andrew should sleep in your bed with you. Like he did before."

Marianne didn't even flinch. "Before what?"

"Before you told him to go away," he said bluntly. "You are going to tell him you didn't mean it, aren't you?"

"I don't know. What makes you think I didn't mean it?"

Eric shook his head at the folly of adults, and Marianne had to resist the urge to hug him. He'd gotten so very wise all of a sudden. And Shannon was growing up. They weren't her babies anymore. "You think about it, Ma," he said gently. "G'night." Taking his sister's hand, he headed back down the darkened hallway.

When it got to the time when her eight-year-old could outthink her, Marianne thought dismally, she was in deep trouble. And maybe the honesty and principles that she'd prided herself on were nothing more than stupidity and pigheadedness. And why was she sitting alone in a candlelit bedroom when she wanted to cry from wanting Andrew?

It took Mrs. LaPlante's oldest teenaged daughter, Millie, half an hour to get there. She arrived with a six-pack of Tab under one arm and a transistor radio under the other, a nightgown and a stack of old Cosmopolitans in her tote bag.

"You sure your mother does't mind your spending the night, Millie?" Marianne questioned anxiously, brushing out her thick chestnut hair.

"Nah. She said she's just as glad to get rid of me," Millie confided with a swig of her Tab. "What time you figure you'll be back tomorrow?"

"Oh, not too late," Marianne said vaguely, wondering if she should try to dig up her antique supply of makeup. She could always borrow some of Millie's. She seemed to be wearing enough to supply an entire

Miss America pageant. No, it would be a waste of time. Cameron would have to accept her the way she was. If he wanted a painted woman, he'd have to look further.

"The children know you're going to be here," she said, pulling on a light sweater against the gathering night chill. "They should sleep straight through, though. I don't expect you'll have any trouble."

"Don't expect I will. Got anything to eat?"

Marianne cast a critical glance at Millie's pasty, starch-filled form. "Help yourself," she said cryptically. "What's mine is yours."

The night was still and beautiful as Marianne drove across the island. All the houses were dark, all the few streetlights extinguished by the power blackout. The moonlight was enough to illuminate everything, and Marianne succumbed to temptation on the back road and flicked off the headlights for a few moments. It was almost as clear as daylight on the narrow road ahead of her, and she reveled in the fairy-tale magic of the night.

She didn't even stop to consider whether Andrew would be at home, whether he'd be happy to see her. She didn't stop to consider whether she could find her way to his cabin in the woods. Once she'd made the decision, she wasn't about to start thinking up problems or she'd change her mind.

Except that she couldn't go back and face Millie La-Plante's vapid blue eyes and Tab belches. She'd burned her bridges, or close enough, and she had to face Andrew.

It took her close to an hour to find the cabin, an hour fraught with panic, near-tears and an alarmed resignation. The woods all looked alike in the moonlight, and the path twisted and curved and joined other paths. She visited the raspberry bushes, the copse of trees where she'd plundered his evergreens, the small, gurgling stream that rushed with the new-fallen rain. She was just about to give up in tears when the last path she had taken twisted around into a clearing, and the log cabin lay in front of her, dark and silent.

Of course it would look uninhabited, she told herself bravely. After all, it was probably after midnight, and the power was off. Cameron would have gone to bed early. That's where she'd find him.

But what, she thought suddenly, if he wasn't alone? What if some lively young creature, one of Millie's skinnier friends, was right now warming that narrow bed of his? The thought was at first so devastating that Marianne nearly crawled back off into the woods, awash in misery.

And then her backbone stiffened. If he was there, lost in the throes of passion, then it was better she found out about it now.

She'd be polite, though. She'd give him fair warning. Striding up to the rough-hewn front door, she rapped sharply, waiting for a sleepy voice to bid her enter.

Not a sound issued forth. She knocked again, and still no answer. She hadn't even thought of that possibility. Maybe he'd gone to Millie's friend's house. Damn it, she had to stop that sort of thoughts. As far as she knew, Millie didn't even have any friends. Cameron had probably flown back to Scotland, as far away and as fast as he could. She'd been nothing but trouble, and he had gotten tired of dealing with her moods.

She reached out and tried the door. It swung open to

her touch, revealing the dark, empty cabin, the power tools at the far end silent sentinels.

"Cameron?" she called softly, her voice just slightly nervous. "Andrew?"

He was well and truly gone. Moonlight streamed in a window over the narrow bed, and she could see the neatly-made covers, the one pillow with not a dent in it. He'd left, without a word.

Her choices were simple. She could try to find her way back through the moonlit forest and face Millie LaPlante's smirking face. Or she could curl up in that narrow little bed and cry herself to sleep.

There really was no choice at all. The night was cool, but the house still held the day's warmth. She stripped off her clothes and climbed naked between the sheets of Andrew Cameron's narrow bed. The pillow smelled like his pipe. Turning her face into it, she let out a quiet little moan of pain.

"Where are you, Andrew?" she said out loud, her voice small and sad in the moonlit room. "Where are you?"

Her dreams were filled with him. With the sound of his voice, the feel of his body, the smell of his pipe. She moved restlessly in the bed, searching for a heavy sleep that eluded her, her senses still filled with the memory of him. And then her eyes flew open as her head left the pillow. The pipe smoke was suddenly very real.

"Andrew?" Her voice was small and plaintive and just slightly nervous in the dark room. The moon had set sometime while she was sleeping, and she couldn't see a thing, could only smell the rich peaty smell of his pipe.

"Right here, lass," he said quietly, moving out of the shadows. She couldn't tell from his voice whether he was glad to see her or not, and his expression was hidden by the darkness. "What are you doing here? Where are the children?"

"I . . . I got someone to stay with them tonight. Millie LaPlante," she said, starting to sit up. And then she remembered she'd taken off all her clothes, and she slid back down again. She wasn't about to expose herself when she was still so uncertain about his reaction. "Where were you, Andrew?"

"I had to drive down to New York. Someone wanted me to build him a hammered dulcimer, and I'd made up several designs. I could have sent them to him, but I decided it might do me good to get away for a while. There didn't seem to be anything to keep me here." He sounded distant, almost philosophical, but he sat down on the bed beside her, still puffing gently on the pipe.

"You weren't gone very long." She wanted to reach out and touch his hand, to pull it to her breast, but she didn't dare.

"No, I wasn't. I wasn't any happier down there, so I figured I might as well come back. Why are you here, woman?"

Suddenly she found she liked the sound of that on his tongue, the rich Scottish burr wrapping around the word "woman." He made her feel like a woman, did Andrew Cameron. Ripe and fertile and feminine to his masculine, and she liked being in his bed.

"I wanted to ask you a question," she replied.

"And it couldn't wait till tomorrow?" He knocked

the dottle from his pipe and turned all his attention back to her. His hands were free now, but he still didn't touch her.

"It couldn't wait another hour." She pulled herself upright, holding the sheet around her breasts. "Cameron, why do you want to marry me?"

"Woman, you know that as well as I do."

"No, I don't," she cried. "All I know is that I don't want to marry you just for the sake of the children. I don't want to marry you to get Tom off my back. I don't want to marry you just to have someone to help me patch my roof or even to conduct sexual aerobics."

"You've made that clear, Marianne," he said wearily, and this time she recognized the thread of pain in his voice, and that pain was her triumph.

"Andrew," she whispered, "there's only one reason I want to marry you, and that's because I love you. I don't want to marry you for practical reasons—I hate being practical. I only want to be with you because we belong together."

He sat there for a long, silent moment, listening to her declaration of love, and her fear began to come back. Only for a moment.

"You stubborn, pigheaded, impractical, nasty-tongued viper," he said, his hands finally reaching out to her. "I ought to beat you. If I weren't such a mild-mannered gentleman, I would. Do you know what you've put me through these past few days?"

She felt her body pulled against his, and she went happily. "Some mild-mannered gentleman," she scoffed. "You're just as pigheaded as I am. And you're the one who's gotten his own way. Do you realize how hard it is for me to admit you're right?" Since he was busy kissing her breasts, he couldn't do any more than give her a muffled assent. "And I don't want you saying I told you so. Andrew?" She let out a little gasp of surprised pleasure. "Andrew!" And then she giggled, an enchanting little ripple of laughter. "Andrew," she said, sighing and leaning back in the narrow bed. "Oooh, Andrew."

# Chapter Thirty-four

The moon had set hours ago, and still Jessica lay there, cradled against Springer's warm body in the narrow dip of the twin bed, watching the shadows move across the slanting ceiling. The house was still and silent all around them, and downstairs Matthew slept soundly. And Jessica lay there trying not to cry.

The body next to hers shifted, and the ancient springs of the iron bed creaked loudly. "Are you awake?" His voice came softly, the breath ruffling the hair above her ear, and she considered keeping silent.

"Yes," she whispered back. She had to say something; she couldn't just spend the rest of the night curled against his body, knowing he was going to leave. She'd have to give him his freedom, before he gave her hers.

"This isn't going to work, you know," she said.

"Isn't it?" He kept his voice neutral. He'd been expecting something like this.

"I thought you might be able to get a job teaching in Burlington," she went on, not really listening to him. "And I realized it wouldn't work. You can't make that sort of commitment; I don't want you to make that sort of commitment."

"All right," Springer said calmly.

"And you've got Katherine to think of. You can't uproot your daughter on a whim. She's been through too much in the past year, what with the accident and everything. You can't complicate her life any further."

"No," said Springer.

"I'll be just fine, you know. I already talked with Buddy LaPlante about firewood for the winter. He's going to deliver six cords sometime in early September. Maybe you could help me stack it before you go?"

"Certainly."

"And you might want to come back and see how we're doing. Maybe at Christmas," she continued, feeling strangely close to tears.

"Of course."

"But I can't make any promises, Springer," she said firmly. "We're not ready for it."

"I understand perfectly," he said, and he did. Far better than she did.

There was a long silence in the narrow bed. Jessica contemplated trying to move away, then changed her mind. She wanted the feel of his body against hers for as long as she could have it.

"Aren't you going to argue with me?" she demanded suddenly.

"No."

"Don't you care?" She sounded lost and waiflike, and Springer laughed, a low, sexy laugh that sounded completely heartless to her vulnerable ears.

"You seem to have it all worked out," he said politely. "It doesn't sound as if it's open for discussion."

"So you won't try to change my mind?"

He smiled down at her lazily. "Of course not."

"You agree with me?" she persisted, not knowing what she wanted from him, only knowing his acquiescence was tearing her heart apart.

"I didn't say that. I just said there didn't seem much point in arguing about it right now," he murmured peacefully.

His body was warm and strong against hers. His mouth was teasing her neck, his teeth nipping lightly against the sensitive skin, and she could feel the fires stirring and building deep within her once again. "When do you think you'll be leaving, then?" she managed to ask on a slightly strangled note as the wanting began to take over. She turned in his arms, feeling him hard and urgent against her.

He smiled down at her, and she would have said there were warmth and love in that smile. "Whenever you really want me to leave," he murmured against her mouth. "I'll stay until you tell me to go." And he deepened the kiss, his mouth pressing hotly against hers as his hand slid up and cradled her slender back. And then there was no longer any time for words.

AUTUMN WAS IN THE AIR. Jessica opened her eyes slowly, staring out the open casement window, and she could feel the promise of fall on the soft breeze. An errant branch of the maple tree outside the upstairs window had turned a flaming crimson against the green leaves, and soon the Canadian geese would start moving south. And Springer would be headed west.

He was so warm, his body wrapped around her smaller form. How many mornings had she awakened next to him? Just once, years ago, in her apartment in New York. And she had gotten up and run away.

She wanted to run away again. It felt too good to be lying beside him, warming herself next to his silken flesh. She always knew it would be—it had been self-preservation that had kept her away. That, and self-destruction. Nothing ventured, nothing gained, she told herself, sighing lightly. And how was she going to survive when he left her?

The distant, snuffling sound floated up the stairs, and immediately the adrenaline shot through her. Slowly, reluctantly, she pulled herself out of bed, carefully enough so that he slept on, his face young and peaceful-looking in sleep. She made it down to Matthew's bedroom, an old bathrobe thrown around her nude body, just in time to forestall his more forceful announcement that he was ready to get up.

"Hello there, munchkin," she cooed, lifting him out of the crib. "I haven't seen enough of you in the past few days. How do you like having your father here? Do you like it as much as I do?"

Matthew flailed his fists at her, managing one of those beatific smiles that never failed to melt her, and she cradled his small, squirming body against hers.

"Yes, I know," she murmured. "You want clean clothes and your bottle. Rest easy, little love. I'll take care of it."

The porch was cool and crisp in the late-summer air as Jessica trailed out there, the bathrobe wrapped tightly around her body. Perching in one of the wicker rocking chairs with Matthew wrapped tightly in a blanket, she leaned back, staring at the lake, while the baby made speedy, peaceful work of his bottle.

It was a glorious day, perhaps the last of her glorious days. Springer would be leaving soon, and the sooner the better for her peace of mind. But she knew deep in her heart that it was already too late. She'd fallen in love with him, let down her barriers long enough for him to make himself indispensable. And somehow things were never going to be the same again.

She looked down at the baby curled peacefully in her arms, those dark, dark eyes of his closed in bliss. Why was she sending Springer away? Why wasn't she giving him a chance to fall in love with her? Why was she determined to sabotage her life in the guise of saving it? What was the good of keeping a whole heart if it meant never feeling anything?

God help her, she didn't want him to leave. And it was time to be brave enough to tell him so. She could spend the rest of her life hiding from love, or she could reach out and fight for it. It was time, past time, for her to let go of the past. A sudden flood of resolve washed over her. She could make Springer MacDowell love her, she could.

Matthew opened his dark eyes, so like his father's, and stared up at his mother's determined expression. "Matthew, my angel," she cooed, smiling down at him, "we're not going to let him go."

"I'm glad you decided that," Springer said from the doorway, and his voice shivered deliciously down her spine. "Because I have no intention of leaving you. Ever." He moved out onto the porch, lithe and graceful and determined. He'd thrown on a pair of jeans and nothing else, and he shivered slightly in the cool breeze. "It's about time you realized we love each other. I'm not going to abandon you like everyone else. You can trust me, Jessie. I'm staying."

She turned slowly, her tear-filled ice-blue eyes meeting his over the silky black head of his son. "I know," she said, and her smile was brilliant in the early-morning sunshine. "I know."

JESSICA HANSEN MACDOWELL stared at the blank page with a combination of determination and malevolence. Matt Decker wasn't going to get the better of her. She'd climbed out of the big brass bed that now reposed in the tiny room under the eaves, crawled out from under the pile of patchwork quilts, leaving her husband sound asleep, and padded downstairs, barefoot, in her oversized Lanz nightgown. The Selectric still monopolized the dining-room table. She'd been stuck for two weeks now, unable to end volume ninety-nine, unable to even come up with a title. Now she at least had a glimmering of how to finish Decker's recent caper, and once the thought entered her mind she wasn't going to let the delicious comfort of her marriage bed stop her.

The house was crammed full of sleeping children. Matthew was still ensconced in his room at the bottom of the stairs, and next to him slept Springer's daughter Katherine, a solemn enchanting pixie of a child, with the same fathomless eyes of her half-brother and her father, and a brace on her right leg. A brace that should be gone by Christmas.

Eric and Shannon shared the front bedroom upstairs while Marianne and Andrew were spending the month touring Scotland. The children had accepted their mother's and stepfather's absence stoically enough, and Jessica was beginning to feel like the little old woman who lived in a shoe. A fitting comeuppance for a little mother, she thought with happy resignation.

Matt Decker was the only cloud on the horizon, but at a quarter past two on a chilly October morning she was about to whip him into shape.

"What are you doing?" Springer stood in the middle of the room, his silky black hair ruffled, the austere planes of his handsome face still dazed from sleep. "Are the kids all right?"

She was staring at the blank sheet of paper. "All sound asleep. I got a brainstorm tonight and decided I could finish number ninety-nine."

"I'm glad my lovemaking was so inspiring," he drawled, crossing the room with his usual lithe grace. He was wearing a dark blue velour kimono and nothing else, and Jessica looked at him with a sigh.

"You're distracting me, Springer," she said with mock sternness.

"Good." He enfolded her in his arms, his clever hands running over her flannel-covered body and dwelling on the soft curves and swells. "Do you have any idea how sexy this damned thing is? I'd take it over satin and lace anytime. You feel so soft and luscious underneath." To emphasize his point, his large hands caught her hips and drew her up against him. She almost consigned Matt Decker to eternal writer's block as she felt his arousal, and it took all her willpower to keep from sliding her hands inside his bathrobe.

"I've got to finish this, Springer," she said, a note of pleading in her voice. "Be good to me."

"I'm trying to be," he said with a groan. "How long will it take you?"

"Only a very few minutes if you stop distracting me," she promised.

"All right." He pulled out the chair for her, positioning himself behind her. "You type, I'll massage your shoulders. It's now—" he peered at the electric clock on the mantel "—two twenty-seven. At two thirty-seven you're coming back to bed with me. If it takes any longer than that, I'm going to do obscene things to you under the table. Then you'll know what real distraction is."

With a martyred sigh Jessica's fingers attacked the typewriter.

*Matt Decker surveyed the carnage around him. Stockholm was a bloody mess, and the amazon by his side looked singed from the trusty flamethrower she was never without.*

*He looked down at Ilse's passion-glazed face, and an amazing transformation came over his iron-hard features.*

*"Decker, are you smiling?" Ilse demanded.*

*Decker ran a hand through his close-cropped hair, and his gunmetal gray eyes were rueful. "Yeah, I guess I am. Sorry about that, babe. It won't happen again."*

"SPRINGER, PUT ME DOWN. I haven't quite finished."

"Yes, you have," he growled in her ear as he ascended the narrow staircase, Jessica held high against his chest. "You've already made sure that Decker and his war bride will live happily ever after. Now you've got to put some work in on us." He angled her in the door, kicked it shut behind them and dropped her on the bed.

"That's it! That's the title," Jessica crowed. "*Decker and the War Bride*! I love you, Springer!"

Springer followed her down on the bed. "I'm glad I have my uses," he murmured in her ear, his tongue making tiny, darting forays into the sensitive interior.

Jessica chuckled as she felt his hands begin to lift the admired nightgown. "Oh, you come in handy every now and then," she purred.

### The Slaughterer, vol. 99: Decker and the War Bride

*Matt Decker surveyed the carnage around him. He'd seen too many bloody battlefields, but this was the worst of all. Ilse, his Nordic goddess, his warrior woman, stood at his side, Beretta smoking.*

*"You surrender, Decker?" she questioned, her icy blue eyes shimmering in the moonlight. "A woman can't spend all her life fighting battles alone."*

*"You need a man by your side, baby," he said. "And I guess I'm that man." He dropped his Walther in the smoking rubble. "Come here, baby."*

*Ilse dropped the Beretta alongside his, kicking the dowsed flamethrower out of their way. "Meet me halfway, Decker."*

*"You got it." Scooping the blond amazon over his shoulder, Decker headed off for his traveling tank. His war bride snuggled up against him, blissfully happy.*

*"You think someday we'll have a little army of our own?" she said, sighing.*

*"You bet," Decker assured his woman. And he dumped her inside the tank, preparing to drive off into the blood-red sunset. "You bet."*

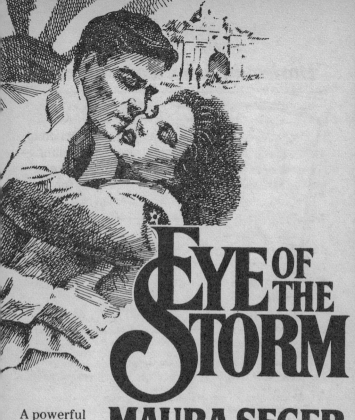

# EYE OF THE STORM

## MAURA SEGER

A powerful
portrayal of
the events of
World War II in the
Pacific, *Eye of the Storm* is a riveting story of how love
triumphs over hatred. In this, the first of a three-book
chronicle, Army nurse Maggie Lawrence meets Marine
Sgt. Anthony Gargano. Despite military regulations
against fraternization, they resolve to face together
whatever lies ahead.... Author Maura Seger, also known
to her fans as Laurel Winslow, Sara Jennings, Anne
MacNeil and Jenny Bates, was named 1984's
Most Versatile Romance Author by *The Romantic Times*.

At your favorite bookstore in April.

EYE-D-1

# Share the joys and sorrows of real-life love with

# *Harlequin American Romance!*™

# GET THIS BOOK
# FREE as your introduction to
Harlequin American Romance —
an exciting series of romance
novels written especially for
the American woman of today.

## Mail to:
### Harlequin Reader Service

| In the U.S. | In Canada |
|---|---|
| 2504 West Southern Ave. | P.O. Box 2800, Postal Station A |
| Tempe, AZ 85282 | 5170 Yonge St., Willowdale, Ont. M2N 5T5 |

YES! I want to be one of the first to discover
**Harlequin American Romance.** Send me FREE and without
obligation *Twice in a Lifetime.* If you do not hear from me after I
have examined my FREE book, please send me the 4 new
**Harlequin American Romances** each month as soon as they
come off the presses. I understand that I will be billed only $2.25
for each book (total $9.00). There are no shipping or handling
charges. There is no minimum number of books that I have to
purchase. In fact, I may cancel this arrangement at any time.
*Twice in a Lifetime* is mine to keep as a FREE gift, even if I do not
buy any additional books. 154 BPA NAZJ

---

Name                                    (please print)

---

Address                                                    Apt. no.

---

City                        State/Prov.        Zip/Postal Code

---

Signature (If under 18, parent or guardian must sign.)

AMR-SUB-1